Bonded

Sapphire was happy to relax into Eduard's comforting arms. In the tiny space left them by the other close-dancing couples, his warm body pressed against hers. She closed her eyes and concentrated on the music. Then she felt his erection pressing against her and caught her breath.

'I think he wants to have you,' said the voice of Jethro Clarke. 'But it's going to be me. We tossed a coin for you and Eduard lost.'

Sapphire glowered straight into the eyes of the lecherous Texan. She couldn't believe what she was hearing.

Other books by the author:

Handmaiden of Palmyra
Odalisque
The House in New Orleans

Bonded
Fleur Reynolds

BLACK LACE

For my wonderful friend Heather G.

Black Lace books contain sexual fantasies.
In real life, always practise safe sex.

This edition published in 2004 by
Black Lace
Thames Wharf Studios
Rainville Road
London W6 9HA

Originally published 1997

Printed and bound by Mackays of Chatham PLC

ISBN 0 352 33192 5

Chapter One

Sapphire Western was driving through the wide open spaces of Texas, wondering if it was time for her to become a sexual being instead of a human adding machine. Perhaps she should let herself go, explore love's possibilities and get emotionally involved. There was a restlessness within her which was unsettling. Was an affair what she wanted? More important – was it what she needed? For certain, she was having trouble restraining her deepest desires.

It was a sunny, warm afternoon and the freeway seemed to stretch before her like an endless black ribbon through the variegated green landscape. The hood of her sleek aubergine-coloured sports car was fastened down and her thick red-gold hair was streaming out behind her. She was wearing dark sunglasses that shielded her beautiful dark blue eyes from the glare of the bright autumn sun. Passing truckers waved. She pretended she hadn't seen them.

Astutely, Sapphire asked herself if her ambition, her work, her drive for independence and total financial security was a substitute for sex. Was she, in fact, incapable of having a loving, sexual relationship? She knew in her heart of hearts she was frightened of losing control, of not being in charge of her own destiny.

Sapphire was terrified of emotional uncertainty. She had a deep fear of being taken to the edge. Then she remembered she took risks in business and held her cool, so why shouldn't she try it with sex and love?

With awful clarity, Sapphire realised that her ambition had not allowed sex into her life. Not since school had anybody got her into bed: and that one foray had been a teenage fumble. She had fancied guys. She'd often dreamt about them. Imagined them kissing her lips, sticking their tongues in her mouth. Fondling her breasts. Parting her legs. Touching her at the top of her thighs. Then she had dismissed those dreams.

Wistfully, she thought back to her university days, when everyone was having a wild time and being totally abandoned, and how she would have none of it. She had deliberately concentrated on her studies, and then on her all-important career. Coming from a family of real achievers, and the only girl, she was determined to be a success. Sex, she had decided, would only get in the way. Also, she'd instinctively realised that the men she fancied were the most charming go-getters who – gossip had it – were the most wickedly sexual. Listening to the students chattering, Sapphire had had a secret and vicarious pleasure from their salacious stories, but had primly remarked that she regarded their exploits as time wasting. She had not had any relationships. And she had not fallen in love. Sapphire had steadfastly resisted all temptation.

She had kept her desires to herself. Nobody knew where her true inclinations lay – not even her best friends, Zinnia and Auralie. She had been prudent with her confidences. Having analysed her choices, she had decided it was less hazardous if she stayed clear of liaisons. They were bound to be dangerous. But now she was having totally different thoughts and ideas.

Sapphire slowed down to check out the sign coming up ahead. Not knowing the territory, she'd studied the map well before leaving Dallas. She'd have to leave the freeway for the smaller roads. The next exit was hers.

She glanced into her driving mirror to see what was coming. Nothing was on her tail. She changed into the appropriate lane, turned and carried on with her journey.

Sapphire realised she was lost when she came across an old Wild West town that she hadn't marked on her route. She drove through slowly, keeping her eyes alert for some sort of indicator. Annoyed with herself, she cruised on past run-down clapboard shacks, a closed down hardware store, a dilapidated railroad station and a tacky superette. Thinking the place looked more like a movie set than a real town, but loath to turn back, she continued on and out the other side. Then she found herself in open country along a narrow tree lined lane. To her surprise, the tiny road suddenly became a formal private driveway. Panic overtook her when she found she was heading towards a palatial mansion, with an Italian sports car coming at her full tilt. It screeched to a halt.

'Were you aiming for Sunshine Ranch, or did you make a mistake?' its occupant shouted.

'I made a mistake. I'm looking for Burnsville,' Sapphire replied, her heart turning over as she gazed at the handsome young man in the driver's seat. It was like a switch had gone on in her being. She found herself shaking and trembling as she took in his black hair, lightly tanned face, blue, blue eyes, wide, full mouth, strong athletic body, expensive clothes and arrogant gypsyish air. He was sexy. Very sexy.

'You're looking for Burnsville?' said the man. 'The polo match?'

'Yes.'

'I'll point you the way,' he said then, stopping in mid-sentence, he got out of his car walked across and leant on the door of her car.

'How did you know?' asked Sapphire, flustered.

'Know what?' he asked, his eyes roaming over her face and her body.

'About the polo match.'

'There's nothing in Burnsville for a beautiful woman –

except the polo. And it's obvious – ' he pointed at her tight white jeans, high brown leather boots and white lawn blouse, ' – that's where you're heading. I wouldn't say, looking at you, that you're going to a cocktail party!' Sapphire laughed nervously. That idea was absurd. 'And,' he continued, 'a friend of mine's just gone to the polo. His aunt owns this little pile.'

Sapphire surveyed the white building and its high doorway surrounded by supporting pillars. Its Palladian style reminded her of the house she grew up in in Connecticut.

'On second thoughts,' he said, making her look back at him, 'if you back up and stop. Let me get in front then you could follow me – at least part of the way.'

'That's kind of you,' she said breathily. The impact of his gaze had turned her limbs to jelly and covered her in goose pimples.

'Not really,' he said. 'I've a plane to catch but showing you where to go will remind me to drive real slow.'

'How gallant of you, sir,' she said teasingly, recovering some of her normal composure.

'No, it'll stop the cops catching me speeding. They give you one helluva heavy fine. It's instant. And they always get you. 'Cos us drivers forget about the speed limit and it's their job to remember. In fact, I think in Burnsville it's their only job. Did they stop you?'

'No, 'cos I did go real slow,' she said. His eyes continued to bore into hers. It was as if he could see into her soul, read her secret desires and know that she was tingling between her legs and had an unaccustomed fluttering in her belly.

'Good. Know something? They've got a new school and a new church – built with the proceeds of those fines. They ain't fools, they put 'em up where you can't see 'em. You drive through real quick, thinking it's a sleepy old town, then wham, the cops are there beside you, all lights flashing.'

He smiled and half-bowed, indicating that she move on, and returned to his own car.

'Thank you,' she said, reversing.

Sapphire followed him, her sex wet with longing, her brain screaming: beware. Halfway towards the freeway there was a small road which she had missed before. He stopped and pointed at it. Sapphire slowed down and hesitated. Should she stop, too? He had the air of danger she always found exciting and normally went out of her way to avoid. But should she avoid it now? Yes. After all, she didn't know him. They had not been introduced. She put up her hand, waved, swung her car left and drove on – fast.

Sapphire was thirty minutes late for the polo match. She parked her car near the exit. Taking out her large, padded and chain-handled handbag and checking she had her camera with her, she wondered off past the cars and the horse-boxes, the grooms and the spectators, to look for her friend Zinnia. Sapphire was at the polo match to meet Zinnia's husband, Jethro Clarke.

Sapphire remembered Zinnia's invitation, her voice purring down the telephone. 'Honey,' she'd said, 'if you're on holiday in Dallas, you've gotta come to polo on Saturday at Burnsville. I'll be there with Jethro.'

But Sapphire couldn't see her anywhere.

To give herself a better vantage point, Sapphire stood on the steps of a horse-box near a great shady oak. In vain she scanned the crowd. After a while she gave up, she couldn't see Zinnia or anybody else she recognised. Sapphire nestled down under a stout and ancient oak tree, half-heartedly watching the game. It was when she propped herself up on her elbows, to get a better view of the best-looking and wealthiest men in Texas, that she noticed one rider in particular. Watching him manoeuvring his body this way and that, Sapphire could feel his sexuality. She was instantly reminded of her earlier feelings and the opportunity she had had to get to know someone new. An opportunity she had so decisively thrown away. Would this man be a good substitute for the handsome rich gypsy who had kindled a fire within her and sent a sudden and deep glow surging through her body?

Sapphire was acutely aware that she had made the wrong decision and was regretting it.

It was the way the polo player wielded his stick which initially attracted her attention. She was impressed by his control and how he managed to manipulate and take advantage of every situation. But it was when a sudden, loud, and inharmonious cry went up from the select crowd around her that she became completely intrigued by his behaviour. She quickly took out her camera and started clicking.

Through the lens Sapphire saw the player ride hard towards his rival, chase him down the field, swerve violently then throw his stick, causing the other rider to miss an open goal.

That doesn't add up, thought Sapphire, realising there was more to the man's action than simple gamesmanship.

The umpires stopped the chukka. Waiting for the furore to die down, and half listening to the arguments with the referee, Sapphire continued taking photographs, thinking she really had to meet that player now. All she knew about him was what she could see: his kit was purple and white and he had a large number three emblazoned on his back. Wanting to know more, she put down her camera and checked out her programme. He was Eduard del Sur, playing for the Los Peregrinos team.

Sapphire took out an exquisite diamond studded mirror from her handbag. She checked the mascara around her beautiful dark blue eyes. She added more vermilion gloss to her full wide lips. With long elegant hands, she nudged her thick tumbling red-gold hair into shape. She was preparing for her meeting with number three of Los Peregrinos. Her sense of regret for the rich gypsy had made her bold for the polo player.

The end of the match was announced. Los Peregrinos had lost. The riders and their ponies (the winners elated, the losers disgruntled) trotted across the turf towards their waiting grooms and respective horse boxes. In their kit, it was hard for Sapphire to recognise anybody. Not that her friend Zinnia would be among the riders, but her new husband should be. Sapphire only knew him by reputation. He was a high goal player, in every sense of the phrase.

From a distance Sapphire saw members of the opposing team intermingling with the spectators. One of them threw his reins to a groom, marched across the field, had a brisk word with a couple of people then climbed into a racy sports car and sped away.

Then she saw three of the Los Peregrinos players coming towards her, leading their animals. One turned to check his pony's bridle. Sapphire saw the large number three on his back. He was Eduard del Sur, the man who had fouled. He removed his helmet. He was handsome, in his thirties, fresh-faced and almost studious looking. He was tanned, with short sun-bleached hair, dark brown eyes and an alluring lop-sided smile.

Sapphire picked up her camera again and took his photograph.

The other two removed their helmets. One was a rangy and tall mousy blonde, the other was older, closer to fifty and craggy, with iron-grey hair. Deep in conversation, they passed by, oblivious of her presence. Sapphire reckoned they must be discussing one of their great loves. Was it women or horses? Or one horse? A treasured pony perhaps? Or was it one woman? Sapphire felt a twinge of jealousy with the thought. She needed to know. Straining her ears and well-hidden behind the tree, she kept clicking, taking snaps. And discovered they were talking money.

'200 million sterling. They had a hole of 200 million!'

Wow, thought Sapphire. That was a big hole in anybody's book.

'I tell you, Kit, the old man's past it. Thank God the son's finally seen sense and gone into the company,' said the older man.

'What do you mean – 200 million down?' asked the

7

tall rangy one, in a very-hot-potato-in-the-mouth English accent.

'Share certificates they couldn't pass on and claim for because of the chaos. Some of them were maturing bearer bonds. It'll limit their ability,' said Eduard del Sur and Sapphire thought she could detect a Latino inflexion in his voice.

'So what did you do?' the Englishman asked.

'Worked on it and got it down to fifty million. The auditors said it was still too large, so a provision had to be made in the balance sheet.'

'And now what?'

'They're sending me to Meriboa,' said Number Three.

'Well that's a tiger economy if ever there was one. In fact, with the military gone and a new democracy in place, it's gonna be the biggest tiger economy of them all,' said the tall young man.

'They've opened up a futures seat on Minmex. I'm activating it.'

Futures. Tiger economy. Sapphire smiled a smile of recognition. These people were no longer strangers. She felt like a traveller in foreign lands suddenly hearing the voices of compatriots. These men were speaking her language: banking. Investment banking. She could wrap up her desire; she knew their sort. They did not have time for long term and loving relationships, and she had no intention of being an easy lay. The only lust that interested these men was their lust for money.

'Need a pee,' said the tall young man with the plummy English voice; he walked away.

'So, are you interested in technology portfolios?' asked Eduard.

'Me? No,' said the older man. 'Got enough.'

'That's where the money is.'

'Goddam it, Eduard, I said no. No more technology,' exclaimed the grey-haired man. 'I first made my money on wheat. I'm a Georgia boy, born and bred. I know a good crop when I see it. I feel it in my bones when a bad harvest's coming. And you know as well as I do, bad harvest in the fields means big money on the exchange. Close to the earth, that's where I am, and I don't stray too far from the natural when I'm playing the market.'

'Then what about the kaw-kaw tree?'

'That's grown in Taiwan. I ain't touching Taiwan, you're talking too many complications, not least the Triads.'

'I'm not asking you to. You see, they've found it in the north of Meriboa.'

'Meriboa's known for rubies and teak, that's solid produce.'

'So's the kaw-kaw, it might become the world substitute for petrol and – '

The other man stared at Eduard incredulously.

' – it could be produced for about three pence a litre,' Eduard continued blithely.

'Stop. Stop. I've heard some garbage in my time.' The older man exploded into laughter. 'Way back, they talked about chicken shit as an alternative. Well now, I don't see too many automobiles filling up at the local egg battery!'

'It would be high risk.'

'Yeah! Like taking out your own private rocket patent for individual travel to Mars! Now, Eduard, you listen to me. You wanna talk commodities, real commodities, then I'm your man; but don't give me any of your hocus-pocus nonsense. Investment, yes. Flights of fancy, no. Besides – '

Sapphire was in full agreement with the more cautious older man.

'Some flights of fancy are investment, investment in the future,' Eduard persisted, interrupting.

Investments. Sapphire knew a lot about investments. Her family's fortune was founded on high-risk investments.

'Well, if it's futures you want, you'll have to hit quickly. I'll be there by the end of the week,' Eduard was saying.

'Won't you be checked?'

'I'll worry about that,' said Eduard, with total assurance. 'What else? You said "besides" and I interrupted.'

'So you did. You've gotta learn to listen more and talk less.'

'What was it?'

'I was gonna tell you I've got my heart set on something else right now.'

'What?'

'Takes time to organise. When it's ready, I'll let you know.'

'A take-over or a buyout?'

'Your impatience ain't your best characteristic,' said the older man.

As she listened, Sapphire felt like a spy gleaning information. Was she in on the beginning of some devious dealing? Then she would have nothing whatsoever to do with the handsome, sexy man. She could not afford to be associated with anyone who was even remotely on the wrong side of the law.

Her naturally careful nature was half-pleased with this outcome. It neatly solved her dilemma. She might have been attracted to Eduard del Sur but now she would banish that attraction. Sapphire promptly did as she always did. She closed down her emotions. That's well and truly nipped in the bud, she thought, as she snapped her camera closed, slipped it into her handbag, snapped that closed too and stood up.

'Anyhow, you know me. Just call, I'll knock the market back, then buy,' said Eduard.

That was the moment he noticed Sapphire.

'Hi,' he said, eyeing her up and down.

'Hi,' she said, feeling the impact of his glance and trembling. She started to walk away.

'I'm Eduard,' he said, putting a hand on her arm. 'Are you waiting for anybody?

'Yes,' she said, endeavouring to extricate herself from his grip and the sweet tingling that came as a result of his touch.

'Pity,' he said, holding her eyes, silently telling her he found her sexually exciting.

Then, despite her own admonitions, she found herself saying, 'Zinnia Clarke. I'm here to see Zinnia Clarke and meet her new husband.'

'Are you Sapphire Western?' asked the older man.

'That's me,' she answered, turning towards him.

'You know this beautiful woman!' exclaimed Eduard. 'You know her and you didn't tell me, didn't mention her. Hey, man, you've been holding out on a good buddy.'

'Zinny described you –'

'Then you must be Jethro Clarke,' she interrupted. She eyed him warily. The king of the corporates. This was the man who had created havoc with various businesses after he'd become their chief executive and had made himself a fortune in the process. Leveraged buyout – LBO – was Jethro's speciality. He'd talk his directors into buying themselves their business with money raised through his Wall Street and City of London friends, meanwhile making certain his own contract of employment was watertight. If they threw him out, he'd get an enormous payment, if they kept him, he'd have a gigantic salary. But then, in order to meet the debts from the bank, the ordinary people – the employees – lost their jobs. Downsizing, it was called. Downsizing for efficiency, it was sold as: downsizing for greed was the truth. Thousands lost out while a handful became as rich as Croesus.

'I sure am Jethro Clarke,' the older man replied, giving her a sexy stare from under his pale hooded eyes as he held out his hand.

Sapphire didn't like the way he was looking at her. It was as if he was assessing her suitability for a romp in the hay. Aware that Eduard had turned her on and that her nipples were erect and showing through her white blouse, Sapphire brought up her arms and crossed them over her breasts to protect them from Jethro's forthright gaze.

'Hello,' she said, formally, not taking his hand. She knew a little trick that was totally disconcerting to men who gave her the unwanted come on. She did it now. She focused on the tip of his right ear and smiled a cool, cold smile. Sapphire was silently telling the legend, the corporate titan, the major Wall Street player that she didn't like him.

Sapphire utterly failed to see what Zinnia had made such a fuss about, or why she had married him. A fifty-year-old man with greying hair, pale hooded eyes and not good looking was not a man who appealed to her. He had an interesting face. He was fit and his bank balance was huge. None of that was enough to recommend him to Sapphire. She thought he seemed avaricious, greedy. She was immune to his charms.

'I've got a note for you,' said Jethro, handing Sapphire an envelope of Zinnia's familiar pale orange high quality paper. 'Zinny tried to call you but your mobile wasn't on – '

'That's right,' interrupted Sapphire. 'I'm on holiday and my phone stays off.'

'She can't be here because – '

Sapphire tore open the envelope and was about to read the letter when she noticed Eduard bend down and pick up a tiny blue flower. She thought he was going to hand it to her; instead, he carefully placed it inside his helmet. Odd, she thought, very odd. Once again his actions intrigued her. Banking and wayside flowers were a strange combination.

The men handed their ponies over to a groom and Sapphire read the note.

> *'Sapphy, sorry babe not to be at polo – had to go to England. Business calls. Stay at the Finesteins' tonight. I'll ring you there. Love Zinny.'*

Zinnia and Sapphire had met the high-minded, virtuous and elderly Finesteins, who lived in a quiet and very expensive suburb of Fort Worth, at an opera gala.

They had a wild daughter, Carola, whom Sapphire disliked and they tried to contain. They were always paying out to keep her scrapes from public knowledge. They hated scandal; they wouldn't have anything to do with anybody, either in business or socially, with scandal attached to their name. Sapphire folded the letter and shoved it into the top pocket of her tight white jeans.

'Told you she had to go to England, did she?' asked Jethro.

'Yes,' said Sapphire, walking away from him and towards her car.

'Hey, Sapphire,' called Eduard. 'You wanna meet me tonight?'

'No,' she said sweetly.

Eduard looked taken aback. She guessed he wasn't used to being turned down. He ran after her. 'Sapphire? Why not?' he asked.

'Got better things to do,' she replied.

'Such as?'

'Mind your own goddam business.'

'Okay, you're playing hard to get. Now normally, I'll play too, but I don't have the time – '

'And I don't have the inclination,' she said, arriving at her car and bleeping it open.

'You're kidding me.'

'No, I'm not,' she said, climbing in and settling comfortably on the fine leather seats.

'You're not only kidding me, you're kidding yourself too,' he said perceptively.

'Goodbye, Eduard.'

'Are you staying in cow town or oil town – Fort Worth or Dallas?' he said, leaning through the window.

'Goodbye,' she said, turning on the ignition.

'My guess is cow town. I'll find you and we'll have dinner tonight.'

'No way,' she replied. 'I never date a guy I haven't been introduced to.'

'I told you, my name's Eduard, Eduard del Sur.

'Not good enough, and – '

13

'Yes?' said Eduard eagerly.

'I don't like men who play dirty,' she said haughtily.

'No? Well now, let me tell you, playing dirty's fun,' he replied, deliberately tinting his words with lascivious overtones.

'Not for this woman,' Sapphire replied brusquely, putting her car into gear and speeding away.

'Try it sometime. You might get a pleasant surprise,' Eduard shouted after her.

Sapphire drove on without a backward glance. She felt well pleased with herself. She had managed to keep Eduard at bay and leave without any complications.

Eduard stood watching Sapphire's car until it was out of sight. She was exactly his type, he thought lustfully. Blonde, long limbed, big-breasted and with that little space, that inviting triangle, at the top of her tight white jeans that turned him on. Eduard had felt his cock rising throughout their verbal exchanges. He had a penchant for big-breasted blondes, and Sapphire fitted the bill. She reminded him of his wife. He wanted Sapphire but suspected he was still in love with Jeanine, who was lost to him forever.

Eduard sighed. He hadn't meant to deceive anyone. It had happened by stealth. Eduard snapped a twig off a tree and sat down on its large knarled root, thinking about the many and major changes in his life since he'd taken Jeanine to Brazil for their honeymoon. And how he, Laurence Vladelsky, had become Eduard del Sur.

He and Jeanine had arrived in Sao Paulo flushed, in love and tired, and had been met by his aunt and her new husband who had driven the long miles to his huge estate. For the entire journey he'd sat holding Jeanine's hand, never quite believing that she was his, that his virginal goddess had agreed to marry him. How he loved her. It brought tears to his eyes as he remembered taking her soft young body in the cool light of a Brazilian dawn.

Absent-mindedly Eduard rubbed the little stick backwards and forwards between his well-shaped hands as he remembered his only night with his bride. How he had caressed her, played with her, seduced her lovingly, making sure she was ready for him. Gently, he had introduced her to the art of love-making.

He re-lived the moment when, wearing a pale silk negligée over a paler silk night-dress, she had nervously approached him lying naked under the sheets. He had loosened the ties of her night attire and pulled her down to him, taking her in his arms. He had kissed her lovely neck, her eyes, her glorious hair, her lips. For hours he had embraced her, languidly fondling her breasts and her nipples. He had shown her how to hold him, how to stroke his penis, how to keep it stiff and not let him come. He had shown her how to suck. How to take his member in her mouth, gliding up and down its full length and exciting him further by gently manipulating his balls. He had lifted her night-dress, revealing her secret place wet with desire and, parting her long legs, had moved between her thighs. He had let his penis slide on her moistness then slowly, moaning and shaking, trembling with passion, he had penetrated her with love.

The next morning, when they had woken Jeanine had been ill. Mosquitoes had got in under their net and bitten her. Not biting him, they had gorged themselves on her body, leaving her with a high fever and unable to accompany him to the planned celebratory polo match. Knowing how keen he was on the game Jeanine had insisted that he go. His aunt had put her private jet at his disposal so that he could return to his bride quickly. He had left Jeanine in her sick room and that was the last time he had seen her. In the heart of the Brazilian jungle his plane had crashed.

He had parachuted down and had trudged and staggered through the jungle for weeks. When the Indians had come across him he had been suffering from many things, including amnesia. Although, due to his knowledge of plant life, he had been in better shape than

15

most people would have been after such an ordeal, he had had no idea who he was. They had taken him to their compound and had nursed him back to health. But the process had taken a long time.

The Indians had given him his new name. Eduard del Sur. He'd been found as the sun came peeping over the horizon, and they'd once had a missionary amongst them, whom they'd liked, a frenchman called Eduard – hence Eduard del Sur.

Gradually, when his memory had returned, Eduard had realised he was really Laurence Vladelsky. He had been about to go storming off back to Europe when he discovered that he had been declared officially dead and Jeanine had collected on his life insurance. By then he had been living with an Indian woman of the tribe. It had been a convenient arrangement and existed until she caught chicken pox and died. Then he'd upped and left. He had rejoined civilisation as Eduard del Sur, got himself a job in a small-town bank and worked his way up and out. He'd discovered he enjoyed banking. He loved stocks and shares and playing the market. Eduard was a born gambler.

'Who was the popsy?' asked Kit, Viscount Brimpton, the tall rangy polo player, bursting in upon Eduard's reverie. He was the wealthy heir to large estates in north-west England and the nephew of the woman who owned the Sunshine Ranch. He adored polo; he had no need to earn a living but, as a four-goal player, hired himself out during the season and made useful pocket money.

'The what?' asked Eduard.

'The blonde bimbo you've just let get away.'

'Sapphire Western. A friend of Zinnia's,' Jethro replied, joining them.

'Wouldn't mind giving her a good rogering,' said Kit.

'That's what I was thinking,' said Jethro. 'But take care, she's no bimbo.'

'Oh? Tell me more,' said Kit.

'She's an auditor,' said Jethro.

'An auditor? How damned uninteresting,' said Kit, and walked off to see to his pony.

'An auditor, she's an auditor? Don't you mean a book-keeper?' said Eduard, who found it difficult to believe a female could hold such a responsible job.

'I said auditor and I mean auditor. I found out quite by chance. The only way of knowing what you can do is finding out what you can't – financially speaking of course – so I went off to Gowan and Grilpin's in London. She's going to work for them. Old William Gowan has taken her on as his trouble-shooter.'

'Gowan has? How do you know?' asked Eduard.

'Was in there one day with my new partner Petrov Vladelsky when –'

'Petrov Vladelsky!' exclaimed Eduard. His uncle Petrov! Was his past sneaking out to haunt him?

Before meeting Jeanine, Eduard had played the field. He'd enjoyed many an orgy at Petrov's, his uncle's extravagant sex monastery outside London, and in Paris at Countess Jacqueline Helitzer's establishment. He'd had men and women, adored and screwed them all. He'd been in Paris having a fling with Auralie, Jeanine's cousin, when they'd met. Poor Auralie. Too slim, too volatile, too vulnerable. Well, she'd found her consolation in Gerry de Bouys.

'Do you know Petrov?' asked Jethro.

'No, no,' said Eduard, hurriedly, lying. 'Heard of him of course. You were saying . . .?'

'Yes, we were walking into G and G's as she was walking out. And there's no passing up on a woman like that. "Jeez", I said. And Petrov knew her.'

'No!' exclaimed Eduard.

'Yeah, said he'd never seen her looking so tasty. Apparently she's a friend of Auralie de Bouys . . .'

'Auralie de Bouys?' Eduard said, quite shaken. How much did Jethro have to do with his family?

'Oh for heaven's sake, Eduard, where have you been?'

'Geneva,' said Eduard.

'Auralie de Bouys,' said Jethro patiently, as if he was

explaining to a child, 'Auralie de Bouys is the woman Gerry de Bouys divorced.'

'Divorced!' Eduard exclaimed.

'Yes.' Jethro looked at him oddly. 'Yes, divorced.'

'I didn't know,' said Eduard, quickly.

'It was one helluva scandal.'

'It was?'

'Yeah, a couple of years back. I reckon a lot of it got hushed up. You know, naughties, S&M orgies and little Miss French Auralie swinging two ways at once.'

'No!' said Eduard, as if completely surprised but remembering just how many ways he'd seen Auralie swinging. 'But I can't believe that Miss Uptight Sapphire Western's got anything to do with that.'

'True. She hasn't,' said Jethro, very definitely. 'I know, because Petrov said how he'd give anything to get between her legs – and he's a dead randy guy.'

'Is he?'

'Oh sure,' said Jethro. 'I heard tell he's got some sort of religious community house, only it ain't.'

'And Sapphire Western?' asked Eduard.

'Petrov said she was at some arty institute with Auralie. He met her once, briefly. Would've liked to have moved in on her, but she didn't stay around long enough.'

'Oh!' said Eduard, non-committally. 'So how did he know she's an auditor at Gowan and Grilpin's?'

'Asked William Gowan what she was doing there. "She's a girl who asks all the right questions," he'd said, "and I've just taken her on as assistant chief auditor." So Eduard, if you intend bedding her, keep that in mind, eh? You don't need anybody asking any questions.'

'Too true,' said Eduard. 'Questions can upset the best laid plans.'

'But, there are always exceptions,' said Kit, returning and butting in. 'Eduard, why the hell did you go for that guy out there?'

'Don't like him or his attitude,' said Eduard. 'Just didn't want him making the goal.'

'Sure, Eduard, sure. So you lost us the match,' said Jethro. 'I think you're losing your touch.'

'What, me?'

'Yeah, that Sapphire woman fancied you – '

'I know.'

' – and you let her go.'

'I'll find her.'

'You don't have to. I'll tell you where she's going.'

'Where?'

'The Finesteins place in Fort Worth.'

'No! How do you know?' asked Eduard.

'Read Zinny's letter.'

'What?'

'Zinny's gone to England – some sort of fund management meetings. And then to an old ladies' party in London.'

'An old ladies' party?' Eduard was mystified. 'What old ladies?'

'Something to do with her old friend Jeanine and – '

'Jeanine? Jeanine who?' asked Eduard, trying to keep his intense curiosity out of his voice. Jeanine was not an everyday ordinary sort of a name. Could it be his wife Jethro was talking about? It had to be. If he knew Petrov, he had to know Jeanine as well.

'Jeanine Vladelsky, of course,' said Jethro. 'Widow of one Laurence Vladelsky.'

It was his wife. Eduard was stunned. He hadn't heard anyone mention her in ages. Nobody had mentioned anyone from that circle in ages. And now, in one day, almost in one moment, he'd heard tell of Auralie, Petrov and Jeanine. He'd have to be careful.

'Do you know her, this Jeanine?' asked Eduard.

'No, but she's Petrov's niece by marriage,' Jethro explained. Noticing the blank look on Eduard's face, he continued. 'Her husband came from your part of the world. South American. Brazilian, I think. I'm surprised you never met him. Supposed to be a botanist but, from what I've heard, spent most of his time playing polo. Got lost in the jungle or something. Died. Apparently, this Jeanine's got her fingers in a lot of pies. Zinny wasn't very specific – anyhow she runs an hotel.'

'She runs an hotel?' exclaimed Eduard, trying to disguise his surprise. When he was declared dead, she would have been left a wealthy woman, so why was she running an hotel? 'Runs it?'

'Owns it,' said Kit, 'and it's very exclusive. I stay there when I'm in town. Of course, you have to be recommended – '

'Excuse me, sir,' said a groom, coming up and approaching Jethro, 'the referees want a word with you.'

'Me! Are you sure you mean me and not this sonofabitch here?' said Jethro in surprise and pointing to Eduard.

'No, sir, you, sir,' said the groom, walking away, and Jethro followed him.

'I say, old boy,' said Kit, 'looks like you've got up everybody's nose today.'

'What?'

'Well, David Lewis told me he wouldn't stay to speak with you. Bad move, that. On the Exchange you don't need enemies. Rumours can kill a business.'

'Oh, Hanway, Rattle and Lewis can go to hell. David Lewis is a cocky bastard.'

'I've always found him most amenable.'

'Yeah, you would. Anyhow he's probably used the opportunity to go see his new woman.'

'What new woman?' asked Kit.

'The one he's infatuated with but keeps well hidden,' said Eduard.

'See what I mean. Bankers thrive on rumour,' said Kit.

'Yeah, you could be right,' said Eduard, laughing. 'Who and what is going up and down! Oh, tell me, Kit, how come this hotel is so exclusive?'

'Jeanine caters for guests with exceptional appetites.'

'What sort of appetites?' asked Eduard.

'What sort do you think?' said Kit.

'Sexual?' asked Eduard, in amazement.

'Of course sexual,' said Kit.

This did not sound like his Jeanine. His Jeanine was a sweet gentle girl. Eduard was a mixture of jealousy and bewilderment. How did Jeanine come to be running an interesting exclusive hotel? Who had introduced her to sex in all its variations? Petrov?

Petrov had leered a few times in Jeanine's direction. He was the one who would have had the time, the access, the inclination and the environment to seduce the innocent beautiful young Jeanine. Eduard would lay a bet that it was Petrov.

'So what's Jethro's wife doing there?'

'Your guess is as good as mine, but they obviously let each other off the leash occasionally,' said Kit.

'Does Jethro know – about that hotel?' asked Eduard.

'No idea. Ask him – here he is.'

'Jethro . . .' Eduard began, but Jethro interrupted him.

'Eduard,' said Jethro, with a look of anger on his face. 'As the captain, the refs have told me that they don't want to see you playing here again.'

'What?' exclaimed Eduard.

'Your foul was well out of order.'

'Yeah, but – '

' – and you know the rules. The refs' decision is final.'

'Yeah. Ah well. I was going to go east, I'll just go there sooner. I'll get a few games there,' he said philosophically. Then he remembered Zinnia. 'Um, Jethro, has your wife been to Jeanine's hotel before?'

'You talking about the one in Kensington, London, England?

'Yes.'

'Yes, she has, quite a few times. Was there six months ago, Ascot time, in fact.'

'And have you been there?'

'Hell no,' replied Jethro. 'Zinny said it's a very staid place, not my scene at all.'

Eduard and Kit exchanged glances.

Eduard was puzzled. Did Zinnia have hidden desires and needs, or was this a bizarre revenge for her new husband's infidelities? Jethro was a well-known womaniser.

Zinnia must have been aware of his reputation when she married him. Everyone who knew him also knew that he would screw anything that moved. Had she hoped to tame him? Hoped that he would be faithful, then caught him in *flagrante delicto*? Or was he so intent on getting it up and putting it around he never satisfied anyone, including his new wife, and this was her secret way of punishing him?

'Apparently there's an old countess coming from Paris and Zinny wants to see her.'

'Oh? What's her name?' asked Eduard, endeavouring to make the question seem as innocent as possible.

'Countess Helitzer,' said Jethro.

'Oh!' said Eduard.

He wanted to laugh but thought that would have been extremely indiscreet. However, he doubted if the stunningly beautiful, sexy and thirty-something Jacqueline Helitzer would have been very flattered by the description. Eduard would have loved to have enlightened Jethro but decided to keep such knowledge to himself. It could be very useful later. He looked quickly at Kit, but nothing untoward seemed to have registered on the young aristocrat's handsome face. He'd obviously never met the charismatic Jacqueline, Countess Helitzer, or been to her mansion in the Bois de Boulogne.

'Do you know this countess?' asked Jethro.

'No,' lied Eduard.

Identity deception did not alter his memories of beautiful people and evenings of sensual delight spent at the Helitzers' impressive and very private home. 'No, I don't know her.'

'Well, apparently she's known Zinny for some time and is going to London for some reunion or another. She has asked especially for Zinny to be there,' said Jethro.

'And you're not going?' asked Eduard, keeping his face and his voice deadpan.

'No, of course not. What would I do at an old ladies' tea party?' asked Jethro.

Eduard's assessment of Zinnia's character went up a

few notches. She had her husband well taped. The perfect way to make sure that Jethro did not arrive if anything risqué was going on was to make it appear to be a gathering of elderly females. Eduard knew, given the principal players, it would be anything but. He was both amused and intrigued. It was almost worth a trip to England to find out – but he would have to go to Jeanine's in disguise. He would think about it. Before or after the Far East? He'd think about that, too.

'And why has your wife suggested Sapphire go to the Finesteins' tonight?' asked Eduard.

'Don't know exactly. But it bugged me.'

'Why?' asked Kit.

'Well, the Finesteins themselves won't be there. They're on a cruise,' said Jethro. 'And their fun loving daughter Carola is – well, on the loose.'

'Zinnia knows that?' asked Eduard.

'Oh, for sure.'

'Interesting girl, your wife,' said Eduard.

'The best,' said Jethro. 'Knows I have my peccadilloes and – er – turns a blind eye, but is utterly faithful to me.'

'Really! Do you think she invited Sapphire to keep an eye on you? I mean, could it be possible that she's worked out you've got the hots for Carola?'

'No, Zinny'd never do a thing like that,' replied Jethro with complete assurance.

'So is it a private party or can anybody join?' asked Kit.

'Oh, it's very private but you can come,' said Jethro, laughing.

'Then I will, too,' said Eduard.

'Good, it's a celebration,' said Jethro.

'Of what, for what?' asked Eduard. 'Your new partner?'

'No.'

'Oh, he won't be there, then?' Eduard said, trying desperately to keep the worry out of his voice. The last thing he wanted was to meet Petrov. Then his cover would be completely blown.

'He doesn't leave Europe much,' said Jethro tersely. 'Which is good for me.'

'So, it's got to be a deal,' said Eduard.

'Yeah, a little deal,' replied Jethro.

Eduard smiled. If Jethro said it was a little deal, he reckoned it had to be mega.

'Yeah, Momma and Poppa Finestein are coming in with me.' said Jethro.

'Oh!' exclaimed Eduard.

'Yeah, there's a company I fancy. So, let the best man win,' said Jethro.

'It won't be you, Jethro,' said Eduard. 'Not as far as Sapphire is concerned.'

'And why not?'

'Got the feeling you weren't her type,' Eduard replied, he had noticed the look of aversion on Sapphire's face. 'In fact, I'd say you're definitely not her type.'

'Are you for real?' Jethro laughed cynically. 'I've always found the combination of my cock and my money gets me any woman I want.'

'There's always one that gets away,' said Eduard dryly.

'I noticed,' said Jethro pointedly.

24

Chapter Two

Jeanine Vladelsky lay back on her sumptuous bed, completely satisfied with life. She had spent the night sucking and screwing her masseuse, the exotic Meriboan, Ana Tai. Countess Jacqueline Helitzer was arriving with her entourage within the next few hours and Zinnia said she was coming soon; exactly when, Jeanine didn't know, but she was looking forward to a few days of utter debauchery.

Jeanine smiled, stretched her beautiful body and gazed lovingly at her home and her exquisite possessions. Ever since she had taken over Auralie's design group, Petolg Holdings, her life had gone well. She had let the company go public and they had obtained even bigger and better contracts. Her various other projects were about to come to fruition. She had been buying up shops and factories that owned their own sites. She was about to buy another one south of the river. And her biggest scheme of all was also her biggest secret. No one yet knew what she was planning.

She had already made more money than she knew what to do with. She had bought the house next door and extended her rooms into it. Her bathroom was much bigger. So was her dungeon. And, to increase her happiness, her latest amour, the incredibly rich and

25

wonderfully handsome Everett de Bouys, had tele-phoned from Texas to say he was on his way back to London and wanted to find her ready and waiting. Jeanine knew exactly what that meant. She slipped off the bed to begin her preparations. First she would take a long leisurely bath.

Wallowing naked in her gigantic marble jacuzzi, she thought back to the first time she met Everett de Bouys.

It had been the week before Ascot at a party in Belgravia, London. She had been chatting to Teddy, Lord Mawson, an amusing little social climber who'd made oodles of money and been newly ennobled, when she had noticed the handsome, elegantly-dressed young man gazing at her lustfully. She had inclined her head graciously then turned away. Her entire demeanour had been demure, almost bordering on submission. Jeanine had made sure that there was nothing about her that was brassy or strident or screamed 'look at me, I'm a sexy bitch'. She had seemed soft and gentle, a real woman and she had deliberately fostered this idea with the clothes she wore.

On that occasion she had been wearing a silk chiffon frock overprinted with lime leaves and violet flowers and a heavier but matching jacket which buttoned to the top of its mandarin collar. Her long shapely legs had been encased in stockings of the softest shade of lilac and on her her feet she had worn high, deep lilac, ankle-strap shoes. When she moved her head, her blonde curls had swayed so that anybody who was interested caught a glimpse of her fabulous long drop diamond earrings and knew she was rich.

Fascinated by the man's good looks, she had eyed him up and down, taking in his strong, masculine face, his black hair and blue eyes; his tall, muscular body had been clothed by the most fashionable and best English tailors; his attitude and dress had creamed money. Jeanine had known he wouldn't be in the room if he didn't have vast amounts of it. She had wondered what he'd be like in bed. Moments later he'd barged in on their conversation.

'Hello, I'm Everett de Bouys,' he'd said.

'I presume you've pushed into our intimate conversation because you want to meet this beautiful woman, who runs the finest hotel in London,' said Teddy.

'You presume correctly,' replied Everett. 'But where is this hotel and why haven't I stayed there?'

'Jeanine Vladelsky,' said Teddy, ignoring Everett's question, 'allow me to introduce Everett de Bouys.'

'How do you do?' said Jeanine, extending a soft and well manicured hand. 'De Bouys? My cousin, Auralie, was married to Gerry de Bouys.'

'And Gerry's my cousin,' said Everett, holding on to her hand fractionally too long. Noticing her wedding ring, he dropped it quickly. 'Not that I've had much to do with him – our respective fathers don't get along too well.'

'Oh?' said Jeanine.

'Jeanine was married to Laurence Vladelsky, the botanist,' said Teddy, quickly.

'Was?' asked Everett.

'I am a widow,' said Jeanine, simply.

'I'm so sorry,' said Everett.

Jeanine could feel he was observing the norms of polite behaviour but felt no sorrow whatever.

'I will not intrude upon your grief,' said Everett, bowing slightly then sauntering away.

'I want him, sweetie,' Jeanine said to Teddy.

'Thought you might,' said Teddy languidly.

'Know anything about him, womanwise?' she asked.

'Not much. A bit of a workaholic, by all accounts,' replied Teddy.

'Lives in London?' asked Jeanine.

'When he's here, yes. A flat above the shop.'

'And where's the shop?'

'De Bouys Merchant Bank in the City,' said Teddy.

'Do you mean that he is the bank?'

'Yes. He finally agreed to go into the family business –'

'What was he doing before, sweetie?' asked Jeanine.

'Computers. Set up his own computer game company, much to his father's annoyance. Only child and all that – you know how important it is to keep the fortune in the family. Keep the family name.'

'Was it successful? Everett's computer games company?'

'Yes, very; sold it and made a mint. His father, old Cecil – nice old codger, but frail and a bit doddery – begged his son to come into the business, otherwise ... Well there was talk of takeovers or even a straight-forward sale,' replied Teddy.

'And that fabulous eighteenth century house near St Paul's Cathedral, they own it – it's still theirs?'

'Oh yes.'

'I want him more than ever,' said Jeanine.

'Careful, honey bun, I reckon he thinks he's God's gift!'

'Oh well, in that case, full frontal attack, no messing about, eh? Why don't you ask him if he'll join us for dinner?'

'Sweetie pie, I've already got my dinner date,' said Teddy.

'Sweetie, darling, the last thing I want is for you to actually join us. You're the ploy,' said Jeanine. 'You can leave us when we get to the restaurant. I'll take him from there.'

Teddy laughed. 'I don't doubt you will,' he said.

'Jeanine and I are going for a little Japanese,' said Teddy, tapping Everett on the shoulder a little while later. 'Care to join us?'

'Sounds good to me, thanks,' said Everett, falling straight into Jeanine's trap.

The three of them squeezed into Everett's long, low, sleek, top-of-the-range Italian sports car and drove to Jeanine's choice – a discreet and very expensive Japanese restaurant in the heart of Chelsea. The lights were low, the food was good and the hot saki flowed. Before they'd ordered their sushi, sashimi, and tempura, Teddy's mobile rang. He took the call, then said he had to leave. He apologised to them both, kissed Jeanine – who was trying hard not to look like the cat who'd got the cream – and departed.

'So,' said Everett, 'you haven't remarried?'

'No,' said Jeanine, choosing her words very carefully. 'But I have a number of close friends.'

'Oh,' he said, missing the irony. 'And what's this hotel you run?'

'It's very exclusive. Introductions only.'

'What do you mean?'

'Only special people can go there,' said Jeanine, knowing she was whetting Everett's appetite.

'How special?' asked Everett.

'Oh very special, very special indeed,' said Jeanine enigmatically.

'Can I go there?

'Only if you're a good boy.'

'A good boy?'

'If you behave yourself,' said Jeanine.

'I wouldn't have thought of being anything else,' said Everett.

'You see, I like people who are honest with their emotions,' said Jeanine softly. 'If they want to do something, I think they should do it – but with finesse.'

'You're talking in riddles,' said Everett.

'Oh, I'm not,' said Jeanine. 'I'm giving you some very good advice.'

Their food arrived and they started talking about banking and equities and options. Slowly, as the evening wore on, the seductive hot saki took effect.

'You're an incredibly beautiful woman,' he said.

'And you're a very handsome man,' she replied, and put a hand on his knee.

Her hand snaked up his thigh. Suppressing a smile she watched him gulp then quickly sip his rice wine. Jeanine was enjoying herself. She stared into his eyes, licked her lips, then ran her other hand up and down the warm saki decanter as if she was rubbing his cock.

He put a hand on her knee. She didn't push it away. He snaked it up under her skirt, finding her stocking-top. She knew he would have a pleasant surprise. She guessed he'd thought she was a prim tights girl. His touch thrilled her. She looked into his eyes and saw a certain inviting wickedness. Her heart started pounding. Her stomach went into a tight knot and she could feel her moistness oozing out between her legs.

Jeanine decided to take off her jacket. Removing her hand from his thighs, she undid the buttons, revealing the low-cut bodice of her chiffon frock and her very rounded full breasts. She knew exactly what she was doing. Everett would be overcome with longing and desperate to feel her luscious breasts. In a moment she'd feel his cock. That would really drive him crazy.

'Some men are leg men,' said Jeanine, boldly, 'others are tit men. Which one are you?'

'Um . . .' He was quite taken aback by her forthright question.

She leant forward; her bodice barely covered her nipples.

'Breasts,' he said, speaking before thinking.

'Do you want to feel mine?' she asked brazenly. 'Would you like to put your hands down the front of my dress and feel my tits?'

'Yes,' he said, his voice croaking with desire.

'Then why don't you?'

'We're in a restaurant,' he said, embarrassed.

'Yes,' she answered, 'fun, isn't it? Nobody'll notice – or if they do, they'll pretend they haven't seen a thing. So,' she licked her lips, 'kiss me, touch me.'

Jeanine leant across the table and their lips met. She forced her tongue through his half-closed lips. He brought up a hand, touched her face, her neck, and let it wander down over her cleavage, she pushed her breasts closer to him. He slid one finger under her bodice and flicked her hard stiff nipples. She gasped, pushed her tongue further into his mouth, lowered her eyelids and wiggled on her seat.

'I want you,' he said.

'Do you now?' said Jeanine, sitting down again and smiling her soft catlike smile. 'Is that what you always say to a woman on your first date?'

'No,' he laughed, 'not always. But then it's not often a woman asks me to feel her breasts in full view of everyone in a restaurant.'

'Oh sweetie, you did it so expertly, I'd have thought you'd done it hundreds of times.'

'No,' he said. 'have you?'

'No,' she lied, 'I haven't. Have you got a hard-on? I like sitting with a man who's got a hard-on. And I like feeling it. I've done that lots of times.'

Under cover of the table, Jeanine quickly undid the buttons on his flies and pushed her fingers through the gap until she was touching his thick and throbbing cock.

'And what else haven't you done?' she asked him, as his prick responded to the firm but gentle pressure along his glans. 'I mean, have you ever been sucked off in a restaurant?'

'No!' he exclaimed.

Jeanine began to move away from him, as if she was about to slide beneath the table.

'No,' he said, hastily holding one of her hands to stop her moving any further, while he quickly closed the gap in his trousers.

'No?' she queried. 'Don't you want me to suck your cock?'

'Um, yes,' he admitted. 'But not here.'

'But I'd like to do it here. I'd like to get under the table, and put it in my mouth and suck.'

'Please, Jeanine,' he said looking around the restaurant. The smart Japanese waiters were gliding soundlessly around the room and their customers seemed intent on their own food and their partners. They were eating without a glance in their direction.

'If you let me suck you here, I'll let you fuck me

31

tonight,' she said. 'That is what you want, isn't it? Well, isn't it?'

'Yes,' he replied.

Jeanine leant forward. Squeezing her magnificent breasts together, she let them flop on to the table then she flicked her nipples with her middle forefinger while looking at him and licking her lips. 'And I want you too,' she said, rubbing her leg against his. 'But I think you want me flat on my back, my legs apart and your cock stuck up hard inside me. I'm very wet, you know. I'm all juicy and tingly – ' Her hand disappeared under the table.

' – and I'm touching myself. She gave tiny gasps. 'Wouldn't you like to touch me like this, run your hands along my sex?'

Jeanine enjoyed talking dirty. It fascinated and excited men. She pushed her sexy tongue between her wide lipstick-covered lips and brought her hand out from beneath the table, putting it under his nose. It smelt of her sweet sex-musk.

'Lick it,' she said. 'And Everett, if you want to fuck me tonight, I suggest you do as I ask. Go on, open your flies. I want to play with you.'

'Um, Jeanine,' said Everett.

Jeanine watched the combination of panic and desire cross his face. 'Yes?' she said looking at him through half-closed eyes.

'Have you ever made love to a woman?' asked Everett, leaning away from her.

'Yes,' she answered, sexily. 'Why?'

'I wondered,' he replied.

'Does the idea turn you on?'

'Yes.'

'Have you ever made love to two women?'

'No,' said Everett.

'What a simple life you've led,' she said, touching the fabric of his trousers at the top of his thighs then moving her hand so it lay full on his crotch. 'Would you like to?' she asked.

32

'Yes,' he gasped.

'Is it one of your fantasies?' she asked.

She had wormed a finger past his fly buttons until once again it was touching his tender, aroused phallus.

'Yes,' he replied.

'Then let me suck your cock now and maybe...' Jeanine didn't finish her sentence. She was under the table and his cock was in her mouth before he could reply. She was taking the head slowly, holding the shaft firmly; she was licking the rim, taking her fingers down. Everett took a deep breath.

'Why don't you come home with me?' she asked, moments later, sitting beside him as if nothing had happened. 'Then we'll see what we can do. You see, I think that fantasies should be lived, acted out, appreciated and enjoyed.'

In the soft light of the restaurant she saw a perplexed expression flit across his face. She was confusing him. Relishing his confusion, she kissed his lips.

'Have you ever been fucked by two men?' he asked.

'Now that would be telling,' she replied.

'So tell me,' he said, his hand sliding further and further up her skirt.

She closed her legs, teasing him, not letting him feel the warm, moist place at the top of her thighs.

'I think I'd enjoy watching you being screwed,' he said, lifting her chin, looking into her eyes.

'Would you now?' she replied enigmatically. 'Well perhaps you could – but first, you'd have to seduce my flatmate,' she said.

'Your flatmate. But I thought you owned a hotel?'

'Oh, I do; but I don't live there,' said Jeanine, telling a half-truth.

'Who is your flatmate?' asked Everett. 'I mean, maybe I wouldn't fancy her.'

'Oh you will, sweetie,' said Jeanine, 'everybody does. But nobody gets inside her knickers.'

'Why not?'

'I think she prefers women,' she said, knowing he'd see this as a challenge.

'Where do you live?' he asked, determined to have her and the other woman as well.

'Kensington,' she replied, 'and I think we should get a taxi. You order it and I'll go to the loo.'

Jeanine had no intention of using the restroom. She went off to make a very private call on her mobile telephone.

In the taxi she had let him kiss her lips and fondle her breasts. She had not allowed him to touch her between her legs but had unzipped his flies, taken his thick throbbing prick from its tight enclosure, and had gone down on him again.

'Leave your flies open,' she said, when they finally arrived at the house next to her hotel. He paid for the cab. Jeanine got out and opened the door with a number of keys.

'Is that you, Jeanine?' a voice called.

'Yes, and I've a friend with me,' she answered.

'Don't forget to lock up properly,' the voice called.

Jeanine treble-locked the door and Everett followed her into the dark womblike hall of the white stucco building. It was part of her enclosed and secluded private world and Jeanine had decorated it with great care. Here, anything could happen – and frequently did. It was a secure and safe place of excitement and debauchery.

A tall thin young Asian woman with cropped black hair, bright blue and green make-up enhancing her dark slanting eyes, and dark almost blue black lipstick on her thick, wide lips, appeared. She put her head around the sitting-room door.

'Hi,' she said. She walked in and kissed Jeanine full on the mouth.

Everett stared.

The newcomer was wearing a rubber outfit slashed from its high collar to below her navel, and its skirt flared out, revealing a few inches of bare thigh before they were encased in rubber stockings. Her high heels had large thick straps buckled around the ankles. There was a ring in her belly button, in her eyebrow and in her lip.

Without any bidding, the Asian took off Jeanine's jacket then, unzipping the back of her dress and allowing the bodice to fall open in the front, she licked Jeanine's full opulent breasts and sucked on her nipples.

'Did you obey me?' asked the black haired woman.

'Yes,' whispered Jeanine, lowering her eyes.

'Are you sure?' she asked.

'Yes,' said Jeanine, softly.

'You didn't let him touch you here?'

She pushed Jeanine against the wall. She lifted the hem of her chiffon skirt and shoved it into Jeanine's hand, revealing Jeanine's soft white thighs, her stocking-tops, and her pure white panties. She pulled Jeanine's knickers down to her knees, exposing her pale blonde mound.

'No, no; I didn't let him touch me anywhere,' Jeanine replied, huskily.

Jeanine was wanting the other woman to touch her, feel her sex-lips. She pushed her hips out, inviting the crop-haired woman to take advantage of the offer.

'You didn't let him touch your lovely pussy?' asked the other woman, and put her finger in her own mouth, sucking on it suggestively.

'No,' said Jeanine.

'You're quite sure? You wouldn't lie to me, would you? You know what would happen if you lied to me.'

'I haven't lied to you. Ask him.'

'Did you play with his cock? I told you you mustn't play with his cock,' said Ana Tai. The Asian girl slowly let her hands roam over Jeanine's body, then one finger began to caress the outer lips of Jeanine's fleshy sex mound.

'No,' lied Jeanine, a long sigh of pleasure escaping from her mouth.

'You didn't play with his cock? You didn't suck his cock in the cab?'

'No,' said Jeanine.

'I don't believe you,' said the Asian girl.

'I didn't,' Jeanine assured her.

'I'm Ana Tai,' said the other woman, unexpectedly turning towards Everett.

'He's Everett,' said Jeanine. She saw that he found it impossible to move. She looked at his crotch and realised his cock was stiff and aching, throbbing; longing to be touched, stroked and caressed. She knew he was mesmerised by their behaviour.

Ana Tai pushed him back against the doorpost. 'Oh, you've got your flies open,' she said. 'Jeanine. Jeanine, what's this? Why should a man come here with his flies open? You disobeyed me. You did, didn't you? Now, tell me the truth.'

'No,' said Jeanine. 'I didn't; really, I didn't.'

'Bend over. Bend over and lift up your skirt. Quickly; you know I don't like to be kept waiting.'

Jeanine bent over, lifted her skirt, exposing her lovely bare buttocks.

'Tell me Everett, did she suck your cock? I have to know,' said Ana Tai, firmly. 'If she did, then she must be punished. And you can punish her. If she sucked your cock in the cab then you must smack her bottom. You would like to smack those round plump cheeks, wouldn't you? I'd give you permission to slap her hard – very hard.'

Jeanine knew Everett's cock was twitching with desire.

'I didn't, did I?' said Jeanine. 'I didn't take your lovely big prick in my hands and put its head in my mouth and suck on it, did I? Tell her the truth, Everett.'

'Yes, tell me the truth,' said Ana Tai, putting her long thin hand tipped with long blue-black nails into the gap of his trousers and easing out his large phallus.

'She did,' gasped Everett.

'She did what?' asked the almond-eyed woman,

caressing his cock, moving her hand exquisitely up and down the length of his shaft.

'She did suck my cock,' he said, with his eyes on Jeanine's bare bottom.

'Show me, Jeanine,' Ana Tai said harshly. 'Show me what you did in the taxi.'

And there in the hall, keeping her knees straight, Jeanine bent over and took Everett's cock into her mouth. While she was sucking his prick Ana Tai stroked Jeanine's bare buttocks.

'You've been a naughty girl,' she said, giving Jeanine's bottom a short hard slap. 'Have you had many women?' Ana Tai asked Everett, looking at him through narrowed eyes as she leant her rubber-covered legs against Jeanine's thighs and embraced her breasts.

'A few,' he answered hoarsely.

With her hands inside his trousers, playing with his balls and her mouth going up and down on his shaft, Jeanine knew he was finding it difficult to speak. She took her mouth away from his cock and answered for him.

'He's never had two women,' she said.

'Quiet,' ordered Ana Tai. 'Everett, for that you can smack her twice. Once for telling me lies, and once for stopping sucking your cock before I gave her permission. Go on. Hard, bring your hand down hard on her bare bottom.'

Everett positioned himself behind Jeanine; Ana Tai took hold of his prick and he smacked. He brought his hand up and then down very hard. Twice. Smack. Smack. Then Jeanine felt his fingers sliding their way into her full, wet, swollen sex. Ana Tai realised what he was doing and pulled him away.

'So you've never had two women,' said Ana Tai. 'Then I think you'd better come with us.'

The slim Asian led the way along the hallway and up the wide thickly carpeted staircase. She opened the door of a dimly lit room where a very large four-poster bed occupied most of the space.

'Everett, take off your clothes,' commanded Ana Tai, 'then lie on the bed.'

Everett did as he was told.

Ana Tai slowly stripped Jeanine. When Jeanine was stark naked, Ana Tai stood her beside one of the bed-posts. Everett watched hungrily as Jeanine put her hand inside the slit-fronted opening of Ana Tai's leather covering and began playing with the other woman's breasts.

'Open your legs.' said Ana Tai. Jeanine instantly obeyed. 'Wider.' At her command, Jeanine opened them wider. Aware that they were giving him a vicarious thrill, the black-haired Asian woman stroked Jeanine's neat blonde triangle, while Jeanine fondled Ana Tai's breasts and the two women kissed.

Titillated and tantalised, Everett lay on the bed and reached for his balls and prick.

'No,' said Ana Tai, noticing what he was about to do. She took his hands away and placed them flat on the bed. 'You wanted two women, so you must wait until we are ready to take you. You will be punished if you touch yourself.'

'Punished?' he asked.

'Oh yes,' she said.

Ana Tai pressed her exposed breasts to Jeanine's, then slowly began to move one finger backwards and forwards along the outer rim of Jeanine's sex.

'I want you very wet,' Ana Tai whispered, but loud enough for Everett to hear.

Jeanine's hips swayed with the undulating sensuous grace of a salsa dancer. Ana Tai stopped playing with her and put both hands on her breasts; then, with her tongue, traced the outline of Jeanine's mouth.

'What am I going to do to you now?' the Asian woman asked.

'I think you are going to suck me,' said Jeanine breathlessly.

'Yes,' said Ana Tai. 'I am going to put my head between your legs and I'm going lick your swollen little clitoris until you don't know whether you are in heaven or in hell; and, after that . . .'

Jeanine arched and jutted out her pelvis, offering herself to Ana Tai who knelt down, spread Jeanine's sex wide with her hands, then buried her tongue in the depths beyond the blonde mound.

From time to time, one or the other of them gave a swift glance in Everett's direction. They wondered how long he would last before trying to touch himself. And then they would punish him. Jeanine swayed and jerked to the rhythm of Ana Tai's exploring tongue and fingers. They saw his prick stand on end and quiver with intense excitement. It was Jeanine who noticed his hands slip across his belly and grip his pulsating phallus.

'Punishment time,' said Jeanine triumphantly.

Ana Tai stood up, walked across the room, opened the drawer of a pine chest and removed a number of articles. Jeanine stayed exactly where she was and Everett blanched when he saw what Ana Tai was carrying.

'We thought you wanted to screw us,' said Ana Tai, advancing on him.

'Yes, yes I do,' sighed Everett.

'But you have disobeyed me,' said Ana Tai. 'I told you if you did you would be punished. You did hear me, didn't you?'

'Yes,' he whispered.

'You touched yourself. You went to masturbate, you wanted to rub your cock when I'd specifically told you not to.' Ana Tai gave his prick a quick flick with her hands. 'Everett, turn over,' she commanded. 'I want you on your belly. Quickly; I need to be obeyed quickly.'

Everett turned over.

'Jeanine, get on the bed with him.' Jeanine did as she was told. 'You, don't touch her until I give you permission. Jeanine, sit with your thighs either side of his head. Now . . .'

Everett was faced with Jeanine's open, moist sex.

'Jeanine, lie back. You, put your arse in the air and your hands on the inside of Jeanine's beautiful thighs.

Keep your hands exactly where they are. Now, I want you to lick Jeanine's lovely pussy.'

Willingly obeying Ana Tai, Everett's tongue lapped at Jeanine's full sex lips, tasting her sweet musk.

'I can't see,' said Ana Tai. 'Put your arse higher.' Ana Tai wrenched him away from Jeanine. 'What do you think you're doing?' she asked, angrily. 'Do you think you're a car mechanic greasing a piece of machinery? Jeanine, tie his hands,' ordered Ana Tai.

From beneath a pillow, Jeanine drew a length of cord, wound it around Everett's wrists and tied it to a bedpost.

Everett raised his head and looked nonplussed.

'Your actions are gross,' said Ana Tai, with derision. 'Your movements are those of a polar bear tearing at a piece of flesh. Have you never learnt? Don't you know that a pussy is a delicate instrument, to be enjoyed gently, softly?'

With force, Ana Tai swished the cane hard across his bare backside. He jumped as it seared his rump. Jeanine gripped his hands so that he was unable to move too far from the stinging bamboo.

'Ow,' he yelled.

Jeanine pushed her sex close to his mouth.

'Punishment,' said Ana Tai. 'Don't move, close your eyes and keep your arse up. And don't touch Jeanine until I give you permission.'

Everett obeyed her.

'Now, I shall tell you how to lick her,' said Ana Tai, her slight Eastern accent enriching her words. 'A woman's sex is something to be treasured and adored. It is a priceless object, fashioned to be loved and relished. How would you like it if I scraped my cane along your penis?' To drive the idea home, Ana Tai prodded the sharp end of the cane along his member. It hurt.

'Ow,' he squealed.

'When a woman is excited,' said Ana Tai, using a dulcet tone, lulling Everett's fear, 'she exudes a sweet honey; she swells, reddens and opens, she longs to be touched, to be stroked. She creates a space within her that longs to be filled. But if she is attacked harshly, that longing ceases. You must lick her gently, taste her nectar lovingly, stimulate her softly and savour the flavour of her. Meander through her exquisite unfolding flower. Indulge your senses and tempt her, invite her to be seduced: then make her beg for more. Now, I give you permission to touch Jeanine again.'

Everett wriggled up the bed so that his face was close to Jeanine's soft enticing flesh. He brushed her labia with his lips and her vulva parted imperceptibly. His tongue trailed along her long vertical opening and Jeanine could feel herself swelling with enjoyment.

'I gave you permission to pleasure my flat-mate,' said Ana Tai, sharply. 'What do you say?'

'Thank you, madam,' he replied.

'Exactly. And I am going to spank you, really spank you, for not honouring me properly. And after each stroke you will thank me, is that understood?'

'Yes.'

'Yes, madam,' corrected Ana Tai; she whipped him hard and left harsh bright red marks across his neat bottom. He cried out with a mixture of pain and pleasure.

'You say "Thank you, madam",' she hissed.

'Thank you, madam,' whispered Everett.

'Louder.'

'Thank you, madam,' he shouted.

The cane seared him again. He flinched and squirmed, but his face was flushed with enjoyment.

Jeanine watched as Ana Tai caressed Everett's reddened bottom, and she smiled. Her new recruit was playing her part very well. Jeanine was pleased she'd been able to slip away from him at the restaurant and organise this pleasant diversion. Soon Ana Tai would slide a finger into his bottom-mouth. But how soon?

Jeanine arched. He was learning quickly. She wanted Everett's tongue deeper. But the Asian woman didn't do as Jeanine expected. Instead, she reached round under his arched pelvis and slowly began to stroke his prick.

'I want him now,' said Jeanine.

Sliding her hand up and down his cock, Ana Tai bent over Everett, realising that her rubber clad thighs would excite him. As if he hadn't been able to hear Jeanine's words, Ana Tai repeated them. 'Jeanine wants you. She is ready for you to fuck her. She wants your dick hard up inside her, and I shall give my permission. What do you say?'

Everett had forgotten to say 'thank you'.

Ana Tai dipped her fingers in some oil and then rammed them hard up inside his virgin bottom-mouth. Everett bucked and leapt into the air. The crop haired woman was ready for him and brought the cane down hard on his trembling thighs.

'Thank you,' she said. 'You will learn politeness and you will say thank you.'

'Thank you,' he said.

'Thank you, what?' she said, letting her prick-holding hand slide down to grip his balls tightly as her other hand swiped the paddle across his buttocks.

'Thank you, madam,' he stuttered.

'Jeanine, open your legs wide,' she said.

Jeanine obeyed.

With her smooth rubber-encased legs gliding against his, Ana Tai let go of Everett's balls. She took his throbbing penis and guided it into Jeanine's wanton wet sex. She stayed holding it as he gasped and charged backwards and forwards. After a while, Ana Tai allowed her fingers to stray on to Jeanine's engorged little bud, giving her extra excitement. Everett invaded Jeanine's moist opening. There they stayed, the three of them, until Everett came with a rich and fulfilling orgasm.

Oh yes, thought Jeanine, playing with herself; she had enjoyed herself that night.

She clambered out of the jacuzzi and enveloped herself in a huge bath wrap. She was wondering if she wanted Ana Tai to join them once again or if she'd take Everett on his own. Perhaps today she'd slip into her leathers and have him all to herself in her dungeon.

Jeanine switched on her intercom. Mrs Maclean answered.

'Henrietta?'

'Yes,' said the American woman who acted as her friend, confidante and general manager.

'Are you busy?'

'Not particularly,' said Henrietta.

'Then come here; I want you. And bring your big friend with you,' ordered Jeanine.

Jeanine slipped out of the wrap and wandered naked into her walk-in closet and took out her special black leather gear. She had just had time to check all the buckles were in good order when Henrietta Maclean appeared. The lewd sight of her excited Jeanine.

Henrietta was dressed in a modern-day version of an eighteenth-century shepherdess costume. Her tits were jacked up over a low cut bodice. The skirt billowed out to the side and fell to her calves. Her feet were laced into tight ankle-length boots, but the middle of her skirt was split down the middle; protruding from it was an enormous thick black dildo.

'You were busy,' said Jeanine, looking at her and thinking that nobody would recognise the quiet subdued, plump, middle-aged American housewife who originally came to stay in her hotel.

'I'd just finished,' said Mrs Maclean.

'Who was it?' asked Jeanine.

'Mr de Bouys. Mr Gerry de Bouys,' she replied. 'And he was very disappointed that it wasn't you.'

'What did you do for him?'

'The usual.'

'Good. So he went away happy?'

'I've seen him happier,' replied Henrietta. 'He'll stop coming if you don't screw him soon.'

'I'm not a tart,' replied Jeanine. 'I don't screw anybody I don't want to. And at the moment I don't want to screw him. He bores me. But his cousin is coming and he, sweetie, is a different kettle of *poisson*. So oil me, stroke me: make me ready.'

43

Jeanine walked over to a massage table in the corner of her bathroom and lay face down. 'Is Auralie back from Petrov's?' she asked.

'No, not yet,' Henrietta replied, taking a variety of oils out of a cupboard.

'Tell her she needn't come back tonight,' said Jeanine.

'You've changed your tune!' exclaimed Henrietta, as she started to pummel and massage Jeanine's lovely body with the sweet-smelling substances.

'I'm feeling magnanimous,' replied Jeanine, squirming with delight as Henrietta prodded and squeezed her breasts and nipples.

'Turn over,' said Henrietta Maclean.

Jeanine turned over and Henrietta climbed on top of her between her legs and rubbed her back and her bottom. Every time she leant forward to massage Jeanine's shoulders, the dildo rubbed between Jeanine's legs, exciting her wet sex lips.

'Is it the double one?' Jeanine asked, squirming.

'Sure is, honey,' replied Henrietta Maclean. 'I've got this goddam rubber cock fastened tight to me and one half is shoved right up my pussy. I'm having a real good time. Why – do you want it too?'

'Yes,' said Jeanine, keeping her torso flattened on the massage bed and raising her arse high in the air.

Henrietta covered her hands with oil; then she spread it all around Jeanine's wanton swollen sex and rubbed.

'You sure are feeling sexy,' said Henrietta, kneeling behind her and allowing the tip of the dildo to enter Jeanine's fragrant honey-pot. 'And what are you planning for Mr Everett?'

'A surprise,' said Jeanine, squirming as the dildo was pushed further and further into her sex. 'Oh that's nice, Henrietta, really nice: but you'd better stop now and dress me. He'll be here soon.'

'He will?'

'Yes, he rang saying he's taking his father's new jet and flying straight to London. And I can't wait,' she said walking into her huge bedroom, which was decorated in shades of cream and gold, with heavy golden brocade curtaining covering one complete wall.

Jeanine's body was glistening and her breasts were fuller, her nipples erect and her sex open and wanton. She sat down and made up her face. Then Henrietta helped Jeanine with the intricacies of the leather corset. The strips crossed her breasts, leaving her nipples bare; those around the tops of her thighs accentuated her pale fleece. Henrietta positioned the slits in the leather exactly over Jeanine's sex and back passage, then brought up the buckles over her rounded belly and fastened them tight.

She piled Jeanine's hair up high and fitted a leather-and-chain collar around her neck; she placed a high feather mask over her eyes, then completed the outfit by covering Jeanine in a cloak of the finest kid leather. Then Henrietta made her perch on a high stool close to her bed while she rolled black silk stockings along Jeanine's thighs.

'Will you be using your pleasure den?' asked Henrietta.

'Oh I think so,' said Jeanine, pushing her feet out for Henrietta to put on her highest of high-heeled black leather boots.

Jeanine clicked a switch. The wall of curtain drew back to reveal mirrors – endless two-way mirrors, and, in the room behind, cages hanging from the ceiling, a high stretcher bed, a vaulting horse, instruments of torture and whips and paddles of every type and design. 'And this time I'll have him all to myself.'

The intercom shrieked. Jeanine answered. It was Terry, her receptionist, telling her that Countess Jacqueline Helitzer had telephoned from Paris to say her plans had changed, her party was postponed for the moment and she didn't know quite when she'd be arriving.

Jeanine was delighted. Now she would have extra time to spend with Everett.

Chapter Three

Zinnia did not go to straight to Jeanine's hotel in London; instead, she hired a car at the airport and drove to a castle in North Wales. David Lewis, her boss at Hanway, Rattle & Lewis, had sent her on a secret mission to see his father Caradoc, the owner of the bank.

After passing through the lush green English countryside, Zinnia drove up the slate-grey mountains into Wales. Arriving at the outskirts of a village, which had a long name consisting almost entirely of consonants, she stopped outside a magnificent pair of wrought-iron gates. The lodge porter checked her identity then let her into the long tree-lined drive. Expecting a stone edifice from the Middle Ages, with a drawbridge and a moat, Zinnia was surprised to discover it was a Manchester cotton baron's Victorian redbrick monstrosity. She pulled up in front of its large, imposing covered portico.

There Zinnia was greeted by an extremely handsome young man, who was dressed in a black suit with a sparkling white shirt.

'Good afternoon, Madam,' he said. 'Mr Lewis has had to go out. He'll be back in a little while.'

'Oh,' she said, quite surprised. She had arrived at the time specified.

'I will show you your room, and you are of course at

liberty to roam the house and grounds. Mr Lewis has an excellent library, should you prefer to sit and read.'

'Thank you,' said Zinnia, following him into the vast mock baronial hall. 'Tell me, what's your name?'

'Francis,' he said.

'And are you the butler?'

The young man stopped dead in his tracks and eyed her haughtily.

'Certainly not,' he said, with a slight shrug of the shoulders and a definite huff in his voice. 'I am Mr Lewis's personal companion.'

'Oh I see,' she said, guessing Caradoc Lewis's sexual inclinations.

Zinnia was intrigued. Why had David asked her to go there? Since her marriage, she hadn't been so close to her boss. Prior to her wedding, they had had an arrangement. He would make an appointment to see her, and if she was bending over her office desk when he entered he knew she was randy. He would lock the door, stand between her legs, pull up her skirt, pull down her knickers, unzip himself, take out his prick and screw her violently until they came. They enjoyed it. The quick furtiveness of it excited them both.

Afterwards, they got on with their work, never referring to their short sharp escapade. However, since her marriage, he had respected her vows and kept his distance. But, Zinnia thought, even if she had been available, she doubted whether David Lewis would have continued with their game. She was aware that he'd got himself entangled with an unknown and, by all accounts, unsuitable woman – who was occupying most of his spare time and some of it which wasn't spare. This surprised Zinnia. David Lewis had always been careful with his associates and relationships.

When giving her the assignment, David Lewis had explained that it was to meet with his father and discuss the possibilities of new fund management.

'Oh, and Zinnia, take a short holiday whilst you're there,' he'd said. 'It'll confuse the enemy.'

But who was the enemy? Other fund managers? Zinnia was too intelligent to believe that discussing or even acquiring new funds was all there was to her trip. Something else was behind it. She could feel it in her bones. And old Caradoc Lewis was known not to approve of women in positions of power within his bank. There had been a major row when David Lewis had brought her into the firm. So why send her to Wales when he could have gone himself? What could be more ordinary than father and son meeting? There was something more in the wind and, for whatever it was, she was being groomed to play her part.

'My father doesn't think women can cope in banking,' David had told her. 'So you'll be a good cover. No one will think he'll give you time of day, let alone believe you got to meet with him.'

Zinnia knew full well, for all their protestations to the contrary, this was very much current thinking amongst the upper echelons of the financial fraternity. Dismayed that most of her sex's good work had gone under-praised and virtually unsung, she saw this assignment as a challenge. In accepting it, she would prove that women were as supremely capable in the banking world as men. Zinnia suspected a hostile take-over was on the agenda, but not of her bank. She wondered which one was being targeted.

Francis showed Zinnia her room, which was spartan but warm. She found that the castle had an ancient and surprisingly efficient central heating system. After a quick wash to freshen up, she went for a wander in the beautifully maintained grounds and noticed that the surrounding moorland was well stocked with partridge and grouse.

When she felt she'd admired nature enough for one day, she returned to the house. The rooms, though dark, were large and gracious. She sat in the library and tried to read. But she couldn't concentrate. Jethro was on her mind.

She kept thinking over and over again about her

present situation. Where she was going with her life? What did she want? She had thought with a good job and being wed to Jethro she had everything, but she was beginning to realise the marriage was a mistake. He was too busy feeling and screwing other women to understand her cravings, her needs. Three days after their wedding she saw him shoving his hands up Carola Finestein's skirt.

Zinnia didn't let him know what she'd seen. She could have forgiven him if he had taken time with her, loved her properly, shown her some affection. But since they'd got married, he'd almost forgotten she existed. She was just another acquired trophy. Something wanted, obtained and, no doubt, soon to be discarded. But things didn't work that way; not in Zinnia's book. Love, she thought, needs to be nurtured. She was fed up with being rolled over in the middle of the night, having a quick fumble that satisfied Jethro but left her wanting. She was fed up with constantly feeling deprived, deflated – almost de-sexed. Nurtured she was not.

Zinnia was going to fight her corner and she was going to fight dirty. She would have Sapphire as her ally. She was pleased with herself. That had been a clever ruse, to get Sapphire to go to the Finesteins' and unwittingly spy on him. She looked forward to hearing about that when she telephoned.

It was early evening when she finally got to meet with Caradoc Lewis. The sixty-year-old banker was sitting in his book-lined study in a large heavily carved high-backed armchair, with a Welsh blanket over his lap. Zinnia decided that, for all his prejudices, she liked Caradoc Lewis. Father and son had the same charm and thin wiry build, also the same mop of dark hair and slightly swarthy skin. Caradoc Lewis was wearing rough country tweeds. His son would have worn an Italian designer suit. Zinnia found Caradoc Lewis sexually attractive.

He took to her, too. He liked the cuddly roundness of her. Her wrists and knees were soft and inviting, they seemed not to have bones. Her long, bouncy, shining auburn hair was piled high in the front but fell over her shoulders in thick curls. She had changed from the formal pin-stripe she had been wearing into a pistachio green silk and cashmere suit which showed off her well-endowed body. Her satin blouse, polo-necked, and skin-coloured, was modest and a tease. At first glance, it appeared she was wearing nothing under her suit. It was a subtle choice, a game she hoped Caradoc Lewis would enjoy.

'Do you play chess?' he asked as they sat appraising one another.

'Yes,' she replied.

'Then we'll have a game before dinner,' he said, pressing a bell close to his chair for the butler.

Francis came in and wheeled a table across the room; he set up the carved jade chess set ready for play.

'Would you care to start?' asked Caradoc Lewis.

'But don't you want to discuss the various new funding projects?' Zinnia asked, perching her briefcase on her knees.

'No, I don't; not now. Later,' he said, adding, 'will you begin?'

'Thank you, yes,' she answered.

Her hand hovered momentarily over the white knight. Should she or shouldn't she move it? And why was he not in a hurry to discuss business? The secrecy of her meeting and Caradoc Lewis' total lack of inquisitiveness towards the papers in her case reinforced her belief that she was there because of an impending happening. She was being tested.

Caradoc Lewis looked at her quizzically. 'The white knight?' he asked.

'No,' she replied. 'But I was wondering if you are.'

Caradoc Lewis laughed. 'No, not me,' he said, enigmatically. 'But you'll do. You'll do. My son's a clever man and he was right to send you.'

Zinnia opened by moving the white queen's pawn two places forward. She lost the game but felt no sense of disappointment. She had played exceptionally well. She discovered much later that Caradoc Lewis was a world class player and realised then that the game had been the interview. When it was over, Zinnia tried again to bring up the subject of funds and their management but Caradoc Lewis had said, 'Another time, my dear, another time. You leave early tomorrow, don't you?'

'Yes,' she'd replied.

'Might have a job for you. I'll talk to David. But how'd you fancy going to the Far East next week?'

'The Far East!' she exclaimed. 'Where?

'Meriboa,' he said. 'Tell me, Zinnia, where are you staying in London?'

'At an hotel in Kensington,' she said. Zinnia gave him Jeanine's number.

Caradoc Lewis gave her a knowing look. 'And how is the beautiful Jeanine?' he asked.

'Very well,' she replied, taken aback that he should know her.

'You visited her before coming here?'

'Er, yes,' Zinnia replied.

'An exceptional woman, and an exceptional establishment,' he said.

'Um, yes,' she said avoiding his eyes.

'A place with tremendous facilities, don't you think?'

'Yes,' she replied.

'It's where I stay when I go to London,' he said.

'You do?' she exclaimed.

'Oh, yes.' Zinnia caught his eyes and he held them. 'I need a clever woman with certain aptitudes for this assignment,' he said.

'I see,' she said, suddenly excited.

'I'm so glad you do. David hasn't underestimated you. You'll forgive me if I'm wrong but, if I'm not very much mistaken, you enjoy being fucked?'

'Yes,' she said, surprised by his sudden outspokenness.

'And you enjoy being sucked, and taking a man's cock in your mouth?'

51

'Yes,' she said, wiggling slightly in her seat. He hadn't touched her. He hadn't moved, yet she was wanting him – wanting him to stroke her, feel her.

'Are you wearing any knickers?'

'Yes,' she said.

'Take them off,' he said.

Standing in front of him, Zinnia lifted her skirt. She undid the one button on the waistband of her pure silk directoire panties and let them slide to the floor.

'Keep your skirt up,' he said.

Caradoc Lewis gazed lustfully at her rounded alabaster thighs and the thick patch of her bright red fleece. He stretched out a hand to her crotch and pulled her to him. 'You are wet,' he said, his finger skimming along her sex lips.

'Yes,' she said.

'I want to fuck you,' he said, as his fingers eased slowly into her opening sex. 'I'd like you to sit astride my lap with your back to me.'

He undid his flies. Zinnia walked backwards on to him. He let the rug fall down to the ground, she felt the hard rasp of his rough tweeds against her soft skin. She heard him tear something and realised he was covering his penis with a condom.

'Bend over,' he commanded, feeling her wet sex from behind.

She put her hands on the arms of his chair when she felt his sheathed cock at her secret entrance. She pressed down as he pushed upwards through her opening and welcoming sex.

When his cock was firmly lodged up high inside her, he brought his hands round and started to fondle her large breasts.

'Pull up your blouse,' he said. 'I want to feel your nipples. I like the look of a woman half-dressed. It excites me. I could take you to my bedroom, lay you down and screw you there; but this is much more exciting.'

Riding him, keeping the rhythm going, Zinnia did as she was told and he pushed up her bra, leaving her great breasts trapped under the tightness of lace and silk. Languidly, his fingers caressed her erect nipples. She brought her hands down between her legs and held the base of his cock as she went up and down on him. Then he shoved his bottom forward. She took his scrotum in her hands and let one finger stroll between the cleft of his buttocks.

At her touch so close to his arse he shuddered and came quickly. But Zinnia was still wanting.

'Stand close and let me play with you,' he said.

Wantonly, with her large breasts displayed under the tight, constricting, bra, Zinnia kept her skirt up and thrust her hips forward. He touched and stroked the excited and swollen button at the inner apex of her sex lips. She rolled her hips to meet his exploring fingers. His touch was light on her full bud and hard within her. He knew what to do: where to feel, when to thrust up and when to pull back. Her calves began to shake. Her belly coiled. She sighed and shuddered. She came and was deeply satisfied.

'Hors d'ouvres,' she said, smiling at him.

'Yes,' he said, pressing the bell beside him, 'and now it's time for dinner.'

Caradoc Lewis did up his flies. Zinnia readjusted her clothing. Francis returned, looked from one to the other, then picked up Caradoc's blanket which was lying on the floor.

'You'll be extra hungry now, sir,' said the young man.

Zinnia, aware of the tinge of jealousy in his voice, watched him walk to a darkened corner of the room and come back with Caradoc Lewis's wheelchair. She'd have to beware of Francis.

Zinnia had had a good, sexual and exhilarating time and her drive to London had been easy, nevertheless, she was delighted to be back in the comforting warmth and seclusion of Jeanine's hotel. It had been a shock to find that Caradoc Lewis's legs were useless, paralysed. She had never screwed anyone without the full use of their body before. She had enjoyed it. Caradoc Lewis had concentrated on other, more esoteric, aspects of love making.

Standing in the elegant blue, cream and gold foyer Zinnia realised that there wasn't the usual hustle and bustle. And some things had changed since her last visit. She looked about her. There was now a large picture hanging over the marble fireplace. It was a painting of the late Princess Olga Vladelsky. She had been killed in an aircraft crash. Whoever had painted it had captured her essence. She gazed down on Jeanine's customers with her familiar glamour and hauteur.

'Zinnia, sweetie, darling,' said Jeanine, coming out of her office to greet her, wearing high spiky-heeled boots and a fine leather flowing cape. As Jeanine moved, Zinnia caught a glimpse of an exotic and buckled leather basque.

'Love your new hairstyle, sweetie,' Jeanine said, pecking her cheek and giving her the once-over, taking in her power dressing, her black pin-striped suit, its short skirt and flesh-coloured georgette blouse. 'And great clothes. You're looking terrific – and as randy as hell.'

'Yes,' said Zinnia.

'Then, sweetie, it's time for games before dinner,' said Jeanine.

'But there's nobody about,' observed Zinnia.

'Oh some people are: the cook, the kitchen staff, Kensit, I think, and Mrs Maclean. Others might be, I haven't checked to see who's back. We've been preparing for the arrival of Jacqueline and her mannikins. They turn the place upside down when they get here. I give everyone time off before she arrives. Most of them have gone to Petrov's.'

'How is he?' asked Zinnia.

'Well, I think,' answered Jeanine. She didn't want to discuss Petrov. 'I haven't seen him for some time.'

'Tell me, Jeanine, is there a new man in your life?'

'Why do you ask?'

'You look so radiant and – ' Zinnia pointed to Jeanine's special outfit.

'Well, yes,' replied Jeanine, coyly. 'What's more, he should be here soon. Actually sweetie, I thought he would have been here by now, but never mind.'

'Who is it?'

'Everett.'

'Everett!' exclaimed Zinnia, in surprise. 'Oh! Didn't I screw him way back in your dungeon with some of your other friends? Wasn't it Ascot week or something? I know it was before I got married.'

'You did, sweetie, darling,' said Jeanine. 'And how is Jethro?'

'Jethro!'

Jeanine caught the disapproval and disappointment in her friend's voice. 'Being a naughty boy, is he? You'll have to send him here. We'll change his ways.'

'He's driving me plum crazy,' said Zinnia. She might have spent the previous day screwing Caradoc Lewis but she was still angry with her husband. She was more than angry; she was furious with Jethro.

'So what's this husband of yours been doing?' asked Jeanine.

'Screwing around. It pisses me off, Jeanine. Really pisses me off.'

'So get yourself a new man.'

'Thought about it,' said Zinnia. 'I thought about it real hard. I think I might, but I'm not sure. You see, what makes me extra mad is that since we married I've been faithful – well almost – but with Jethro I haven't had one moment's satisfaction. He's a goddam five-second wonder.'

'Come downstairs. Let's have some champagne and forget about Jethro,' said Jeanine.

As they stepped out of Jeanine's office, Zinnia noticed a handsome young man in the hotel lobby. Their eyes met. Zinnia knew she'd seen him somewhere before. There was a sweetness about him, an air that she liked. A sudden licentiousness rushed through her body.

Zinnia had instant images of this man kissing her lips and caressing her breasts: his taut, athletic body over hers, his hands roving down over her belly to play between her legs. Zinnia let her gaze wander from his eyes to his mouth. Yes, she definitely wanted to kiss those lips. That idea made her feel sexier than ever. The soft dark flower at the top of her thighs began to moisten. Her sex opened wantonly.

'Ah Jeanine, we have an appointment,' said the man, his eyes sliding away from Jeanine to Zinnia.

'Gerry, I'm afraid not . . .' Jeanine's hard no-nonsense voice trailed away.

Zinnia realised that Jeanine was aware of their mutual attraction. Using a different and far more welcoming tone Jeanine suddenly said, 'I'll be with you soon. Wait here for me.'

So that's Gerry! thought Zinnia. Auralie's ex-husband Gerry that Jeanine had become entangled with; Zinnia was surprised to see him. She thought that relationship had ended some time ago. Zinnia hadn't seen him since his engagement party. Neither had she fancied him – then. He'd seemed callow, too youthful. She certainly fancied him now. There was something extra about him. He'd grown up, become a man. But why was he still playing lap-dog to Jeanine?

Gerry turned to talk to a tall and very beautiful young black guy. Zinnia recognised him as Kensit, one of Jeanine's helpers. Smiling in his direction, Zinnia followed Jeanine down to her private apartments. She was wanting to ask questions, but that wasn't allowed. She went through the double doors that opened on to Jeanine's sitting room.

'So Jethro's being a pain in the arse,' said Jeanine. 'Well, sweetie, darling, a massage would seem to be a good idea and then maybe some games, eh?'

'Why not?' replied Zinnia.

Jeanine pressed the intercom.

'Mrs Maclean, please.' Jeanine waited. 'Ah, Henrietta, sweetie. Now, Henrietta, I have a friend with me. Zinnia.

Remember her? She's in need of some relaxation.' There was a pause, then Jeanine added, 'Yes, the very same thought had crossed my mind. I'll leave you to arrange it.'

Jeanine walked over to a wall cabinet and took out a couple of champagne flutes. Zinnia sat in one of the deep armchairs bedside the white marble fireplace and glanced at the long wall of heavy beautiful curtaining. She knew from her previous visits that behind that tasteful luxury was Jeanine's room of tortuous delights.

Jeanine took a cold bottle of Moet from her baby fridge, poured some of the sparkling liquid into the blue-tinted crystal flutes, then handed one to Zinnia.

'Take it in the bathroom,' she said. 'You'll see I've made a few changes since you were last here. I've bought the house next door. Extended my domain. And it's very special. I've learnt a lot. All the work's been done to my very specific orders. Come and see my new bathroom.'

Zinnia moved into the bright newly extended and re-decorated bathroom. It was a room of mirrors with two showers, a large bath, a jacuzzi, a sauna and a massage couch.

'Bathe, sweetie, then lie on the couch,' said Jeanine, closing the door.

Zinnia ran the water, poured in soothing bath oils, undressed then stepped into the bath. She lay enveloped in the steaming water, allowing her worries and cares to float away. Once out of the bath she draped a large bath towel around her plump shoulders, sat on the massage table and sipped her champagne.

Mrs Maclean came in carrying a tray of bottles. Zinnia, who had visited the hotel not long after it had opened, had found Mrs Maclean installed as Jeanine's manager. Apparently she had arrived for a holiday at a disastrous moment in Jeanine's life and had stayed, to their mutual benefit and all-round satisfaction. Zinnia looked up at her and smiled.

'Hiya, honey,' said Henrietta Maclean.

Then another woman walked in. She was a tall thin

Asian with short masculine cropped black hair, large slanting eyes and rings in her lower lip and eyebrows. She, too, was wearing a white surgical coat, but when she moved Zinnia caught a glimpse of black rubber covering her belly and her legs. She also wore long rubber gloves.

'This is Ana Tai. She's going to help me.'

'Hi,' said Ana Tai, in a soft lilting voice.

Henrietta Maclean removed the huge bath towel from Zinnia's plump, rounded body and laid her down on her back, putting her legs together.

Ana Tai looked at her lustfully. She stretched out her long narrow arms and dipped her gloved fingers into a pot of sweet-smelling oils. Then she ran one hand along the inside of Zinnia's closed thighs and let the other hand rest on her sex mound, allowing one finger to nonchalantly play on Zinnia's clitoris while the other anointed her outer lips, enticing them to open so that she could slowly enter the willing moistness beyond.

'Ah,' sighed Zinnia, raising her hips and opening her legs to welcome Ana Tai's exploring fingers.

'Honey, you know you must keep very still and in the position I put you, so close your legs again,' said Henrietta, lubricating her breasts with more of the oils.

Zinnia offered her body up to their expert ministrations. Up and down they went, over Zinnia's shoulders, breasts, belly, legs and feet, pummelling, squeezing, and rolling. They turned Zinnia over. Up and down, pressing here and there, round, up, down and round and up. Every so often, one or the other made a foray between Zinnia's legs, massaging softly on her sex lips. Opening her, preparing her. They massaged her young alabaster skin again and again until her plump white body was glistening and smelling of sex-musk and completely relaxed. And then, without saying a word, Ana Tai left them.

'Where's Jeanine?' asked Zinnia, sliding down from the table and walking towards the door.

'She's had a friend come calling,' said Mrs Maclean. 'And she's asked that you don't come out naked.'

'Oh,' said Zinnia, stopping in her tracks. There was a note of disappointment in Zinnia's voice; because of the unexpected visitor, was her game to be curtailed?

Henrietta Maclean opened one of the mirrored wall cabinets and retrieved an Egyptian dancing girl's skirt and bodice.

'She asked that you wear this,' said Mrs Maclean, holding up the flimsy and semi-transparent garment.

Mrs Maclean tied the skirt around Zinnia's waist. She wound the folds of fabric over Zinnia's voluptuous breasts and adjusted her breasts so that they spilled out over the top of the multi-coloured bodice.

'You look beautiful,' said Mrs Maclean, in admiration of the redhead's comely figure. 'And good enough to eat. Now put on these shoes.'

Mrs Maclean placed a pair of exceptionally high-heeled red shoes in front of Zinnia, who stepped into them. They were practically impossible to walk in, so whoever it was who'd called was either leaving soon or going to enjoy the *hors d'ouvres*. Zinnia was full of anticipation. She couldn't wait to find out who it was.

'Is it Everett?' asked Zinnia. 'Has Everett arrived?'

Zinnia wondered if they were going to have a three or four-way session in the dungeon. She'd enjoyed it last time. The hands roaming, the tongues licking, the cocks plunging, and Jeanine whipping.

Mrs Maclean didn't answer.

'Henrietta? Who?'

'Zinnia, you know you never ask questions here; never,' replied Mrs Maclean sternly. 'Jeanine wants you to wear this as well.'

Mrs Maclean held up an elaborate feathered mask. It fitted neatly across her eyes and over the bridge of her nose and blocked out all light.

'Now hold out your hands.' Zinnia obeyed and Mrs Maclean fitted a pair of handcuffs around her wrists. Then she guided Zinnia from the bathroom into Jeanine's sitting room. As they approached the double doors, Zinnia heard Jeanine's voice speaking softly and enticingly and deep sexy male laughter. They entered and there was total silence.

Zinnia heard the swish of the curtains and Mrs Maclean, holding her by one arm, took her through into the room beyond. There unknown hands took her handcuffed wrists and fixed them to a chain, pulling her arms upwards. Then hands began feeling her breasts, parting her diaphanous skirt, touching her thighs, her belly and her very round, very pale pink bottom.

There was no noise in the room. No one said anything. There was complete silence except for Zinnia's soft sighs as she thrilled to the unseen fingers trailing through the cleft of her buttocks. She felt cool lips on the back of her thighs. She offered her luscious bottom to the lips and to the exploring tongue, her hips gave a movement backward as if to say, 'yes, take me, take me now'.

Zinnia teetered on her extremely high heels as large masculine hands gripped her rump, tipped her forward and exposed her neat puckered hole. A slim hard wet tongue began to work its way inwards. She shuddered with excitement. An extra tingle rushed through her as she felt a stiff penis rub against her knees and sidle up on the inside of her tender thighs. Then another, larger, penis pressed against her belly and other hands took hold of her heavy breasts. Fingers clasped and caressed her erect nipples.

Zinnia sighed and twisted on her chains. She was high, excited almost beyond endurance. She wanted those unknown hands sliding between her perfumed and oiled thighs. She wanted those fingers entering her, playing with her sex, opening her wider. She wanted to feel a penis in her hands and guide it into the depths of her aching moist sex.

One of the men was exciting her more than the other. One seemed to have a chemistry that blended with hers, his fingers made her tremble. Zinnia felt that man slide down her imprisoned body and his tongue touch her engorged clitoris. She jerked violently and let out a long gasp of pleasure.

It was a thick exploring tongue, and it was entering every tiny secret place within her. It was sucking and slurping at her juices, opening her, enabling Zinnia to give vent to her visions of total wantonness. She moved her muscles in an attempt to draw the tongue upwards. The tongue withdrew and nibbled on her clitoris. The deprivation of sight heightened her sense of feel and touch. The mouth kept changing direction, one moment pushing the tongue deep inside her sex and the next moving upwards, pulling and biting on her full sex bud; all the time, hands massaged her inner thighs.

Another, slimmer, harder tongue began exploring her bottom-mouth and was joined by a finger oiling her, easing open her dark red-brown muscle. Zinnia began to experience alternating and exquisite pinpoints of high pleasure. One moment the feeling was in her womb, the next in lips and in her nipples. When a stiff, warm and throbbing cock began rubbing harder between her thighs, it seemed to Zinnia as if the pleasure spread, suffusing her entire body. Every inch of her was an erogenous zone.

She gave herself completely to the trembling fever encompassing her, until thoughts of Jethro forced their way into her mind. She thought of his trim body, his broad chest, his slim hips and his wayward cock. His cock which had never elicited from her the same undulating sensuous response as the unknown tongue and fingers now thrusting and penetrating her hidden being were able to do.

Zinnia was used to sex, real sex, with all its variations: and now she was getting it. Would Jethro enjoy the sight of her bound, blindfolded and being pleasured? She told herself she didn't care if he did or if he didn't. She was being fulfilled.

The hands belonging to the man sucking at her sex and massaging along her thighs moved. The fingers shifted and touched her gently, touched her swollen wet sex as if to enter. She tingled and waited expectantly for those fingers to move again. There was a tightening in her throat and a gripping in her belly. Zinnia wanted those fingers up inside, exploring her secret self.

'You – ' Jeanine must have pointed at one of the men ' – you, fuck her.'

Zinnia was spread open. Hands lifted her up by her large globes and held her so that she was easily, but slowly, very slowly, impaled on the tip of a large, stiff phallus.

Zinnia could feel the man's breath against her cheek, his chest against her naked breasts, his sweet smell assailing her nostrils as he stealthily edged his way into her sex. She had a strong desire to murmur words of love into his ear. She wanted to wind her arms around his neck and hold him close as he began to thrust into her. Joy and ecstasy were overwhelming her and she let out little moans of happiness.

An extraordinary thought crossed her mind. Was it Gerry who was fucking her? Was it his cock hard up inside in her inner depths? She'd find out when the blindfold was removed. The thought excited her more and she thrust and wiggled closer to him.

The man behind her kept one hand on her backside, steadying her, and brought his other hand round to gently and softly play on her clitoris. Then the man screwing her from the front lifted her up and away from his cock, leaving the other man's strong hands on her clitoris and backside. He took her weight and then she was turned on her chains and felt another cock poking at her swollen wet sex entrance, driving in hard up to the hilt.

'Now remove her blindfold,' commanded Jeanine.

She was instantly obeyed. Zinnia was able to see who was taking her, touching her, fucking her. Only one person. There was only one man in the room, but Jeanine was sitting on a high stool in her basque and holding a whip like a master of ceremonies. Zinnia knew there had

62

been two men and two cocks and four hands exploring and taking her alabaster body.

She turned her head to make sure. Whoever it was had gone. Left. Departed. Zinnia felt an acute sense of disappointment. She was sure it had been Gerry, but it was Kensit who was screwing her. She squirmed and thrust out her hips to meet and blend Kensit's ebony body with hers. Black and white intermingling. Zinnia gave a huge and satisfactory grin as she thought how Jethro, from the southern state of Georgia, would kill her if he ever found out. She thrust her hips higher to take him deeper.

Some time later, Zinnia trailed up the beautiful staircase, wondering when Jeanine would install a lift. Inside her elegant bedroom, she wearily removed her suit and blouse but kept on her exquisite flesh-coloured silk bra and directoire knickers. Zinnia threw herself down on her large bed and fell instantly asleep.

A knock on her door wakened her.

'Come in,' she called.

To her surprise, Auralie walked in with a tea tray.

'Auralie!' Zinnia exclaimed, smiling and holding her arms open.

'Madame,' said Auralie, as if she didn't recognise Zinnia, and pulled a table over beside the bed. For a moment Zinnia was speechless. She stared at Auralie and wondered where the faint clanking noise was coming from.

'Auralie, what are you doing here, serving and . . .?' Zinnia was nonplussed. On previous visits, Zinnia had always asked about Auralie and was told she was working hard on her fabric designs, putting her collections together. But she had never seen her. Not even when she'd gone to Petrov's had Zinnia seen Auralie. What was she doing at Jeanine's dressed like a chambermaid?

Zinnia surveyed her thoroughly. She was wearing a crisp white cotton blouse with a Peter Pan collar, pin tucks over her pert breasts and pearl buttons along the front opening. She wore a very short bias-cut black skirt and a white bib-fronted, lace-edged apron. Her feet were shod in high-heeled lace-up shoes, her legs were encased in black stockings, and perched on her head was a small frilly cap.

When Auralie bent down to place the tray on the table, Zinnia noticed the small chains around both ankles rising up her legs.

'Auralie, what is this?' asked Zinnia.

'Tea, madam; I thought you'd ordered it.'

'No,' Zinnia was quite perplexed. 'Auralie, it is you. Auralie, why – ? I mean ... Auralie, speak to me; it's Zinnia.' She jumped off the bed. 'Auralie, what's going on? I see the name of your company everywhere. I know it's successful. Why are you pretending you don't recognise me, and why are you dressed like that?'

'I hope your tea is to your liking, madam,' said Auralie and started to walk out of the room.

'Oh no,' said Zinnia, grabbing hold of her. 'Auralie, please ... And what are these chains?'

'Jeanine's chains,' said Auralie.

'Jeanine's chains!'

Zinnia lifted Auralie's skirt and saw the chains disappearing under the elastic of her crisp white schoolgirl knickers. 'You mean, you are – '

'Her sex slave, yes.'

'How?' asked Zinnia. 'You, of all people. I'd never have thought it. You were the goddess. The leader at Petrov's. How did it happen?'

'Well ...'

'Auralie.' A stern voice was heard from the doorway.

Both women looked up and saw Jackson, a huge burly black man, carrying Zinnia's suitcases. Swiftly, Zinnia swiftly dropped the hem of Auralie's skirt.

'Madam has been calling for you,' he said advancing menacingly into the room.

'I was bringing Mrs Clarke her afternoon tea,' said Auralie meekly.

'And that was why she was lifting your skirt?' said

Jackson. 'Madam will have to be informed. She told you to stay downstairs, didn't she?'

'Yes,' said Auralie, lowering her head.

'Madam will not be pleased, will she?'

'No,' said Auralie.

'Madam will have you punished for disobeying her orders, won't she?' said Jackson.

'Yes,' said Auralie.

'What do you think that punishment will be?' asked Jackson, coming closer and standing threateningly in front of Auralie. Zinnia sat on the bed, about to protest that it was she who had held Auralie back and had been responsible for lifting her skirt. She felt guilty. It was her curiosity that had landed Auralie in trouble.

'Whatever you suggest,' said Auralie. There was a note of acquiescence in her voice that made Zinnia keep quiet.

'Yes,' said Jackson, with a smile of satisfaction. 'And I suggest that, as it was here that you disobeyed, your punishment will have to take place here, in front of Mrs Clarke. Kneel down.'

Auralie knelt in front of him.

'Open your mouth,' he commanded as he slowly undid the flap of his trousers. Zinnia watched, mesmerised, as Jackson took out his massive, throbbing jet-black phallus and held it to Auralie's wide lipstick-covered lips.

'Suck,' he said, easing his balls into his own hands.

Auralie licked the cap of his huge stiff warmth, then covered it completely with her mouth. Moving her tongue over its head, she clasped its stem with both her hands and, with a firm but gentle strength, she stroked it down to its base. Then, taking Jackson's soft sac into one of her hands and running her other hand between his thick muscular thighs, she let her mouth glide up and down on his shaft.

Zinnia was hypnotised by the big black man. She lay on the bed, staring back at him, feeling desire fermenting in her belly and exploding down through her womb into that expectant willing pink opening, which was made more moist and more juicy as she looked at his thick prick sliding in and out of Auralie's mouth.

She wanted to feel his huge bulk on top of her, his dark hairless body enveloping her, those enormous black muscular thighs lying between her soft white legs and his great phallus pressing in, stretching her, easing its way up through her warm, wet sex. Almost of their own accord, her hands began to snake down over her body and under the waist elastic of her wide-legged silk knickers.

'Auralie. Auralie. You're wanted,' they heard Henrietta Maclean call.

Auralie turned her eyes up towards Jackson, who nodded, and gave her permission to depart. Silently she left the room, closing the door behind her.

Zinnia and Jackson were left staring at one another. The tension between them did not allow either of them to move. She lay immobile; even the finger lying on her pleasure bud was still. Then, very slowly, never letting his gaze wander from her pale blue eyes, Jackson sauntered over to her, reached out, and caught her nipples in a scissor-like grip with his long strong fingers.

'Mrs Clarke,' said Jackson, bending down and licking first one nipple then the other, 'please open your legs.'

He took her hands from her sex and placed them around his rampant phallus. His hands prowled over her body. One finger touched her hidden bud and her body was instantly kindled. She sighed and wiggled her hips invitingly. Licking his lips and keeping his eyes on hers, silently promising her excitement and wickedness, he massaged her moist sex.

'Wider, open your legs wider,' he said. 'I want to fuck you.' And then he took a condom from his trouser pocket and eased it over his prick.

He swivelled around on the bed so that he lay between her legs and put a hand under her buttocks, lifting her hips so that the point of his penis met her wanton, wet opening.

'You want me, don't you?' he asked, his large dark brown eyes staring into her pale blue ones.

'Oh yes,' she said, clasping his shoulders and putting her legs around his waist. 'Oh yes.' Zinnia crossed her ankles over the small of his back and raised her hips.

'Oh yes,' she sighed, 'I really want you.'

'To do what?' he asked.

'To fuck me,' she said.

Jackson gave short teasing thrusts into her moistness with his full thick throbbing black shaft. Then he swooped in and rode her hard. He rode her slow. He moved her so that she lay with one leg under and one leg over his, but with their bodies curved apart. His fingers played with her pleasure button. Her hands cupped his balls and ringed his penis as it continued charging into her depths.

Zinnia writhed. She danced horizontally. She moved and stretched, opened and jerked. She tensed and stroked. They were both rising, quivering, shaking, coming to their climax, when the door opened.

'Zinnia!' shouted Jethro Clarke.

Chapter Four

Sapphire took the freeway to Dallas and coasted along within the speed limit, her mind turning rapidly. Zinnia's note disturbed and worried her. Which friend was it she had rushed across the Herring Pond to do business with? Was it male or female? And why hadn't she said who it was?

Sapphire knew that her late father, Sir Bevis Western Untermann III, the owner of Western Untermann & MacGrogan, one of the world's biggest investment banks, and Caradoc Lewis, Zinnia's employer, had a running battle; they loathed each other's guts and were always trying to out-do one another. But Zinnia didn't know she was Sir Bevis's daughter. Not many people did. Sapphire made certain of that.

Anyhow, her father had been dead for a few weeks. If it was some fresh mega-deal, what was the need for secrecy?

Sapphire was finding tying up her father's vast concerns a nightmare: highly lucrative for various lawyers across the globe, but extremely inconvenient to her. The will had not yet been read. The lawyers gave as their excuse that all his papers and financial projects had to be collated before that could happen. Meanwhile, she had to remain in constant contact with them, as this could happen at any time and anywhere.

Sapphire had always been closer to her father than her mother. When she was little, they'd called her 'little Bev', as she was so like him in character – though not so similar to him in features. Occasionally people made odd comments about her appearance, as she didn't resemble her mother either.

Sapphire had high cheekbones, a small straight nose, a full wide mouth and beautiful thick blonde hair with hints of red. She could almost be called a strawberry blonde; whereas her mother had naturally lank, mousy-brown hair, a pronounced patrician nose, a small mouth and light brown eyes.

Also, Sapphire did not have her mother's ability to defer to Sir Bevis. Sapphire defied him. From a tiny baby she was defiant. She would do what she wanted. This exasperated her forbearing mother, who was happier coping with her easy-going and lazy son who, it was obvious to anybody seeing them together, was the child she preferred. As he got older, Sapphire realised her brother was a great disappointment to her father. He was constantly getting himself into debt; his financial affairs were a disgrace. He didn't seem to have any aptitude for making money, only for spending it. Sapphire thought that he was a scoundrel and not a lovable one.

Sapphire was quite different. Bright and very pretty, she had grown up with dinner-table talk of companies, profits, shares and options, and had lapped up everything to do with finance. It held no mystery for her. Basically, she thought it was simple; there was no need for wide-eyed awe. Spread the load and never lend any more than ten per cent on one project. She was only too well aware that some banks had lent more, ending in deep trouble and usually the ruin of the bank. Anyhow, lending more than ten per cent of a bank's loan capital on one investment was illegal. It could also be fraudulent: something she would be checking into with her new job.

She had recently left banking to become a roving

auditor. It was a big responsibility, and meant bigger bucks. She smiled a smile of deep satisfaction. If her father knew, he would have been proud of her. But he would never know. She would never be able to tell him. The thought made her sad.

Sapphire remembered how Sir Bevis used to indulge her tantrums until she had refused to go into the family bank after leaving university. Sir Bevis' business, handed down through three generations, was greatly respected in the City of London and on Wall Street.

There had been a monumental row when, after gaining her first class degree in economics, Sapphire had turned down his offer of a job because she believed it was based on nepotism and not because he trusted her ability.

'You'll never treat me as an equal,' she had yelled at him. 'I have to choose you, not the other way round. I won't be your pretty little lap dog. You are not going to control me like you do everyone else.'

'Being a woman, you're lucky I asked you in at all,' Sir Bevis had said.

'That's exactly what I mean,' Sapphire had replied indignantly. 'And, being a woman, I'll make my own way and I'll leave my brother to do the crawling. I'm going to London to study art.'

She was throwing him off the scent; although she did study art at the Courtauld Institute, she also went to the London School of Economics.

'Why, you ungrateful little hussy,' Sir Bevis had shouted at Sapphire's retreating back.

By only using the Western part of her name, Sapphire had severed connections with her family and its business. At the Courtauld, she had met her friend Auralie. They'd lost touch, which was a pity. Sapphire was expecting to go to Europe for the reading of her father's will and hoped to link up with Auralie again.

After her course in art appreciation, Sapphire had gone back into the money world, where she felt at home and happiest, and had found herself employment with the smaller finance houses in the City of London.

Sapphire and her family hadn't been reunited until her mother lay dying. She had told Sapphire that her father also was very ill with little time to live. When she'd learnt this, Sapphire had returned to the States. Her time in England had proved highly profitable and when she got back – with her record for diligence and reliability – she had landed a plum job.

Sapphire drove towards Dallas, thinking how investment banking was a ferociously competitive world. It was also a comparatively close-knit community. Did she know anyone in it called Eduard? Sapphire racked her brains. No. But then he was talking tiger economies. The Far East. Meriboa. That was not her territory. But it might be, in the future. She didn't know where her company would send her and her razor-sharp mind to ferret out frauds.

As she got closer to her destination she thought about Zinnia again. Why had she married Jethro Clarke? It was a mystery to Sapphire. But then Zinnia, too, was a mystery. Nobody knew her background or where she came from. Sapphire had never been to her home.

She supposed Zinnia had met Jethro on the mega-deals he frequently did through Hanway, Rattle and Lewis. Sapphire knew most of Zinnia's New York City associates and didn't like them very much. She thought she knew all Zinnia's London friends. They were not many, and most of them were the Vladelskys. There had been a rumour that Zinnia had got herself embroiled with Petrov Vladelsky. Sapphire didn't believe it. She had asked Zinnia, who had denied it completely.

Sapphire had met Petrov once. He had perturbed her. He was charming and polite, with old fashioned good manners: a big-built man with piercing grey-blue eyes, a magnetic presence and a raffish air. Sapphire had found him physically overpowering and louche.

She realised it was this quality of loucheness, bordering on depravity, that she had sensed in Zinnia's husband. It was that that had repelled her – his air of sexual licentiousness, not monetary greed. Perhaps Zinnia had a more varied sex life than she had ever admitted to? Maybe there was some truth in the Petrov rumour after all. On second thoughts, Sapphire dismissed the idea. She was being unusually bitchy.

Sapphire wondered if Zinnia had gone to see Auralie de Bouys. Auralie was one of the few people who did know she was Sir Bevis Untermann's daughter. But Auralie was in a completely different line of business.

Delicate, sweet, artistic Auralie had left the Courtauld Institute to study fabric design and then had set up her own company, Petolg Holdings. Sapphire knew it had gone from strength to strength, especially after her marriage to Gerry, Sir Henry de Bouys' only son. She had heard that Auralie had obtained huge contracts, the biggest was re-designing all the fabric for Sir Henry's world-wide fleet of passenger aircraft.

Since then, she had divorced Gerry and gone public, floating Petolg Holdings on the stock exchange. Then her company had taken over, eaten up and swallowed other smaller design companies. Was it possible that Auralie's company was about to take over or merge again, and that's why Zinnia had high tailed it to London?

Sapphire had always thought Auralie de Bouys was the epitome of a sexy French woman and had envied her dark, enigmatic good looks. She had longed to be like her. Petite and chic. But nobody had heard from Auralie for ages. No doubt she was too well occupied with business to socialise.

Sapphire knew and liked Auralie; surely Zinnia would have said if she was going to see her? Who else did Zinnia have contact with? Auralie's cousin, Jeanine? To the best of Sapphire's knowledge, they had only met once – at Auralie's engagement party, where she and Zinnia had watched various men milling around Jeanine, sighing and panting for a piece of her soft fragrance and her fragility.

'That Jeanine's about as sweet and fragile as an old boot,' Sapphire had said to Zinnia – who had agreed with her when she'd said that she had found Jeanine too submissive, simpering even, with her dewy downcast eyes and her shy smile. Sapphire thought they were the sort of mannerisms that might fool a man but didn't fool any woman. She could see that Jeanine was a calculating bitch of the first order. Since then, Zinnia had never mentioned her and, from that brief acquaintance, Sapphire didn't think they would have much in common.

Sapphire was still worrying about the whys and wherefores when she arrived at her hotel in Dallas. She showered and changed into a heavy linen navy blue and white suit. Feeling refreshed she packed her luggage, paid the bill and drove to the Finesteins'.

She was still niggled and irritated by the contents of Zinnia's note. She calmed down when she entered the beautiful mansion and heard the elegant sounds of Beethoven's 'Spring' sonata. Sapphire's irritation completely vanished as she stood in their great hall and enjoyed the sight of some of the greatest impressionist paintings in private ownership.

Her heart sank when the maid opened the huge door into the main reception room. She was faced with a sea of unknown people dressed in very expensive, glamorous and sexually blatant cocktail wear. Sapphire had assumed that, except for the Finesteins, the mansion would be empty. She was not dressed for a party. She felt completely out of place in a travelling suit. She also felt at a disadvantage. These people were not the nice staid friends of the old Finesteins.

'Hiya, hiya,' said a voice.

Sapphire's heart sank. Carola Finestein. That explained everything. Their out-of-control, rotten apple daughter was giving the party. The little mouse was playing while the big cats were away.

Sapphire couldn't bear the sight of Carola and her present appearance didn't lessen her aversion. Carola had her long, dyed platinum-blonde hair piled up on top of her head, and was wearing the highest pair of ankle-strap shoes, and the shortest, most hip-hugging purple leather shift. Her huge breasts were bulging over the top of her low décolletage. Sapphire was disgusted by such a downmarket display of cheap sexuality, but she nodded politely and smiled.

'So glad you could come,' said Carola, grabbing Sapphire's hand and weaving her through the throng of guests. 'Now, honey, I insist you enjoy yourself. We've got the finest champagne in the whole of Texas.'

'Only fruit juice for me, thank you,' said Sapphire stiffly.

'I didn't know you were teetotal.'

'I'm not, but I'm driving.'

'You can stay the night.'

'No, no –'

'Anyhow, one glass won't do you no harm.'

'No, thank you.' Sapphire wanted a clear head.

'Suit yourself, hon,' said Carola peevishly.

She showed her displeasure by instantly leaving Sapphire in the middle of a group of complete strangers. They stared at her, then turned their backs. She was hemmed in. A sense of threat and panic engulfed her. These were not her sort of people. She couldn't put her finger on what it was, but it seemed to Sapphire as if there was a heavy, almost threatening, sexuality hanging in the air.

Sapphire closed her eyes and told herself it was all in her mind. Nothing was amiss. She was in stress. Finding herself attracted to Eduard had upset her equilibrium. What on earth had Zinnia been thinking about, to ask her here when the Finesteins were away? Zinnia knew very well what she thought of Carola. Sapphire's instinct was to get the hell out. Then she remembered Zinnia was telephoning.

'I didn't have to find you,' said a familiar and sexy voice in her ear, 'you found me.'

'Eduard,' she murmured, smiling a genuine smile. Dressed for the occasion, he looked more handsome than ever.

'I believe you're pleased to see me,' he said, and put a hand on her shoulder.

'I – I don't know anybody,' she said, her voice faltering as he gently stroked her neck. 'In fact, I don't know why I'm here.'

'Because you're very beautiful,' said Eduard.

The music stopped. There was a moment of silence, then a full orchestra surged out with the strains of various Viennese waltzes. Eduard put his other arm around her waist and pulled her close.

'Dance with me,' he said, wanting to fondle her breasts, roll his tongue around her nipples and let his hands drift between her legs.

Completely forgetting her previous resolutions, Sapphire was happy to relax into the comfort of Eduard's enveloping arms. In the tiny space left them by the other close dancing couples, his warm body pressed against hers. Sapphire closed her eyes and excluded everyone else. Only the two of them existed. She concentrated on the music and keeping in time with Eduard.

His hand slid down to her bottom and pulled her closer. She felt his erection against her pubic bone and caught her breath. His other hand grazed past her neck and down over her left breast. It lingered on her nipple, playing with it gently, exciting her, making her moist. Sapphire sighed softly, wallowing in the tension in her belly and in her sense of anticipation.

'I think he wants to fuck you.'

Sapphire's eyes flew open at the sound of those words. She stared straight into the hooded pale eyes of Jethro Clarke. Unlike Eduard, she noticed the arrogant bastard had not changed his clothes. He hadn't even left his whip at home. He prodded Eduard with it.

'But I will. I'll be the one. It's me who's going to fuck you,' said Jethro.

Sapphire could not believe what she was hearing. She was mesmerised by the older man's audacity and was momentarily speechless.

'I don't think so,' she said, finding her voice, and huddling closer to Eduard.

'Oh I do,' said Jethro, 'and when this woman here's finished pleasuring me, I shall pleasure you.'

Jethro turned slightly, allowing Sapphire to see Carola kneeling on the floor in front of him. His riding breeches were wide open. One of Carola's hands cupped his generous balls; the other held his massive erect cock as it slid in and out of her mouth. 'She gives a good blow job, but it's a fuck I want, and I can't wait to come between your thighs.'

Sapphire was amazed that no one else seemed to take any notice. They just continued slow dancing.

'Carola, let the pretty lady see the size of my cock.' Carola obeyed him, taking her mouth up to its tip and her hand down to its base so that Jethro's large throbbing prick stood proud. 'See, I'm gonna have you squirming on the end of that. If not now – later. Any time later. I can wait. I've learnt patience.'

'I wouldn't have you touch me if you were the last man on earth,' said Sapphire, and spat at Jethro.

'We'll see,' said Jethro and laughed. 'You see, Sapphire baby, we tossed for you and I won. Remember that, Eduard – I won.'

'Go to hell,' she hissed, wrenching away from Eduard. 'Both of you, you – you bastards!'

'It's not true,' said Eduard, trying to catch hold of her. 'Sapphire, it's not true. Please, believe me, it's not true.'

And it wasn't true. Jethro had told a blatant lie, but Sapphire was in no mood to listen to Eduard's pleas.

'And you, you hooker, you can get out of my way,' said Sapphire to Carola, almost falling over her as she sucked on Jethro's penis.

Half-crying, Sapphire pushed her way through the mass of people. It was always the same whenever she fancied someone – decadence when she wanted romance, and licentiousness when she needed loving. Now, her only desire was to get away as quickly as possible. Sapphire ran out of the house, got in her car and drove. She drove to the airport. If Zinnia had gone to London there was nothing stopping her following.

Sapphire was on holiday. She was a free agent. And she wanted some explanations.

All the direct flights to London had departed. She boarded one to New York but ended up in Geneva with a very interesting proposition.

Chapter Five

'*D*arling,' said Jacqueline, Countess Helitzer – the well known fabulously rich society hostess who gave outrageous parties. 'What changes are you planning?'

Jeanine didn't answer immediately; she just smiled her catlike smile and turned up the sound on the video. The two stunning-looking blondes were in Jeanine's sumptuous private apartments watching pretty, plump Zinnia being ravished, enjoyed and pleasured by a couple of handsome men.

'Oh, darling, she looks as if she was really enjoying it,' said Jacqueline, who was rumoured to have been a penniless Hungarian but had arrived in Paris with an introduction to the elderly Count Helitzer. He had fallen madly in love with her, married her within three days of their acquaintance and died a few months later, leaving Jacqueline an extremely wealthy woman.

Jacqueline turned off the video, and glanced at her sleek self in Jeanine's cheval mirror. She was well pleased with her new outfit, a satin-silk tangerine tunic, made by a new couturier in Paris.

'Oh, she was enjoying it, sweetie, darling, most definitely,' said Jeanine.

'A lovely body she's got. I always had great satisfaction between her legs. So abandoned, so ripe, so sexy,' said Jacqueline, remembering the times she had had Zinnia flat on her back in her mansion in the Bois de Boulogne. 'And who was that who used his tongue so well? He was gorgeous, darling, absolutely gorgeous. Loved the blue eyes and the black hair. A gypsy. A sexy gypsy,' said Jacqueline, kicking off her high-heeled brown kid shoes then rolling down her fine silk stockings and throwing them carelessly on the huge bed in front of the vast wall of luxurious curtaining.

'If he is, he's a very rich, sexy gypsy,' said Jeanine dreamily, but didn't offer any further information.

Jacqueline was intrigued. She gazed across at Jeanine in her heavily-embroidered kimono with her flaxen hair piled up on top of her head, almost Japanese-style, and thought how beguiling she looked.

'And Kensit, his splendid black cock gliding in and out – that was exciting, darling, really exciting. Did she know she was being filmed?'

'No,' said Jeanine, who was sitting in a hard-backed brocade-covered chair and wondering why the countess had arrived late and with none of her entourage in tow. 'And neither did he.'

'When did you film that?'

'Earlier in the year. Ascot week, I think. We were going to the races, I know. Yes, I'm sure it was Ascot and not Goodwood – before she married.'

'Is her marriage okay, darling?' asked Jacqueline.

'I wouldn't say so,' replied Jeanine.

'That's what I thought. I was surprised when she accepted my invitation. In fact, it was sent out by mistake. Where is she now?' asked Jacqueline, adding some bright tangerine lipstick to her well-shaped lips.

'She's rushed off somewhere. Which was just as well, because her husband turned up unexpectedly,' said Jeanine, smiling while checking out her nail lacquer. 'And he found her screwing Jackson.'

'Jackson!'

'Yes, sweetie, Jackson. Zinnia's husband had no idea what his dear little wife could get up to.'

'Oh darling! Oh *mon Dieu!* So, what's wrong? Is her husband not performing properly?' asked Jacqueline.

'Not performing at all,' answered Jeanine.

'Oh, has he been losing money? That can make a man lose his libido. Such a fragile thing, darling, a man's libido. Money down the pan, no sperm up the spout.'

'Apparently, his libido is fine,' said Jeanine, 'as long as he's chasing other women.'

'Oh God, she's got herself a butterfly. Well, she was right to come to here,' said Jacqueline, pulling on a pair of long fine chocolate-brown leather kid gloves.

'And she said she's looking forward to your party,' said Jeanine.

'So tell me, what happened about Jackson?' asked Jacqueline.

'Jethro went berserk. Absolutely crazy. Zinnia went off somewhere – God knows where; I haven't seen her since but she said she's going to divorce him. This place was like a mad house. Anyhow, I calmed him down. We talked business. He's got a big deal on. A mega-deal.'

'What?'

'I don't know. He said it was secret and tricky. Well, if my knowledge of the city is anything to go by – they're all tricky. I think it's a take-over of some sort, and he doesn't want any hassles. He's got enough trying to find the millions he needs for whatever it is he's got planned. I told him he needed to relax. He said no, he didn't. Then he saw Ana Tai and – '

'Who's Ana Tai?' asked Jacqueline.

'The new massage girl, from the Far East – Meriboa.'

'Oh, really?'

'Yes. But massage only. No extras. That's what I've agreed.' Jeanine saw no reason to explain the rest of her agreement to the countess. 'Now, sweetie, tell me why you decided to have your party here?'

'Darling, I was bored in Paris. I wanted to see you,' said Jacqueline, opening the front of Jeanine's kimono.

'Mmm, very pleasing ... Very alluring.' Jacqueline kissed her full on the mouth.

Jeanine held her breath as Jacqueline began fondling her ample breasts. Sweet, delectable sensations of pleasure were concentrated in her nipples as Jacqueline nipped them with her gloved fingers. Jeanine undid her kimono belt.

'No,' said Jacqueline, covering her up again, 'not yet, darling. Stay like that – for the moment. Tell me about these changes you're planning.'

'Now?'

'Oh yes. Business, darling,' said Jacqueline, leisurely stroking Jeanine's neck, 'business comes first. Without it, how can we afford our beautiful indulgences?'

'I want to be rich,' said Jeanine.

'But you are, darling,' said the countess.

'No, I want to be incredibly, horribly rich, sweetie. And I'll make sure I am. I don't care what it takes, what I suffer.'

'You suffer? Oh, Darling! No, it's other people who suffer when someone wants to get horribly rich.'

'Oh sweetie, there speaks somebody who already is,' said Jeanine, pouting.

'I earnt it, darling.'

'Yes, flat on your back!'

'Oh no, not always,' said the countess. 'So how are you going to make all this money?'

'I want to buy back the company,' Jeanine announced, with a triumphant note in her voice.

'I thought you owned the hotel,' said Jacqueline.

'I do,' replied Jeanine. 'I'm not talking about the hotel. I've not spent vast sums acquiring the place next door and having it specially fitted up, only to sell it. I'm talking about the design business, Petolg Holdings. Have you forgotten we went public?'

'So you did – with some help from Sir Henry, as I recall. And you've been buying up other companies ever since.'

'Yes, shops and factories who own their own sites,'

81

said Jeanine. 'And, in most cases, the property is worth more than the businesses. I bought a wonderful place the other day: a factory and not that old and not too far from the Globe Theatre on the south side of the Thames. Just divine, sweetie. Just divine.'

'The south side of the river? Divine? Really, darling! I don't think so,' said Jacqueline.

'It will be divine. And it's practical, very practical. You see, sweetie, the new bridge across the river will make it very easy for the City and my customers, my wonderfully rich customers, to get to me.'

'You mean you're going to have another hotel, an hotel like this?'

'Of course. It's a successful formula – why should I change it? Looking from the outside, who would know? Looking in, who would know?' Jeanine lowered her voice. 'Who would know that I have one of the best sex dungeons in London, eh? Nobody. So, yes, sweetie, there's fat to cream off – and I want to do it.'

'How?'

'Buy it back. But I don't want Petrov or Auralie to know just yet. Petrov's lost a lot of money, thanks to that old insurance company.'

'Oh he was one of the many, was he?' said Jacqueline. 'He still comes to my soirées.'

'Petrov's not broke – far from it; but he hasn't got what he had. The profits from Petolg Holdings are very handy. Keeps him in acolytes! Actually, the whole design business is boring me. . . We don't have any real competitors. Every contract we go for we get. We got another de Bouys one.'

'What for?' asked Jacqueline. 'I thought Sir Henry had completely refurbished all his airlines and his air terminals?'

'He had,' replied Jeanine. 'This one was extraordinary. Top secret.'

'Oh, tell me,' said Jacqueline conspiratorially. 'I love secrets.'

'It was for a space station.'

'A space station!' exclaimed the countess.

'Yes, a space station on earth.'

'You mean, like NASA?'

'Yes. Satellites. He's put money into that now, too. What doesn't Sir Henry own? Anyhow, we had to design the fabrics for the apartments and living quarters for the personnel, as well as for the offices.'

'Oh, *très extraordinaire!*' said Jacqueline. 'You never think of people like that sleeping or screwing or doing anything except watching their funny little dials, do you? Where is it, darling?'

'Sorry, can't tell you,' said Jeanine, remembering how she had refused to go to the Matto Grosso and see the site. For all her lifestyle, memories of her dead husband, Laurence, were still strong. A part of her was wedded to him forever. Bonded, she thought, even after death. His disappearance in the heart of the Brazilian jungle the day after their wedding had left her devastated. Aware that Jacqueline might pick up on her sorrow and thence where the secret location was, she quickly and cheerfully added, 'But it's a fabulous contract. We deliver our bid for it in a few days.'

'Oh, you haven't got it yet?'

'No, tendering for it. But it's a foregone conclusion – Mummy being married to Sir Henry and all that.'

'Oh, yes. And you want to throw all this – this industry away?'

'Not throw it away, Jacqueline, make money on it. You see, there's no risk any more. No high.'

'But what would happen to Auralie?'

'Auralie? She's my slave; she'll have to accept whatever I do.'

'But if she didn't and went?'

'My mother would be well pleased.'

'Why's that?' Jacqueline asked, with feigned innocence.

'She can't stand her.'

'Ah, *oui!*' Jacqueline said. 'That was *bonne chance,*

darling, *n'est-ce pas*? Your mother marrying the great industrialist, just as you took over the business.'

'It was excellent, sweetie, excellent. And when the company was floated, Sir Henry bought loads of the shares. Handy, eh?'

'What? Sir Henry?'

'No, love. Handy that he's in love with my mother and will do anything, absolutely anything for her,' said Jeanine, smugly.

'Tell me, does your mother know about your other enterprise? This hotel?'

'This hotel? Yes, of course.'

'And its added extras?'

'No!' exclaimed Jeanine with horror, 'of course not. Does your mother know about your mansion?'

'My mother is dead,' said Jacqueline.

'Oh I'm sorry. When did she die?' she asked.

'More than twenty years ago – and if she hadn't, she would have been my permanent guest!'

'She would?'

'Oh, yes, she had a most interesting life; but she loved too well and badly. Auralie reminds me of her.'

'Auralie does?'

'Yes.'

'Where did your mother die?' asked Jeanine, feigning interest. She wasn't interested in anybody Jacqueline liked or loved being similar to Auralie.

'In Meriboa. On a stop-over. She was coming back from Australia. She'd been staying with her friend Rosamund de Bouys.'

'Who?'

'Rosamund de Bouys, Sir Henry's cousin, and – '

'That's what I thought you said. Do you know her?' asked Jeanine.

'She's my godmother, and she was – '

'Oh, really? And where exactly is Meriboa?' asked Jeanine, cutting across Jacqueline's words. She was completely indifferent to anything that did not immediately concern her. Meriboa, she did want to know about. She had heard about it recently, in conjunction with things financial. Jeanine was very interested in all things financial.

'Meriboa's near Singapore. And it's beautiful, really beautiful; so's the atmosphere, now they've got rid of the military. I went there years ago before all that – ' Jacqueline stopped. She noticed the look of boredom on Jeanine's face. 'Is she here now?'

'Who?' asked Jeanine, suddenly aware that the countess was addressing her.

'Auralie.'

'She is. She came back this afternoon. She's been at Petrov's.'

'Darling, do I have your permission?' said Jacqueline, indicating the bell pull.

'Of course,' replied Jeanine.

'Poor Auralie,' said Jacqueline.

'Poor Auralie!' exclaimed Jeanine peevishly. 'Why poor Auralie? She's a little bitch.'

'I feel sorry for her,' said Jacqueline. 'I remember Olga telling me how she lost her parents as a child; that's got to affect you.'

Jeanine was unaware that Jacqueline was speaking from the heart. Nobody knew about Jacqueline's childhood. She chose not to tell them: that her father left before she was born and that her mother had died when she was nine. Jacqueline had been brought up by a series of foster parents.

'Oh, don't give me pyschobabble,' said Jeanine, with an irritated wave of her hand. 'My parents looked after her, did everything for her – and look how she repaid them.'

'How?' said Jacqueline, very interested; no one had heard the full story of the family rift.

'Betrayal and disloyalty,' said Jeanine, 'and I don't want to discuss it.'

'Well, whatever,' said Jacqueline, recognising intransigence when she saw it. No way was Jeanine going to tell her any more. 'Auralie's very beautiful but she's always the one who loses out. I think her problem is she loves – '

'Loves? That little bitch couldn't love anything except herself,' said Jeanine. 'That's why I get such pleasure when I make her kneel down and suck me and even more when I whip her bottom.'

'I think she feels and loves intensely,' said Jacqueline. 'And yes, Jeanine, she will accept your decision, but she won't like it. And she's a good designer. You need her.'

'No I don't,' said Jeanine. 'Oh no, I don't. I assure you I don't. Anyhow, she can stay on as my slave,' said Jeanine, dismissing the subject of Auralie and returning to herself. 'I thought I'd go in for some real speculation.'

'A sin fund, darling?' said Jacqueline.

'No, sweetie, they're old hat; an ethical fund, that's much more me.'

'Ethical? You!' Jacqueline gave a throaty laugh.

'Truly,' said Jeanine. 'Everett was here the other day and he told me how much I'd have made if I'd invested in one of those pure flower oil, no animal experiments companies. A lot. And with far less effort than I've put into Petolg Holdings. You just hand over the money and grab the profits.'

'Or maybe not,' said Jacqueline sagely.

'But that's where the high comes in: in the maybe not, the gamble. Also, he told me about something called the kaw-kaw tree – now, that sounds very interesting.'

'The kaw-kaw tree? What is it and where's it from?'

'From Meriboa. They think it could be used as an alternative to petrol.'

'Oh Jeanine, don't get carried away with stupid ideas.'

'Jacqueline, if it doesn't work, I don't lose too much, and if it does – '

'It'll be brought up by the gasoline companies and squashed,' said Jacqueline flatly.

'Yes, but I'll have made a pile. So what the hell. And then there's futures. It's an interesting time we're living in. Zinnia does frightfully well as a fund manager.'

'When's she back?'

'Zinnia?'

'Yes.'

'God knows. In time for your party, hopefully. I thought I'd pick her brains and, of course, Everett's . . .'

'Everett, Everett? This is the third time you've mentioned him. Who is he and have you fallen in love?'

'He's Gerry's cousin, and yes, I have fallen in love with him.'

'Gerry's cousin? Gerry de Bouys?'

'Yes.'

'And you've fallen in love with him?'

'Yes.'

'And what does Gerry think about it?'

'He doesn't know. He's yesterday's news. Auralie can have her husband back for all I care.'

'Does he still come here?'

'Oh yes. He gets what he pays for and nothing less. He loves a good spanking – but these days, mostly, I get Mrs Maclean to do it.'

'And Everett?'

'He's the handsome one with the tongue in the video with Zinnia.'

'I see. Well, darling, he's not bad for the weekend, or even,' said Jacqueline, licking her lips, 'even for a while longer. Is he around? You must invite him to my party.'

'He was, but had to rush away.'

There was a knock on the door.

'Enter,' called Jacqueline, as once again she took Jeanine's magnificent breasts into her gloved hands and playfully squeezed her nipples.

'Such beautiful breasts,' sighed Jacqueline, staring at the young woman who had entered. 'Don't you agree, Auralie?'

Jeanine ran a hand under Jacqueline's tunic, pushed aside her silk knickers, and touched the countess's excited engorged little button.

'Yes, madam,' said the young woman, who was holding various oils and potions and love toys on an oval-shaped eighteenth-century rosewood tray.

87

Auralie waited by the door, not daring to take a step until ordered. Her only movement was to lower her eyes, showing her submissiveness. But she had seen in a glance what the two women were up to. Auralie could imagine where Jeanine's fingers were; her thumb would be on Jacqueline's clitoris, her middle finger creeping along the wet slit, while the other two fingers rubbed either side of Jacqueline's full fleshy sex lips.

The countess smiled at Auralie. She thought the petite young Frenchwoman looked enchanting and enticing in her lime green satin corselet, laced tightly at the waist. She approved of the design and how the halter of dark green leather wound around her neck, criss-crossing the satin, outlining her covered upright breasts but encircling her exposed, large and rouged nipples. The short skirt, falling from the hem of the corselet, consisted of floating fine black lace. Her dark green lacy stockings were held up with green garters. Her suede shoes were very high and of the same matching dark green. They were tied with strips of leather around her slim, elegant ankles, then wound up over her calves and finished above the knee. Her deep auburn hair was bobbed and she wore a black spotted lacy eye mask.

'You rang, madam?' said Auralie.

'What took you so long?' asked Jeanine.

'I was helping Jackson,' answered Auralie.

'Come here,' commanded Jacqueline.

Obediently, Auralie ventured further into the room. As she did so, she revealed a tantalising glimpse of her nakedness, her availability, beneath the layer of lace. And Jacqueline was reminded of the first time she saw the petite green-eyed beauty.

She had been brought by Princess Olga to Jacqueline's most private, sumptuous and sensuous world: the well guarded and electronically-controlled Helitzer mansion on the edges of the Bois de Boulogne. On that occasion, Auralie had been wearing a black leather two-piece; the boned top had had a scooped neck, long sleeves and criss-cross thongs running the length of the bodice. The skirt had been a skin-tight fit over her hips and fell in wide bias cut strips to her ankles. She had worn silk stockings and her long auburn hair had been piled up on top of her head with sexy tendrils escaping, making her appear both sexy and vulnerable.

The maître d' for the evening had seated Olga and Auralie at a table in the centre of the ballroom – a ballroom which Jacqueline had lovingly restored. It was opulent, exotic and erotic, and very Art Nouveau, with its sparkling chandeliers and swirling shaped mirrors. Jacqueline had watched Auralie obey Olga's instructions and swish her skirt upwards before sitting on the harsh, itchy, plush velvet chair.

During dinner, Jacqueline had revelled in the astonishment on Auralie's face as she had realised what was happening to the diners on the balconies surrounding the room. While the beautiful women and their handsome male partners were gorging on their food, a group of liveried midgets walked under them, stroking, playing, teasing her guests' sexes with feathers. But Auralie's astonishment had not lasted for long. Jacqueline watched her become aloof, almost cool – as if she was seeing their delicious debauchery through a haze of detachment. And that had made her subsequent announcement all the more puzzling.

And then there had been Carlo. Muscles-bulging Carlo, who had gross eyebrows hanging over tiny piggy eyes, a squashed nose and thick lips. He was small – very small in stature – but large in sexual appetite. Carlo was raw sex. He was also the ugliest of Jacqueline's liveried mannikins; and he was very well hung.

Auralie's face had been a picture of controlled surprise as Princess Olga had unbuttoned his frock coat and revealed his excessively large, semi-flaccid cock hanging free from his breeches. Cupping his balls in one hand and nodding her approval at his size, Olga slowly began to rub the ugly little man's massive prick. And it grew hard and erect under her expert handling.

Suddenly the ballroom lights were extinguished and

Heidi, a statuesque redhead draped in slinky red, had appeared on the raked stage, singing. She had a good voice and had belted out the first verse of the old Ruth Etting number 'Ten Cents Dance' and then, with a swishy arrogance had waltzed from the stage through the diners until she had arrived at Olga's table.

At that point Jacqueline's attention had been distracted by the arrival of Count von Straffen and his current *amore*, Daisy. The next time Jacqueline had looked up Heidi was bent over Olga's table and Carlo was standing between the singer's outstretched legs, masturbating. His mouth was level with Heidi's sex and he was slurping at her luscious wet pussy.

That had been too much for Jacqueline. She had begun to feel left out. Everywhere she looked, her selected guests were enjoying each other's bodies. At her own table, Count von Straffen's cock was being stroked by Daisy. His hands were under the table and Jacqueline felt certain that Daisy was sitting on them, his fingers rammed up inside her wetness.

Needing attention, Jacqueline had sashayed over to Olga, snuggled her hands down Olga's bodice, tweaked her nipples then kissed her lips. Auralie had seemed impervious to their greeting. Her eyes were firmly fixed on the diners on the balconies. Jacqueline followed Auralie's glance. She noticed Olga's ex-husband Petrov.

Petrov was sitting naked, being entertained by a woman who was on her knees in front of him, sucking his cock. Olga waved. He returned her salutation. Auralie gave a slight gasp.

Jacqueline saw Olga's glance slither from Petrov to his tall beautiful black acolyte, Leyisha. She was bent over the balcony rail and moaning in ecstasy. A blond and suntanned man was screwing her arse. He had arrived with Petrov, that much Jacqueline knew, but Olga realised it was Laurence mounting Leyisha. The same Laurence who had fucked Auralie earlier in the day, had taken her virginity and caused her emotional pain.

Swiftly, Olga's eyes went to Auralie's face. Anguish

was written all over it but she sat bolt upright. Olga could read a certain steely determination in her look. She was not surprised when Auralie made the announcement that had amazed Jacqueline.

'I want to be screwed,' Auralie had said defiantly.

'Then you shall be,' said Olga, who had insisted that Jacqueline guide Auralie up on stage.

A spotlight was trained on the two women, one tall and blonde and the other petite and auburn-haired. It had followed them up on to the stage and to the huge bed covered with white satin sheets and plenty of pillows.

Jacqueline had sat Auralie down, blindfolded her and unlaced the leather thongs on her bodice; then placed her hands above her head and tied them to a post. She had spread Auralie's legs wide and tied her ankles firmly, but allowing plenty of slack on the rope which was attached to rings on either side of the bed. With a series of white satin pillows, she had raised Auralie's buttocks so that her swollen sex was exposed and clearly visible. Then she had taken a small vibrator from under a pillow, turned it on and held it against Auralie's wanton sex; then let it whisper gently, very gently over her expectant clitoris.

This had sent waves of pulsating desire through Auralie's body and unimagined fantasies steaming through her mind. Auralie was open and wanting and Jacqueline slid quietly off the bed, giving the vibrator to Carlo.

Jacqueline and her guests then watched with vicarious pleasure as the ugly little man teased Auralie's juicy excited sex, first with the vibrator then with with the tip of his enormous throbbing phallus. Not knowing who or what, but high as a kite and crazy with desire, Auralie had raised her hips off the pillow, wanting whoever – whatever – to enter and plunge into her depths. She had lain pinioned and blindfolded on the bed, moaning and begging to be fucked.

Someone had swivelled the bed on the stage so that

Auralie's head lay towards the audience and Carlo was shown in all his glory, his cock full, stiff and at the point of entry. Slowly he had eased his huge member into Auralie and her gasps of pleasure had echoed around the room.

The spotlight was turned off and the footlights came on. The audience were able to see that most of Jacqueline's little men, wearing their trousers with cut-outs around their crotch and flaunting their erect cocks, had joined Carlo. One was kneeling behind Auralie's head, his knees against her ears and his penis in her mouth. Another one was putting her tied hands around his thick prick, making her rub it. Another two lay either side of her, feeling her tits while gyrating against her hips.

Jacqueline remembered how Auralie had given a wonderful and natural display of wanton sexuality, and had continued to do so long after her initiation had been complete. And now she was Jeanine's sex slave. Yes, Jacqueline did feel sorry for Auralie, because she thought the young woman did not enjoy her position.

'Closer, Auralie, closer,' said Jacqueline, 'I can't see what you've got on the tray from there. Bend down.'

Auralie did as she was told. Her skirt rose, revealing her neat, high rounded naked bottom and bare shaven sex. Jacqueline noticed but ignored the criss-cross of red stripes patterning her posterior.

'Ah, some toys, *ma petite*,' said Jacqueline, releasing her hands from Jeanine's breasts to hover across a selection of the objects.

'How were you helping Jackson?' asked Jeanine.

From a row of assorted dildoes and whips Jacqueline chose a small vibrator. She held it between her hands, caressing it backwards and forwards. She watched Jeanine squirm. Her tongue hovered on her lips and Jacqueline knew Jeanine was excited.

'Bend over further with your legs apart,' said Jacqueline to Auralie, parting her skirt, stroking her between her legs then placing the vibrator on her clitoris.

Auralie's response was instant. She jerked and shuddered as tiny waves of pleasure hit her full, ripe, shaven and juicy sex.

'Keep still,' said Jacqueline, asking the virtually impossible. 'Don't move.'

'How were you helping Jackson?' Jeanine asked again.

Auralie lowered her head but said nothing.

'Were you screwing him?'

'Oh no, madam.' she said.

'Then what were you doing?'

'He asked me to suck his cock, madam.'

'He asked you to suck his big black cock?

'Yes, madam.'

'And what did you do when he asked you?'

'I bent down, undid the flap of his trousers and took his balls in my hands. His cock was very stiff, madam ... but ... Ooh...' Auralie's voice wavered as the vibrator continued exciting her clitoris and Jacqueline's cool fingers were slowly stealing into her sex.

'Did I give you permission to suck Jackson?'

'No, madam.'

'Then you have disobeyed me.'

'But, madam, I thought ... You told me that I had to obey Jackson,' said Auralie as Jacqueline's fingers began to push a dildo up into her soft pink wantonness.

'Only when I'm not here,' said Jeanine, excited by Jacqueline's activities.

'Jackson said – Well, he said you were with the countess and not to be disturbed. And he had a new friend with him.'

'Auralie,' said Jeanine, reaching out a hand and raising the lace-edged skirt up and over Auralie's soft pink bare bottom. She saw the fresh dark weals. 'You said you obeyed Jackson, so why are there fresh whip marks here?'

'I didn't do all he wanted, madam,' panted Auralie.

Jacqueline pushed the vibrator deeper into Auralie's sex as her fingers continued to work their enchantment on her clitoris.

93

'What do you mean?' demanded Jeanine.

'He wanted me to spread my legs, madam, and be fucked by his friend whilst I was sucking his cock,' said Auralie, with half-closed eyes as she rolled her hips up and down, taking the soft and hard instruments of pleasure.

'And you didn't do it?' exclaimed Jeanine with genuine surprise.

'Not immediately; no, madam.'

'Why? What made you disobey?' Jeanine was really interested.

Auralie kept her face down so that Jeanine could not see the inkling of a smile of triumph on her face. But Jacqueline noticed. 'I disobeyed, madam,' said Auralie slowly, savouring every word, 'because I thought you wanted to screw Jackson's friend first.'

'I wanted to screw him?' screamed Jeanine, jumping up out of her chair. Jacqueline quickly stepped to one side, removing the pleasure instruments from Auralie's sex. 'I wanted to screw him? Why would I want to do that? There's only one man in the world I want to screw.'

'Exactly, madam,' said Auralie, very softly, almost contritely. 'I have just been screwing Everett de Bouys.'

Jeanine picked up a small whip from the tray and brought it down hard on Auralie's backside.

'He's here! He's arrived. You've screwed Everett!' she screeched.

'Oh yes, madam,' said Auralie.

Jacqueline was aware of Auralie's sense of triumph. She was fighting back, even though she stayed bent over, accepting her punishment.

'Where is Jackson now?' asked Jacqueline.

'In his room, I think,' replied Auralie, biting her lip.

Jeanine stalked out of the room.

'Darling,' said the Countess Helitzer to Auralie, 'you were right to hesitate, but I think you need more love and less violence. Come here.'

Auralie stood silently beside Jacqueline, who kissed her lips. Then she touched her erect rouged nipples, kissed them. Slowly, Jacqueline ran her soft hands up over the girl's stocking-tops and caressed the flesh at the top of her thighs.

'You're not happy, darling, *n'est-ce pas*?'

'No,' said Auralie, softly.

'Spread your legs,' said Jacqueline. 'I want to suck you.'

And the beautiful Countess bent down in front of Auralie. Delicately parting the Frenchwoman's sex lips with her fingers, she licked her sweet-tasting musk and sucked on her excited little bud. Auralie swayed backwards and forwards with the rhythm of the ripples of pleasure.

'How dare you?' hissed Jeanine, storming into the room and grabbing Auralie by her hair. 'You whore, you hooker, you slut!'

'Jeanine,' said Jacqueline softly, 'you are spoiling my enjoyment.'

'And she has spoilt mine,' countered Jeanine, in a temper. 'She's a liar. A damned liar. Get out. Get out, Auralie.'

Auralie quickly left the room, a quiet smile of triumph on her pretty face.

'Why did you do that?' asked Jacqueline.

'She's my slave.'

Jacqueline stood up, sat on the bed, and put on her stockings and her shoes.

'What are you doing?' asked Jeanine.

'I was enjoying her. You have implied that I did not have the right to pleasure myself with your slave. So I will go,' said Jacqueline.

'No, no,' said Jeanine. 'Stay. Please stay. I'm sorry. I'm sorry.'

'How sorry are you?' asked Jacqueline, opening Jeanine's kimono, letting her hand rove over her body and under the waistband of her knicker elastic.

'Very sorry,' gasped Jeanine as Jacqueline's forefinger touched her hidden bud. 'But she lied to me. She told me she'd screwed Everett.'

'And hadn't she?' asked Jacqueline

'No, he hasn't even been here,' said Jeanine. 'I've been waiting and waiting. She was saying it to make me mad.'

'And she succeeded,' said Jacqueline. 'Darling, anger is not good.'

'Jacqueline, I'm in love with him. I'm in love with Everett de Bouys. He was due to arrive a couple of days ago. He phoned me from Texas to say he was coming – and then nothing. Absolutely nothing. Jacqueline, he's the man I want to marry.'

'Marry?'

'Yes, marry,' said Jeanine, with tears in her eyes. 'It'd be good to be a wife. You forget I was only married for a day. One day, and then Laurence was killed in that plane crash. I thought I still loved him; maybe I still do. But he's gone and Everett's here. Handsome, clever, and very rich Everett. Yes, I will marry Everett.'

'I'm sure you will, darling. You always get what you want. Now, lie on the bed,' said Jacqueline, removing her shoes, stockings and her tangerine tunic.

'What?'

'Darling, do as I say. Allow me my pleasure. Lie down. Turn over, put your arse high and open your legs,' commanded Jacqueline, as she took a large dildo from the tray, strapped it on, and hovered with it at Jeanine's point of entry. 'I'm going to fuck you.'

Without warning, the door opened and Jackson came in.

'Madam, Madame Vladelsky,' he said. 'You have a visitor.'

'Who is it?' asked Jeanine.

'Your mother,' said the big, burly black man.

Chapter Six

Sapphire stormed into the civilised surroundings of the first-class lounge at Dallas airport, still smarting from the incident at the Finesteins. Needing to be quiet and calm before taking her flight, she sat down, opened up the Wall Street Journal and began to read it.

'Hello,' said a deep male voice. 'How was the polo?'

Sapphire looked up and quivered at the sight of the man she had met in the driveway of the Sunshine Ranch.

'Fine,' she said, almost in a whisper, quickly lowering her eyes in the faint hope he wouldn't see the effect he was having upon her.

'We didn't have time to introduce ourselves last time. My name's Everett.' he held out his hand.

'Sapphire,' she said, taking it.

'Are you going to New York?' he asked.

'Yes,' she said, pulling her slim hand away from his large one. She did not want him to feel her trembling.

'There is a God!' he exclaimed. 'Sorry but, you see, I've been sitting here cursing my father for taking our jet to Mexico when I wanted to get to London, England. All the direct flights have gone, so it's change-over time in NYC. Perhaps we could sit together?'

'Yes,' she said, trying to look and sound cool, calm and collected.

'Good. I'll organise it,' he replied, and walked off, looking for a steward.

Sapphire and Everett sat side by side. As they settled into their seats, he turned his head and she found herself staring at the nape of his neck. There was something about the curve of the muscle just where it joined his shoulders that Sapphire found completely fascinating. She had an overwhelming desire to lick that spot, that space, that juncture of his lightly tanned skin. Disquieted by her own thoughts, Sapphire quickly sat back in her seat, fitted the belt over her lap, picked up an inflight magazine, stared at it studiously and promised to keep her emotions at bay.

Everett clicked on his safety belt.

Sapphire then noticed his elegant, well manicured hands and immediately imagined them caressing her, feeling her nipples, fondling her breasts and travelling down over her belly, between her thighs to her secret self, which was slowly growing moist with desire. Having such sexual and libidinous thoughts, and the strength of her fantasy, made Sapphire tremble with anxiety. She was determined to stay calm and cool and keep herself to herself.

She concentrated on the magazine, attempting to read it.

'Interesting?' he asked.

'Very,' she said, keeping her eyes on the page.

'We were destined to meet,' he announced.

'Really?' she said, keeping her eyes down, gazing at the various advertisements, only half-seeing them until one took her fancy: an announcement for a sale of works of art by twentieth-century women at one of the big London auction houses. She marked the page with her pencil. There might be something there she could afford.

'You like art?' he asked.

'Yes,' she replied.

He eyed her queryingly but she had no intention of offering him any further information. She'd leave him intrigued. She knew that corporate management, banking and art were seemingly an odd combination.

'And champagne? Do you like champagne?' he asked.

'Yes,' she said.

'Then let's get some.'

When the Krug arrived, they clinked glasses and his sexy come-to-bed eyes bored into hers. Sapphire was excited but frightened. The danger that she had always avoided, she sensed was there. She felt Everett drawing her into a mysterious and foreign world – the world of carnal lust and love. When their hands accidentally touched, she broke out in goose pimples. An untamed charge of electricity raced through her whole body. Her womb tightened. Her thighs gave an involuntary outward movement, as if welcoming him to her hidden tenderness.

However, Sapphire thought, if he believed he could loosen her tongue with alcohol, he'd have another think coming. She'd keep the conversation formal. They ended up talking about paintings and sculpture, post-modernism and de-constructualism, and where it was leading. And it proved very interesting. But throughout, she kept her head clear and resisted every effort on his part to discover what she did for a living. She let him drink most of the champagne, while she called for and drank pure mineral water.

'We're moving towards a greater tolerance,' she said, keeping her body upright, contained and away from his.

'Do you think so? Do you really think so?' he asked, slurring.

'Oh yes. It's hard to believe but art doesn't reflect its time, it heralds it and then becomes it,' she replied, desperate to touch him but not daring to give an inch.

'And you think art is heralding tolerance?' he asked, letting his leg lean against hers.

'Undoubtedly,' she replied, easing her leg away from his and noticing the 'fasten your seat belts' sign flashing red. They were getting ready to land. 'Because there's a spirituality out there that isn't fey; it's real. It harks back to things forgotten, almost stamped out, by our western civilisation, but it is there.'

'What is that?' he asked

'Shamanism,' she replied. The rest of her words were drowned out by the captain's microphone loudly thanking all his passengers for flying on their airline.

'Why are you going to London?' he asked, a note of panic in his voice.

'To see a friend,' she replied.

'Work?'

'No, I'm on holiday,' she said, opening her handbag, hunting for her lipstick and taking out the roll of film from the polo match by mistake. She must get it processed.

'If you're on holiday, why don't you come to Geneva?'

'Geneva?' she exclaimed, finding the correct container and applying the bright red to her wide sexy lips. 'Why should I want to go to Geneva?'

Sapphire stood up. He stood up too and followed her off the plane.

'Because I'm going to Geneva,' he said, walking behind her. 'And having lost you once, I don't want to lose you again. Sapphire, please, please say "yes".'

'I'll think about it,' she said.

'Look, don't think too long, my father's here with his jet. We're going right now and Switzerland's not far from London.'

Sapphire walked fast up the ramp and into the main airport, her emotions going haywire. She wanted to go with him. She could go with him, but . . .

'We have a few paintings you might find interesting.'

'I'll do whatever I want,' she said imperiously. 'I don't need bribes.'

'No, of course not,' he said, contritely and reached for her hand. 'Sapphire, I'm sorry. I want you to come with me. Do you want to?'

'Yes,' said Sapphire.

Once more she surprised herself by the alacrity of her reply. She had spent all the time on the plane resisting his unspoken advances, talking so that she wouldn't have to look into his eyes, keeping it intellectual so that he would never guess what she was really thinking and feeling, and then, when he'd asked her to go with him to Geneva, she'd instantly said yes.

Sapphire admonished herself for being a rash fool. Her puritan upbringing had left her with a deep distrust of her sensuality. She was terrified of the turmoil raging within her, and yet fascinated. Torn between her head saying 'beware' and her body screaming 'take me, caress me, I want you', she had gone with her body.

Suddenly, she felt pleased. She had stopped punishing herself. She was taking life on the wing.

Everett made the arrangements and had her baggage hauled off the regular flight to the UK. A little while later, they went aboard a brand new Gulfstream V, which was wonderful and sleek but held no real interest for Sapphire. As long as transport got her comfortably from A to B, she didn't care about it.

After Everett had had a brief conversation with his elderly, frail father, he had introduced Sapphire. It was many hours later that she realised that none of them exchanged surnames. Somehow it didn't seem to matter. All three got on and enjoyed one another's company. Everett, Cecil, and Sapphire was enough.

'Well, father, what was so important in Mexico?' asked Everett.

'A painting,' said his father.

'A painting?' exclaimed Everett, but he should have known. Since Everett's mother's death, his father had transferred his passion for her into works of art.

'Yes, a painting; I will show you when we get home,' said his father.

'Sapphire loves paintings.'

'Do you?'

'Yes, I studied at the Courtauld.'

'Really?'

When the plane touched down in Switzerland, Cecil

101

suggested that she stay with them and not book herself into an hotel.

'My dear, unless you really want to, it's a complete waste of money,' said the old man. 'We have a house which is more than adequate.'

Sapphire accepted his invitation and they climbed into Cecil's waiting limousine and drove into the city.

'How near are we to your home?' Sapphire asked.

'The next block,' said Everett.

'Is there a photographic place nearby?'

'Yes, on the corner.'

'Could we stop? I've a roll of film I want developed,' she said.

Cecil gave the order to pull in but the shop had closed.

'I'll do it tomorrow,' she said.

The chauffeur drove on, deposited everyone's luggage inside the front door of Cecil's house and departed.

From the moment she entered, Sapphire knew that Everett's father was the master of understatement. Their Swiss home was beautiful and vast, designed as if the architect was practising for the Guggenheim Museum in New York City.

There were no hallways as such and no staircase, but a gently spiralling ramp curving up and up and up from a central sitting space. It was an eclectic place, awash with light and colour, where Sapphire felt instantly comfortable. The finest antique Persian carpets were scattered over polished parquet floors. In contrast, instead of the usual leather armchairs, there were Mies van der Rohe loungers.

The walls were a muted cream. As she gazed around her with growing astonishment, Sapphire began to realise (due to her history of art course) that every one of the fabulous and vibrant paintings on the walls were done by women. Women from the past, the far distant past, and women of now.

Sapphire turned to Cecil, who was standing beside her, watching her awe-struck expression.

'It is amazing,' she said, 'I can't believe it. It's the most incredible collection I've ever seen.'

'My wife, Olivia, began it,' Cecil explained. 'I was only interested in money. She was only interested in spending it.' He gave a wry laugh. 'But she spent it well and, after she died, I carried on. Come, walk with me while Everett sorts out some refreshment.'

Everett disappeared through an archway. A few moments later the whole building was flooded with the sounds of music.

'My son has a passion for jazz,' said Cecil, as the virtuoso tones of Ella Fitzgerald's scat jazz recording of 'Lady be Good' echoed around them.

Sapphire and Cecil strolled slowly up the ramp, her eyes roving avidly from one masterpiece to another to the accompaniment of Ella; then the tape changed to Norma Winston singing 'It Amazes Me', and later Betty Carter's 'Make Him Believe'. By the time they arrived at the top of the house, they were hearing Sarah Vaughan's extraordinary version of 'Smoke Gets in your Eyes'.

And all the while, Sapphire was gaping at the treasures on the walls. There was a beautiful eleventh century German psalter illustrated by a young nun called Claricia, a miniature portrait of a courtier by the fifteenth century Parisienne painter, Anastaise, a breviary from Florence with a self portrait by Maria Ormani. She walked on amazed to see that Cecil owned not only one of the self portraits by Sofonisba Anguissola, who worked in Italy and Spain between 1550 until 1580, but also one of her outstanding portraits of Elisabeth de Valois, Queen of Spain.

Then Sapphire looked up and saw various examples of the astonishing work of women painters from sixteenth century Bologna. Sapphire gasped out loud when she saw that he possessed a large, powerful, energetic and stunning version, which she had had no idea existed, of 'Judith Killing Holofernes' by Artemisia Gentileschi.

'They think that one was painted about 1610, before

the more famous one of "Judith Beheading Holfernes",' said Cecil. 'Now, take a look at this.'

From under a glass cabinet he brought out an ancient catalogue. 'It's a tulip book, commissioned by the bulb dealers of the Low Countries in about 1630,' he told her, 'and it's illustrated by the Dutchwoman Judith Leyster. And here are some water colours by the German-born Maria Merian, done at about the same time.'

'I'm astounded,' said Sapphire, staring at meticulous paintings of caterpillars on parchment. Sapphire knew that this woman's work on insects had revolutionised the sciences of zoology and botany. 'I just can't take it in that you own all this. Do you ever open it to the public?'

'No,' he said, 'but scholars come in from time to time.'

'It's wonderful to see, but how sad to keep all this beauty hidden. If I owned it, I'd open it up and call it the Olivia de Bouys Collection.'

'Would you?'

'Oh yes,' she said fervently as the two of them continued their winding journey along the sloping ramp.

Sapphire passed examples of eighteenth century tapestries and beautifully executed ninteenth century needlework, especially the US quilts. The latter had been mostly made to raise money for the abolition of slavery; the patterns in some even told the slaves where the 'safe' houses were.

'May the points of our needles prick the conscience of the slave owners,' said Sapphire. 'Isn't that what one of those women said?'

'Yes, indeed,' said Cecil, taking her arm as they carried on walking past the works of the early Victorian painters – Rosa Bonheur and Rebecca Soloman and Elisabeth Thompson.

It was as they progressed to the top spiral where there was a large gap in the wall, obviously leading to a whole other part of the extraordinary building, that Sapphire saw the American sculptures.

'Oh but that's Zenobia,' said Sapphire, pointing to a

half size model in marble of a woman in chains. 'The great Palmyrene queen who headed up her own armies and drove the Romans out of Syria, Egypt, Asia Minor and back to the Hellespont.'

'It is indeed,' said Everett, joining them and carrying a tray with steaming liquid in elegant 1930s cups. As Sarah Vaughan had finished and Billie Holliday began singing 'Me Myself And I', Everett had come out of an elevator that was disguised by giant murals on its doors. 'Old Bentley's having difficulty getting up today,' he said. 'But he's seeing to our luggage.'

'Old Bentley's our butler,' explained Cecil, laughing. 'He should have retired years ago but we can't bear the place without him, and he couldn't be without us. So we have a pact. He stays here and we do the work!'

'And I think those are made by Suzie Cooper,' said Sapphire, smiling as she pointed to the cups.

'Yes, cups by Suzie Cooper and – ' said Everett, smiling happily because Sapphire seemed so relaxed in his surroundings, ' – and peppermint tea by me. You do drink peppermint tea?'

'Oh yes,' said Sapphire eagerly, she was very thirsty.

Each of them took a cup and began to sip.

'Harriet Hosmer made this small statue about 1853,' said Everett, carrying on where his father left off, 'before the bigger full size version of that famous Palmyrene queen, which as you know caused an uproar when it was first exhibited. And here, this bust of a politician is by Anne Whitney and this one of freed slaves is carved by Edmonia Lewis, who, as I expect you know, was part-black and part-native American – and a terrible life she had too.'

Sapphire sat down on a nearby stool. 'I'm speechless,' she said, her body swaying slightly to the sounds of Miss Holliday and her eyes alighting on the sculptures of Barbara Hepworth and Elisabeth Frink. During their conversation on the plane he had argued on certain points, but had not let slip that he was particularly well-informed on art or that his father had such an incredible collection. She wondered why.

'There's more,' said Everett, pointing to a domestic scene in oils by Berthe Morisot and a superb drawing of a sensuous woman stepping out of her bath by Suzanne Valadon. But what finally left Sapphire catching her breath in total admiration were Cecil's acquisition of modern-day works by the Americans Sylvia Sleigh, Judy Chicago, Jayne Quick-to-See Smith and Barbara Kruger. There was a huge and haunting canvas by an unknown Australian aborigine; she was the painter and recorder of her tribe, but her name had eluded everyone. Whether this was genuine or by design, no-one knew.

There was a painting by the New Zealander, Alexis Hunter, two Englishwomen were represented; there was a mixed media work by Helen Chadwick, and a strange – almost macabre – Surrealist painting by Leonora Carrington. Sapphire looked past them to one of the goddess paintings by the Swedish artist Monica Sjoo and then saw a couple of extraordinary sculptures, using the natural fabric of her environment – whale-bone, antlers, stone and fur – by the Inuit artist, Elsie Emuk.

There was a depth of feeling in the whole house, a spirituality that plugged into Sapphire's new and heightened state of awareness, brought on by her sudden discovery of sex and the beginnings of love.

'It's wonderful,' said Sapphire, beaming at Everett.

The three of them sat on Mies van der Rohe loungers and Sapphire forgot to be shy. In her enthusiasm for the work around her, she forgot to hold back on her emotions and took hold of Everett's hand and squeezed it. 'It's all quite wonderful.'

'My mother's doing,' said Everett proudly, squeezing Sapphire's hand in return.

'As I told you, Olivia, my wife,' said Cecil, 'my very dear late wife introduced me to these artists and insisted I buy them. At first I wasn't sure, but now – now I see the altered mood, the different perspective, that these women offer, and they are among my favourites.'

It was then that there was a sea change in Sapphire's thinking. She looked at the work of the women over the centuries, work that had frequently been denied by historians, or under-rated, and she felt angry. As the anger welled up inside her, she realised that she too was part of that conspiracy. She had underrated her sexuality. She had denied her sexuality. She had played the game of keeping her virginity. She had not allowed her passions full rein. She hadn't allowed them any rein at all. She hadn't allowed herself to be. She had not allowed herself to find out who and what she was.

A part of her was hidden even from herself. She had no idea of what her body could do, where her emotions could take her. She knew about her brain. She had been born with a good one and had used it – but sex, her sex, her sexuality, was a talent lying dormant.

She looked up at the man sitting beside her. Danger? Yes. Dangerous? Yes. But her armour had cracked. Her hard shell, her coldness had evaporated. She was a soft, loving, pliable, moist woman. Sapphire was absolutely determined to find out what that meant. And she decided she would find out with Everett. Wherever he led, she would follow. Willingly. Sapphire had discovered her own new perspective.

'Father, are you going to show us now what you bought back from Mexico?' Everett asked, as his father stood up.

'Yes,' said Cecil.

'He likes you,' said Everett, watching the painted elevator doors closing on Cecil's frail figure.

Sapphire sipped her tea. Alone again with Everett, she felt the tension rising. The longing to touch him overwhelmed her.

The two of them stayed silent. She stared at the paintings.

'Sapphire?' he said.

'Yes?' She turned quickly and their eyes locked.

'Sapphire, will you – will you have dinner with me tonight?'

'Yes,' she said, and was saved any further conversation as Cecil came back with his latest acquisition: a painting, raw in its intensity, by Frida Kahlo.

'This is the reason for my trip to Mexico,' Cecil announced. 'This beautiful long-forgotten painting by a brave woman who suffered so much; and yet her art grew out of her pain. Love can, too. Love and pain and healing.' Tears began to roll down the old man's face. Hugging the painting, he walked back into the elevator.

'He's remembering my mother,' said Everett. 'We'll leave him. He'll be alright. This happens from time to time, and he prefers to be by himself when it does. Now, have you been to Geneva before?'

'No,' Sapphire replied.

'Then I'm taking you somewhere special. It's a café with a cabaret. Bentley told me that tonight only there's a special performance by an opera singer.'

'Opera? But you like jazz,' Sapphire exclaimed. Opera wasn't high on her list of priorities. Big, fat, loud and ugly opera singers who screeched was not Sapphire's idea of a romantic dinner-date.

'This is different. This opera singer is young, slim and very pretty, and she can sing jazz – which she's doing.'

'She can?'

'Oh yes. You do like jazz, don't you?'

'Yes, very much.'

'She's Swedish. Her name's Sara Ljungberg and I've heard her before, in London and Stockholm. She's wonderful. So do you fancy that? Or we can – '

'Sounds great,' said Sapphire.

'Fine. You'll want to freshen up.' Everett guided Sapphire through the arch from the terraced ramp. 'Your suite,' said Everett, his hand hovering on the handle of a closed door. 'I'll call for you in half an hour.'

He pushed the door open and walked away. Sapphire found herself staring at Everett's rear, thinking how neat and high and well-shaped it was. It had hollows in it where other men's filled out. She had the strongest desire to trace those hollows with her fingers. She pursed her lips, drew in a sharp breath, and told herself to stop her ridiculous thoughts.

Stepping into the room, Sapphire saw an essay in white. Virginal white: Sapphire guessed the room had never been occupied. The walls were bare and devoid of all decoration. The furnishings – an armchair, a side table, the bedside tables, the bed, the bedhead, the bedside clock – everything was white. It was elegant, but not cosy or snug, and Sapphire felt uncomfortable. The room lacked a soul. It had no essence, no story to tell.

Even when she noticed that someone had tried to soften the harsh effect by tying high feathers with long trailing ribbon to each of the iron struts of the bedstead, it didn't relieve her sense of the meagre. She walked over and turned down the heavily embossed white coverlet. The linen and lace pillowcases, the linen sheets, even the box of chocolates put on the bedside table were a startling white, as was the ice box which was seated on top of a long row of white built-in cupboards.

She opened the fridge and found a selection of white wines, champagne, mineral waters, fresh fruit and salad. She took a white peach and bit into it. Needing relief from her glacial surroundings, Sapphire strode over to the vast window, drew back the heavy white silk damask curtains, opened the French windows and stepped out on to a huge cantilevered balcony.

Eating, deliberately allowing the juice to run over her lips and down on to her chin, she gazed up at the chill, clear, midnight blue autumn sky, where distant stars twinkled. It was infinitely more fascinating than the stark white room. The unknown dark forces of the night and those within her imagination were luring her into temptation.

With a sudden flash of illumination, Sapphire realised why she felt uncomfortable in the room. It was an echo of herself. A room without experiences. A room where nothing had happened. She was as emotionally blank as the room. She was as a page without writing or a canvas without brushstrokes.

A breeze caught her hair, she shivered slightly. She wondered if, by morning, she would have marked that page. If Everett moved towards her, would she be able to take it on the wing – cope with his physicality, his desire, her own disposition and inclination? Or would she withdraw, retreat into her habitual shell? Would she be able to hold out against the power of Everett's gypsy charm and his compelling dark blue eyes? Sapphire was torn between a longing to know and a need to keep herself pure. But she knew her resistance waned with every moment she spent in Everett's company.

Sapphire kicked off her shoes and padded back into the warm room and across the thick white carpet to the white stereo unit to see what discs were there for her to play. She discovered a selection of music: some classical, some pop, some funk and some jazz. She picked up one, a new recording by the half-Swedish pop and folk singer, Sonja Kristina. 'Sonja's Jazz Classics'. Sapphire put it on. As the pure strains of Sonja's rendition of 'In My Solitude' drifted into the room, Sapphire undressed.

Before taking her bath, she took from her suitcase her toiletries bag and her baby-pink satin pyjamas. The nightwear she put at the foot of the bed. The bag she took with her into the huge, sparkling white marble bathroom, where she eschewed the shower. She would have a jacuzzi and think what she would wear for her evening with Everett.

Sapphire travelled light but well. A café with cabaret deserved a cocktail frock. She had bought one in Dallas – clinging maroon silk devorée with a V-neck and an ankle-to-mid-thigh split.

Out of the bath, she towelled herself dry and eased the frock up over her body. It was cut so that the fabric from the left hip fastened with three buttons on the right shoulder and vice versa, forming the V of the cleavage and, even with her large breasts, she didn't need a bra. It would have spoilt the softly flowing line. She put on flesh coloured high-cut knickers that gripped her rounded buttocks and then drew on hold-up flesh coloured silk stockings. She thrust her slim feet into black leather stiletto-heeled shoes.

She piled her thick, red-blonde hair up on her head and placed a solid gold torque around her swanlike neck. She checked her fingernails for any chips in the maroon lacquer. There were none. She made up her face with soft grey eye liner and dark red, almost maroon coloured lipstick. She popped an extra lipstick in her black leather handbag and was ready for Everett precisely thirty minutes later.

The café was not what Sapphire had been expecting. She had imagined a dark cavern, plenty of smoke, a funky atmosphere – almost cosy. Instead it was open and light, everyone could see everyone else and all heads turned when Sapphire and Everett entered. Even the DJ stopped to gape.

The place was anything but intimate and it reflected their mood. Everett and Sapphire were not easy with one another. Their previous camaraderie had vanished. They walked apart, and were controlled in their actions and their words. The prying gaze of the other customers made Everett walk close to Sapphire.

She stalked behind the head waiter and sat stiff and unbending at the table. Everett called for champagne and they just managed to get their food order when the taped music stopped and Sara Ljungberg came on and began to sing. A slight, slim young woman, with very pale skin and short dark brown hair, she was beautiful and had an aura, a stage presence, that was irresistible.

Everett and Sapphire sat opposite one another, but evaded each other's eyes. They half-turned towards the singer who sang hauntingly of love found and love lost and love betrayed and slowly, very slowly, Everett and Sapphire melted and relaxed.

'You are the most beautiful woman in the room,' said Everett, after the waiter had poured their drinks. 'And I would like to drink to us.'

Sapphire lowered her eyes.

'Sapphire,' he said, putting his hand under her chin, raising her face to his. 'Sapphire, I've fallen in love with you.'

'You don't know me,' she said.

'I know enough,' he replied. 'Sapphire, listen to me; I've fallen in love with you.'

His other hand reached for hers, holding the flute of champagne. She trembled. He stared into her eyes and she stared back. She was lost, completely lost. The whole of her body was aching for him, screaming for him, wanting him. She tried to stop herself shaking, but she couldn't. His hand gripped hers harder. He picked up her hand and brushed his lips over her fingertips. His touch seared her and fused their flesh.

At the end of Sara's set, the waiter bought their food, but all Sapphire could do was look at it. She wasn't hungry any more.

'What's the matter?' he asked.

'I don't know,' she lied. She knew full well what the matter was. She wanted him to make love to her but was too reserved and shy to make the move.

'If you are ill, perhaps we should leave?' he said, his eyes holding hers.

'Yes,' she said, her heart fluttering. She inclined her head, and jerked her hand away from his.

They left the café and their untouched food and wine, and it wasn't long before they were back again at the extraordinary house. As Everett opened the door on to the gently lit central space, she felt his hot breath on her neck. Her mind reeled off into a whirr of lascivious fantasy. Every part of her, every nerve ending, was aching and waiting to be caressed.

Sapphire tripped on the edge of the Persian carpet. Everett caught her in his arms. They stayed close for a moment. She attempted to break away.

'I shall carry you upstairs,' he said, lifting her up and cradling her in his arms before she could protest, he strode fast up the sloping ramp.

112

In the bedroom, he didn't turn on the light and didn't put her down. He just held her tight, looking at her in the moonlight. And her world stood still. With their eyes locked, their hearts pounding, their bodies trembling, he lowered his lips to hers. His touch was exquisite. And the hunger within them spurted up, flooded into and was concentrated in their mouths. Then they fell back on the bed. She could feel the desire in his body, the hardness of him as he lay over her. And one of his hands went up along her spine and the other down over her bottom, frightening Sapphire.

'No,' she said, jumping away from him. Danger was close and she wasn't ready yet. She wasn't ready for the consequences. She had to put some space between them, but she didn't want him to leave the room. 'No, I can't – I can't.'

'A drink, you need a drink,' he said, calmly.

'Yes, yes.'

'Champagne,' he said, coming to stand beside her.

Sapphire moved away from him and sat in one of the armchairs. Everett popped the cork, poured the fizzy corn-coloured liquid into a couple of cut crystal flutes and handed one to her.

'Cheers. Do you know Mari Boine?' he asked, turning from her to look through the disc collection.

'No,' she said.

'She's a Saami.' He put a CD on the player.

'A what?' she asked.

'A Saami. That's what the people from Lapland are called; Saami.'

'Oh,' she said.

Sapphire had never heard the tender soft invocations of Mari's pure coloratura before. She stopped drinking and stood quite still listening. The notes the woman was singing seemed to be her notes. The chords were chords she recognised from deep down within her, echoes of her own spirit. Gradually, the singer's voice was joined by a clarinet, a dulcimer, and then a drum.

The drum. The drum was Sapphire's thumping heart.

The singer was speaking to her of longing and yearning and of life. As the composition moved and changed, its extraordinary resonance heightening Sapphire's emotions, it was also the harbinger of ecstasy.

'To us,' whispered Everett.

'To us,' she repeated, and moved back to the bed thinking, Oh my God, now what? And every portion of her body screamed 'touch me', but she was frightened of him doing it. Frightened, because she wanted it, but couldn't escape – she didn't want to escape. Sapphire avoided his eyes, eyes that seemed to bore into her soul. She sipped at the wine then, not knowing what to do with herself, she sipped again and again, faster and faster, until the glass was empty. And the music continued.

'Have some water if you're thirsty,' said Everett, getting up and taking a bottle of sparkling mineral water from the ice box, pouring some into a tumbler and handing it to her.

'Yes,' she said hoarsely.

'Perhaps you are hungry, too?' he asked.

'No – I mean yes,' she said.

She watched as Everett peered into the ice box and took out peaches, bananas, mushrooms soaked in vinaigrette sauce, carrots and cucumbers. Then, from the cupboard, he took some sparkling white china plates.

'What do you want?' he asked.

'What is there?' she asked.

'Mushrooms – ' he began.

'I'll have some,' she interrupted.

Everett ladled the dark little buttons on to a plate and gave them to her. She took the plate and their fingers met. Shaking with anticipation, Sapphire gave a slight gasp, held her breath and swallowed hard. His touch sent exciting tingling messages along every part of her skin.

'More wine, I think,' said Everett, holding the champagne bottle. She reached for her glass on the bedside table and held it out. He started to pour fractionally too

114

early. A couple of cool drops hit the side of her hand and slopped on to her maroon devorée frock.

'So sorry,' he said, and stroked her hand where the liquid had spilled. She froze, suspended between desire and fear. 'There, that's better,' he said, and finished his glass of champagne.

But it wasn't better for Sapphire. She was aware of every nuance in her body, every movement, every tremble. He appeared oblivious of her feelings.

Sapphire turned to put her glass on the bedside table and was suddenly flushed with shame as she realised the slit in her frock had parted and he could see a flash of bare thigh and stocking top.

'Sapphire,' he said.

She looked at him. Their eyes met.

'I think I should leave you to sleep,' he said.

She had been a fool. She was going to lose him. Why couldn't she let go, enjoy, take?

In the moonlit room, there was a stillness in the space between them, but their bodies were trembling and the music was now reaching its own ecstatic heights.

'No,' she whispered. 'No, don't go – kiss me.'

Sapphire said what she wanted but saying it surprised her.

Never letting his eyes leave hers, Everett pulled her up towards him. In one swift movement he clasped her around her waist and bent her backwards. Her hands went up to touch his handsome wild gypsy-like face. His hands followed hers and clasped her wrists. She could feel the strength of him, the exciting hardness of him pushing against her belly. Sapphire held her breath. As if there was a forcefield around them, their lips seemed to touch before they did. And there were instant sparks on ignition.

Every erotic dream she had ever had sprang to life as the wide, red softness of his mouth touched hers; his tongue, his smell, his taste heightened her lust. Passion fused them. They rolled, in unison, backwards and forwards across the huge white bed. They stayed locked together in a long and ardent embrace. His tongue pushed past her teeth, entering into the small cavern beyond.

When he moved his mouth, his tender lips touching her eyes, her nose, her cheek and her ears, the whole of her body quivered. Each kiss found her more heady, as if she had taken the most powerful drug. Everett painted a portrait of her with his lips as they travelled from her mouth to her cheeks, to her ear lobes and back again to her mouth.

He nuzzled her neck and a quick spasm, a rash of goose pimples, broke out where his lips met her flesh. He took her higher and higher. Erotic desire flooded through her. Exquisite sensations squeezed into and out of her womb. Her mind ceased to think, to plan, to observe. Emotion and desire were paramount.

Respond. Respond, cried her tongue, her mouth, her breasts, her arms, her legs and her opening ripe sex. Her whole body was his, a landscape waiting to be painted. He was the painter. And the singer was still singing. But now Sapphire's notes of joy and release were echoing through the room in harmony with hers.

'I love you,' Everett whispered in her ear. 'I love you and I want you.'

His potent words, the words she wanted to hear most, let loose her womb. Everett loved her. Nothing else mattered. She could give herself to him completely. The swelling, the moistness of her inner self, increased as his questing hands caressed her neck then journeyed down to hover at her cleavage. He made no attempt to remove her frock. Instead, with infinite delicacy, the tips of his fingers inveigled their way through the V of her neckline and touched her hard erect nipples. Sapphire gasped. Everett closed her mouth with his.

Sapphire lay back, taking his tongue, entwining hers with his, thrusting. His fingers gradually increased the pressure on her nipples so that from gentleness the feeling progressed to heightened pleasure, then to pain, then to a combination of the two. Sapphire could not tell where one sensation ended and the other began, but it was extreme.

'Open your legs,' he whispered, pulling at the hem of her frock.

Sapphire obeyed willingly. Still kissing her, Everett eased the dark silk up along her pale stockings.

'Spread your legs wider,' he said, as his fingers lightly, gently, stroked past her stocking-tops to the whiteness of her soft thighs. Sapphire let out a series of short sighs that were almost the notes of a song. Her hands, imprisoned by his, wanted to touch the nape of his neck and the curve that had excited her earlier.

Her breasts were aching to be fondled, and her own hands wanted and needed to caress him. The yearning within her to be taken and ravished grew stronger. He was playing with her like a master with his slave. She wanted him to teach her to obey his every whim. She no longer had the capacity to tell her body to do anything. It responded to him naturally. As his fingers lingered over the top of her thighs, she felt her buttocks tense and rise. Brazenly, she lifted her hips towards him, offering herself, yielding, yielding to him, opening, swelling – combining moisture and tingling, excitement and fear but, more than anything, desire.

His fingers travelled further up. They skimmed the outside of her high-cut briefs and she held her breath as his fingers trailed with infinite care across her closed-in and covered sex. One finger. One finger started to ease its way under the elastic. One finger touched her sex lips. One finger touched her sex lips with a whisper of a movement and she cried out in short breathy gasps.

The softest slip across her labia was almost a torture as he lingered on the swollen moistness of her wet sex. She held her breath. She wanted more. She raised her hips again. Two fingers pushed under her knicker elastic and touched. She gave short moaning gasps. Two fingers and tiny currents of torment rushed through her as, with the tenderest pressure, he squeezed her sex lips together.

Not entering – just the slightest pressure and the sweetest squeezing.

With an intake of breath, Sapphire made a long low sound, then let forth an extended wail – the sound of desire at the beginning of fulfilment. And issuing from the speakers was the the sweet high sound of the flute together with Mari's voice, their music mirroring Sapphire's feelings and her cries.

Very slowly Everett's fingers began pushing into her juicy wet sex. Sapphire's body moved this way and that. She found her own natural rhythm, her hips rising and lowering, the muscles within her opening and closing. Through his exploring fingers they both discovered her innate licentiousness.

'Hold on to the bedstead,' said Everett, placing one of her hands around a rigid strut. 'Grip it hard, and don't move,' he said. Then he poured some more champagne into a glass and lifted it to her lips. 'Drink,' he commanded. And Sapphire drank the fizzy liquid, making her more heady, more abandoned.

'I want to make love to you,' he said, nibbling at her ear lobes. 'I want to pleasure you. Would you like me to do that?' And he delicately pressed her nipples between his thumbs and forefingers. 'I want an answer from you, Sapphire. Say yes or no. Do you want me to pleasure you?'

'Yes,' she whispered.

'Yes, is that all you can say? Tell me what you want me to do to you.'

'I . . . I don't know . . .' she said, confused.

'Would you like me to kiss your breasts, suck your nipples, or go down between your legs?' Sapphire drew in a sharp breath as his lips touched her thighs just before her sex. 'I see, so you want me between your legs. But, Sapphire, do you want my tongue or my cock?'

Sapphire was silent.

'If you cannot choose, I must choose for you, but I must do it my way. And that means you submit.

Whatever I want to do to you I'll do. Do you agree to that?'

'Yes,' she whispered.

Sapphire had no real idea what he meant but wanted him to caress her more, she wanted him to fondle her breasts, wanted him between her legs. And she wanted to touch his penis, feel its strength and erect hardness.

Everett leant forward, took the ribbons that trailed from the bedhead and, firmly, but giving her plenty of leeway, he tied Sapphire's wrists. Then he lifted her skirt up around her waist, pulled her panties to one side and lightly licked her moist sex. Sapphire tensed and raised her buttocks, welcoming him. But Everett stopped and kissed Sapphire's eyes, and then her lips, checking at the same time that the bindings were totally secure.

'Spread your legs,' he said. 'Wider. I want you spread-eagled across this bed and I want you watching everything I do to you. And remember, you obey me. Is that understood?'

'Yes,' she whispered shamelessly.

Everett stood up and quickly undid the slim leather belt of his trousers and threw it on the floor beside the bed, then he undid his flies and removed his trousers, his tie, his shirt, his shoes, socks and his underpants. He was completely naked. With the moonlight streaming in through the vast window, Sapphire was able to admire his beautiful firm body, big full balls and a very large, very stiff cock. She had a wild desire to take its erect fullness into her mouth.

Everett knelt on the bed, putting his knees either side of her hips and letting his cock and balls move gently on her belly; he reached up and undid the buttons on the shoulder of her frock. Between undoing each button he kissed her lips. When each button was undone, he sensuously stroked her skin. He pulled the fabric down, revealing the beautiful white swell and contours of her large breasts. He bent and tenderly licked them.

Deftly, he massaged her nipples, enjoying the sweet sound of her sexual whimpering. Then, taking a feather from the bedhead, he caressed her erect nipples and swept it down over her belly to her panties. He pushed the elastic of her pantie legs to one side and she felt his tongue licking her thighs and then the outer, very pink and very swollen, lips of her sex.

Her entire body was trembling. Tiny tremors of pure excitement shuddered through every nerve ending, every part of her body, whether she had ever considered it sexual, erotic, arousable or not. Sapphire was amazed to find sex did not stop in and around the top of her legs but was made up and heightened in each particle of her living being.

Snake-like, he eased his hand under the waistband. With his middle finger he found her hidden bud, her aroused clitoris. In one fast movement he spread his whole hand over her sex, then gripped and held her hard, only his middle finger continuing its salacious work.

The slowness of the feather and the swiftness of his sex-grab caught Sapphire unawares. She let out a long high note, the sound of a bitch on heat, and he felt the moisture and dampness increase between her legs. His fingers slid inside her palpitating and swollen flesh.

The sensation Sapphire experienced with his fingers gliding inside her exceeded anything she had ever imagined. She was completely lost to all reality except the fever his fingers wrought within her. Then he slid her panties down her legs, removed them, and changed his position. Kneeling beside her head, he placed his large and rigid cock in her hand.

'Play with it,' ordered Everett.

Willingly, Sapphire let her hand trail its length, finding his large balls. Letting her fingers glide over his testes she took her hand back up along his glans, under the hood, then played up and down between the rim of the cap and the head. Each stroke she gave him gave her pleasure. This was what she wanted, where she wanted to be. With Everett, in a bed, making love – and she didn't care what he did to her, what he asked of her. She was utterly his and would obey him.

'Suck me,' said Everett, turning her head towards his prick.

'Suck you?' she exclaimed. Sapphire had had the desire but she had never done it before.

'Yes, take my cock between your lips and suck on it,' he said.

Shamelessly, she opened her big red mouth and took its urgent roundness inbetween her soft lips. Everett swivelled his body so that his face was towards her womb. He had tapped into her pure and natural love of sex that so far was unsatisfied. He put his head down between her legs and the next moment Sapphire felt the most delicious sensation surge through her taut body as his tongue enjoyed the soft sweet sea-smelling tissue of her inner body.

But it was when his tongue came up and licked at her clitoris, softly and with utter gentleness, as if he was taking nectar from the most precious, the most fragile object in the world, that her mind and body exploded simultaneously – not with an orgasm but with uncontrolled sexual abandonment. She writhed and squirmed and gasped and sighed and erotic visions flooded into her brain. She didn't care what he did as long as his tongue didn't stop its extraordinary work. And she stayed sucking his prick.

'Lift up your bottom,' he said, moving away from her mouth.

'What are you going to do?'

'Don't ask questions,' he commanded.

Sapphire raised her hips. Everett put three pillows under her buttocks.

'Now lie back,' he ordered, gazing at her.

She was aware that she must seem to him utterly abandoned – her red-gold hair falling over her face, her full rounded white body naked except for the gold torque around her neck, the stockings on her legs and the black high-heeled shoes on her feet.

He sat down beside her; with one hand he began caressing her aching nipples and with the other he took a dark oily mushroom from the white china plate and trailed it through her sex. The cold wet squashy feel of the mushroom dipping into her was so unexpected that Sapphire opened wider, wanting more, wanting that strange feeling again. She rolled her hips from side to side and moaned with delight. Everett insisted that she watch him as he took the mushrooms one by one, rubbed them on her beautiful swollen red flowering sex, and ate them.

'Now stay exactly as you are,' he said. 'You mustn't move. Keep your legs open and your hips high.'

Everett walked over to the ice box and removed the long, cold cucumber.

'See this?' he said. 'I am going to play with you with this.'

Everett began to roll it along her thighs; on the outside, on the inside, taking it further and further up, letting his fingers stray on to her wet labia as he rubbed its icy coldness between the tops of her legs.

'Hold your breasts,' he ordered. 'I want to see you clasping your own breasts, massaging your tits, playing with your nipples. I have allowed you enough ribbon so do it, my love, do it.'

It excited her to have him watch as she caressed her aching breasts. Then, slowly, he began to insert the cucumber into her soft pink opening, its hard cold stiffness easing gently into her warm and wanton wetness. He watched her sex clasp it like a sea anemone, her muscles closing around it, gently accepting it. When he had thrust the tip in, he left it hanging lasciviously from her sex and took another mushroom, and rubbing it up and down on her clitoris to stimulate her hard little bud.

Jerking the cucumber a little further into her, he lay his head beside her feet. He took off her shoes, then pulled off her stockings. He took her left foot in his hand and sucked and licked every toe. Then he repeated the process with her right foot. And all the time Sapphire felt his prick pressing against her legs. Then, licking as he went, slowly he clambered along her body. He shifted his position. His hands and his tongue went higher and higher. She could feel the hardness of the cucumber inside her juicy wet entrance, then the urgent warmth of Everett's penis on her inner thighs. And the whole of her was crying out for him, his cock, his prick, his penis, to enter her, penetrate her, dominate her.

The lewd pleasure of his assaults on the aroused membranes of her sex was bringing Sapphire almost to the point of climax.

'Please,' she moaned, 'please take me.'

'Take you?' he asked. 'What do you mean, take you?'

Sapphire hesitated. Could she say what she meant? Could she say the word?

'You must tell me what you want.'

'I want – please will – please fuck me,' she whispered.

'No,' he said, dipping his fingers into the oily vinaigrette sauce and smearing it over her luscious breasts, encircling them and tweaking her rose-bud nipples. 'No.'

He gave the cucumber a further shove and she opened her legs to welcome it further. She was powerless to do anything except let her body go with his outrageous desires.

'I want you to drink,' he said,

'No, no, thank you,' she said, realising her bladder was already filling up from the wine and the water.

'Sapphire, it's not a request it's an order.' He poured some more champagne into her glass and lifted her head. 'Drink. You promised to obey me, now, drink. All of it.'

She sipped but he tipped her head back and she was made to drink the lot. What she didn't drink fell over her well-oiled and glistening body. He massaged it into her breasts and her belly. She was drunk with the wine and intoxicated with her own ribald and erotic thoughts.

Everett smiled and leant his body over hers. Sapphire gasped. She had been longing to feel the strength of him against the yielding rounded softness of herself, her erect nipples, and her womb. Sapphire was longing to be fondled and fucked.

'Sapphire, I want you to turn over,' he said, holding the cucumber in place. 'Turn over, keep your tits flat against the bed, and put your bottom up high.'

Sapphire did as she was told. The ribbons which held her in place were long enough to allow her to turn over, but not loose enough to allow her to escape. More thoughts came into her mind; she wondered what it would be like to suck another man's cock as Everett played with her. To have another man's hands roam over her body, another man in the room watching her being fucked. She flushed with shame at her debauched thoughts but eagerly moved her hips up and down as he guided the cucumber further and further into her sex.

He slid his body under her so that his cock was level with her mouth and his mouth with her bottom. Sapphire suddenly realised, with a deep sense of mortification, that her tiny hidden puckered place was on view. She tried to close her legs.

'No,' he commanded. 'You keep your legs open.'

He slapped her buttocks hard then licked her chastised flesh. Everett worked her sex with the cucumber and her clitoris with his middle finger; his hand slid along the cleft of her buttocks. She clenched again.

'Don't do that,' he scolded, and began to move a finger on to that other hole, her tight-hidden forbidden hole. 'If you do, I shall have to punish you. Now, suck me,' he said, easing the finger deeper into her tight dark brown hole. She clenched once more. 'No, no, you stay open.' He smacked her bottom very hard.

Sapphire was startled to find herself revelling in the combination of hurt, depravity and delicious sensuousness.

'And keep sucking my cock' he ordered.

Then she felt something long, thin and supple, she was reminded of the leather belt he had taken off, trailing along the soft tingling flesh of her vulva and through the cleft of her bottom. Suddenly, and without warning, that same small forbidden hole was being flicked. Flick; and then her sex was stroked. Flick and her sex was stroked again. She was opening and closing, the flicks were strange but oddly pleasurable.

The strength of each tiny lash-stroke was increased. Pleasure became pain. In between the pain there was a sudden stab of bliss as a finger played on her excited and swollen clitoris. She was wet and open and could do nothing except sway and moan and cry out with the unexpectedness of the extreme desire she was experiencing and wallow in it.

Everett poured more of the vinaigrette sauce over her buttocks, not caring if it slopped on to the sheets, the pillowcases: not caring what it marked. Not caring about the stains. Wanting it. They would be there forever, a token of their love night. He massaged the oily liquid into her naked rounded flanks and she shuddered and shivered with delight, her body bathing in waves of licentiousness. Then she felt a burst of fire across her oiled bottom as thin leather scorched her bare buttocks.

Sapphire cried out. She did not know whether she was crying with pleasure or pain, or whether it was a mixture of the two that led her to yell.

Everett's soft hands immediately came down on her buttocks and more oil was massaged into her rounded raised bottom. The massage eased the pain of the stripe. He turned her over. He pressed on her belly, on her full bladder, at the same time as he moved the hard elongated cucumber within her.

'Please,' she moaned. 'No, please – don't do that.'

'Why not?' asked Everett, increasing the pressure so that she was almost spilling her water.

'I might . . . I might . . .' Sapphire faltered.

Unexpectedly, Everett kissed her lips. 'You might what?' he asked.

'I might not be able to hold my water,' she said.

'Oh but you must,' he said, and began to play with her sex, stimulating her again.

Everett took the cucumber from her ripe wet pleasure

place. Then he changed his position and knelt between her open legs. He put on a condom and, with his arms outstretched taking his weight, slowly he drove forward into the dark pink depths of her wanton sex.

There was an agony in his taking her, agony in her bladder each time Everett's pelvis met hers, the pressure sent an exquisite piercing through her vulva and her womb. Everett edged his body to one side. His hand foraged between their sticky damp bodies and found her clitoris.

Until that moment, Sapphire would never have believed that such a delicate touch could have produced such a frantic intensity, such a raging frenzy within her. She thrashed around the bed, rolling this way and that as he swooped and pierced and rode her hard, lunging and pounding into her inner depths.

With his fingers massaging her hard over-excited little point, she felt she would burst: not only with the love juices flowing down from her womb, but with water needing to flow out from her bladder. She tensed in order to stop it happening. Everett knew full well what she was doing and increased his pressure on every part of her that was affected. She could only moan and sway.

Everett put one hand under her bottom and gripped it hard. He dug his nails into her rounded flesh and continued to thrust into her. Sapphire was twisting and turning on her bindings like a woman possessed.

He moved his hand to her belly and once again she was subjected to the sensations of acute pain.

'No,' she said.

'No, what, my love?' said Everett.

'I can't, I can't hold my water . . . I can't. You're – you're . . .'

Keeping his cock inside her, he made her put her legs around his waist. He undid the ribbons on her wrists, gathered her up in his arms, took her into the bathroom and placed her down in the shower against the cold tiled wall. He grabbed her bottom and pressed his prick against her belly and kissed her lips. His hands trailed down over her large white breasts, down towards her sex. And then he pressed. He pressed on her full bladder and she gave a short cry; her water trickled out and down his legs. Tears welled up in her eyes and she flushed with shame.

'No, no, my darling, don't, don't cry. You're so beautiful, Sapphire, so beautiful,' he said, kissing her neck, her lips. 'Everything, I love everything about you. I wanted you, I wanted to feel your golden rain. It's pure, it's you.'

He kissed her again and again, and caressed her breasts and turned on the shower. The two of them stayed there as the water flowed over them while he kissed and cradled, fondled and embraced her soft and pliant body.

Then he covered her in a huge bath towel and dried her, and she dried him; they were laughing together, all shame forgotten in the enjoyment. She nuzzled at his earlobes and his neck. He carried her back on to the bed and put on another condom. Kissing her passionately, with her arms around his neck, her legs far out to the side and shuddering, her hips raised, their heads moving with a fluency of motion, sliding and gliding on each other's love-sweat, he entered her, took her with all the urgency of his hot fiery body. He immersed himself in her, blending her body with his. They were completely one. They came together and lay exhausted and loving in one anothers arms.

'Sapphire,' he said some time later, his hand over one breast, her head on his shoulder. 'I meant to ask you, what do you do – for a living, what do you do?'

'Is it important?' she asked, kissing his nipples.

'No, but I'd like to know.'

'And I'd like to know your name, first,' she said.

'You know it,' he replied, surprised.

'No I don't, I know you are Everett and your father is Cecil and you've got a fantastic house with amazing paintings, but I haven't got a clue who you are.'

'Now that's amazing,' he said, kissing the top of her

head. 'I've spent the most incredible evening of my life with a woman who drives me to distraction and I don't even know her name and – she doesn't know mine!'

Sapphire burst out laughing; her hand snaked down and reached for his penis.

'Hello,' she said, 'I'm Sapphire Western.'

His hand roamed down over her belly and held her pubis.

'And I work in a bank and my name's Everett de Bouys,' he said, not having any idea of the bombshell he had dropped.

'De Bouys?' she exclaimed, half sitting up in the bed.

'Yes, de Bouys,' he said. 'Why?'

'De Bouys bank? You've got to be because you're Everett and Gerry is Sir Henry's son.'

'Yes,' he said, looking slightly mystified.

'I know Gerry's wife, well, ex-wife, now – Auralie,' she said, innocently. 'She was the friend I was going to see in London. Isn't that extraordinary?'

'Extraordinary,' he said. 'When did you meet Auralie?'

'When I was a student at the Courtauld.'

'Oh!' he said.

'And you've got your father's gift for understatement,' she said, giggling and snuggling into him. 'You don't just work in a bank, you and your father own the bank.'

'Yes,' he said. 'How do you know?'

'Because – ' Then she hesitated. She didn't want to tell him she was Sir Bevis Untermann's daughter. 'Because I've worked in banks too. I changed my job recently. Soon, I'm starting work as an auditor for Gowan and Grilpins.'

'An auditor!' he exclaimed. 'You're an auditor? At Gowan and Grilpin's? That, I'd never have guessed. Oh my sweet darling, that's wonderful, wonderful.'

'Why?'

'You're just the person we need. You're on holiday, you say, but could you – would you – do something for us?'

'What?' Sapphire asked warily.

'Meet me at the bank tomorrow. I'll have to square it with my father. I don't think there'll be much trouble there, but – and this is top top secret – we're missing some bonds. Bearer bonds, about to come to maturity.'

'That's terrible,' she said. 'How many?'

'Too many to be healthy,' he said. 'We've searched in various places, to no avail; now we think they must be in our vaults here.'

'And if they're not?'

'Then it leaves me with a terrible suspicion.'

'What's that?'

'That the man father sent to Meriboa to open up our futures base is a thief.'

'That is an awful conclusion to come to,' said Sapphire.

'I know,' said Everett. 'I'll have to be very careful. If they're not here, I'll have to go to Meriboa. Fancy a trip out East? We'll take the jet. Father won't be able to go, he's too frail and the climate wouldn't suit him. Would you do that? Come to the bank tomorrow and help us?'

'Yes,' she said, and kissed him lovingly. 'Yes, I will.'

'You see, there's something else, as well,' he said, holding her tight, feeling it safe to tell her what had been worrying him for ages. 'I think someone's moving in on us.'

'A takeover?'

'Yes, a takeover – but a hostile one. We don't want it. Father was thinking of selling, but then I agreed to come into the business.'

'You haven't always been a banker?'

'No; in fact, I said I wouldn't ever be one. I love computers – computer games, thinking them up. I had my own company but I looked at the old man and thought I can't, I just can't let him spend the last days of his life unhappy. So here I am, where I never expected to be.'

'With me!' she laughed.

'With you, certainly, but also as part of de Bouys. Father and I are happy with our present arrangement,

129

but the loss of those bonds is not going to help us,' he said.

'No, it isn't,' she said. 'Who do you think it is, wanting to takeover?'

'On that front, I'm not sure,' he said. 'They've got to be big. The likeliest are Caradoc Lewis of Hanway Rattle's or – if he hadn't died – I would have suspected Sir Bevis Untermann.'

Sapphire stiffened when she heard her father's name. Everett didn't notice. He was too far away in his musings.

'There was no love lost between Sir Bevis and the de Bouys.'

'Oh? Why not?' asked Sapphire, intrigued.

'Don't know,' said Everett. 'I never did. Sir Henry and Sir Bevis used to be friends. I expect a deal went wrong somewhere.'

'Could it be a woman?' asked Sapphire. It crossed her mind that there could be aspects of her father's life she didn't know about.

'No. No way, Sir Bevis was happily married to the same woman for years,' said Everett, laughing, taking her in his arms again and holding her close. 'So the most likely bidder is Hanway's, because our bank would give them access to markets they don't have at present.'

Sapphire breathed a sigh of relief, but she wondered if he was right. Could it be Hanway's? Was that the business that Zinnia had been called to London for? That would make sense.

Sapphire was sorely tempted to tell Everett whose daughter she was, but decided discretion was the better part of valour and stayed silent.

'Maybe, it's a nightmare,' said Everett. 'Maybe we'll find those bonds tomorrow, together, tomorrow,' he said, and kissed her again. 'Now, my sweetest darling, time to sleep.'

Sapphire, who was used to wearing night-clothes, slipped into her pyjamas and curled up in his arms. Warm, comfortable and happy, she drifted off into sleep.

She awoke next morning feeling odd and strange, as if she had dreamt an incredible dream. She and Everett had spent a wonderful night together. He had taken her, loved her, sucked and licked her. He had said he loved her. Was it true?

The trail of her clothing across the room, shoes and stockings abandoned anywhere they landed, told her it was for real. She lifted the bedcovers, saw the marks on the sheets, smelled the smell of sex on her and the bedclothes and smiled. The room now had a history. It was occupied. And it had her name on it.

Contented, Sapphire lay quite still in the vast bed, staring up at the sunbeams playing on the ceiling. A cloud passed over, obliterating them. She shifted her gaze and noticed a letter on headed notepaper on the bedside table.

'Couldn't wake you; you looked too perfect. Breakfast downstairs and lunch on us,' it said. 'Meet you at the bank at 11am. The address is on the top. Take a taxi. Father thinks you're wonderful and so do I. Love E.'

Sapphire looked at the clock. Half past nine. She, who never slept beyond eight o'clock, had broken one of her own patterns. She had broken two patterns. She had made love and woken late. Sapphire jumped out of bed and opened the French windows.

She stepped out on to the balcony and spread her arms as if welcoming the world. She breathed in the morning air and looked down to the avenue below. Geneva in the morning. The hum of traffic, the honking of horns. Trees glistening from a brief downpour of rain, the sun lighting up droplets on the leaves like particles of crystal. And somewhere out there was her lover. A man who loved her. She was happy. Supremely happy. Sapphire had never known such happiness.

Sapphire had fallen in love.

She turned from the view and began searching through the clothes she had brought with her in an effort to find something to wear that would fit her mood. Her evening with Everett had left her glowing, aware of her

131

body, proud and confident. Naked, holding up each item in turn, she discarded it as not suitable for the day ahead: a visit to Everett's bank, then lunch. Looking at the few clothes she'd brought with her, she decided nothing suited. She would wear the same severe suit she'd arrived in and go to the shops. She'd find something new and wonderful in one of the local boutiques.

Sapphire bathed, using some of her special herbal bath salts, and washed her glorious hair. Then she put on her white cotton underwear which was trimmed with the finest Belgian lace: a low cut bra which showed off her cleavage and high cut bikini panties which hugged her rounded bottom. Over her shapely legs, she drew on pale flesh coloured hold-up stockings. She liked stockings – her thighs could breathe and she did not need to wear a garter belt. She thrust her feet into navy blue suede brogues and chose a matching navy blue shoulder bag.

Walking along the avenue, Sapphire was oblivious to everything – passing limousines and taxis, even shops she would normally have dawdled at. She was floating through a world of her own. Sapphire was on automatic pilot. However, nobody was oblivious to her, she was impossible to ignore. Flushed with love, Sapphire was radiant. Passers-by smiled, cars stopped for her to cross, public transport drivers waved.

Her mind was thinking, concentrating on Everett. And the same thing happened to her as had happened in the restaurant the night before. A shiver of excitement enveloped her. Her heart fluttered and her womb tightened. Her nipples hardened and a tingling rushed through the softness of her hidden self, leaving a moistness between her legs.

She sauntered into the first boutique she came to and, in a daze, purchased an outfit that she would not normally have bought, a wool and silk suit. White-ecru with a hint of pink, it had a short flared skirt and a single breasted fitted jacket. To wear it properly, to its greatest advantage, she had to dispense with her bra. It was a far cry from her normal prim clothing. To complete her ensemble, she bought a large floppy black hat, black-framed sun-glasses, an ecru-coloured leather handbag with a fabulous large-chain strap, and sling-back, black, very high heels with straps that crossed over her instep.

She was ready to meet Everett at his office. When she got there, his secretary opened the door. Happily, Sapphire walked in, to find a woman clothed from head to toe in erotic black leather, her hand on Everett's crotch and kissing him full on the lips.

Sapphire gasped in horror and amazement. The woman turned to see who had entered.

'Carola!' exclaimed Sapphire.

'Sapphire Western, you prissy little goddam cow, what are you doing here?' drawled the Texan. 'Don't tell me it's 'cos you want a fuck, 'cos I won't believe that. But I do, honey.' She raised one of her leather clad legs along Everett's thighs.

'Sapphire – ' Everett began.

Carola held him in her a vicelike grip.

Sapphire crumpled inside. Tears welled up in her eyes. Betrayed again, she turned sharply on her heel and stalked out of the room, with Carola's rasping Texan voice hitting in her ears.

'Jeanine's missing you, hon; she wants you real bad and has some interesting information – '

The rest of her words were lost to Sapphire. Her only thought was to get away from Geneva as fast as possible.

Then she remembered she had to telephone her father's lawyers to find out when and where they were reading his will. Was it going to be in London or some place else? She found a public telephone box and called them. Meriboa, they said.

She didn't bother to return to Everett's house. He could keep her clothes, do what he liked with them. She never wanted to see him or them again. She took a cab back to the boutique she'd been in earlier, bought some new outfits, and left the ecru one behind, telling the assistant it was hers if she wanted it. Sapphire had decided it was unlucky and, though sensible, she had superstitions, or – as she preferred to call them – instincts. She took another cab, made him stop and wait while she bought some new luggage and then got him to take her to the airport.

Sapphire had some sense of satisfaction. Whatever her father had done, whether he left her money or not, she was more than capable of supporting herself.

She was angry. She felt duped, but at least for once she had risked. She had made love, been made love to. She was liberated from the shackles of virginity.

Sapphire took the next plane out of Switzerland, bound, with stop-overs, for a country she'd never heard of before. At least, she thought, there she wouldn't meet anyone of her acquaintance. Getting some of her old fighting spirit back, she decided that maybe she would risk again and have some real fun.

Chapter Seven

'Sorry, Mr de Bouys, but madame's rushed off to see her mother,' said Terry, the receptionist, putting down the newspaper he was reading when Gerry came eagerly up to the desk. 'She left early, very early. They're having breakfast together, I think. Lady Penelope called in yesterday but – um – madame wasn't able to see her.'

'She will be back, though, won't she?' asked Gerry.

Gerry noticed the newspaper was open at the gossip page and that Lady Rosamund Ware de Bouys was in town. Perhaps Jeanine would be having breakfast with her, too. Madam Jeanine would have to be on her best behaviour with his Australian aunt. Lady Rosamund de Bouys had a reputation for being fearsome and very proper – very proper indeed. It was only to be expected from the widow of a major general. There was no scandal there: no scandal associated with that side of the family.

'She's expected, sir,' said Terry. 'If you'd care to wait?'

'Very well,' said Gerry, crestfallen, acutely disappointed and slightly agitated.

'Hello darling,' said a husky female voice. A beautiful, stunning-looking, superbly-dressed woman was sitting on the long settee facing the main door. Gerry looked nonplussed. He didn't know her.

'I'm Countess Helitzer, Jacqueline Helitzer,' she said,

languidly holding out a hand to be kissed. 'And you're Gerry de Bouys. We've never met but I know your wife – your ex-wife, little Auralie.'

'Oh!' he said, looking around the room, vaguely expecting to see her. Deep inside, he was still angry with Auralie.

A part of him had not recovered from the shock he'd had when he found out that, instead of being the sweet young virgin he thought she was when he'd married her, she was a member of Petrov's sex-sect. Petrov's High Priestess, enjoying orgies at his mansion in Lower Wycombe.

Gerry had employed a private detective to follow her, to discover exactly what she was up to. And he had had a full report. Screwing men and women, spanking men and women. Hotsie Totsie, the unctuous Mr Norris had called her. Gerry had been profoundly embarrassed. His wife. His precious wife had behaved like a slut, just when he'd been chosen to represent a safe Home Counties seat in Parliament. Gerry had had to give that up. The party would never have allowed him to become an MP. There had been enough scandals; no more were needed.

He had had to divorce her – a nasty, messy divorce. He would have preferred to have kept it hushed up but Jeanine had insisted. 'If you love me, you will get rid of her,' she'd demanded. So he had. Not that he'd regretted it. Auralie had betrayed him. She had completely buggered up his life. Because of her he was not now sitting in the House of Commons.

His father had not been pleased. Sir Henry had hoped that Gerry would have achieved that status. Gerry had the vague feeling that occasionally he was a disappointment to his father. Sir Henry had told his son that he was too busy making money to become an MP – in any case, he was hoping for a peerage – but Gerry should get close to the power-base; the law makers. Be a law maker himself.

Gerry remembered bitterly when he had first discovered that something was wrong with his marriage.

Auralie had been denying him her body. On various pretexts she had stopped him making love to her. Her main excuse had been pressure of work, organising her collection. She had said that it left her exhausted and with no desire for sex. But she had been lying. She had lied to him.

One day, Gerry had returned home unexpectedly, to find his dear little wife screwing a nun. Auralie had had the woman tied to the bed post in their bedroom and was kneeling between her legs, slurping at her sex. Then she had spanked the nun. Even now he was conscious of the vicarious thrill it had given him as he'd watch the cane sear across plump Sister Margaret's naked buttocks.

At the time, he had stood silently in the doorway, the unobserved watcher, and had played with himself. His cock was rising even as he thought about it. He wondered how long it would be before Jeanine put in an appearance. Some time, he had to get back to his office and make his report. With his father in town, he had to be prompt.

'Auralie's not here,' said the beautiful blonde Jacqueline, interrupting his thoughts. 'She's gone shopping for me. I just adore shopping, darling but couldn't, today. I'm waiting for friends to arrive. So – ' Jacqueline patted the seat beside her, ' – come and sit by me.'

Jacqueline put an elegant, red nailed and bejewelled hand on his knee. 'How good are you at sucking pussy,' she asked, quite suddenly, stroking his inner thigh through his fine cashmere suit.

Gerry's cock shot up.

'Oh, that excites you, does it?' said Jacqueline, as her hand touched his crotch. 'I'd like to feel your cock. I'd like to unzip your pants and take it out and suck it.'

Jacqueline let her hands trail over his zip. Gerry held his breath. Not here, dear God, not here, he was praying. He glanced up to see where Terry was. The reception desk was empty.

'What about playing with pussy?' Jacqueline asked lasciviously.

137

She stood up. She was wearing a soft grey silk suit. The jacket fastened to her neck with large gold buttons, the skirt was straight and fell to her ankles.

'Now, darling, as I said, I am waiting for friends to arrive and you are waiting for Jeanine. And I hope she arrives in a better temper than when she left. Oh dear, what a fuss. Pulling moodies, she was.'

'Why?' asked Gerry, curious.

'What I propose – ' the countess ignored Gerry's question completely, ' – is that we have a little enjoyment. Put your hand on the settee.'

Jacqueline turned her back to him. The skirt was cut with a slit at the back from hem almost to waist. Gerry had sight of Jacqueline's stocking tops, a glimpse of thigh and the curve of her bare bottom. His cock strained along his trousers.

'I need a little attention,' said Jacqueline. 'So when I sit down, I want to feel your fingers.'

'Where?'

'In my pussy, darling,' she said.

'Here?' exclaimed Gerry, agitated. 'Oh no, we can't – you can't – I can't.'

'Why not?' she asked, perplexed.

'Jeanine does not allow it. It is absolutely forbidden. What happens anywhere else in the house is okay but never ... She never allows anything sexy to take place in the foyer.'

'Oh? What's her hang-up?' asked Jacqueline.

'Well, once someone put up some very naughty photographs of her performing.'

'Performing?'

'Um, yes, having sex, sucking someone off.'

'Really? Who was she having sex with?'

Gerry looked sheepish.

'You?' said Jacqueline. 'Was it? Was she having sex with you?'

'Yes; it's a long time ago but it freaked her at the time and, ever since, she says – '

'Well darling, rules are made to be broken.'

'Look, sorry, but she'll be angry.'

'So?' exclaimed Jacqueline. 'Won't she punish you if she's angry?'

'Yes.'

'Gerry, Gerry, I thought you'd have liked that.'

'Um – '

'Come on, tell me,' said Jacqueline, using her best wheedling voice. 'Don't you get a thrill if she spanks you?'

'Yes.'

'So what are you worried about?' asked Jacqueline.

'She won't let me fuck her.'

'Is that so terrible?'

'Yes,' he said. 'I don't want to do anything to upset her. And if I . . . If I touched you, played with you and she caught me doing it here – well – '

'There's one answer to that,' said Jacqueline.

'What's that?' he asked.

'Don't let's get caught, darling,' she drawled.

Jacqueline walked over to the desk and banged on the bell. 'Terry,' she called, leaning over, giving Gerry a fuller view of her naked bottom. Terry came out from the office. 'Terry, is Jeanine really with her mother?'

'That's what she told me, madam,' Terry replied.

'And when exactly are you expecting her back?'

'She said about now, but if she's with her mother and they're talking business, it could be hours.'

Terry went back inside the office and Jacqueline returned to Gerry. 'Terry doesn't think she'll be back for hours,' she said. 'Now I think you're very sexy, and very handsome and I fancy you, but I can't leave here because I'm waiting for people. So darling don't be boring and put your hand down – ' Jacqueline flicked the separate parts of her skirt to the front. She pushed her buttocks close to his face. 'Put your hand on the seat, darling,' she said, 'I want you to feel me.'

Gerry, his prick stiff and erect at the sight of Jacqueline's naked arse, and with all resistance gone, did as he was told. Jacqueline lowered herself on to his upright fingers and her sex opened willingly to his touch.

'There,' she said, 'isn't that quite delightful?'

'Yes,' he said.

'Now, darling, we shall have a little talk. We shall sit here, quietly discussing our stocks and shares, while you play pussy; and if you do it properly, no one will know. So tell me, what have you heard on the street? Is it a bull or a bear market?'

Gerry couldn't think. He didn't want to think. Stocks and shares: that was business. Business was for another time. Now was play. In any case, Gerry didn't have to worry much about work and business. He worked for his father, Sir Henry de Bouys. As long as he put his time in, enough for people to know he was there, he could coast. His father would never sack him. And Sir Henry's business was doing just fine.

Gerry had no intention of thinking or talking business; but he was worried about Jeanine's imminent arrival. The thought of being caught fingering Jacqueline's squashy, warm, moist and inviting sex moving and squirming on his fingers in the foyer both excited Gerry and caused him some consternation.

What would Jeanine do to him if she found out? She would spank him, for sure. Would she whip him? Would she tie him up in the dungeon and mask his face and suck his cock? Would she put her legs around his waist and let his cock glide up inside her? Would she deny him access to her body?

Gerry wanted Jeanine's body. Would she ban him from her presence? He shuddered as that thought crossed his mind. Or would she spank him harder? Would she let him fuck that gorgeous redhead again? Gerry didn't know who she was, but that woman had fired him. He had adored seeing her in that dancing girl costume. He remembered how jealous he had felt when Jeanine ordered him away and he had to watch Kensit's cock thrusting . . .

'Gerry? Gerry.'

Jacqueline had noticed a far-away expression on his face.

'Um, yes?'

'Stocks and shares not your forte?' she asked, opening and closing her inner muscles around his exploring fingers.

Gerry shook his head.

Jacqueline looked down at his crotch. His large bulge was giving him away, showing her how excited he was. She wiggled. Maybe she'd unzip him and suck him off. Gerry eased his fingers further into Jacqueline's moist vulva.

'Or shall we talk about this?' asked Jacqueline. 'What do you like most? Is it the women who spread their legs for you? Or do you like it when one of Jeanine's slaves sucks your cock, or thrusts their fingers and their tongue into your arse? Does that excite you? Keep playing with me, darling, keep playing. I love your touch; you've got good fingers. Tell me what it is you like. Maybe I can do it to you. Maybe Jeanine won't come back and we can play some games together.'

Gerry felt a raging hunger storming through his body. He wanted her to stand up and lift her skirt above her waist so that he could stroke her thighs and bury his head in her sex. 'I like everything possible,' he whispered hoarsely.

Gerry had thrown caution to the wind. Now he wanted this beautiful blonde. He wanted her between his legs. He wanted her with her thighs spread apart and him coming up and feeling his cock at her entrance. He wanted to feel her luscious breasts, caress them and suck them. His hips started to move in anticipation with little jerking movements. And his tongue was flicking in and out of his mouth. Oh yes, he wanted to fuck the beautiful countess.

It was then that Henrietta walked in with Ana Tai. She had her usual lip and eyebrow rings adorning her face. Her slim boyish figure was emphasised by the short, white surgical coat, nipped in at the waist by a wide

141

rubber belt. She was not wearing her usual rubber outfit and Gerry could see her slim legs and part of her pert rose-bud breasts. The top buttons of the coat were undone and Gerry caught a glimpse of her nipple rings.

'Keep playing with me, darling,' said Jacqueline, sitting harder on his hands so that he could not escape. 'Oh, Henrietta,' called Jacqueline, drawing attention to them both.

Gerry wanted to die. He wanted the floor to open up and swallow him. If Henrietta realised what he was doing he would be most severely punished.

'Henrietta,' said Jacqueline again.

Then to Gerry's complete astonishment Jacqueline stood up and walked away from him, leaving him frustrated and abandoned. Leaving his hand with nothing to do, his prick upright with desire and his body trembling.

Henrietta turned queryingly. Jacqueline's skirt fell back and she looked her usual svelte self.

'Hello, Mr de Bouys,' said Henrietta, glancing at Gerry's crotch.

Gerry tried hard to hide his bulge and Henrietta turned her back on him.

'Henrietta, darling, please introduce me,' Jacqueline said, smiling at Ana Tai.

'Countess Helitzer, meet Ana Tai, she's from Meriboa and she's our masseuse in the other house.'

'Oh, darling, how exciting,' said Jacqueline, and Gerry watched the two women lock eyes.

'Madam,' said Ana Tai, acknowledging the countess haughtily.

Gerry wanted satisfaction. He was in agony. He wanted the licentious countess back sitting on his hand.

Jeanine's office door opened and Terry came out with a fax in his hand.

'Countess,' he said. 'This is for you.'

Jacqueline took it and read aloud; that, due to something or other, the rest of her entourage were delayed in Calais.

'Well,' she said. 'It looks like I'll have to change some of my plans. Have you heard from Jeanine? Has she rung in?'

'No, madam,' said Terry.

'Then I want a massage now, with Ana Tai,' said Jacqueline.

'Ana Tai is booked,' said Henrietta.

'Darling, you must unbook her,' the countess replied.

'I can't do that,' said Henrietta.

'Why not? Who's so important?' she asked.

'Zinnia's husband,' said Henrietta. 'But you can have the appointment afterwards.'

'What!' exclaimed Jacqueline. 'Do you mean Jethro Clarke?'

'The same,' said Henrietta. 'Madam wants him kept happy. He said he wanted a massage and, like you, he insisted on having Ana Tai. Of course it was explained to him – Excuse us, one moment.'

Henrietta disappeared into Jeanine's office with Terry.

'What was? What was explained to him?' asked Jacqueline.

'That I only give massage. No extras. That's the deal,' said Ana Tai.

'Really? How interesting. Why's that?'

'I don't like men,' said Ana Tai, giving Jacqueline a slight come-hither smile.

'And what else do you do here?' asked Jacqueline.

'Why do you think there's anything else?' Ana Tai replied with a question.

'I know Jeanine,' said Jacqueline. 'There's got to be an 'and'.'

'Sometimes we play flatmates,' said Ana Tai.

'Oh? What does that mean?'

'If Jeanine fancies a guy who's never been here, she brings them to the flat next door and I play with her in front of him.'

'Oh, so you work in pairs, eh?'

'Sometimes.'

Henrietta Maclean came bustling out of the office.

'Mr de Bouys,' she said, 'Mr de Bouys, there's been a message. Can you come?'

Gerry, who had been listening and enjoying the two women's conversation, was disappointed to be drawn away, but he obeyed Mrs Maclean.

The moment he walked through the office door his arms were pinioned behind his back. A leather hood was slipped over his head. His clothes were removed. He was left naked and made to sit on hard, plush velvet, a commode on wheels which scraped and itched his bare bottom. Terry instantly strapped his arms behind him, and his legs to either side. As the brake was on, Gerry had no idea what he was sitting on.

'You disobeyed madam,' hissed Mrs Maclean, close to his ear. All sounds were muffled by the enveloping hood.

'No,' said Gerry, with difficulty. His lips were constrained, tight, pushed through a narrow slit.

'Don't lie,' said Henrietta. 'Terry was watching you. He saw the countess lift her skirts and sit on your hand. You know that is forbidden. There are not many rules in this house but that is one of them. No sexual activity in the main foyer. Terry – '

There was something threatening in Mrs Maclean's voice. Gerry, in complete darkness, trembled with anxiety and his penis shrivelled.

The next moment, Gerry felt hands on his thighs. Someone was kneeling in front of him. Lips suddenly encompassed his penis, licking him slightly. His cock jerked. Delicious.

He was lulled into a false sense of security. Gerry opened his legs wider and tipped his hips forward so that the mouth could take him deeper. Cold hands were on his balls. Desire and erotic thoughts flooded through him. Gerry moved his shoulders, his hips. Sweetness. Gerry began to gasp. His cock was swelling.

Then something cold was put around the base of his prick. Cold and metallic. A cold metallic cock ring was being squeezed tight close to his balls. Tight and tighter.

Cold hands also began playing with his penis, stroking it. Warm lips were licking it, sucking it. It swelled up under the gentle onslaught of hands and lips.

There was a pain inside him, an aching. The more the lips sucked on his member, the greater the pain was from the cock ring. But he could not stop his desire or his tumescence. The mouth was expert.

Hands came over his shoulders and touched his nipples. Flicked them, squeezed them. Other hands played with his balls and the lips kept sucking, pulling on his cock, making certain that it grew, enlarging and lengthening. Gerry's penis, which had shrunk under the attack, was being brought back to full size. Gerry was at full stretch, and his mind was working overtime. Would they take him down to the dungeon, where Jeanine would be waiting? Would he be spanked? Would Jeanine sit on his face? Would he be able to fuck her? Gerry knew something would happen.

'You did enjoy yourself, didn't you, Mr de Bouys?' said Henrietta menacingly.

'When?' he asked.

'In the foyer, playing with the countess's pussy.'

'Yes.'

'Good,' she said, releasing the brake on the commode.

'What . . .?' he exclaimed, as he felt the chair moving.

'You're going back outside.'

'No,' he squealed through his tight constricted lips. 'No.'

'You wanted to play sex games out there,' hissed Mrs Maclean. 'We are obliging you. We are going to leave you like this in the foyer, facing the front door.'

Gerry, totally humiliated, bound, gagged and blindfolded, had no way of knowing whether the place was full of people or if it was empty.

In the foyer, Ana Tai was sitting on her own. Jacqueline had gone upstairs to her room with the one member of her entourage who had arrived, an exceedingly ugly dwarf. Ana Tai turned to stare as Gerry, sitting in the commode, hooded, naked, his penis erect and swollen and held tight by the cock ring, was wheeled into the reception area by Mrs Maclean and Terry.

'Mr de Bouys is being punished for disobedience,' said Henrietta in a loud, clear and carrying voice. 'He will sit here like this until Madam Vladelsky returns and decides what to do with him. Normally, we do not allow sex out here, but on this occasion should anyone notice that Mr de Bouys penis is losing its erection they have permission – in fact they are encouraged – to arouse it. Suck it, play with it. The choice is anybody's.'

Henrietta positioned the commode slightly to one side but in full view of the main door. She put the brake on and was about to walk back into the office when a tall busty blonde, dressed in tight leathers, strode into the hotel. She marched straight up to the reception desk without noticing Gerry.

'Hi,' she said, 'I sent a fax. I'm Carola Finestein.'

'Ah yes, Miss Finestein,' said Terry, noticing how her jacket barely contained her full, high, jacked-up tits. 'We are expecting you.'

'Is Jeanine in? Has Jethro Clarke arrived?' she asked.

'No Miss, but Mr Clarke's due any minute. That young lady over there is waiting for him.'

Carola turned to see who Terry was pointing at and struck a provocative pose. She thrust her tits out and pouted, stood with her legs slightly apart, the tightness of her trousers outlining her vulva, and eyed Ana Tai up and down. 'Why?' she asked petulantly. 'Why's she waiting for him.'

'He's asked for a massage,' said Ana Tai.

'Oh, you have a gym and things here? Good. I'll book myself in. You have reflexology, too?'

'No,' said Henrietta.

'Pity. Well, I'm here now, and you can cancel that massage. Jethro says I give him the best,' said Carola.

'We couldn't do that,' said Mrs Maclean, firmly.

'Who are you?' asked Carola.

'Mrs Maclean. The manager.'

'Oh! Jeez!' exclaimed Carola, noticing the naked hooded Gerry. 'Jeanine like kinky statues or something?'

'Statue?' asked Henrietta.

'Okay, waxwork, call it what you will. But that, that is weird. To have that in reception!'

'It's a man,' said Henrietta.

'No kidding! Jethro told me this was an hotel, not a goddam brothel, and I've given my parents this number. What's he doing there like that?'

'He's been a naughty boy,' said Henrietta Maclean, standing beside him so he could hear. 'He's been a very naughty boy. Haven't you?'

'Yes.'

'Yes, what?'

'Yes, madam,' he squealed.

'It's his punishment.'

'Wow!'

'He broke a house rule.'

'For real?'

'Yes.'

'So what happens? He just stays there?'

'Sort of.'

'What does that mean – sort of?' asked Carola.

'His cock has to stay erect.'

'It does? How does he keep it up?'

'He doesn't. We do,' said Henrietta.

'You mean he gets his cock sucked every time it goes down? Like he's due for it right now?'

'Exactly.'

'Some goddam punishment!' said Carola. 'You do it?'

'Anybody who's here who wants to can do it,' said Henrietta.

'I can do it?' asked Carola.

'If you feel so inclined,' said Henrietta.

'I think I do,' said Carola, smirking. She was going to show off her talent. 'Jethro says I give the best blow job ever, and he's not here, so I'd better do some practice.'

Ana Tai and Henrietta exchanged glances as they watched Carola move in between Gerry's spread legs

147

and her gloved hands encompass his semi-withdrawn penis. Softly, using small movements, taking it a little at a time, Carola enticed his cockhead into the open. When his cock was very stiff and throbbing she took it into her mouth and licked and sucked.

'Hell! What d'ya know!' exclaimed a voice. 'Carola up to her favourite pastime.'

Carola jumped up. She had recognised Jethro's Southern drawl. Once again Gerry was left abandoned.

'Jethro!' said Carola, running over to him. 'Your goddam wife has gotten me thrown out of my home.'

'What d'ya mean, honey?' said Jethro, staring at the naked hooded man.

'I mean she telephoned my parents and told them she was gonna cite me in her divorce petition, and they said that I was godless and no child of theirs. They're gonna cut me outta their will, stop my allowance, and – '

'Jeez, who's that?' asked Jethro.

'Mr Clarke,' said Henrietta, ignoring Jethro's question. 'Ana Tai is waiting for you.'

Jethro's eyes skimmed the room, alighting on Ana Tai. Although he had seen her before, it was the first time she had seen him. She inclined her head very slightly and blinked her lovely almond-shaped eyes in silent acknowledgement.

Jethro had no way of knowing that Ana Tai had been taken by surprise. For once in her life she liked what she saw: a tall, craggy looking, fit and athletic man with iron-grey hair. He was stylishly and very expensively dressed and arrogant.

Without speaking to him, she could tell that. His stance was arrogant. Late forties, early fifties – whatever, there was something about him that appealed to her. It was, Ana Tai thought, a pity Jeanine hadn't taken a fancy to him. They could have played their games with him. Or in another time, in another place, she and Auralie could have him.

Ana Tai was missing Auralie. They had not managed to snatch any secret time together for the past few days.

And now, when Jeanine was out, when it would have been possible, Jacqueline had sent her shopping. The countess took too much for granted. She thought she could do what she liked, have anybody she wanted. Well, not Ana Tai. She had taken against her, and that had squashed any lustful feelings she might have had for Jacqueline Helitzer.

'Mr Clarke,' said Henrietta, 'I told you, Ana Tai is waiting.'

'Yeah, okay, but who's that? Why's he there? It's goddam out of order. Tied up – a hood over his head' Jethro was genuinely disgusted. 'And what's he got on his cock?'

'A cock ring. He's being punished. If you break the house rules, you are punished. Terry, you see to him. He needs a little uplift. Give him a suck,' ordered Henrietta Maclean, pointing to Gerry's member, which was slowly withdrawing into itself.

'Yes, Ma'am,' said Terry.

Ana Tai saw the look of silent astonishment creep over Jethro's face as Terry began to play with Gerry's penis.

'Jeez!' said Jethro, bewildered.

Jethro had an innocence that Ana Tai liked.

'Would you like to do it, Mr Clarke?' asked Henrietta Maclean.

'No, I fucking would not. I'm not a goddam faggot,' said Jethro, utterly horrified.

'Jethro, Jethro, did you hear what I was telling you?' said Carola, tapping him on his chest.

'I sure did, honey,' said Jethro,

'You've gotta stop it,' continued Carola.

'Yeah, sure,' he said.

'Well, where is she?'

'Who?' said Jethro, staring at Terry attending to Gerry's penis.

'Your fucking goddam big titted, red headed whore of a wife,' shouted Carola. 'Where is she?'

'I don't know,' he replied. 'But I'm finding out.'

'Oh, er, Mr Clarke,' said Henrietta, 'Ana Tai does have

another appointment. And you will remember. No extras. If you want anything else you come and see me. But Ana Tai is out of bounds. That's one of the rules here.'

'Did he break that rule?' asked Jethro.

'No, sir.'

'You mean you don't get to fuck that skinny Asian?' said Carola. 'Aw shucks, hon, you can have a goddam massage later. I've booked a room here and I'm horny as hell.'

'Sorry, Miss Finestein,' said Henrietta. 'Mr Clarke must take his appointment now or he'll lose it.'

Ana Tai cast a haughty look in Jethro's direction. Jethro caught her glance and held it.

'Hell! I've got another idea, why doesn't she give him a massage while he's screwing me?' said Carola.

'No,' said Ana Tai, very firmly; she walked behind the reception desk to collect her various lotions. Her instant dislike of the brash American woman was in direct ratio to her unaccountable liking for the American man.

'I made her a most interesting proposition. And I'll pay,' said Carola to Mrs Maclean.

'Ana Tai does what she wants,' Henrietta replied.

'But I'm horny,' whined Carola. 'Jethro, I wanna fuck. Jethro – Jethro, don't you wanna screw me?'

'Course I do, hon, but I got a lot on my mind. I need a massage. I need relaxing.'

'But Jethro, you always say I give the best – '

'You do, hon, you do. The best amateur. Right now, I need a professional.'

'You goddam jerk!' said Carola angrily. 'You ain't such a great fuck to be putting me down like that! I'll go screw someone else. There's gotta be someone in this lousy town.'

Furious, Carola surveyed the people in the lobby. She plonked herself down on the settee. 'I'll wait here for Jeanine. I'm sure she's got some acquaintances who'd help a girl out of her predicament.' Carola looked up at Henrietta Maclean. 'Or maybe you know someone?'

'Wait one moment,' said Henrietta, going behind the reception desk, grabbing Ana Tai's arm and propelling her into Jeanine's office.

'Ana Tai,' said Henrietta, as the Meriboan loaded her tray with various artefacts. 'Ana Tai, where's the countess?'

'Upstairs,' she replied.

'Good, maybe I can get her to – '

'She went up when one of her men from Paris arrived. He missed the train and came by 'plane,' said Ana Tai.

'One of her men?' said Henrietta. 'What's he like?'

'Why?'

'That bitch on heat out there wants a fuck, we'll get her one.'

'He'd be perfect,' said Ana Tai, smiling wickedly. 'Shall I ring the countess and ask her if her man could help our dear friend? I'm sure he would. But, Henrietta, tell Miss Finestein she's got to be blindfolded.'

'Ana Tai!' said Henrietta, intrigued. 'Why? Why should she be blindfolded?'

'Because the countess's friend is short, fat and ugly. An ugly dwarf. I'll qualify that. He's very short, not too fat, but incredibly ugly; and, if what I thought I saw was real and not padding, he's hung like a donkey.'

'Truly?'

'Yes.'

'A blindfold it is. If she wants a fuck, she'll get it,' said Henrietta, smiling at Ana Tai conspiratorially. 'I'll ring the countess and tell her.'

Ana Tai took a thick strip of black wool, covered on one side with black rubber, down from a peg on the wall. She put it in her pocket, then walked back out into reception where Carola was still pleading with Jethro to change his mind and Terry was still sucking Gerry's swollen, aching cock.

'Terry,' she said, sternly, 'stay on the desk and wait for madam. Miss Finestein, I think I may have solved your problem. We have a countess staying here, a – '

'A countess!' exclaimed Jethro.

'Yes, a French countess,' said Ana Tai.

'Is that the woman Zinnia came to see – the old lady?' asked Jethro.

'Old lady!' exclaimed Ana Tai. Then she laughed. 'Zinnia told you that, did she?'

'Yes.'

'Your wife has a sense of humour,' said Ana Tai.

'A French countess! I ain't into women . . .' wailed Carola.

'She has a friend with her. Apparently he's shy. Has his own little foibles,' said Ana Tai, coming closer to Carola. 'He can't get it up unless the woman is blind-folded. We each have our turn-ons, and that's his. He doesn't like to know who he's screwing. And he doesn't want anybody to know him.'

'Oh. Is he famous or something?'

'Could be, I'm not at liberty to say,' said Ana Tai.

'I've met a lot of famous people who do that. I've not done it myself, so this could be a whole new experience.'

'It sure could,' said Ana Tai.

'Well, Jethro, you have your goddam massage and I'll go fuck this guy. I'll tell you about him later.'

'Sure, hon,' said Jethro.

'One thing's for fucking sure, he'll be better than you.'

'Yeah, yeah,' said Jethro.

'Miss Finestein, if you'll put this on, I'll take you to his room,' said Henrietta coming out of the office and taking the blindfold from Ana Tai's pocket.

'Um, nice smell, what's it made from?' asked Carola as Henrietta wrapped it around her eyes.

'Wool and rubber,' said Henrietta, tying it in place. 'You look wonderful. Leather and rubber: it's gonna drive him wild.'

Carola smiled like the cat that got the cream. 'See you later, Jethro,' she said, in her best imitation Marilyn Monroe voice.

'Sure hon,' said Jethro. 'Have a good time.'

'We'll talk about your motherfucking wife later, okay?' said Carola.

'Okay,' said Jethro, with a sigh of relief as Mrs Maclean guided Carola up the beautiful staircase.

Ana Tai buttoned up her surgical coat and Terry, now back where he should be behind the reception desk, handed her her tray of oils and lotions.

Ana Tai had an odd combination of feelings. She was worried about Auralie. She should have been back by now. Shopping for the few things Countess Helitzer wanted did not take as long as she'd been gone. Also, she was puzzled by her unlikely attraction to a middle-aged man. A man of any sort was strange, but a middle-aged one was even stranger. She stood close to him. Ana Tai admired the trim shape of his body. She smelled his personal odour. It was sweet, without manufactured chemicals from various bought products. It was his smell that she found so attractive.

'Mr Clarke,' said Ana Tai, 'please follow me.' She led the way out of the hotel and into the house next door.

In the massage room, while Jethro undressed down to his jockey shorts, Ana Tai lowered the waist high table.

'How long have you worked here?' asked Jethro, excited at the prospect of her long brown hands roaming over his body.

'Long enough,' Ana Tai replied, as she busied herself with the various preparations.

Jethro noticed her white surgical coat was gaping between the buttons. He caught a glimpse of her tawny breasts and desperately wanted to touch them. Asian she might be, but Jethro's prejudices were crumbling. He had a flash of belly and thigh. He had the strongest desire to stroke her legs and search for her secret place. But visions of the man in the hood, bound and secured and displayed in the foyer, stopped him from violating the rules.

'Where do you come from?' he asked, staring. He had suddenly seen the rings hanging from her prominent nipples.

'You ask too many questions,' said Ana Tai witheringly,

putting a fresh towel on the bed and adding, 'lie face down.'

She left his hairless back bare, put a towel over his lower parts, then sat astride him and began to work on his shoulders. As she bent over him, Jethro was bemused by Ana Tai's tone. She had seemed friendly, almost attracted by him. Had he misread her signals?

Jethro felt the hardness of her starched surgical coat, then the soft yieldingness of her rose-bud breasts and her firm thighs gripping his hips. And her sex. In the small of his back, he could swear he felt her naked sex. And rings. He wanted to look. She had rings in her lips and eyebrows; he realised she must also have them in her labia. As her hands continued to flow over his body, this thought kept him spellbound.

He, who took women quickly, how and when they came, was fascinated by the brown skinned, exotic Meriboan. Women for him were depositories for his desire and release. He had no thought for their needs. He had never stopped to consider that he might enjoy sex more if he gave more. He had never put his head down between a woman's legs. Their musky sex smell was not something he found alluring.

He suddenly had a yen to bury his head between Ana Tai's thighs. His cock was hidden inside his shorts but it was rising as he felt her gliding on top of him. He could do with her hands around his prick, rubbing it. He wondered why the restriction, why no extras. Why couldn't he ask for it? Was she a dyke?

Jethro found that thought very exciting. If she was a dyke, he'd show her. He'd show her what a man could do. He'd show her his stiff prick. He'd shove it up inside her, give her a good time. Jethro was immensely proud of his penis. Maybe he could get her to talk dirty.

'So you like women, eh?' he asked, as she pummelled his shoulders.

'Yes,' she said softly. 'Don't you?'

'Sure I do,' he said. 'But you don't like men, right?'

'What makes you think that?' she answered.

'You not giving extras. A lot of women like doing that.'

'Do they?'

'Sure they do.'

'You're certain of that, are you?'

'Yes.'

Ana Tai laughed. 'I'm not,' she said. 'Anyhow, I don't have to do anything I don't want. And I don't want.'

'Don't you like a man's cock? Don't you like it hard? Hard and up inside you?'

'No,' she said, simply. Her oily hands were easing the way around his spine and hips.

'So you're a goddam lesbian! Jeez! I could show you a thing or two,' he said.

'You could! What?' she asked.

'How to have a real good time.'

'Oh, but Mr Clarke, I do,' she said sweetly. 'Whatever makes you think I don't – we don't?'

'Well, what d'ya do? Strap on a fucking dildo, when you could have the real thing?'

'No,' she said, her hands going up to his neck. She poured some more oil over his skin.

'So what, then? Tell me,' he barked, trying to control his pent up frustration, his spoilt child's rage. He wanted this woman and he wasn't going to get her.

'Women stroke,' she said. 'Women stroke lovingly. Gently. Women arouse. Turn over, Mr Clarke, please.'

He did as he was told and Ana Tai spread herself across his belly, her knees taking her weight, imprisoning his arms between his hips and her legs. She leant forward and oiled his pectorals. She completely ignored his massive bulge, his prick stiff, the tip of it peeking out over the top of his shorts.

Jethro lay back, staring at the gaps in her coat. He could see her breasts, her nipple rings, he let his eyes slide down her body, searching for the other gaps between her buttons. Yes, she was naked, naked under the starched white coat. He could see her navel, and her navel ring. And, as she rose up taking her hands up to his neck he could see her shaven sex.

Jethro started to tremble. She was so near and yet so far.

'You were telling me,' he said.

'About what, Mr Clarke?' she asked, standing up.

Jethro thought for a brief moment that his session with her was at an end, but she was only changing her position, kneeling with her back to him. Her sex hovered over his balls.

'Women,' he said, endeavouring to catch sight of her buttocks as she raised her body before slithering down along his legs to massage his feet. 'Women stroke lovingly.'

'Don't you know this?' she asked, trying to keep the sarcasm out of her voice. 'Don't you know that women like to be treated gently, loved?'

'Yeah, sure,' said flippantly.

'Then there is nothing more to say,' she replied.

'I like it when you tell me. It relaxes me,' he said. 'I've got a heavy day ahead. Your voice, it's soothing. Please, tell me more.' It was the closest Jethro had ever got to begging in his life. He waited with bated breath to see what she would do and say.

'Well,' she said, turning her head to look at him and bringing her body almost upright as her hands roamed from his thighs up to his scrotum. 'Well,' she said, easing herself back, her bare sex softly touching – almost not touching – hinting at touching the tip of his cock.

Jethro closed his eyes. The slightness of it gave him the deepest sensation. Blood suffused his body. Desire overwhelmed him. He wanted to move his hands but she had her knees firmly in place. It would have meant a struggle. He didn't try it. He opened his eyes. Her coat seemed to have risen up. He could see the curve of her milky coffee-coloured buttocks.

'Well,' said Ana Tai, leaning forward towards his knees and massaging his inner thighs. 'I will take a woman's hand in mine and put it over my breast. "Touch my nipples," I will say.'

Jethro swallowed hard.

Ana Tai tilted forward. She seemed to have gathered up her coat and he saw her sex: open, swollen and ringed. She was excited. This thrilled him. She stroked his knees, his thighs. Up. Closer. Closer to his prick.

Jethro tensed his buttocks as she made short circular motions inwards towards his aching balls. Oh please. Please, touch me. But she didn't. She brought her body up again, almost on his phallus. His stiff prick was held by his jockey shorts tight to his belly. Then she moved her buttocks and sat on it. He felt her muscles, the muscles in her buttocks, in her sex, tense and loosen. Tense and loosen. His hands, unable to get at her, opened and closed on the air. He closed his eyes again, imagining. Imagining. Then, languidly, she rolled away from him and off the bed.

'What?' he asked, bewildered.

But she was only changing back again to her initial position. Jethro wanted to fondle her breasts. He noticed that a button had come undone on her coat. Her beautiful rose-bud breasts were displayed in front of him. His hands ached to feel them.

'What do you say, then?'

'To my woman?' she asked.

'Yes.'

'Touch my nipples. Embrace them.' Ana Tai lingered on the word. The word itself was an embrace.

He closed his eyes once more.

Kneeling beside his hips, Ana Tai was making circular movements over his belly and up to his chest. It seemed as if by accident that, as she said the word 'nipple' she caught his between her fingers and squeezed.

Jethro caught his breath, swallowed hard, and wallowed in the sensation she was giving him.

'Kiss them, suck them,' said Ana Tai, using her best, haughtiest and most commanding voice. Jethro's eyes flew open. 'Not you, Mr Clarke, not you,' she said, rising up again, her sex hovering over his prick.

Was she going to touch it, this time? He waited. No. She stretched herself forward, lifting up and away from his cock, her hand roving over his chest and round his neck.

'Then?' he asked, trembling. 'What then?'

'Then,' she said, 'we feel each other.'

'How? How do you do that?' he asked. He wanted to know more. He wanted to imagine it. The feel of her hands travelling over his body was exquisite.

'Like this, really,' she said, squeezing her thighs into his hips and massaging his chest. 'I'll tell her to lie under me. I straddle her – like this. The same as I'm doing to you Mr Clarke.'

'And then what? There's got to be more.'

'Oh, there is, Mr Clarke, much more,' said Ana Tai sensuously.

'What?' he asked eagerly. The whole of his body felt on fire, consumed with passion and desire.

Ana Tai looked at Jethro. He swallowed and licked his lips. 'I tease her.'

Ana Tai leant back on her haunches, both hands trailing over Jethro's thighs – higher, higher, meeting at the top of his thighs. Would she? Would she? She did. She let them float tenderly over his balls and stiff prick.

'Then I ease my way along her body.'

'Do it,' he begged. 'Do it to me. Show me. Please.'

Her middle fingers had found the tip of his erect and quivering prick. They glazed over it. Whispering at it. He gasped. Ana Tai hesitated. 'Perhaps not,' she said.

'I promise. I promise I won't touch you,' he said. Almost desperate. He would promise her anything. The world. She could name a price for whatever she wanted. He didn't care. Just as long as she didn't stop.

'You will be punished if you do touch me,' she said sternly. She knelt up and began undoing the buttons on her coat.

Was she going to take her coat off? Was he going to

see her lovely body completely naked? No. Just one button was undone. Then she stood up.

'Put your hands above your head,' she commanded, as she straddled his chest and nestled her knees into his armpits. Keeping the coat on, she undid the remainder of her buttons, revealing all of her beautiful, slim, supple and beringed body.

Jethro trembled and shuddered. His cock was pulsating. His heart was pounding. Never had he been on such a high. Could he refrain from touching her? He must. The image of the hooded naked man in the foyer, wearing a cock ring and having his prick sucked, loomed up before his eyes. He must not give way to temptation.

Ana Tai put her hands under her bottom and moved her hips. She moved her hips forward towards his face. He clasped his quivering hands together. The urge to caress her was strong. Almost too strong. Her tawny-brown swollen sex, devoid of all hair, was coming closer to his mouth. Gold rings were hanging from her aroused labia. And in the divide her excited dark pink inner lips were unfolding, peeping out, inviting him to caress and touch.

Ana Tai looked him straight in the eye. She allowed the tiniest of smiles to hover around her mouth. She put out her long tongue and wiggled it at him. She eased her thighs open a fraction more. The hand on her buttocks, she brought round and placed on her belly.

'Then I do this,' she said. She held his gaze. Her sex had opened wider. Her juices were oozing out. He watched in an agony of desire as her oily perfumed hand snaked down over her pubis and, with infinite delicacy, she stroked her flushed juicy inner lips.

'Lick me,' she whispered, her finger slowly disappearing into her swollen wanton flower.

Jethro couldn't believe his ears. Did she say it or was it wishful thinking?

She let out her tongue and wriggled it from side to side as her hips danced and her fingers played.

'Lick me,' she said, louder this time.

Jethro lifted his head and stuck out his tongue. Ana Tai nodded, then moved her sexy musk-smelling hand to the back of his head.

She had meant it.

Gently, he put his mouth to her sex and kissed. Her entire body trembled. She sighed. His tongue slid along her moistness. She closed her eyes and moaned, a long low beautiful moan. A song of desire, a song without words. His tongue began its exploration, deeper, deeper inside her. She gasped. And panted. Fervently.

'Yes, oh yes, lick me. Suck me, find the spot.' Ana Tai was shaking.

She clutched at his head, pulling it tight, holding it hard between her legs as she leant back. And the hand that had been on her buttocks crept down over Jethro's body.

He issued a long series of sighs, the moment her fingers slid under his shorts and found his thick, stiff prick.

His tongue slithered on her wet sex. Her oily hand glided on his erect and throbbing cock. He wanted her. It was his all consuming thought. He wanted her flat on her back. He wanted her now. He wanted his thick cock straight up inside. He wanted to fuck her.

'Jethro, Jethro,' a loud Texan voice shouted. Carola marched into the room. Neither of them had heard the door open.

'Jethro! Oh my God! You're sucking the bitch!' Carola went up to the bed and grabbed Ana Tai by the hair. She dragged her away from Jethro's hungry mouth.

'Jethro! Listen, listen to me,' shouted Carola. 'I've just had the life shagged out of me.'

'Good,' said Jethro, completely bemused and wondering who had let her in.

'No, you don't understand,' she cried. 'I've just had the life shagged out of me by a goddam dwarf.'

'A small person,' said Ana Tai, quietly.

'What?' exclaimed Carola.

'It's not politically correct to say "dwarf". They don't like it.'

'Well, fuck politically correct,' said Carola, defiantly. 'I suppose you've gotta say "vertically challenged". Well I tell you his goddam cock wasn't!

'Did you enjoy it?' asked Ana Tai, sweetly.

'No. No, I did not,' said Carola vehemently.

'Then get your money back, sweetheart,' said Jethro.

'I didn't pay any goddam money,' Carola screamed at him.

'Then what are you complaining about?' he asked.

'I was blindfolded. I didn't know,' she cried.

'Look, Carola, I don't know how you got in here but I was having a massage . . .' said Jethro.

'You goddam liar,' shouted Carola. 'You were sucking her off.'

'No, he wasn't,' said Ana Tai.

'What's with you two? I saw you. Jethro, you had your head buried in her pussy. And she was rubbing your cock.'

'You are mistaken,' said Ana Tai, she didn't want Jeanine finding out that she'd been giving Jethro Clarke extras.

Carola looked from one to the other. 'Jethro,' said Carola, giving him a sly smile, 'I think we need to talk.

'Sure hon, sure,' said Jethro, as Ana Tai was wondering how he could get rid of the meddlesome bitch and get back to seducing her. 'Later. I'll talk to you later. I have prior engagements.'

'Yeah! Well, let me tell you, Jethro,' said Carola. 'Jeanine gave me the keys to get in, 'cos I just had a fax from my Daddy. He says he won't have his reputation dragged through the mire of a divorce and – unless there's a public reconciliation, and very very soon, like in the next couple of days – he's withdrawing from your project.'

Jethro blanched.

'So, hon, you might think I'm a goddam no-good white trash bimbo, but I understand banking. You've got a deadline and if you don't meet it, the corporate raiders, those fine gentleman, will move in and your one hundred million greenbacks will go floating down the Swanee. So I think your first priority is to find your whore of a wife, don't you? And, as luck would have it, your partner Petrov Vladelsky phoned – and he said Zinnia's in Geneva.'

Chapter Eight

'*B*ut why isn't Petrov here?' asked Auralie petulantly. 'You said he would be and it's important.'

'Yours is not to reason why,' said Mrs Klowski, sternly. 'You are rude. Your rudeness will be reported and punished.'

Auralie had telephoned the mansion much earlier that morning and had asked to speak with Petrov. Mrs Klowski had answered, telling her that he was unable to come to the telephone. As Petrov had a mobile, Auralie knew what that meant – Petrov was screwing and had given instructions not to be disturbed. Auralie hadn't explained that it was urgent.

Auralie congratulated herself on taking advantage of a number of events and finally escaping from Jeanine's clutches. If she'd planned it, it couldn't have been better. A fine combination of circumstances had added up to her run for freedom: Jeanine's mother insisting on seeing her daughter early that morning and Jacqueline asking her to do some shopping. Auralie had got in her car and fled up the motorway. But not before she had gone to see her stockbroker.

'Sell all my Petolg Holdings shares,' she'd told him.

Auralie had remained inwardly fuming ever since she had overheard Jeanine telling Jacqueline about her intentions for buying back the company. Well, she was done with the simpering bitch. She could have it, the whole lot. It was hers. Or anybody else's.

Auralie was aware that Jeanine held all the cards because Sir Henry was madly in love with her mother, Lady Penelope. But something that Miss Prissy Jeanine had forgotten: good designers are hard to find. Auralie knew it was her designs that were the backbone of the business. Let Jeanine sink or swim without her. Auralie was also well aware that if she held on to her shares, the moment a buyout was publicly known she could make lots more money than by selling them now. But she didn't give a damn. Auralie wanted out, now. And she'd sent Jeanine her letter of resignation.

Within minutes of her shares going up for sale, Auralie had received a very good price. Excellent, in fact. With that money she would start again, perhaps with Ana Tai. She was good with her hands, good at massage and aromatherapy; recently, Auralie had shown her how to embroider in the Western tradition. She had discovered Ana Tai had a real aptitude for it. Maybe they could set up a new company in Meriboa. What she'd done once, she could do again.

Auralie was arriving at Petrov's monastery to give Petrov the news of Jeanine's intentions. She was late, but not because of her share sales. The miles of road-works on the highway had resulted in a slow crawl and she had arrived tired, thirsty and bad tempered. Her disposition was not improved when she discovered that Petrov was not there.

The strict Mrs Klowski, with her prim uniform, her sharp face, mannish haircut and clanking keys, ushered her into the hall of the great Tudor mansion.

'Monsieur Petrov won't be long,' said his formidable housekeeper. 'Are you thirsty?'

'Oh yes,' said Auralie.

'Good. There is a pot of tea waiting for you,' she added, handing Auralie a dark green religious habit to change into. 'I will come for you when Monsieur arrives.'

Auralie removed her clothes, put on the habit and waited in the seductive warmth of the banqueting room.

Sitting in one of the high-backed Jacobean chairs in front of the large stone fireplace, Auralie quickly drank the herb tea. When she'd finished, she gazed about the room at the heavily-timbered ceiling; the minstrel's gallery was at one end, facing a large dais at the other. There was also the long oak refectory tables surrounded by carved oak dining chairs.

As time wore on and Petrov didn't appear, Auralie was left contemplating Petrov's extraordinary and highly erotic tapestries. They could, Auralie thought, be woven from pictures taken at orgies she had taken part in, in that very room. Then Auralie realised the herb tea was having an effect. Her bladder was full. She needed to pee. She got up and tried the door that led to the lavatory. It was locked. Auralie was about to try another door when Mrs Klowski marched into the room.

'He is ready for you now,' she said. 'I hope you are ready for him.'

'I want to use the lavatory,' said Auralie.

'That's not possible,' said Mrs Klowski. 'You should have gone before.'

'But . . .' Auralie started to protest. She had been a fool. The herb tea was more than a thirst-quencher. It was a diuretic.

'Bend over,' said the housekeeper.

'Why?' asked Auralie.

'You don't ask why – you obey,' said Mrs Klowski, sharply. 'Bend over the chair with your legs apart and lift up your habit.'

Auralie submitted to the hatchet faced housekeeper's demands, revealing her nakedness and the rings in her labia and the inviting neat plumpness of her soft pink buttocks.

'Your rudeness has been reported,' said Mrs Klowski, fondling her thighs then giving Auralie a sudden and very hard slap on her bare rump. 'Monsieur Petrov has

165

given me permission to punish you today and now your bottom's a lovely red.' Mrs Klowski slapped her again.

Auralie wondered if anybody was watching her humiliation through the various spyholes. She felt Mrs Klowski's small stubby hands easing upwards, parting her sex lips, rubbing her, making her wet. Then, pressing slightly on Auralie's lower abdomen, Mrs Klowski inserted two metal balls inside her vagina.

'Keep them there,' said the stern housekeeper, 'and follow me.'

Mrs Klowski's arrival anywhere was heralded by various sounds: clanking keys and high heels tapping on the parquet floor. Auralie knew that Petrov would realise they were heading towards the confessional. She wondered what he would be doing on his side of the cubicle. Would he be playing with himself, or would he have an acolyte in with him sucking his cock? Mrs Klowski unlocked the door to the tiny room behind the dais and pulled Auralie inside.

'Stand there,' said Mrs Klowski, raising the habit high, revealing Auralie's bare reddened bottom.

'Now sit down,' she said.

Auralie lowered her buttocks on to the harsh fabric of a small stool in front of the grille.

'Welcome, Auralie,' said Petrov. 'I hope you are comfortable.'

Auralie squirmed on the seat. Comfortable she was not. Her bladder was too full; each time she moved and the metal balls pressed within her, the dull ache increased but she lowered her head submissively.

'Yes, thank you, Petrov,' she said.

'Good. Does Jeanine have a message for me?' asked Petrov.

'No,' said Auralie, 'She doesn't know I'm here.'

'Then how did you manage to leave the hotel?' asked Petrov.

'I did her a favour the other day, so – '

'Oh? And what was that?' he asked. Petrov knew there was no love lost between the two women.

'I stopped Jeanine's mother catching her as Jacqueline was about to screw her,' said Auralie.

'Oh, did you?' he said. 'That was very noble of you.'

'I thought so,' said Auralie, remembering why Jeanine's mother loathed her.

For most of her early years, Penelope had looked after Auralie. After her parents had been killed in a car crash, Penelope had brought her up as her own. Auralie's mother had been Penelope's twin sister, she had married Boris Vladelsky. Years later Penelope had met Boris's brother, Stefan, and had married him. Stefan had been the cause of the trouble and the event that upset the family had happened on Auralie's eighteenth birthday.

Penelope and Stefan had been living in Paris. Jeanine, being younger than Auralie, had still been at boarding school in England. Penelope had given a huge party for Auralie in their elegant Parisian apartment. For the first time in her life Auralie had got drunk. Feeling very strange, she had made for the nearest room to lie down. Scarcely knowing where she was, Auralie had wrapped herself in the silken draperies on Penelope's massive cherry wood double bed and had gone to sleep. When she awoke she had found Stefan fast asleep and stark naked beside her.

Stefan had been slim and athletic and also an exceptionally handsome man, with deep-set green eyes and a shock of black hair. Auralie had sat up and gazed at him. It had seemed to her that he was in a deep, deep sleep. She had looked at his body and admired it. She had especially admired his penis. It had lain to one side, inert but beautiful. Auralie had had the strongest desire to touch it. To feel it. To see what would happen if she did.

Slowly and carefully, with great trepidation and with the lightness of a feather, she had reached out a hand and gently stroked it. He had stayed fast asleep but his prick had quivered. She had stroked it again. Its rounded tip had pushed out from under the furrows of concertined flesh. Utterly entranced, she had touched it again along the ridges of its emerging cap. Auralie had continued to touch it. Stefan's penis had continued to quiver and grow.

Auralie had watched with a quiet fascination as it had thickened and extended. When it was proud and upright, she'd felt she had to hold it. Its stiff erectness, combined with its soft movable warmth, had made her want to stroke it. Up and down. Up and down. Then she had felt the strongest desire to take it in her mouth and suck it.

She had looked at Stefan, who had been lying quite still, his breathing never changing. Careful not to touch any other part of his body, Auralie had knelt up on her haunches beside his waist. Completely oblivious to everything, she had opened her mouth wide and had guided his beautiful large prick between her lips and had sucked on the head. She had been so completely immersed in the pleasure of licking and sucking on his penis that she had failed to hear the door open and Penelope enter. She had been unaware of Penelope's arrival until the older woman had screamed.

Auralie had been thrown out of the house without ceremony and had taken the guilt with her. It was some years later when Auralie finally realised that Stefan must have known what she was doing – and that Penelope must have known that Stefan had been a very willing participant. And it was that knowledge that made Penelope loathe Auralie.

'So Penelope's been to Jeanine's,' Petrov said. 'That must have been interesting.'

'Not as interesting as it might have been,' said Auralie.

'Does she know about her daughter's activities in her hotel?'

'No, but she nearly did,' said Auralie, giving a slight smile.

'And what did Lady Penelope want?'

'To see if Sir Henry's designs were ready, she said.'

'Were they?'

'Oh yes, and I happened to have all the swatches and things to hand, which was fortunate. I gave them to her and told her that Jeanine was away. As you know, she hates me, so without her daughter there, she didn't stay around.'

'We shall start calling you Saint Auralie, soon,' said Petrov acidly. 'So why the acts of kindness, Auralie?'

'Jeanine's the bitch, not me,' she said.

'So what have you come to tell me?' asked Petrov.

'Important news – and I didn't trust faxes or telephones. You needed to hear it direct. I'm talking about betrayal.'

'Gossip,' said Petrov flatly.

'No, real betrayal; but I'm telling you first. I'm leaving. Going. Taking my freedom,' said Auralie, pressing her face against the grille.

'I see,' said Petrov, slightly perturbed.

'We had an agreement, Petrov,' she said. 'I could go whenever.'

'Where do you want to go with your new-found freedom?' asked Petrov.

'Meriboa,' said Auralie.

'Oh, really?' said Petrov, intrigued. 'Why do you want to go there?'

'It's a long way from anywhere else,' said Auralie, not wanting to tell him her real reason. She wanted to go to Meriboa with Ana Tai.

Auralie had fallen in love. From the moment she had seen Ana Tai working in Jeanine's other house, Auralie had been stricken with love. Ana Tai had told her how she wanted to return to her homeland. But she wanted to return rich. She had taken the job as masseuse at Jeanine's to make her money. But Ana Tai would not screw a man. She had made that clear during her initial interview with Jeanine.

'I will play games with them,' Ana Tai had informed Jeanine. 'I will play with their cocks, I will tease them – but I will not be screwed.'

'In that case, I shall give you a role. I shall call you my flat-mate,' Jeanine had said, 'you will help me excite and seduce the men I want. The rest of the time you can be the masseuse.'

Ana Tai had told Auralie of her agreement with Jeanine when the two women had secretly made love.

'Oddly enough,' said Petrov, 'I was thinking of going to Meriboa myself.'

'You were?' she exclaimed. 'Why?'

'I expect for the same reason as you,' he replied. 'Now, Auralie,' he continued, 'before you say another word, I think I should tell you something and I want you to find out if my current information is correct.'

'What's that?' asked Auralie.

'That Jeanine is planning a buy-out.'

'You know!' exclaimed Auralie, almost bursting into tears. Tears of frustration and anger welled up in her eyes. 'But that's what I've come to tell you. It's terrible. Terrible. All those companies she's been buying up and now ... Petrov, you know what happens afterwards. They sell off bits piecemeal to pay for their profit. But what does Jeanine care? She didn't build up the design business; she didn't put her heart and soul into it. She just put in money.'

'And you're frightened you'll lose your position,' said Petrov.

'No, I'm not,' said Auralie.

'Well, you should be,' he said, seriously. 'Look at what she's acquired. Similar companies, all with their own designers. She could let you go and bring in one of those.'

'Yes, she might,' said Auralie, wondering who had told him about Jeanine's intentions. Suddenly she decided to be cagey.

'You're not bothered?'

'She's a bitch,' said Auralie. 'With her, anything is possible.'

'It could just be a rumour. Our Jeanine's quite good at rumour, when it suits her,' said Petrov.

'I overheard her telling Jacqueline,' said Auralie. 'Who told you? Did Jacqueline tell you?'

'Never mind, but you've confirmed my worst fears. If you want to go to Meriboa, I will make the arrangements. You can go with me.'

'With you?' said Auralie. This was not the outcome she'd expected. Auralie did not want to go to Meriboa with Petrov.

'Yes,' said Petrov. 'But there's something I want.'

'Oh? What?'

'A girl at Jeanine's.'

'Just tell Jeanine,' said Auralie, 'and she'll arrange it.'

'No, I can't,' said Petrov.

Auralie's heart sank a little. Was she going to hear what she didn't want to hear? 'Why not?' asked Auralie, warily.

'I've already mentioned it to Jeanine, but she has a pact with this girl. No screwing. No dicks. Girls only, and only with Jeanine's permission.'

'What's her name?' asked Auralie in a timorous whisper.

'Ana Tai,' said Petrov. 'She's Malaysian or something; tall and thin, got rings in her lips and –'

'She's Meriboan,' said Auralie.

'Is she? You know who I mean, then?'

'Yes,' said Auralie, her voice faltering.

'I want her,' said Petrov. 'I want her here.'

'No.' The word escaped Auralie's lips before she could hold it back.

'Auralie,' said Petrov, sternly, 'do I detect an unwillingness to obey me?'

'No,' she said, quickly. Nobody knew of her affair with Ana Tai and, against all odds, Auralie intended to keep it that way.

'Good,' said Petrov. 'Now, it seems our little Eastern flower prefers women; she doesn't like men. I want you to be the bait. I want you to seduce her. That shouldn't be a difficult assignment. Perhaps you have already?'

'No,' said Auralie.

'You wouldn't lie to me, would you?'

'No,' said Auralie, lying. 'But Jeanine?'

'I'll sort it out with Jeanine,' said Petrov, pressing his face to the grille. 'Now, as you're in the confessional, what else have you got to tell me?'

'Nothing,' said Auralie.

'Has anything interesting happened at the hotel recently?' Petrov asked.

'No,' lied Auralie.

'Oh really? Nobody new's turned up?' he asked. 'Nobody I'd be wanting to know about?'

'No.'

'Are you sure?' said Petrov.

'Quite sure,' she said, without complete conviction, dithering inwardly. Should she mention Zinnia and the unexpected arrival of Zinnia's husband? No. Auralie would lay a bet that Petrov already knew. However, Zinnia had sworn her to secrecy when she had left for Geneva. Auralie had no intention of betraying her friend.

She wanted to smile as she remembered Zinnia's description of her husband's face when he found her flat on her back with her legs in the air, her sex being plundered by big, burly and jet-black Jackson.

'I'll divorce you, you hooker,' Jethro had screamed, yanking Zinnia off the bed.

'You'll have to cross-petition then,' Zinnia had snarled back at him. 'Cos I've already started proceedings and I'm citing Carola Finestein.'

Zinnia had used that moment to wrench herself free from his grip. Grabbing her clothes, she had fled downstairs, to be told by Terry that Caradoc Lewis was on the telephone. He had ordered her immediately to Geneva.

'Auralie,' Zinnia had said, 'please can you go back to my bedroom, get my bag and my passport, and promise me you won't tell anyone where I'm going? Not anyone.'

Auralie had retrieved Zinnia's things and had found Jethro sitting on the bed, his head in his hands.

'I was mad,' he was saying to Jackson. 'Just plum mad. I don't really want a divorce.'

'Then you'd better do something about it,' said Jackson. 'Cos I think she does.'

Auralie thought about Petrov's question carefully. Zinnia wasn't new. Zinnia had been to Jeanine's and Jacqueline's and the mansion in the Bois de Boulogne. She could truthfully say no. After all, what Petrov knew, he knew; what he didn't know was Zinnia's secret. Anyhow, what was it to him?

'I think you're lying,' said Petrov, and called for Mrs Klowski, who immediately entered the small confessional box, and without being told, tied a blindfold around Auralie's eyes.

'Stand up and take off your habit,' commanded Mrs Klowski, gruffly.

'I want her punished,' said Petrov.

Mrs Klowski tied Auralie's hands behind her back. Naked, the rings in her labia glinting in the gloom, she was marched into the banqueting hall and up the steps on to the dais.

'She's been disobedient, Mrs Klowski,' said Petrov, his voice now echoing from the minstrel's gallery.

Mrs Klowski stood beside Auralie, holding a thick black pizzle in her hand, stroking it lovingly.

'I think we need to see her bare bottom,' said Petrov.

Two young men stepped up beside her as Mrs Klowski turned Auralie so that her rear was facing the minstrel's gallery. Very slowly, Mrs Klowski caressed Auralie's neat rounded buttocks while trailing the pizzle down over her sweet rose-bud breasts, over her belly and down to her shaven and ringed pubis.

'And she has lied to me. Disobedient liars need spanking,' said Petrov.

Mrs Klowski took a long thin cane from a quiver in a tall jar on the dais.

The two young men beside her were now holding their own pricks. They were thick and erect and almost at bursting point.

'No, I wasn't,' said Auralie. 'I wasn't disobedient and – '

'Petrov thinks you were,' said Mrs Klowski, striking her roundness with the long thin cane.

Auralie jumped. Mrs Klowski caressed her reddened delectable rounded soft bottom then quickly took up the cane again and gave her another two stripes. Auralie screamed with a combination of pain and pleasure.

Mrs Klowski stroked the weals she had left on the Auralie's backside, then licked them. Bending Auralie over, she stroked her thighs and pressed on her belly.

'No,' cried Auralie, her full bladder aching 'please no – no.'

'Don't let go your water,' said Mrs Klowski menacingly.

Mrs Klowski increased the pressure on Auralie's belly. Playing with her sex lips, the stern housekeeper slowly pushed the metal balls up inside her until Auralie couldn't take it any more and her water began to leak out over Mrs Klowski's hand.

'She is extremely disobedient,' said Mrs Klowski in a very loud voice, as Auralie's water streamed out and down her legs.

Auralie tensed her body for the crop but, instead of that searing pain lighting across her body, she felt lips clamped to her nipples and her breasts gently caressed. The softness of the touch, the delicacy, relaxed her. When the lash came the pain was sharper, more intense, more beautiful.

Her legs were spread apart. Moments later, she felt a thick fat tongue licking her outer sex lips, then forcing its way between the inner furls of her moist private self. She knew that it was Mrs Klowski's tongue.

She moved her muscles in an attempt to draw the tongue upwards. The tongue withdrew and nibbled on her clitoris. She pushed her hips out to meet the challenge of the exploring tongue. Bare, bound and unseeing, Auralie enjoyed the tongue starting its magical work again: one moment deep inside her, the next moving upwards, wriggling expertly, flicking her clitoris and licking her bottom-mouth.

She heard someone behind her and felt hands over her shoulders, felt hands clasping her breasts – kneading

174

them, playing with the nipples. Then she felt another person kneeling in front of her, stroking her legs. The tongue moved and the fingers of the person in front delved deep into the space left by the tongue. The hands playing with her breasts pulled her backwards while her arse was penetrated by an exploring finger.

Then hands held her sex wide open and she was penetrated from the front without ceremony. Someone pushed his long thin penis in suddenly so that she jerked towards him and he thrust. And he kept thrusting and penetrating. Auralie was being enjoyed and enjoying. She was shaking and squirming and loving every minute, never wanting it to stop.

'Release her,' boomed Petrov.

Auralie couldn't bear it. She wanted more. She wanted the fucking to continue. She was desperate to come.

'Take her to her room. Leave the chains and blindfold on,' he ordered. 'This is your punishment, Auralie. To be left wanting. Chain her so that she cannot touch herself. Perhaps one of us will come and avail ourselves of your body; perhaps we won't. Take her away, Mrs Klowski.'

Auralie was taken to a small cell with a single bed up against a wall. Her hands were chained above her head – not uncomfortably, but she couldn't reach down and play with herself. Her legs were spread apart and chained to either end of the bed, and a small vibrator was turned on and put at the entrance of her sex – just inside her labia, and just enough to keep her excited, wet and tantalised.

Some hours later, Petrov came in to see her. He checked the battery in the vibrator, then pushed it up into her wanton sex. She shuddered expectantly, and rolled her hips sexily. Surely Petrov was going to take her now – take her, screw her and release her from her longing? She needed to come. Auralie was desperate to come.

'You will stay here and not return to Jeanine's,' he said, touching her aroused and sensitive clitoris and making her sigh with delight and desire.

'Yes,' said Auralie, obediently.

'And I have an old friend of yours with me,' said Petrov.

Behind the blindfold, Auralie felt lips lick her sex. Thick lips, and a thick tongue. She raised her hips lasciviously. The vibrator continued just inside her labia, driving her to distraction. She felt a body scramble over hers and a cock was put between her lips.

'He wants you to suck his cock,' said Petrov.

Auralie opened her mouth and a thick long cock slid into it.

'Suck it properly,' said Petrov, massaging her breasts.

Auralie took as much of the huge cock as she could. In and out, playing with her tongue along its ridges.

'Good, good,' said Petrov. 'Now he's going to fuck you. You want to be fucked, don't you, Auralie?'

'Yes,' she said, panting, as the penis was taken from her mouth and the vibrator from her sex.

A pillow was put under her bottom, raising her open swollen sex. The body moved over her and she felt the thick cock at her entrance. She gave a long slow sigh of relief as the prick drove slowly into wet tantalised wantonness and she started to come. Once, twice, three times she came and was ready for more.

Petrov leant over her. His penis touched her face. She opened her mouth to take it. He put it between her lips. Petrov mouth-fucked her as he removed her blindfold.

Then she saw she was being screwed by Carlo. Carlo, the ugliest of Jacqueline's little men. The one with the biggest penis. The one who had taken her, to the delight of all onlookers, in the mansion in Paris.

There was something erotic, depraved, and totally debauched about the ugly little man who was jerking on top of her, who leant down and clamped his thick lips over her breasts. She raised her hips higher to take him.

'You will miss us if you leave,' said Petrov. 'But don't worry, we're filming you now and we'll give it to you to keep you happy.'

Petrov spurted into her mouth. Covering his nakedness with a habit, he looked at the spreadeagled and chained figure of Auralie who was being mercilessly shagged by Carlo.

'Auralie,' he said, 'I shall leave you to Carlo for a few days. I'm going to Geneva. I believe your friend Zinnia is there and, if my scouts are right, she's having the life fucked out of her by some randy old banker.'

Petrov turned to leave the room.

'Oh – and, Auralie, don't tell me lies again, not even the lie of omission,' said Petrov. 'And – er – no need for you to contact Ana Tai. She's at the airport with Jethro Clarke. All three of us are going to Geneva. It's a pity you didn't tell me the truth, or you could have come, too.'

Chapter Nine

Zinnia had taken the plane to Geneva as Caradoc Lewis, the chairman of Hanway, Rattle and Lewis, had ordered. At the airport, she had been met by Francis. He had escorted her to a waiting limousine, then driven her to a small chateau in the mountains.

He ushered her into a heavily beamed, formal drawing room, lit by candles and with a log fire burning to take off the chill off the autumn night air. Francis had indicated that she sit in a hard-backed chair with curving wooden arms. Then he served her with a large, sweet and highly potent cocktail, which he told her was the chateau's speciality. He departed as his employer wheeled himself in.

Caradoc Lewis was clothed in the same rough tweed suit and with the heavy Welsh blanket over his lap. 'Your husband is worrying me,' he said, placing himself beside her chair and not stopping for any of the niceties like 'hello' and 'wonderful to see you'. 'There's something going on and I need you to find out what it is.'

'What sort of something?' she asked, quite taken aback by his abruptness.

She knew that Jethro was keeping his head down while trying to put a deal together. She reasoned that it could only be a small deal because big ones always went through Hanway, Rattle and Lewis. What it was, she had yet to discover.

But, as always, Jethro wouldn't want any publicity until he pounced. Especially bad publicity. And any leakage of a possible divorce from her, so soon after their marriage, could mean his usual partners – like the Finesteins, with their strict moral code – withdrawing their support. Then the deal, if not off, would certainly be postponed: costing him time and, in the end, possibly the deal itself.

'There's a young man Jethro's friendly with who's trading for de Bouys in Meriboa. He needs to be investigated. I want you to do it. I want you to go under cover and find out more about him. And find out why Jethro's dealing with him and not with us.'

'Me?' she exclaimed.

'Yes, you.'

'But I'm trying to keep out of Jethro's way at the moment, not walk into him,' said Zinnia.

'Oh, don't worry, Jethro's not in Meriboa,' said Caradoc Lewis.

'Where is he?' she asked.

'London, I believe,' replied Caradoc.

'But why me?' Zinnia asked.

'Because, my dear, you have the right qualifications,' he replied, gazing at her lustfully. 'Undo your blouse; I want to feel those big breasts of yours. I want those nipples.'

Zinnia did as she was told. She took off her suit top and then she unbuttoned her blouse. She stared at him, watching the bulge under his blanket grow large with excitement at the sight of her huge breasts, which were only partially covered by her skimpy satin and lace bra.

'Come here beside me,' he said and, when she did, he reached out and eased her long nipples from their lace covering. Expertly he rolled them between his thumb and forefinger, exciting her as he increased his pressure almost to pain. She felt a sharp stab of pleasure leave her breasts and connect with her womb. Zinnia licked her lips, wiggled and opened her legs slightly.

'Now sit there in front of me,' he said, noticing the signs and recognising the beginnings of wantonness. She sat down, her short skirt rising high. 'Don't cross your legs. Are you wearing knickers?'

'Yes,' she replied.

'Take them off,' he said. 'I want to be able to see your sex. I also want instant access.'

Zinnia stood up and pulled her knickers down, dropping them to the floor.

'Now give them to me,' he said.

She handed them to him.

'They're damp,' he said, feeling the crotch. 'So you're wet, are you? You're wanting my cock, are you? Well maybe, and maybe not.' He lifted her knickers to his nose and sniffed. 'A sweet musk,' he said. 'A sweet sexy musk. Now, open your legs a little further. Stay like that until I tell you to move. Now, this trader's name is Eduard del Sur . . .'

Zinnia gave a short gasp. 'I know him,' she said. 'He's a friend of Jethro's, plays polo with him from time to time. Might even have been playing down in Texas.'

'He was,' said Caradoc, 'but what's interesting about this young man is he seems to have appeared from nowhere. He's a Latino, that much we've found out – but who or what he is . . . Well, there we've drawn a blank, beyond de Bouys in Geneva. However, he appears to have the Goldsmith touch. In and out to great advantage, faster than the blink of an eye. Same with women, too. He screws around but there's no one woman. We need to know more about him.'

'You want me to seduce him?'

'Yes,' said Caradoc. 'You can fly out in the morning. Francis and I will stay here. I have a number of other odds and ends to sort out. You will fax me through, informing me of your success.'

'You're certain I will be successful?'

'I have no doubt of it,' said Caradoc. 'Are you still going ahead with the divorce?'

'Oh, yes.'

Zinnia knew Jethro was desperately trying to locate her to stop the divorce. Auralie said he'd gone crazy when he'd discovered she'd gone from the hotel. Well, there was a lot of craziness about. She'd heard through Caradoc – though how he knew, she hadn't yet discovered – that Auralie had upped and left Jeanine's. That was a surprise. But life was full of them. Caradoc Lewis's opportune telephone call had been another.

'Good; your talents are wasted on a man like Jethro Clarke,' he said. 'But they aren't on me. Will you have another drink?'

'Yes, thank you.'

'Now, Francis, you know,' said Caradoc, wheeling his chair beside Zinnia's and stroking her thighs.

'Yes.'

'He's an accommodating young man,' said Caradoc. 'He'll go far. Started life as a trader in the City.'

'He did? Which city?'

'The City of London,' said Caradoc. 'I met him and persuaded him to come and work for me here.'

'Why?' Zinnia asked.

'I told him he could learn more by being closer to the head,' said Caradoc mischievously. 'And, as he's ambitious . . . Spread your legs wider,' His hands strayed up and began touching her sex lips. 'Oh, my dear, you really are quite wet.'

'Yes,' she gasped as his fingers gently opened her, sliding backwards and forwards on her soft, rose-coloured, highly sensitive, inner corral.

'Stay still,' he said. 'Stay absolutely still.'

From under his blanket Caradoc brought out a thick, long pink leather dildo with extra large balls.

'Move your bottom towards the edge of the chair and put one leg over the arm.' Zinnia obeyed him. Her sex was open and on view. 'That's beautiful, quite beautiful,' he said, gliding the dildo on her moist and swollen sex lips but not entering. 'I can see you're very excited.' He touched her clitoris with the tip of the dildo. Zinnia let out a quick gasp as a thrill ran up her body.

'You like that, eh?' he asked.

'Oh yes,' she gasped.

'Good,' he said, slowly Caradoc inserted the big false penis, pushing up into her hungry wetness. 'And this?'

'Oh yes,' she sighed.

'Right,' he ordered, 'now you take hold of it by its balls and shove it up hard into yourself. I want to see just how much you can take.'

Zinnia's red-nailed fingers clasped the fat round plastic balls of the pink leather dildo and she pushed. She pushed and opened, pushed and opened, as gradually the whole prick was swallowed by her wanton and ravenous sex.

'I want you to sit there, fucking yourself, while I get Francis to pour us some more drinks.'

'You want Francis to see me playing with myself?' she asked.

'Yes, my dear,' he said, tweaking her nipples. 'And I want more than that.'

'How much more?' she asked, between thrusts and gasps.

'I'll let you know,' he said. 'But whatever I decide, I will enjoy it and so, I believe, will you. Now stay as you are while I call him.'

Caradoc pressed the bell on his chair.

Zinnia half-sat, half-lay in the chair. With one hand she pushed the dildo in and out of her wet sex, with her other hand she played with her large breasts and massaged her own nipples.

'Beautiful,' said Caradoc.

Francis, wearing a stiff white starched shirt, black trousers and a black jacket, answered his master's call. He couldn't see what Zinnia was doing as she had her back to him.

'You called, sir,' said Francis.

'Yes. I want a whisky,' said the head of Hanways, Rattle and Lewis' merchant bank. Francis opened an antique baroque cupboard where the drinks were stored, and poured one for his master.

182

'And for madam, a cocktail?' he asked, turning towards her. If he was surprised to see her legs spread apart and the dildo moving fast up and down inside her displayed sex while her hands roved across her magnificent breasts, he didn't let it faze him. 'Or would you like something else?'

'Definitely something else,' said Zinnia.

'And that would be?' he asked.

'A Drambuie,' she said. 'A large Drambuie.'

Francis poured the sticky sweet liquid into a crystal glass and handed it to her.

'I think she'd like a Drambuie and your cock,' said Caradoc.

'Oh no, sir,' said Francis. 'I think you must be mistaken.'

'I am never mistaken, Francis,' said Caradoc.

Taking her cue from Caradoc's words, Zinnia took the glass from Francis, sipped some, then, leaving the dildo inside her, she reached for Francis' crotch.

'You see, I was right,' said Caradoc, as he watched Zinnia stroking Francis between his thighs.

'Yes, sir, but – ' said Francis, embarrassed as his penis started to react to her ministrations.

'I have explained to Mrs Clarke that you are a most accommodating young man, so accommodate her. She obviously wants to feel your prick, so let her.'

'Oh, sir!'

'Come on, Francis, hurry up; pull down your zip and let her see your lovely cock. Let her feel your lovely cock. Or shall I do it? But you know what happens if I do, don't you? You know what happens if you don't obey me fast enough.'

'Yes, sir.'

'Tell the luscious Mrs Clarke what happens if you don't obey me fast enough.'

'I . . . I . . .' Francis stuttered.

Zinnia was squirming on the dildo but she kept stroking Francis between his thighs and she could feel his member swelling.

'Tell her,' commanded Caradoc, sternly.

'You spank me, sir.'

'Yes, I spank you. Did you know that, Zinnia? Sometimes this young man has to be spanked for disobedience. He has to bend over and put his bare bottom in the air and I have to discipline him, spank him. How do I spank you, Francis?'

'It depends, sir.'

'How did I spank you the last time that you didn't obey me fast enough?'

'With a paddle, sir,' said Francis, and Zinnia felt his cock shoot up at the memory. It was now hard and straining against his black trousers.

'This time, I might decide to cane you,' said Caradoc.

'Oh no, sir,' said Francis, taking quick sharp breaths as Zinnia's hand found the outline of his penis and was letting her fingers flow up and down it.

'Then undo your zip,' said Caradoc.

'Yes, sir,' said Francis, instantly obeying his master. Zinnia put her hands inside his flies and manoeuvred his short thick erect penis out from his constricting trousers.

'She's got a lovely big red mouth,' said Caradoc, 'I want her to taste your beautiful cock. I want to watch her suck it.'

'But, sir – '

'Obey me,' said Caradoc Lewis sternly.

Zinnia wiggled on the chair, jerking the dildo up, while her fingers ran along Francis' prick. She picked up her glass of Drambuie, looking up at him and holding his eyes, she aimed his prick down into the glass and dipped it into the liqueur. Then, her big breasts flopping to one side, Zinnia bent her head and licked his cock head.

'Delicious,' she said, and licked again and again. She wiggled some more, making sure the dildo stayed in position, then eased Francis' balls out of their imprisonment. She poured some of the sticky Drambuie over his testes, then juggled them whilst continuing to lick his prick. And he gasped. He gasped and swayed his hips. He lunged slightly, wanting his cock deeper inside her mouth, but she kept it back with her hands.

'I want you to fuck her,' said Caradoc. 'I want you to lift her out of that chair and lie her on the floor, here in front of me, and I want to watch your delightful cock charging in and out of her.'

'No, master,' said Francis. 'No, I couldn't. Not in front of you.'

'Francis, are you being disobedient?'

'Sorry, master,' said the young man submissively, while thrusting his cock in and out of Zinnia's mouth.

'You will be,' said Caradoc, wheeling his chair closer to Zinnia and the man she was sucking. 'Take your trousers down.'

'Oh no, master,' said the young man, his hands finding their way to Zinnia's breasts and fondling them. 'Please.'

'Zinnia,' said Caradoc, 'it's easier for you to reach than me. Undo his belt and take his trousers down.'

Keeping her mouth over his cock, Zinnia felt Francis shudder slightly as she reached her hands up, unbuckled his belt, unhooked the fastener and pulled. Francis' neat bare bottom was within easy reach of Caradoc's hands.

Caradoc stroked Francis' buttocks.

'Like I said, he's an accommodating young man, aren't you, Francis?' said Caradoc, as his fingers parted the lean slim cheeks of his rump. 'Do you know what he does for me each night before I go to bed?'

'No,' said Zinnia, stroking his balls.

'Please sir, don't tell her, sir,' begged Francis.

'Quiet,' said Caradoc, sternly. 'Francis sucks my cock.'

'He sucks your cock?' repeated Zinnia, her fingers drifting up and down on the handsome young man's tumescent member.

'Yes. Don't you, Francis? You sit me on my bed and kneel down in front of me and then you suck my cock.'

'No,' said Francis. 'No, I don't.'

'Oh yes, you do, only sometimes you don't do it

185

properly, and then I have to smack you. Smack your bottie.'

There was a loud slapping sound as Caradoc's hand hit hard at Francis buttocks and his hips jutted forward, his cock reaching further into Zinnia's mouth. Francis tensed. Zinnia pulled back. Caradoc produced a cane.

'And I think I'll have to do that now. I think your arguing with me warrants a caning.' Caradoc ran the bamboo over Francis' bottom cheeks then up between the cleft of his arse. 'Oh yes, disobedient young men must be punished.'

'No, sir, I'm sorry, sir. I'll do anything you want, sir,' said Francis, squirming as the cane traced lightly over his backside and Zinnia put his cock back into her mouth and sucked. 'Do you want me to bend down now, sir, and suck your cock? Is that what you want?'

'No, not now,' said Caradoc, tapping the cane continuously with short sharp strikes on his bare bottom, stinging and marking his rounded flesh.

Zinnia took Francis's prick from her mouth and embraced it with her sticky hands. She dipped it into the Drambuie. She dribbled some over his balls, then she poured some over her fingers. Placing his very sticky cock between her massive breasts, she held it there while her hands travelled down between his legs, lubricating him with the dark liquid along his balls and his perineum, moving closer, ever closer to his expectant, waiting and wanting bottom-mouth.

Francis stood beside Zinnia, his eyes closed, enjoying her soft touch.

Suddenly, Caradoc brought the cane down hard three times in succession on his naked flanks.

'Thank you, sir,' said Francis, accepting his punishment.

'You will do as I tell you, won't you, Francis?' said Caradoc harshly.

'Yes, sir,' he replied, submissively.

'Bend over then,' ordered Caradoc. 'I want to see her stroke your arse.'

Zinnia's fingers trailed between the crack of his buttocks. They made small round movements over his bottom-mouth. Round and round she went, circling his tight resistant hole. Round and in. Round and in. She did it again and again. Gradually, he relaxed. She felt him opening beneath her persistent onslaught.

Caradoc moved his chair closer to Zinnia. She lifted her leg high. He was rewarded with the sight of her full luscious sex glistening with her own sweet honey. Caradoc took out the dildo, dipped it in the Drambuie, then pressed it up inside Zinnia. Up and down, up and down; and she got wetter and wetter.

Then she turned, took the dildo from her and faced her full, open, wet and wanton sex directly at Francis' cock.

'The lady wants to be fucked,' said Caradoc, 'and I give my full permission.'

Zinnia raised her hips. Francis put his hands under her bottom. The tip of his stiff and sticky, Drambuie-drenched cock touched her open wetness and Caradoc handed him a condom which he put on. And then he lunged. He lunged and he fucked. Fast and furiously he fucked and, unable to contain himself, came quickly.

'Mmm,' said Caradoc, surveying their activities. 'Yes, that pleases me. And I've been thinking. I have decided we'll all go to Meriboa tomorrow. I've made up my mind. I shall buy de Bouys bank. That'll be one in the eye for Henry de Bouys. He won't like that at all, his brother out of the business. But things aren't exactly going their way at the moment. I've heard the rumours. Missing bonds, it's said,' Caradoc laughed, then he caught the look of surprise on Zinnia's face.

'Sir Henry and I were friends when we were younger,' he added, by way of explanation. 'He took a woman I wanted and then compounded it by grabbing a business I'd set my heart on. Well, the time of reckoning is nigh. You see, my dear, the de Bouys have got a thing about keeping things in the family. And I shall get it. Yes, me. The old de Bouys bank will be owned by the new

Lewis's. The old order changeth and all that. Poor old Cecil! My heart bleeds; so many millions and too old to enjoy them. A shame, my dear, isn't it? Oh yes, Henry de Bouys, watch out. This is one deal you won't get and I will.'

Cecil rubbed his hands with glee.

'And when I've bought it, Hanway's will have access to their Minmex operations. And you, Zinnia, will head that office for me.'

'I will? Why not your son?'

'David understands New York,' said Caradoc. 'He's good on Wall Street. I think a woman should be in charge in Meriboa. One must go with the times. New democracy, new exchange, new attitudes. Change equals expansion, my dear. Oh yes, I've decided. You will head up the Meriboan office for me.'

Zinnia was thrilled. At last her talents were being properly recognised. She leant over and kissed the top of Caradoc Lewis's head.

'But that's wonderful,' she cried, happily. 'Just wonderful.'

'Eduard,' said Jethro, shouting down a crackly telephone line. 'Eduard, is that you?'

'Yes,' said Eduard, holding the receiver slightly away from his ear.

'Look, I've just heard my fucking bitchkin wife is out there in Meriboa,' said Jethro.

'Zinnia?' exclaimed Eduard.

'Yes, goddam it; I don't have another one – at the moment,' replied Jethro.

'Hey, Jethro what's the matter? When I last saw you, she was a great girl; now suddenly she's – '

'She's a whore,' shouted Jethro, interrupting him. 'A fucking goddam whore.'

'But – ' said Eduard, trying to mollify long-distance.

Jethro wasn't having any of that. 'No buts,' he said. 'She's out there and she's working for Hanway, Rattle and Lewis.'

'She always has been,' said Eduard. 'When you introduced us, you told me that.'

'Yeah, well,' said Jethro, calming down a fraction. 'I used to do business with them.'

'Used to?' said Eduard, suddenly really interested. Jethro had used the past tense. Could that mean business – big business – coming his way?

'Yeah, used to,' said Jethro. 'But no more. I ain't gonna do business with any goddam sonofabitch that employs my hooker wife.'

'Jethro, what's she done?' asked Eduard.

'I know, and that's enough,' replied Jethro. He wasn't going to tell Eduard that he'd caught his wife screwing big black Jackson. 'And the bitch is threatening to divorce me. Me! After what she's been up to. I'll have her. Man, I'll fucking have her. I'll stir so much goddam shit, she won't know whether she's on this planet or another – but not yet. I've lined up a deal and a messy divorce ain't part of my present scenario.'

Jethro paused for breath. Eduard wondered what exactly this telephone call was about. 'So what do you want me to do?' asked Eduard.

'I want you to screw her,' said Jethro.

'You want me to screw her?' exclaimed Eduard. 'How?'

'Screw her!' shouted Jethro again.

'Do you mean literally?'

'Of course I mean literally,' said Jethro, his temper rising again at Eduard's obtuseness. 'Get your goddam cock out and screw her.'

'But – ' Eduard was bemused. 'I've only met her a couple of times.'

'Jeez!' exclaimed Jethro. 'Listen, man, I want you to fuck her, okay? Seduce her, screw her, have an affair with her – anything. But get it going and I'll be over in a few days.'

'You're coming here?' asked Eduard.

'Yeah, I'm coming there,' said Jethro, 'And I want to find you in flagrante – '

'You want to find me with her?'

'Yes, you goddam parrot, that's what I said. I want to find you screwing her and I'm gonna take photographs.'

'Jethro, you're not supposed to tell me things like that,' said Eduard.

'I'm telling you because I won't have interference with my deals, and my goddam wife and her divorce petition is interfering. And it's gotta stop. I'm gonna make it worth your while. I've got some business I'm gonna put your way. Real business, real money. Without me, you can't do it. With me, you can.'

'What sort of business?' he asked. Eduard liked the idea of screwing Zinnia. She was sexy, hot to trot, he'd guessed it and, after his conversation with Kit at the polo match, he was certain she was a real goer. But if he was going to be used as a pawn for Jethro, it had to be for something extra good.

'There's a company I want to buy,' said Jethro. 'I need a few million extra. You do have a good few million to spare, Eduard, don't you? Don't bother to answer. I know you have.'

'How do you know?' asked Eduard, stunned by Jethro's accurate knowledge.

'You think I was born yesterday?' said Jethro. 'Some call it the Midas touch, others call it something else. I'm right, aren't I? I know I am. So, interested?'

'What's the company?'

'Tell you what Eduard,' said Jethro, ignoring his question, 'give in your notice to de Bouys today, screw my wife and give me fifty million.

'Fifty million! I can't,' said Eduard.

'That's how much you – er – acquired, wasn't it?'

'Thirty million,' said Eduard, quickly. 'I can give you thirty million.'

'Fine. Thirty million's just dandy,' said Jethro. 'After all, better to give it to me than to the police, eh?'

'Police?' squeaked Eduard.

'Yeah; I heard on the grapevine that de Bouys is minus about fifty million in bearer bonds,' said Jethro.

'How did you hear that?'

'Ways and means,' said Jethro.

'Jethro?'

There was a moment's silence. Eduard thought the line had gone dead. 'Jethro? Jethro?'

'Yes?'

'Does this mean we're a partnership?'

'Sure,' said Jethro. 'You're putting thirty million sterling into the deal; I'd call that a partnership, wouldn't you?'

'But, Jethro, cried Eduard, 'I don't even know what I'm buying.'

'Trust me,' said Jethro. 'Just do as I've told you and trust me. After all, Petrov and I have gotta trust you!'

'Oh yes, Petrov!' said Eduard, with a shiver. 'He's in Europe, right?'

'No, he'll be in Meriboa; and you're gonna get to meet him.'

'I couldn't believe it was you,' said Eduard, leisurely-clad for the sticky Meriboan heat in an oatmeal linen suit and a white shirt of the finest Egyptian cotton.

He was sitting opposite Zinnia, enjoying a dawn cup of coffee in the high-rise high-tech office which Hanway, Rattle and Lewis had rented in the capital of Meriboa. And he was pleased with himself. Against all the odds, against her prevarication, he had managed to pin her down, persuaded her to agree to his suggestion. Eduard had it all planned. He was going to screw Zinnia, then do a runner. The former would be a pleasure; the latter was a necessity. With Petrov arriving, who would recognise him instantly as Laurence Vladelsky, Jeanine's 'dead' husband, and Jethro guessing he was responsible for de Bouys' missing fifty million pounds worth of bearer bonds, he had no option but to disappear again – and fast.

Zinnia was wearing a shocking pink silk suit and black high-heeled shoes. She sat at a broad ebony wood desk which rested on short squat legs. In front of her was a vast window. Behind her stretched a wall of mirror that reflected her vista, the bright blue sky and the early hazy heat drifting off the palm tree-edged bay and out to the Andaman Sea.

'So, you didn't believe it was me,' said Zinnia, smiling a gorgeous seductive smile at him. 'And I couldn't believe it was you, either.'

'I'm real amazed to find you here,' said Eduard, lying. 'I thought you were in London.'

'I was,' said Zinnia, 'but the climate didn't suit. It's real good here. The atmosphere, the feel of the place: there's such a buzz. Everything's happened so fast since the military went. I mean, the buildings – '

'The Exchange – ' said Eduard.

'The life, it's good.'

'You're having fun, then?'

'Oh sure, the best,' she said. 'You can't get much more fun outta life than I'm getting.'

And what was that? Eduard wondered, as he watched a horny expression flit across her face. He felt instantly randy. He was going to enjoy fulfilling his part of the deal with Jethro. He'd wanted her before. He wanted Zinnia more than ever now. But that wasn't his initial reason for insisting on the meeting. He was under orders, but he also wanted a mystery cleared up.

He put the coffee-cup down on its saucer and looked her over. She had an easy way of walking. Sure, she was too short and plump to be a model in a glossy magazine but her hour-glass figure meant she was a real woman. And her red hair, tumbling down over her shoulders, was an enticing and sexual invitation. She reminded him of a lollipop and he had a wild desire to lick her from top to bottom. Prim, uptight Sapphire was forgotten. Zinnia turned him on.

'I believe we have a friend in common,' he said.

'Oh?' she looked at him questioningly.

'An old lady,' he said, taking up his cup again and sipping carefully.

'An old lady?' exclaimed Zinnia, reaching out across

the desk for the coffee pot. 'Would you like some more coffee,'

'No, thank you,' said Eduard, watching her skirt riding up, giving him a good view of her stockings tops and her bare thighs.

'How is Jethro?' she asked. Better to be up front; it saved a lot of agony.

'Ringing me in a couple of hours. He should be arriving any day soon,' replied Eduard guilelessly.

'Oh,' she said. 'Business?'

'Yes.'

'With you?' she asked.

'Yes,' he replied.

'But, he always works with us, with Hanway's,' she said.

'Not this time,' he said.

'Oh, small time, eh?' she said patronisingly.

'I wouldn't say so,' replied Eduard, slightly needled.

'Flotation or take-over?' she asked.

'That's for me to know and you to find out,' said Eduard, hedging. He was still in ignorance of Jethro's intentions.

There was a slight silence. They looked at each other. She smiled. When he saw her smile, he relaxed.

'So we've dispensed with coffee and Jethro, any more questions before you answer mine?' Eduard asked.

'Yours?'

'Yes. Countess Jacqueline Helitzer; I believe you know her,' said Eduard. 'That's what your husband said, back in Texas.'

'Jacqueline?' exclaimed Zinnia.

'Yes, Jacqueline,' said Eduard lazily, letting the information sink in. 'What Jethro actually said was you'd gone to see an old countess who was giving a tea party in London.'

'Oh,' said Zinnia, catching Eduard's eye and realising he knew what she knew about Jacqueline.

'Tell me, how was the um – er – tea party?' he asked.'

'It didn't take place,' said Zinnia.

'Oh, it didn't? Why was that?' he asked.

'People and things didn't arrive and then some people and things disappeared – left without warning. Upset various plans.'

'Jeanine's plans?' he asked.

'Yes, and Jacqueline's,' replied Zinnia. 'You know Jeanine, too?'

'I've met her once or twice, a long time ago, before she started up her 'hotel',' he said, conjuring up visions of his wife. 'I believe she runs a very interesting place.'

'Yes, she does,' said Zinnia.

'But Jethro hasn't been there,' stated Eduard.

'Oh yes, he has,' contradicted Zinnia.

'Did he like it?' asked Eduard.

'I don't think so,' said Zinnia.

'He didn't?' exclaimed Eduard, thinking that explained a lot. If Jethro didn't like, or want, the various opportunities that were purported to be on offer at Jeanine's, then he really was a quick in-and-out merchant with little or no understanding of sex and love and lust. And lust was uppermost in Eduard's mind. Zinnia was sexy – very sexy – and he wanted to get his hands on her luscious breasts. He could feel himself rising and crossed his legs.

Zinnia stood up and put her coffee-cup on a tray.

'Well, Eduard, nice to meet you again,' she said, holding out her hand as if she was dismissing him.

Eduard didn't move. He didn't want her to see his erection. Not yet.

'Zinnia,' he said.

'Yes.' She walked round the desk and towards the door.

'Tell me, who were you fucking when Jethro arrived at Jeanine's?' Eduard asked, making an inspired guess.

Zinnia stopped in her tracks, turned to look at Eduard and saw his hard-on.

'Jackson,' she said, smiling at him, letting her glance roam over the bulge in his trousers.

'Who's he?' asked Eduard, thinking, yes, that would have made Jethro Clarke really mad.

'A big black man with a very large cock,' she said, coming closer to the desk and Eduard's chair. 'In fact it's not only large, it's beautiful. I couldn't resist it.'

She let a hand rest on Eduard's knee, looked up into his face and licked her lips. Then the intercom rang.

'It's Sunday!' exclaimed Eduard.

'We're workaholics, here,' said Zinnia, bending over her desk to take the call, her skirt riding up again. This time he got a view of her silk directoire knickers and the curve of her bare bottom. It was too much for Eduard. His cock shot up to full size.

'Yes?' said Zinnia into the mouthpiece, her voice businesslike. There was a moment's silence while she listened to the voice at the other end. 'Yes. Very well. Yes, I will.' She replaced the receiver. 'My boss,' she said, 'reminding me of something I have to do.' She stayed bending over the desk, searching through various yellow, blue and green coloured papers.

Eduard came behind her, letting her feel the stiffness of his prick pressing against her buttocks as he put one hand between her legs, while the other undid the buttons on her suit top. She was wearing a pink satin and lace bra. Her large erect nipples poked through cut-outs. The sight of them stiffened his cock an extra few centimetres. His fingers caressed one breast, then the other, squeezing and tweaking her aroused nipples.

'That's nice,' she purred and wiggled her large well-shaped bottom.

Eduard's hand began to prowl along her thighs, experiencing the sensuousness of the silk stockings and then her soft firm flesh. Zinnia spread her legs and stuck out her buttocks. He knew she could feel the stiffness of his cock through his linen suit.

'Fuck me,' she whispered.

'What did you say?' asked Eduard.

'Fuck me,' she said; only this time she said it with more force and louder.

'You are a randy bitch,' he said.

'Did you think anything else?' she asked.

'No, not after I found out you knew Jacqueline Helitzer,' he said, undoing the buttons on his flies. 'So you've been to her place in the Bois de Boulogne?'

'Oh yes,' she said, and wiggled her bottom again. 'Oh yes, I've been there . . .'

Keeping her legs straight, she flattened her torso over the desk. Eduard pushed up her skirt, displaying her pink silk knickers clinging to the roundness of her buttocks.

Eduard put on a condom and rubbed his cock against her thighs. Leisurely, he stroked her through her silk panties. He wound his fingers up under the damp material, touching her wet sex lips and then her clitoris. With her arms outstretched, holding hard to the far edge of the desk, Zinnia tensed her belly and jerked towards his exploring penis, inviting him to enter her wet self.

He pulled down her panties – but not to the floor. He let them rest below her bottom globes. He patted her hard, marking her pale pink rump with a deeper red. Then he lay his prick on the elastic of her knickers, its head just touching her wet sex. She gasped as his thick, warm, throbbing tool skimmed her swollen labia, backwards and forwards. The sweet chafing of the elastic gave him pleasure as he put the tip of his prick at her wanton entrance. He gave a couple of tiny movements, enough to tease her but not to penetrate.

'Oh please, please, fuck me,' begged Zinnia.

Eduard bent his legs and slowly let his cock trail along her thighs. Zinnia gasped. He touched her clitoris with one finger. Zinnia clenched her buttocks, raising them high, inviting him to enter her. Eduard put the tip of his prick at her warm wet inviting sex again and gave a couple of tiny movements, still teasing her and not penetrating her.

'Hard,' said Zinnia. 'I want you to fuck me hard.'

Eduard pushed again at the entrance to her sex. She opened at his touch. He slid in slowly, very slowly, and she took his large cock that was stiff and wanting her. Holding her love handles, he slid in. She gasped with each pressure, with each jerk he gave, invading her little by little, further and further, until she had taken his large cock to the hilt. With a gentle rhythm he rode her and then he caught sight of the mirrored wall parting, opening.

Two slim, handsome, dark skinned Meriboans stood like a couple of sentinels immediately inside the split wall. They were dressed identically in tight black leather trousers, which emphasised their genitalia, and metal rings and studs and keys were paraded on their heavy leather belts. Neither wore a shirt but they did wear long black leather gauntlets.

'You are not to fuck in the office without permission,' said one of them.

Zinnia lifted her head. 'And who are you?' she asked, angrily.

'Lu and Du,' they answered, 'and we must see your permission.'

'Now?' she said, rising up, displaying her huge breasts and her erect, aroused nipples poking through their specially-made apertures.

'Yes,' they said in unison.

Zinnia scrabbled amongst the pieces of green, yellow and blue coloured paper on her desk then handed a blue form to one of them. He read it.

'No, not good,' he said. 'Please to come with us.'

Before Eduard knew what was happening, the two men had leapt across the desk. One forced him out of Zinnia, pinioned his arms behind his back and clamped handcuffs around his wrists. The other took off Zinnia's knickers. And a third man appeared and marched Zinnia out through the split in the mirrored wall into the solid darkness beyond. The mirror closed fast behind her. Eduard was left alone with the two men, Lu and Du.

'You were a very naughty girl,' said Caradoc Lewis, reaching for her bare round bottom as the third man placed her in front of his chair.

'I was, wasn't I, but did you enjoy it?' said Zinnia, rolling her hips.

'Oh, yes, very much,' he replied. 'See.' He took her hand and guided it to his lap, where his prick was peeking out through his trousers.

'Who is he?' Zinnia asked, pointing at the third man who had retreated into the shadows.

'That's Mu,' he said. 'So Jethro's planning something big.'

'You think so?'

'Yes.'

'Why? Why do you think that?'

'Because when you hinted that it could only be a small deal he got irritated, as if you'd insulted him. We've got to find out what it is,' said Caradoc.

'What are they going to do with Eduard now?' Zinnia asked, closing her fingers around Caradoc's upright member and feeling all its ridges as she let her hand run up and down, up and down.

'Sit on my lap, watch and listen; the office is, as you've guessed, wired for sound,' he said.

In the soft gloom of the room Zinnia positioned herself either side of Caradoc's immobile legs and eased her wet sex down on to his erect penis. Both of them looked towards the wall that had just closed. They had a perfect view of the office through a huge two-way mirror.

'That's Du holding his arms,' said Caradoc.

They watched Lu saunter over to Eduard, kiss him firmly on the lips then goose him with one of his black leather gauntleted hands. The next moment, Lu's fingers were burrowing inside Eduard's flies. Eduard had gone limp when he'd been jumped on by the two Meriboans. Lu withdrew Eduard's semi-flaccid prick and let it lie outside his trousers.

'We thought white men had big cocks,' said Lu. 'Yours is puny. Look, Du, a little prick.'

'What do you think he's going to do now?' asked Caradoc. 'Will he play with him or suck him?'

'Bet you a thousand he'll bend down and suck him,' said Zinnia, slowly lifting herself up, letting Caradoc feel

198

her inner muscles contracting around his penis before sliding down quickly, making him gasp.

Lu walked around Du, who was holding Eduard still, and undid Du's flies; his long, thin, brown and very erect cock sprang out. Lu then eased Du's balls from their tight leather casing. Then he undid Eduard's trousers and pulled them to the floor. Du slid his penis against Eduard's hips. At the licentious feel of another man's cock on his sensitive skin, Eduard's prick swelled forward with desire.

'Maybe not so small,' said Lu. 'Maybe worthy of attention.'

Lu bent down, ringed Eduard's sex tool with his gloved fingers and stroked it; then he opened his mouth and placed Eduard's prick between his lips. Moving his head up and down, he slowly encompassed his entire member.

'One thousand pounds to you,' said Caradoc, sneaking his hands around Zinnia's large breasts and massaging her nipples.

Zinnia, who had perfected the art of squeezing a cock with her inner muscles, squeezed and smiled. Before she could reply, her eyes were caught by Lu unzipping himself. He pulled his own long thin erect prick free from his leather trousers and began rubbing it himself while he carried on sucking Eduard's cock.

'You didn't have a pink form,' said Du.

'A pink form,' said Eduard, bemused.

'We will have to report you,' said Du.

'Report me?' exclaimed Eduard. 'Where? To whom?'

'To the man who owns this building,' said Du. 'This is a respectable office; we cannot allow sex to take place here.'

'But – ' Eduard started to say. He was bewildered. He looked down at the man working his cock and at the other man's sliding against his hips. 'What are you two doing?'

'We have permission,' said Du. 'Now walk.'

Du gave Eduard a prod in the back and marched him

to the side of the desk, where he could easily be seen by the hidden watchers.

'Bend,' ordered Du, pushing him in the small of the back. With his hands manacled behind his back, Eduard keeled over towards the desk. Du brought his hand round and started to massage Eduard's thick cock. Lu stood up, undid Eduard's lawn shirt and pulled the sleeves down past his shoulders, to his elbows. Then he took the tail end of the shirt and rolled it around the fabric stretched across Eduard's back: his neat bum was on view and ready for fucking.

'You see what you have done by your outrageous behaviour,' said Caradoc, his cock moving inside Zinnia; she carried on riding him, excited by the players in the mirror.

Lu knelt down on the floor and brought out hidden chains with ankle irons that were attached to the base of the short squat desk legs. He clapped the irons around Eduard's ankles.

'They weren't there yesterday,' said Zinnia.

'No, my dear,' Caradoc replied. 'I had them put there late last night. I thought there was a possibility we might enjoy using them.'

'And now what?' Zinnia asked.

'Watch,' said Caradoc, squeezing her nipples.

Du jumped on the desk, took hold of Eduard's hair, pulled his head back then stuck his cock into Eduard's open mouth.

'Suck it,' he ordered.

Lu removed a key from a key-ring on the heavy leather belt around his waist. He unlocked a desk drawer and removed a whip. He stroked it lovingly, then drew it up between Eduard's outstretched legs.

'Before we report you for violation, we have to punish you,' said Lu, standing to one side so that Caradoc and Zinnia had a full and complete view of Eduard's bare buttocks and Du's prick charging in and out of his mouth.

Feeling the thin strips of leather stroking his legs while

sucking on Du's cock excited Eduard, he began to shake with anticipation.

Lu moved closer to him, took hold of Eduard's cock with one gloved hand and gently rubbed it. Eduard swayed and closed his eyes with pleasure. Lu began moving the whip along the crack of Eduard's bottom.

Zinnia moved her hand down to play with her enlarged excited bud.

'No,' said Caradoc, 'I will.' He put his own hand down so that he could feel his cock easing in and out of her while he touched her aroused and well lubricated clitoris. Zinnia sighed as his fingers hit the spot that made her tremble.

Caradoc pressed a bell on a small table beside him. The mirrored wall slid open. Caradoc talked into the intercom. 'Bring him to me,' he ordered.

Lu removed the chains from the desk legs, but kept the irons around Eduard's ankles and locked the chains together, holding them as he marched Eduard into the darkness to be confronted by Caradoc Lewis.

A light was shone on him. Eduard was unable to see Zinnia sitting on her boss's lap, screwing him.

'Something tells me you were looking forward to the lash,' said Caradoc menacingly. 'But you will only know complete humiliation if you tell us what Jethro Clarke is doing, coming here to Meriboa.'

'He's coming here to work,' said Eduard.

'That much we know already,' said the older man. 'what is he coming here to do?'

'To make a deal,' said Eduard.

Feeling the whip trailing across his naked buttocks and then being poked into his bottom-mouth made Eduard shudder with fear and excitement. Lu decided to add to both by unexpectedly bringing the whip down hard on Eduard's rump.

Eduard jumped.

'What sort of a deal? Is Jethro Clarke coming here to buy?' asked Caradoc Lewis.

Du jerked Eduard's arms up his back; Lu brought the

whip down harder on his neat backside. Harder, much harder. Eduard screamed. Du took hold of Eduard's penis and massaged it, rubbing his own against Eduard's naked thighs.

'Is Jethro Clarke coming here to buy?'

'Yes.'

'What?'

'A company,' said Eduard, experiencing the delightful but almost unbearable combination of pain and pleasure. Du carried on playing with him. Lu started to trail the whip across the burning marks on his bottom. Eduard stiffened.

'Relax,' said Caradoc, softly. 'Relax; there is no need for anything but pleasure. Would you like to screw Mrs Clarke again?'

'Yes,' said Eduard, hoarsely.

'Very well, you can – you will – but not right now. Because right now, I'm fucking her.'

The light was switched from Eduard on to Caradoc in his wheelchair, with Zinnia sitting astride him, visibly riding Caradoc's penis.

'Mrs Clarke is enjoying herself, aren't you, my dear?'

'Oh yes,' she said, and massaged her own nipples to show Eduard just how much pleasure she was giving and receiving.

'Fucking me and watching him having his backside tanned. You like that, don't you?'

'Yes,' she said.

Caradoc played with her clitoris as she rode up and down on him. 'Mrs Clarke enjoys being fucked, don't you?'

'Yes,' she said, rising up so that Eduard could see the full length of Caradoc's cock, then slowly easing down on him again.

'But her husband might not enjoy seeing the evidence we have of you screwing her,' said Caradoc.

And Eduard laughed.

'He doesn't believe us,' mocked Caradoc Lewis.

Immediately on a wall in front of his eyes, Eduard

watched film of himself taking down Zinnia's panties and placing his cock at her warm, wet and wanton entrance.

The video was turned off and the spotlight swivelled back on to Eduard.

'Believe us now?' said Caradoc. 'Or would you like us to show you as you were a moment ago, sucking Du's cock while Lu fingered your bare arse? I got the feeling your friend Jethro wasn't too keen on deviants. Especially deviants associated with himself. So, Eduard, what's it to be? Don't fool around with me, or my friends might get nasty.'

'Oh, yes?' said Eduard sarcastically.

'Very nasty,' said Caradoc. 'Talk, Eduard del Sur – if that is your real name. Talk. I want to know about Jethro Clarke.'

'Do you?' sneered Eduard.

'Yes, I do. You see, I need to know what he's up to. But, most of all, I need to know who he's gone into partnership with.'

'What makes you think he's gone into partnership with anybody?' asked Eduard.

'Because I know Jethro, and he's careful. He never uses all his own money for anything. He's planning something and he's planning it with someone. You, I know about. But you're small fry. He needs someone with clout, real clout. It's usually us. Now this means we're losing out. So I want to know who it is.'

'Tough,' said Eduard.

'Sit him down in that chair,' ordered Caradoc.

Zinnia realised he didn't appreciate Eduard's attitude and was burning on a slow fuse. Mu appeared and placed a chair behind Eduard. Lu pushed him into it. 'Now bring me the board.'

A strip of wood half a metre long by fifteen centimetres wide and five centimetres thick was brought and shown to Eduard. 'Place it across his lap and put his cock on it. And don't try to struggle,' he added, to Eduard, 'there's no point.'

Du put the board across Eduard's lap. Lu placed his cock on it. It had shrivelled at the thought of harm but Lu's fingers started working him again and unsatisfied lust took over. Eduard's cock surged forward with Lu's expert handling.

'Now, unless you tell us exactly what you're doing with Jethro Clarke, I shall ask my friends here to nail your foreskin to that plank,' said Caradoc, indicating to Mu to come forward with a hammer and some long sharp tacks.

Zinnia couldn't believe her ears or her eyes. Games were one thing, but this was wicked. Wickedness had no part in her life.

'There are some people who would regard it as a pleasure but I have a feeling that you are not one of them,' said Caradoc.

Eduard began to struggle. Du held him down. Lu squeezed his cock, extending his foreskin along the plank. Mu advanced with the hammer and tacks.

Zinnia was appalled. This was going beyond reason. This was not fun. She knew Caradoc Lewis was ruthless, but she hadn't guessed how ruthless. What he could do to Eduard, he could do to her. How could she have been taken in by him? Perhaps she was a rotten judge of character.

Well, now that she'd discovered Caradoc's real personality, his cruelty, she wasn't going to be a party to it. Zinnia decided at that moment she no longer wanted to be employed by Hanway, Rattle and Lewis. She certainly didn't want to screw Caradoc Lewis ever again.

Mu was holding a long thin tack against Eduard's stretched foreskin.

'No,' screamed Zinnia. 'No!'

'Be quiet, you stupid cow,' said Caradoc Lewis, and pushed her. Zinnia fell in a heap on the floor.

Mu began to stick the sharp tack into a piece of Eduard's highly sensitive foreskin.

'I'll tell you,' said Eduard, dreading the coming pain.

'How very sensible of you,' said Caradoc.

'Jethro Clarke is after a company, a blue chip company, and he's doing it in partnership with me,' said Eduard.

'You? You?' shouted Caradoc. 'He can't possibly do it with you. You need millions. And you haven't got enough.'

'I've more than you,' said Eduard calmly, almost smugly.

'More than me?' said Caradoc. 'You're crazy.'

'No,' said Eduard. 'No, I'm not. There's a whisper on the street that Hanway, Rattle and Lewis are about to take a tumble.'

'What? What did you say?' hissed Caradoc Lewis, wheeling his chair up in front of Eduard.

'Your bank's about to crash, that's what they're saying on Wall Street,' stated Eduard.

'You're lying.'

'No. Your son. Wrong decisions. Maybe Jethro heard it too and isn't taking any chances.'

'Get them out of here,' screeched Caradoc, wheeling himself around the room in a temper, almost unable to contain his fury. 'Get them out of here. I want to call my son.'

Lu and Du undid the Eduard's chains. Mu opened up the mirrored wall. Eduard walked through, put on his clothes and departed.

Moments later, shaken by the preceding events and without a word to Caradoc Lewis, Zinnia followed Eduard out of the building.

Outside in the bright sunlight, Zinnia saw Eduard looking up at the building, waiting for her. She was walking towards him when a man appeared from nowhere and tapped him on the shoulder.

'Laurence?' he said. Zinnia saw Eduard jump, startled. 'Laurence Vladelsky, I am arresting you for fraud and misappropriation of funds.'

Chapter Ten

Sapphire was trying to avoid the heat and the sun of Meriboa as she made her way to her father's lawyers' offices. She was wearing a new chiffon and devorée cream suit, with a large floppy black hat and sunglasses, and was walking the one block from her hotel to the huge steel and glass skyscraper where they were situated.

She was nervous and apprehensive. She had a deep mistrust of the lawyers and this had made her all the more determined to look glamorous and let them think, as men frequently did on first meeting, that she was a silly little thing with not a thought in her head. She had no inkling of what to expect. Would she be rich, moderately well off – or had her father cut her out of his will for not pandering to his every whim?

She was deep in thought when a sudden gust of wind came up and whipped off her hat into the kerb by a set of traffic lights on red. She was grateful for that – otherwise her incredibly expensive hat would have been completely crushed by an enormous limousine waiting for them to change. She ran after it, her lovely red-gold hair shining and glowing in the sunlight. The lights changed to green but the car didn't start, allowing her time to pick it up. She then waved and smiled a thank you to the driver.

'Sapphire?' the driver shouted at her as the windows rolled down electronically.

Sapphire peered in.

'Auralie!' she exclaimed in joy and amazement. 'Auralie, what are you doing in Meriboa?'

'I could ask the same thing, *chérie*,' said Auralie. 'Get in quickly, before the lights change again.'

Without thinking, Sapphire did as she was told.

'Oh, Auralie! It's wonderful to see you,' said Sapphire.

'Sapphy, you're looking amazing, quite amazing,' said Auralie. 'Very chic and very sexy.'

Sapphire gave a soft smile. 'So are you, but then that's usual,' she said, seeing the building looming up ahead and remembering she was virtually at her destination and with only minutes to spare before her appointment. 'Auralie, Auralie – stop. I'd love to chat but I can't. I have an appointment there that I must keep.'

'Oh, that's a pity,' said Auralie. 'It must be with a wonderful man.'

'Er ... No,' replied Sapphire, wondering whether to tell Auralie about the lawyers and her father's will then deciding against it. 'Business.'

'I'm going to the airport and will be back in an hour; why don't we meet then?' asked Auralie.

'Sure,' she said; then, not knowing how long the meeting would take, added, 'No, not a good idea. I might be late.'

'I'll wait,' said Auralie. 'Look, Sapphy, there's a café by the entrance I'll see you there in one hour: and don't worry, I'll have a drink and stay until you arrive.'

'That's just great,' said Sapphire, pecking Auralie on the cheek and feeling quite relieved to see someone she knew, and more than happy that it was Auralie. It was nice, too, to hear her pet name again. Comforting – and she needed some comforting. 'You can tell me all about yourself too. Your company's been doing very well.'

'Not my company, any more,' said Auralie.

'No? I thought you had shares in it,' said Sapphire.

'Have you sold them? What's going on? I've been travelling and not seen a paper for days.'

'I'll tell you all about it later,' said Auralie, slowing down to park.

While Auralie brought the limousine to a halt, Sapphire replaced her hat on her head and checked her lipstick. With a brief wave, she swung her long legs out of the car and, without a backward glance, went into the building to find out what her future would be.

Auralie drove on to the airport where she was going to pick up Jacqueline. She had difficulty finding a parking place and was slightly later than she'd intended to be. Jacqueline was already through customs and waiting, but not alone. She was sitting on a bench, talking intimately to an elegant older woman.

Not wanting to interrupt their private conversation, Auralie stood to one side, assessing Jacqueline's companion. She was tall, with a good figure, in her forties; she had striking dark blue eyes, high cheekbones and a full wide mouth. Tendrils of red-blonde curls escaped from her neat turban; she looked as fresh as a daisy in her Paris couturier clothes. Then a chauffeur arrived, picked up the other woman's baggage and, with a quick touching of cheeks, the older woman left and Jacqueline looked around for Auralie.

'Darling,' said Jacqueline, clasping Auralie to her breast. 'What a flight!'

'So who was she?' asked Auralie, full of curiosity.

'An old friend,' said Jacqueline.

'I met one too, just now, on my way here,' said Auralie, interrupting. 'Sapphire Western.'

'She was Lady Rosamund Ware de Bouys,' said Jacqueline.

'De Bouys!' exclaimed Auralie angrily – and the anger stopped her train of thought. That was the last name she expected. 'Oh God! I can never get away from them, even here. Sir Henry, Everett, Gerry, and now –'

'Yes Gerry. Poor Gerry. I was watching him in London.

Jeanine has your poor little husband exactly where she wants him. How do you say, by the short and curlies?' said Jacqueline.

'Time he grew up,' said Auralie, dismissively. She pitied Gerry, these days. She'd tried to get him to do something for himself. One day, while he was sitting waiting lovelorn for Jeanine, Auralie had talked to him, told him it would be a good idea if he did something for himself – stopped hanging around Jeanine and cut himself off from his father. But he wouldn't; he said he couldn't. Auralie was frightened for him. There could come a time when Sir Henry might push him out into the world and then where would he be? What would he do?

'Now, darling,' said Jacqueline, linking her arm through Auralie's, 'where's the limo and what have you got planned?'

'The car's in the car park and I haven't planned anything until you got here, except I've booked us a suite at the Hotel Lin Chiau.'

'Is it good?'

'Oh, yes. It'll suit us very well; it's discreet.'

'Excellent,' said Jacqueline.

They collected the car and then drove into the city along the coast road, past palm trees and golden sands and the blue, blue sea.

'Oh, darling, it's beautiful here,' said Jacqueline, gazing out of the window. 'Maybe this is where I should have my party.'

'There's something familiar about that woman you were talking to,' said Auralie, returning to her earlier train of thought. 'Tell me about her. I mean, how does she fit in? Where did you two meet? What's she doing in Meriboa?'

'I've know her most of my life. She was my mother's best friend and she's an Aussie, so it's not surprising she's here in Meriboa. It's a stopping-off point between Australia and Europe. She's Sir Henry's cousin – and apparently here on family business.'

'Is she the proper, proper one that lives in Darling Harbour, Sydney?'

'That's the one. I asked her to come and have a coffee but she said no. She has an appointment, some matter that's got to be cleared up. She married a James something or another – a major general in the British army. They travelled all over and when he died, she went back to Australia, reverted to her maiden name and stayed put.'

'They didn't have any children?'

'No, they didn't,' said Jacqueline, emphasising the 'they'.

'She did?'

'Yes and it was all hushed up, darling, a big secret!'

'Underage?'

'No, but almost,' said Jacqueline. 'She'd had an affair with somebody or another. I never knew who and if my mother did, the secret died with her. I worked it out that he had to be rich and unsuitable. Rich, because he paid all the bills, so her family would never discover what she'd been up to; and unsuitable, because she was free to marry and didn't. And in those days, if you got pregnant, you married. A year or so later, she met and wed this James. I don't know what happened but it was rumoured she couldn't have *les enfants*. Of course, sometimes it is just a little rumour because men, especially Forces men, cannot bear to think they can't procreate. Whichever, she didn't have any children by him.'

'So she had an abortion?'

'No; she had the baby and it was adopted.'

'Oh! Was it a boy or a girl?'

'No idea,' said Jacqueline.

'Do you think she thinks about the one she did have?' asked Auralie.

'I don't know,' said Jacqueline. 'I would. I think most women do, when a child is adopted.'

'Do you know her very well?'

'No, darling, I wouldn't say that. She was my unofficial godmother; she kept an eye on me from a distance. I always knew I could rely on her if things got bad.

'Did they?'

'Oh yes. Very bad, darling, very difficult. Once, when I was very young and living with this man in Wales. He was awful, cruel. I was virtually a prisoner in his castle but I managed to make one telephone call – to Rosamund, in Australia. And she helped me. She told me to get to Paris and gave me an introduction to the Count. "He's looking for a young wife," she said, "and he's a silly old fool. He wants an impossibility. Very beautiful, very old-fashioned, very soft and gentle: so you be that and you'll never need to worry again." So I was all those things, darling, and he died three months later, a very happy man. And I became a very rich widow.'

'What did you have to do for him?' asked Auralie perceptively.

'Why do you ask?'

'Usually you have to do something special for a rich old man.'

'You're quite right,' said Jacqueline dryly. 'Poor Rosamund; she couldn't have known what Helitzer wanted wasn't old-fashioned, soft and gentle. It was submissiveness. Total submission to his every whim. And I realised, darling. I obliged. And he married me. At first it was hard, but the idea of poverty was worse so – '

'What did he want?'

'Games, darling, always games. He was the master and I was his little lap dog. Every evening I had to take off all my clothes. He put a strong metal studded collar around my neck, which was attached to him by a long lead. I had to curl up in a basket beside him. He would stroke my back and my bottom while he watched the news on the television. Then, when it was dinner time, I had to crawl on all fours and sit under the table at his feet. He would throw me the food he didn't want. Half-eaten food, the bones – just like you do to a dog.'

'Did you eat it?'

'Oh yes, I had to. That's all I got until morning.'

'And then?'

'He would get up from the table, call for the butler and say he was taking the dog for a walk. I had to crawl behind him. The butler collected his coat and helped him into it. Then he handed him his single-thonged leather dog whip, and we would go out into the garden. I had to crawl behind him until we got to a certain tree, where I had to lift my leg and pee. He would stand watching, staring at my stream.

'When I'd finished, the butler would come out with something wrapped in paper. "The bitch has misbehaved again, sir," he would say, showing the count whatever was in the package. And the count would say, "Bad dog, you're a bad dog and you must learn your lesson." And out there in the garden, with the butler watching and holding the leash, he would whip me. The lash would come biting down on my buttocks, and I would squirm.

'He would mark me until the welts were purple and then would kneel behind me, spread apart my burning halves and take me, take me at the back. When he'd finished, he'd say to the butler, "Put her in the kennel." And the butler would lead me away to a small room near the kitchen, where there was a dog bed. There he would chain me to the wall and, before he left for the night, he would screw me. After that, I could sleep. At first light the butler would come back and unhook me from my chains. I could bathe and be the elegant countess again, until the evening when the count came home.'

'Every day?'

'Most days, yes. Unless there was some special event, or a reception when we both had to be present.'

'Did Rosamund know this?'

'No, darling, no. I think she would have been shocked: very shocked indeed.'

'How old is she?'

'Forty-something. She was younger than my mother,' said Jacqueline.

212

'That's what I thought,' said Auralie. 'Oh, and Zinnia's here.'

'No! Where?' asked Jacqueline.

'Staying at the Staples Hotel. That's why I didn't book us in there. I saw her yesterday, coming out and getting into a cab with a very handsome young man.'

'How do you know she's staying there?'

'I rang the hotel and asked to speak to her.'

'Oh yes, that was sensible. So now what? Shall we go to Minmex and see if Jethro's there?'

'Minmex?'

'Minmex, the exchange,' said Auralie. 'Jethro won't be far from the money. And where Jethro is, we'll find Petrov and Ana Tai.'

'First the hotel. I need a rest and a bath, darling,' said Jacqueline.

'*Oui, naturellement,*' said Auralie, feeling a great swell of gratitude towards the Countess who, seeing her plight and her emotional state, had engineered her escape from Petrov's mansion as soon as he had left for the airport. The two of them had planned on going to Paris but, at Geneva airport, Jacqueline had met Carola Finestein who told her she'd seen Jethro and Ana Tai taking the plane for Meriboa. Leaving Jacqueline to go to Paris to attend to some business, Auralie had gone East.

'What was Carola doing with Everett de Bouys? Did you find out?' asked Auralie.

'She said – and wait for this, darling – Jeanine had sent for him. Carola was his sexy little messenger and she was taking him back to London so that he could marry her.'

'Marry who? Carola?' asked Auralie, bewildered.

'No darling, Jeanine.'

'Jeanine!'

'Yes. Madame Jeanine's getting her own way again,' said Jacqueline.

'Oh, *mon Dieu*; everything just falls into line for that bitch,' said Auralie.

'Well, some things were going wrong, darling,' said

Jacqueline, cheerfully. 'Such a temper she was in before she went stalking off to see her mother. Such a temper.'

'Why?' said Auralie.

'Don't know, exactly. All I do know is she wanted Everett. She told me so. "That is the one, sweetie," she said. You know how she talks. She told me this Everett has everything. He's good in bed, very imaginative. He has plenty of money, so he won't be after hers. And you and I know that whatever Jeanine wants, Jeanine gets . . .'

'Oh yes,' said Auralie, remembering Laurence. Her love, Laurence. And Jeanine had swooped in and taken him. 'God help any other woman who likes or loves Everett, she'll take him.'

'I don't think there is anybody else,' said Jacqueline. 'I didn't get that impression. I don't think Carola is his type.'

'Lucky for her,' said Auralie, pulling up outside their hotel.

Once inside, they bought a couple of newspapers, then retired to their suite. Jacqueline took a bath and Auralie sat whiling away the time, reading the various journals from cover to cover, including the financial pages.

'This is weird,' Auralie said to Jacqueline as the countess got out of the bath and began to dress.

'What is?' asked Jacqueline.

'Petolg Holdings' price is down,' said Auralie. 'It shouldn't be. Somebody must be selling short. But why? With Jeanine wanting a buy-out, the price should be going up.'

'Well then, aren't you glad you got out when you did?' asked Jacqueline, slithering a striped black and maroon silk frock over her superb and naked body.

'*Mais oui, chérie*,' said Auralie sincerely. 'I gave Jeanine my resignation, you know.'

'Did you?'

'Yes, the day I went to Petrov's. I thought, she's so greedy and nasty I don't want anything more to do with her. So I wrote the letter and posted it. That's the end of her as far as I'm concerned.'

'Excellent.

The telephone rang. Jacqueline answered. 'Oh, darling,' said the countess, handing the receiver to Auralie with a look of surprise, 'it's for you.'

'Who is it?' asked Auralie warily. She didn't think anybody knew where they were.

'Who is it?' asked Jacqueline, and paused. 'Gerry?'

'Gerry!' exclaimed Auralie, taking the phone from Jacqueline. 'Where are you?'

'Here, in Meriboa,' he replied.

'Who told you we were here?'

'Carola,' he said.

'Carola did?'

'Well, she told Jeanine she saw you at the airport and I overheard her. Auralie, my father wants to see you.'

'Your father wants to see me?' she exclaimed. 'Why? Why does Sir Henry want to see me?'

'I don't know,' he said.

'Look, Gerry, I don't understand any of this. Where are you?'

'At the Staples Hotel,' he said. 'With my father. Could you make it over for lunch?'

'What time?'

'Noon,' he said.

Auralie checked her watch. It was almost 10.30. Time she went to meet Sapphire.

'No, I can't,' she said. Jacqueline looked at her queryingly. 'Late lunch, say 2.30? I can do that.'

'Fine,' he said.

'Why couldn't you see him at noon?' asked Jacqueline as Auralie replaced the receiver.

'Because I've just remembered I said I'd meet my friend Sapphire. Do you want to come with me?'

'No, thank you. I'm a little tired. I'll wait for you here.'

'Do you want to see Sir Henry?'

'Not particularly, but I'm intrigued. That's two weird

things so far today,' said Auralie, replacing the receiver. 'There'll be a third.'

'What was the other one?' asked Jacqueline.

'Petolg Holdings' share price, of course,' said Auralie.

'So what will you wear, darling, for this mystery appointment with your ex-father-in-law?' asked Jacqueline.

'Oh, if I'm going to see him, something very strait-laced and respectable, don't you think?'

'Yes, darling,' said Jacqueline. 'Wear the dark green with the A-line skirt.

Auralie took it from the wardrobe and put it on. 'But I won't wear any panties,' she said, smiling sexily at Jacqueline while putting a wide-brimmed exotic creation on her head. 'Access at all times.'

Sapphire was sitting drinking iced coffee in the cool, chrome and marble air-conditioned café-bar.

When she'd first arrived and expecting Auralie to be there, Sapphire had been bursting with her incredible news. She hadn't been able to take in everything that had happened in the lawyer's office. She was in deep shock and thought by repeating it, telling what had occurred to someone, especially an old friend, might make the whole episode feel more real.

But as time ticked by, the impact mellowed and gradually Sapphire began to change her mind. When Auralie eventually appeared, Sapphire had definitely decided to keep her information to herself. She was not going to tell anyone what she'd learnt and that, apart from some minor bequests to her brother and various family retainers, she was her father's sole beneficiary and an incredibly rich woman.

'So sorry I'm late,' said Auralie. 'Gerry phoned me.

'Gerry? Your ex-husband Gerry?'

'Yes; he wants me to have lunch with him and his father, for some reason. Can't think what for, so that's why I'm going, but I made it later so we can have time together. Now tell me, Sapphy, how was your business?'

'Fine,' replied Sapphire.

'Très bien,' said Auralie. 'In that case, chérie, stop the coffee and let's drink cocktails. I'll need some Dutch courage for my meeting. I'll have a Kir Royale – and you?'

'A Bellini,' replied Sapphire.

Sipping their drinks, the two young women talked and chatted; gradually Sapphire had opened up her heart to Auralie, telling her how she'd fallen for a man and how beautifully he had seduced her. She hadn't got as far as telling her friend how Carola Finestein was in his office before Auralie interrupted.

'Does this paragon have a name?' asked Auralie.

'Yes; Everett de Bouys,' replied Sapphire shyly.

'Everett de Bouys?' exploded Auralie. 'Oh, mon Dieu! Forget him, chérie. Forget the bastard.'

'Why?' asked Sapphire, quite taken aback by the vehemence in Auralie's voice.

'I've just heard he's going to marry my bitch cousin, Jeanine.'

'Jeanine?' exclaimed Sapphire. 'Everett's going to marry Jeanine?'

'That's what I heard.'

'Oh no,' said Sapphire and burst into tears.

'Oh, I'm sorry,' said Auralie, putting an arm around Sapphire. 'Now you must forget him.'

'It's not that easy,' said Sapphire tearfully.

'Yes it is; you fuck someone else,' said Auralie defiantly.

'Auralie!' said Sapphire, her old-fashioned primness returning. Then she thought, well, perhaps Auralie had the right idea. 'Who?'

'I don't know who,' said Auralie, her eyes wandering over her friend's chest. 'Have you ever had a woman?'

'No; don't be ridiculous,' said Sapphire, quite shocked, but less shocked than she would have been had she not drunk three Bellinis. 'Why, have you?'

'Yes.'

'Oh!' said Sapphire, leaning across the table. 'What's it like?'

'Exciting, *chérie*,' said Auralie. 'Soft, and – ' Auralie licked her lips. ' – and juicy.

'What do you do?' asked Sapphire.

'Kiss, and stroke and suck,' said Auralie, lingering on the word suck.

'Suck?'

'Yes. Another one?' asked Auralie, indicating the empty cocktail glass.

'Yes,' said Sapphire, throwing all caution to the wind. 'What do you suck?'

'Pussy,' said Auralie, hailing the waiter.

'Pussy! You mean, down there?'

'Yes, that's right; between your legs,' said Auralie; then as the waiter came up, added, 'two more please.'

'Oh Auralie, how naughty you are. I'm sure you're just teasing me,' said Sapphire.

'You could say that,' said Auralie.

'You'll be telling me soon you've had a man and woman together,' said Sapphire.

'I have,' said Auralie.

'No!' said Sapphire. 'Oh, Auralie!'

The waiter brought their drinks and Sapphire quickly sipped hers. She was fascinated and appalled.

'Are you wet?' asked Auralie, not drinking her cocktail.

'What?'

'Are you wet? I mean can you feel yourself opening?' asked Auralie again.

Sapphire didn't want to answer straight away. She was ashamed of the tingling in her belly, the sudden feeling of excitement that was flooding through her lips into her belly and then down to her sex.

'You are wet, aren't you, Sapphy?'

Sapphire, not trusting herself to say anything, looked around the room, as if that would help her with her answer. 'Yes, I am,' she admitted, nodding her head.

'Have your nipples gone stiff?'

'Yes,' said Sapphire; then, in a whisper added, 'tell me about it, Auralie. Tell me.'

'You've never done it?'

'No!'

'You've never been laid by a woman?'

'No.'

'You've never been screwed by two people?'

'No,' said Sapphire, draining her cocktail down in one.

'*Chérie*, what have you been doing with your life?'

'Making money,' said Sapphire honestly.

'Oh, *chérie*,' said Auralie, 'fucking is much more fun.'

'Yes, I agree,' said Sapphire, lisping drunkenly and remembering her night spent with Everett. 'But who can I fuck here?'

'Somebody'll turn up,' said Auralie. 'I have great faith in what you're wanting and needing suddenly arriving.'

'Well, I need my bed,' said Sapphire standing, leaning on the table as the room started to go around.

'I'll get you there,' said Auralie, taking her arm and guiding her out of the café.

The sticky heat hit Sapphire. She was suddenly much more drunk than she had been in the cool restaurant and nearly collapsed.

'It's not far,' said Auralie, as she looked up and down in vain for a passing taxi. 'Lean on me, *chérie*.'

Auralie took a small side turning on their way to the Staples Hotel. The narrow walkway turned into a street full of beautiful old colonial houses: leftovers from the British Empire. Hidden from the main drag, leafy from the many trees overhanging the high walls and without the relentless sun burning down, it was cooler. It was there they met Jethro.

Sapphire saw him first, which surprised her; she thought she was past seeing anything.

'Auralie, there's Zinnia's husband, Jethro Clarke,' slurred Sapphire.

'*Mon Dieu!* So it is,' said Auralie, endeavouring to hold Sapphire upright.

He was closing the high gates set into the equally high

wall of a large private house before entering his waiting chauffeur-driven limousine.

'He wanted to fuck me,' said Sapphire blatantly.

'I'm sure he did,' said Auralie.

'I suppose this is where you're keeping Ana Tai?' Auralie shouted. 'But I know where Zinnia is.' Sapphire began to slip from Auralie's grasp. 'Sapphy, stay here a moment,' she said, and propped her up against the limo. 'No, don't slide down. Hold on to the car if you feel yourself going.'

'Yes,' said Sapphire, who was quite happy to hold on to anything as the street came up and met her eyes and the palm trees floated off to greet the sun.

Auralie grabbed Jethro by the sleeve. 'Jethro,' she said, 'you're a dealer; and dealers deal. Now, I've got something you'd like, and you've got something I want. So, let's swap for the information that you need. You have Ana Tai. I want Ana Tai. You want Sapphire. I have Sapphire. And – and this is the big one, *chérie* – I know where Zinnia is.'

'Fine,' he said. 'Where?'

'Is Ana Tai here?' asked Auralie, pointing to the house behind them.

'Sure is,' he replied.

'Let's go there; then we're both certain of achieving our objective,' said Auralie.

Jethro hesitated.

'What's the matter, Jethro?' asked Auralie. 'Oh, you've chained her up, have you?'

Sapphire was vaguely aware of their conversation and then, as she slowly slipped down, noticed Jethro looking at her. The next moment she was high on his shoulders, being carried through the gates and into the garden of a luxurious modern house. Hazily, Sapphire noticed that the garden was well-established but the house was very new. Somebody had obviously pulled down the previous edifice and built this one in its stead.

The roof had a Far Eastern, Chinese feel to its shape; the huge picture windows were surrounded by stained black wood. Inside there was a sparse but vast open-plan reception room, which was decorated in a theme of shades of white, grey and black. The walls were a milky grey, the marble floor tiles black and white, and the chairs and settees covered in black silk. There were a few strategically placed paintings, chosen for their designer quality and suitability for the décor rather than for any artistic merit. Large black ceiling fans whirred against the humidity of the atmosphere. It was anonymous, well designed, expensive and completely impersonal.

'Whose house is it?' asked Auralie: the question Sapphire wanted to know the answer to.

'Petrov's,' replied Jethro, carrying on walking through the open-plan reception rooms and up the glass staircase to the bedrooms.

Jethro opened a door on to a cell-like room with narrow slit uncurtained windows set close to the ceiling. The floor was a dark grey marble, covered in thick black and white Chinese silk rugs. In the centre of the room was a queen-sized bed.

Jethro put Sapphire down on the large bed occupied by Ana Tai, who was lying asleep on its grey silk coverlet. Sapphire gave a sudden intake of breath and tried to get up, but Jethro pushed her down again. Sapphire tried once more but her legs had turned to jelly. She was too drunk to stand.

She lay there and looked at the girl, who was blindfolded and wore a neck-iron with chains leading to a padlocked hook on the wall. Her wrists were handcuffed together and were locked above her head. She was clothed only in a sparkling white shift, which showed off the beauty of her brown body. The rings in her labia were clearly visible and were attached to chains which ran down her legs and ended at padlocked anklets. Her buttocks were bare and there were deep welts across her rump. Somebody had given her a good whipping. The whips were arranged around her but just out of her reach. On a table beside the bed was a selection of dildoes and a tray full of various sweet smelling oils.

'Ana Tai,' Jethro called softly, and stroked her bare buttocks.

'You want me again?' asked Ana Tai, spreading her legs wide.

'No,' said Jethro, letting Sapphire slither on to the bed. 'I've brought a friend for you to play with.'

Jethro sat on the bed, gripped the whole of Ana Tai's sex, forced her back and kissed her mouth.

'Ana Tai!' exclaimed Auralie. 'He's a man!'

'Yes,' answered Ana Tai sweetly, raising her hips.

'Don't you want Sapphire?' asked Auralie jealously.

Jethro looked at the almost comatose figure on the bed. 'Yes,' he said, and reached out a hand and began fondling Sapphire's breasts.

Scarcely knowing what she was doing, Sapphire responded in a lazy, hazy way, her nipples stiffening under his caresses. She half-closed her eyes and decided to enjoy Jethro. She would be abandoned, take risks, have fun. Sexual fun. And later, if she regretted it, she would tell herself she was drunk, so it didn't matter.

Sapphire watched Auralie slip off her skirt and jacket but keep on her high-heeled shoes and her hold-up stockings. She admired her friend's neat body, her small pert breasts and neat rounded bottom. Auralie climbed on to the bed and fastened her mouth over Ana Tai's; she snaked her hands up under the white shift and began caressing Ana Tai's nipples.

Sapphire gasped audibly with a sudden rush of pleasure as Jethro played with her breasts, raised her skirt and let his fingers trail up over her long white legs, until he reached the outer fleshy moist lips of her sex. She was not just feeling sexual; Sapphire needed to be ravished. She sighed and squirmed with excitement as his finger moved backwards and forwards over her silky blonde down. She opened her legs and spread her arms, enjoying the excitement of something forbidden and dangerous.

Sapphire turned her head to see what Auralie was doing. She was kneeling over Ana Tai's mouth and putting her hands between her own legs, she displayed herself, and moved her hips from side to side. Ana Tai rubbed a finger along Auralie's swollen labia, gently touching her stiffening bud.

Auralie tensed her muscles, and jerked her hips forward as if asking for more, more pressure on her clitoris. Ana Tai obeyed; Auralie gave a tiny gasp of delight and began kneading her own breasts. Sapphire watched Ana Tai as she began to ease her fingers inwards, feeling the delight of the soft ridges and the tender juiciness of Auralie's vagina.

Ana Tai reached down her chained hands and grabbed at one of Sapphire's hard nipples. Sapphire raised herself slightly and put her head level with Ana Tai's moist opening. Auralie jutted her hips closer to Ana Tai's mouth, offering herself to the Meriboan, who buried her tongue in Auralie's sweet perfumed rosy flesh and licked her. Ana Tai moved her tongue along Auralie's swollen edges, teasing her, her nose devouring her special erotic smell; then she bit gently on Auralie's engorged clitoris. Auralie moaned with abandonment.

Jethro took hold of Sapphire's fingers and placed them on Ana Tai's belly.

'Stroke her,' he ordered as his fingers slowly, gently, tenderly, opened Sapphire's wet and hungry sex.

Sapphire quickened with anticipation. Then, when he placed his fingers at her sex opening, she trembled and he lunged. He plunged in, taking his fingers to the apex of her love channel. Sapphire squirmed and sighed, letting her fingers roam over Ana Tai's body and the young Asian woman's shaven and beringed sex lips. Hesitating and unsure of herself, Sapphire allowed her fingers to proceed tenderly.

She savoured each second of pleasure, the pleasure of touching another's woman's sex. Not used to the touch of herself, Sapphire became very excited by the softness and the yielding furls and ridges; she was fascinated and surprised by the strength of Ana Tai's inner muscles. They contracted around her fingers, clasping them, holding them, exciting her further and drawing her into hidden depths. Only very gradually did Sapphire completely penetrate Ana Tai's vulva, wallowing in her soft, creamy, sensitive wet sex.

She watched, fascinated, as Auralie bent over and kissed Ana Tai passionately. Then her attention went back to Jethro as he undid the fastening on her skirt and pulled it off, leaving her sex exposed. He removed her shoes and stockings. He bent down and licked her between her legs. She raised her hips.

'Turn over,' he ordered. 'Turn over and kneel.'

Sapphire obeyed him and her face was now at Ana Tai's sex, her rounded bare bottom high in the air.

Auralie knelt with her back to Sapphire and shoved her hips forward so that Ana Tai's tongue could lick and suck at her wanton pussy.

With speed Jethro removed his own clothing, put on a condom and came up behind Sapphire.

'Suck her,' Jethro commanded, pushing Sapphire forward. He stuck his stiff prick between her legs. He rubbed on the outside of her sex but didn't enter. He played and teased her, exciting Sapphire beyond endurance. He stroked Sapphire's round bottom, his hand climbing up her spine under her suit jacket. He was enjoying the sight of her semi-clothed, her long legs and her sex on show giving him immediate access and yet her breasts remaining tantalisingly half-hidden.

'Sapphire, I want to see you put out your tongue and lick Ana Tai; lick her between her legs. Lick her sex lips,' he commanded.

Jethro let his finger rub again and again on Sapphire's wetness but she didn't lick the other woman.

'Suck, I said,' he ordered, dipping his fingers into a saucer of oils. Then he began circling her tight puckered forbidden hole. Slowly he let his fingers ease their way into Sapphire's anus. As he suddenly thrust into her, she jerked forward and her head was forced on to Ana Tai's labia. Excited and willingly impaled by Jethro's fingers, Sapphire squirmed and licked.

With every orifice plundered, Ana Tai was emitting squeals of bliss. Ana Tai pushed her shoulders back, making sure Jethro could see her erect nipples straining through the fabric of her shift.

'He's got a great cock and now he's learnt how to use it,' said Ana Tai proudly.

'And you can watch me screw Sapphire,' said Jethro, standing behind her, his fingers playing with her arse.

With his prick hovering, letting Sapphire feel the merest whisper of his stiffness against the moist wetness of her swollen sex, his cock began making small forays into her engorged and welcoming vulva. She gasped with excitement and lust. Jethro's prick instantly gained length. He jerked forward as if to enter her but Sapphire, drunk on alcohol and desire, had other ideas and pulled back from him.

'I want them both to watch me being screwed,' said Sapphire brazenly. She took a short sharp breath of pleasure and anticipation then, swallowing a lump in her throat, she wiggled her hips and smiled. Capriciously she turned her head towards Ana Tai's sex and put her hands on the Asian's brown thighs.

'Now watch,' she whispered.

Sapphire wanted his cock sliding into her, that hard knob pushing her open, its long shaft inching its way upwards into her squashy pink swollen and lustful flesh. She wanted to feel the full impact of Jethro's pleasure, stretching her, taking her, fucking her, fucking her fast and furiously – his anticipation finally realised.

Auralie eased her body to one side so that Ana Tai could witness Jethro's entry. Sapphire rocked backwards and forwards and, little by little, Jethro's cock gradually felt its way into her lascivious sex and was enveloped by her wanton willingness.

As he bent over Sapphire, he brought his hands round, kneaded her breasts and licked her neck. Then, when she had got used to his soft luscious gliding rhythm, suddenly, and with one quick movement he thrust, pushing his thick engorged penis in up to the hilt. She devoured him, taking every inch of him. He rode her like a horse but she wouldn't let him come. She put her hands down between his legs; she felt his balls, squeezed them, and pressed on the base of his shaft.

'Oh yes,' said Ana Tai, sexily. 'Fuck her, fuck her.'

Sapphire saw the flash of jealousy cross Auralie's face and wasn't as surprised as she would have been a few hours earlier, when Auralie picked up a crop that was lying near and slowly – but with great assuredness – trailed it along Ana Tai's sex lips, pressing on but never entering the Meriboan's soft juicy beringed wetness.

'No, madam, no,' moaned Ana Tai, enjoying Auralie's touch and moving her hips, trying to make the crop glide into her silken warm opening.

'Yes, I will: and don't argue with me,' said Auralie, standing up.

Sapphire, rocking on Jethro's cock, saw Auralie turn Ana Tai over on to her belly so that her sweet luscious soft brown buttocks were displayed ready for the crop.

'Sorry, madam,' cried Ana Tai.

Auralie poked her fingers into Ana Tai's vulva. Ana Tai let out little sighs of pleasure.

'You are very wet, very wet indeed,' Auralie said seductively, shoving her fingers up and down inside Ana Tai's sex, making her dance and squirm.

Ana Tai let her rounded bare buttocks go loose and floppy. Auralie trailed the crop up between Ana Tai's legs, then, with tiny circular movements, poked first at her bottom hole and then at her soft open sex. Ana Tai trembled with excitement as the thin hardness of the crop touched her rosy creamy-wet flesh.

In a flash Auralie brought the crop down on Ana Tai's thighs.

'Thank you, madam,' gasped Ana Tai.

'One is not enough,' said Auralie, sternly. 'Six stripes. And Jethro will administer your punishment.' She handed the crop to Jethro.

Jethro licked his lips in anticipation.

Sapphire realised that even though he was screwing her, there was a bond between him and Ana Tai. And that he desperately wanted to touch the young Asian woman but refrained. Every minute that went by, every minute that Auralie touched and felt and played with Ana Tai's private places made Jethro randier and randier. Sapphire knew instinctively that he wanted to feel her lusciousness quivering beneath his touch. He wanted to touch the open wet juiciness at the top of Ana Tai's thighs, even though he was taking and pleasuring her. Jethro was yearning for Ana Tai's body – and Sapphire could understand why. She thought her big blonde heavy-breasted body compared badly with the Meriboan's sleek, slim figure.

Ana Tai caught and held her breath. Sapphire stuck her hips out, keeping Jethro's cock hard up inside her. Jethro brought the crop swishing down hard over Ana Tai's round buttocks. Between each stripe, Auralie rammed her fingers into Ana Tai's wet and wanton sex and Jethro, suffering pangs of acute envy, thrust harder into Sapphire.

Sapphire could see that the exquisite mixture of pain and pleasure almost brought Ana Tai to the point of orgasm. Each time the crop came down, Ana Tai cried out, begging it to stop, but to no avail.

When her punishment was over, Auralie inspected the red weals on Ana Tai's bottom, then gently kissed and caressed the marks.

'What do you say?' asked Auralie.

'Thank you, madam, thank you,' she said.

'And how are you going to show your thanks, your true thanks?' said Auralie lecherously.

'Your pleasure is my pleasure,' said Ana Tai submissively.

Auralie, who now had her own legs wide apart, her thumb on her clitoris and two fingers inside herself, lay in front of Ana Tai's mouth.

Sapphire once again stroked the soft erogenous zone

of Ana Tai's inner thighs. Facing Jethro, Auralie positioned her sex over Ana Tai's mouth and Ana Tai sunk her tongue into Auralie's wetness.

'Thank you, madam,' said Ana Tai.

Auralie, sitting astride Ana Tai, gazed lasciviously at Jethro's prick charging in and out of Sapphire's sex. She slithered off Ana Tai's hot sweat-soaked body, leant forward and took Jethro's cock in her hands. Sensual and very erotic thoughts flooded through Sapphire as she felt Auralie's fingers tightening around Jethro's stiff cock and fingers straying on to her wet sex and swollen sex-lips. Jethro began to shake and pant. The tantalising sensation of Auralie's hands on his prick was almost too much for him to bear. He was close to coming, but Auralie gripped his penis at the base and held his orgasm back.

'Feel her,' Jethro ordered Sapphire.

Auralie took Sapphire's forefinger, hooked it around her own, then trailed it along the top of Ana Tai's legs. 'She's very wet. Sapphire, put your tongue just where I've got my finger.'

Sapphire moved her head and did as she was told. Sapphire licked at the outer rim of Ana Tai's vulva. Auralie splayed Ana Tai's sex-lips so that Sapphire's tongue could slurp easily at her soft juiciness.

'She wants to be fucked,' said Auralie, stroking Jethro's phallus. 'Take her. Take her fast.'

Jethro moved back from the kneeling Sapphire and positioned himself against the chained woman. Ana Tai remained utterly motionless. Auralie aimed his prick at the entrance to Ana Tai's sex. Jethro placed his hands on Ana Tai's breasts and thrust his cock into the Asian's girl's willing and wanting sex. With the force of his enthusiasm, she arched. He lifted her up against him and started to pound. Auralie began to feel herself with soft tantalising strokes. Ana Tai rolled and heaved, and rocked and swayed, taking every last inch of him. Their bodies were totally together, blended.

Sapphire moved to one side, lay on her back and

watched. Auralie found a whip with a thick handle and rubbed it between Sapphire's thighs; Sapphire swayed her hips licentiously.

'Jethro, what are you doing?' roared Petrov, charging into the room and grabbing hold of Jethro, forcing him to withdraw from Ana Tai.

Sapphire looked up with blurry vision to see who it was who had so noisily invaded the lazy sexy heat of their room. She recognised Petrov and was quite surprised. He did not seem to recognise her. She turned her face away but raised up her hips, giving him full sight of her beautiful, soft, white and rounded bottom.

'You should have been with me, not here, screwing,' said Petrov angrily; but he was instantly captivated by the sight of Sapphire's buttocks.

'Got well-laid,' replied Jethro flippantly. 'Anyhow how did it go? Did my new partner turn up?'

'No, he did not,' said Petrov.

'He didn't?' cried Jethro. It was Jethro's turn to be both surprised and angry. 'He didn't turn up? He didn't arrive?'

'That's what I said,' said Petrov.

'Then something's gone wrong,' said Jethro, jumping off the bed and hurriedly putting on his clothes.

'Where are you going?' asked Petrov.

'The Exchange.'

'Oh, you think it's that important?'

'Oh, yes,' said Jethro. 'Something real bad.'

'Aw, come on,' said Petrov.

'No. Come on, nothing,' replied Jethro. 'If my new partner hasn't kept his appointment ... Hell, Petrov, that's real bad news. He was bringing thirty million sterling in cash.'

'What?'

'Yeah. You got the message now? It ain't just my instinct.'

'Then – ' Petrov looked wistfully at Auralie and Sapphire lying on the bed. 'Then I'd better go with you.'

'No, you stay here,' said Jethro.

'Are you sure?' asked Petrov, feeling relieved. Money was nice but sex was better.

'Quite sure. I'll sort it. Come along, Ana Tai,' said Jethro, unpadlocking Ana Tai's chains and lifting her off the bed.

'Hey!' said Auralie. 'Jethro, that's my woman.'

'We'll talk about that,' said Jethro.

'No, we won't. You're a man, a married man and she's mine,' shouted Auralie.

'Now's not the time to discuss it, Auralie,' said Jethro.

'I think it is.'

'I know it's not,' said Jethro.

'Hey, hey, I'm not a piece of merchandise,' said Ana Tai. 'I'm brown; I'm Asian; it looks like I'm bi-sexual, I'm a masseuse; I'm learning how to sew; I'm Meriboan and I'm telling you all, I'm not going anywhere – except to take a bath and then go to sleep. So you can put me down, Jethro Clarke.'

'Yes, ma'am,' he said.

Ana Tai marched out of the room, quickly followed by Jethro.

'Auralie,' said Petrov, his huge stiff prick throbbing and erect and seeing the crestfallen look on Auralie's face. 'Stay with me and play. You've got another lovely little friend here.'

Petrov was admiring Sapphire's long legs. He bent over her, put his hands out and rubbed her buttocks suggestively.

Auralie dipped her fingers in the oil and rubbed some over Petrov's cock, then on Sapphire's body.

Petrov began rubbing his cock. 'You, you're the one I want,' he said,

Petrov's cock twitched and stirred, betraying his intense sexuality. Auralie stroked Sapphire's breasts and rolled her over so that her rump was available for Petrov's whip. Sapphire didn't realise what Auralie was intending and stared into the other woman's eyes with growing lust. Sapphire wriggled her bottom, raising it slightly and enticing Petrov.

'Auralie, I wouldn't want to stop your pleasure,' said Petrov, 'But who is she? What's her name?'

'Sapphy,' said Auralie. 'I thought she should have some fun. She got a little drunk but I think she's had the fun.'

'I'll give her some more,' said Petrov. 'She gorgeous. I want to fuck her.'

'Don't know if I want to let you,' said Auralie, nibbling on Sapphire's earlobes while stroking her breasts.

'Auralie, obey me,' commanded Petrov.

Auralie ignored him.

'Then this is for insolence,' said Petrov. He lashed at her. He struck Auralie again and again, catching her soft belly and the precious sweet soft flesh at the top of her thighs, giving her the feeling of exquisite pain curdled with pleasure. Auralie bit her lips and tried to lie still, accepting her chastisement.

Petrov smiled lecherously. He eased his hands down between Auralie's legs and found the fleshy pad between her vulva and the puckered orifice of her anus. Lightly he fingered that patch, exciting her; her excitement thrilled him, making his cock stiffen further. It made him roll his hips, and made his mouth salivate with unharnessed desire.

He'd punished Auralie; now he'd screw Sapphire. Petrov dipped his hands into the bowl of oil. With care and very slowly, he massaged every inch of Sapphire's body while she was stretching languidly and kissing Auralie full on the mouth. Petrov's fingers went round and around, down Sapphire's spine, across her buttocks and then up along and down through her crease.

'Hold my cock,' commanded Petrov, keeping his own hands busy and moving his body slightly so that his long stiff penis was pointing at Sapphire's stomach.

Sapphire's long delicate hands gripped Petrov's large erect prick. She held him at the base and cupped his balls. She gave tiny slippery caresses to the collar ringing its head, moving her finger over its neat cap, and watched droplets of liquid appear in its neat slit. Then, in one firm movement, she pulled the skin hard back down; she pressed, holding momentarily at the bottom of the Petrov's quivering shaft before starting up again.

Sapphire could see that her actions pleased Petrov. He obviously liked a woman who knew how to handle a cock. Especially his cock. Petrov began to pant.

'Oil my prick,' Petrov ordered. He leant over the bed and picked up the whip. He stroked it lovingly and flicked the strands apart. Then he held the ends of the long thin leather strips so that she was able to see its cruel bulbous-ended phallus-shaped leather handle.

'You're too tight,' he whispered, bringing some rope from under the bed and quickly tying Sapphire's hands. 'Bend over, keeping your hands out above your head, your bottom raised and your feet slightly apart.'

Sapphire had no alternative but to obey. Petrov wasn't satisfied. He took a couple of pillows and placed them under Sapphire's belly. He fondled Sapphire's wanton moist sex, making sure she stayed wet and wanting, then tapped her legs apart with the whip.

As he struck Sapphire across her neat bare buttocks with the long tailed whip, she jumped with the sudden flash of pain. Tears sprang into her eyes. Auralie quickly embraced her.

'No, no; go with it, Sapphy,' she said. 'It's wonderful; it can be marvellous. Let him do it.'

With exact precision, Petrov began to skim the whip across Sapphire's bare buttocks. Then he brought it down hard, marking her with a deep dark welt. With each stripe she experienced a wincing high curt pain, coupled with a refined sense of pleasure as the tail of the whip seared her soft inner skin.

'Raise your buttocks higher,' Petrov ordered.

Sapphire obeyed. Then she felt her flanks parting and slowly Petrov inserted the well-oiled head of the whip into Sapphire's tight back passage. Flushed with shame, she let her head droop. She knew it was senseless to struggle. She must go loose and accept the invasion.

Slowly Sapphire's well-lubricated channel began to

take the invasive instrument, and embrace its pleasure. Her muscles clutched at it as it passed upwards and let it go easily on the downward stroke. Sapphire opened and ripened. She wanted more. Deeper. Faster.

Aware of Sapphire's mute acceptance of his cruel thrusting leather phallus, Petrov pushed the bulbous head up harder. Then, languorously, he slid a hand round her belly and gripped her sex.

Sapphire was panting. The pain and pleasure was exquisite. She was rolling backwards on to the dildo. The leather whip strips were dangling down enticingly between her legs. Petrov caressed her swollen red and wanton flower, up and down, up and down. Her entire body was quivering. Give me more, give me more, she was secretly yelling.

'Play with me, Auralie,' Petrov ordered, letting his hands ripple down over Sapphire's belly and thrusting the leather whip-end backwards and forwards into her newly-stretched anus.

From her bent over position, Sapphire glanced at Auralie rubbing Petrov's cock, seeing the way she took his hard erect and throbbing phallus, stroking his glans, playing with his balls; Sapphire flashed back on her night with Everett. Instantly her emotions towards him were of anger and longing, though neither had the chance to be uppermost. Her thoughts were dramatically cut short by the sight of a large burly dark brown Meriboan servant walking into the room.

'Master Petrov,' said Kim Long, watching his master lying on the bed, his cock being played with by the redhead and the whip handle lewdly hanging from the blonde. 'Do you need any assistance?'

Kim Long was trussed into a black leather body harness which encircled his massive, erect cock, and his balls were thrust through a silver ring in the leather. He held a long whip.

'Can I suck your cock, master?'

'No, but you can fuck me,' said Petrov licentiously.

He squirmed and wriggled his buttocks to the edge of the bed.

Kim Long's huge brown hands came down on his master's flanks. He spread Petrov's cheeks, displaying his crease. He put his huge prick to the opening, pressing slightly.

'Hard,' cried Petrov. And Kim Long plunged into his depths. 'And you – suck me.' Petrov yanked Sapphire close to his cock head as he squirmed with every thrust of Kim's prick. He loved the twin feelings of Kim Long's large sac banging against his padded flesh between his buttocks and his balls and his cock rammed up hard inside. Sapphire took his phallus slowly into her mouth.

Petrov turned his head towards Kim, who picked up the crop which lay on the bed. Petrov nodded, then withdrew his prick from Sapphire's mouth. Kim Long brought the lash down hard on Sapphire's rump. The pain scorched her. She jumped. The leather whip handle in her bottom began to ease out.

'Don't you dare let go of that,' said Petrov, pushing the handle back again. 'And keep your hands above your head.'

Kim held the short crop at Sapphire's mouth. 'Kiss it,' he said.

Sapphire bent her head and kissed the lash.

Kim scourged her again across her buttocks. Again and again. Harder, more cruel. And Sapphire jumped, and screamed.

Sapphire turned her head to look at the big brown man. She found something deeply erotic in the sight of him, a leather collar around his neck, chains connecting the collar to a leather apron over his navel with his cock hard and stiff sticking through the cock ring. She wondered what his cock would feel like inside her. Almost as if the servant read her thought, she received another stripe across her flanks, stinging and bringing tears to her eyes. She felt humiliated and angry, yet wet. Very wet. And Petrov kept touching, feeling and caressing her body, invading her sex.

Sapphire trembled; her knees shook and her womb tightened. There was an unreal quality to the state she was in. In her wildest dreams she'd never thought that she would have been ordered by a man, almost enslaved by him and obeying his commands – obeying and enjoying. Enjoying the freedom of total eroticism, the sensuality. She should have found it deeply humiliating. Instead, it was deeply thrilling. Sapphire was loving her role of slave, a pleasure-slave being pleasured.

Sapphire watched again as Kim, with his stomach muscles tight and his balls like two stones, thrust harder and harder into Petrov's anus. Kim dropped the whip. He snaked his hands round Petrov's waist, took hold of his long full phallus and rubbed with the same rhythm he was ploughing him. He knew exactly what his master wanted. Perfection. Kim Long lay over Petrov, kissing his shoulders; he sucked, leaving red-ring marks, and came. They came in unison. And Sapphire was left depleted, unwanted, not given release. And Kim Long smiled with pleasure that she had been denied his master's satisfaction.

The two men relaxed and fell asleep.

The two women lay looking at one another, watching the men deep in slumber. Auralie drew Sapphire to her and stroked her breasts and her belly.

'You want to come, eh, *chérie*?' she asked.

'Yes,' said Sapphire.

Auralie played softly and gently with her body, bringing Sapphire to her climax. Then, leaving the two men where they were, they gathered up their belongings and tiptoed out of the room. Sapphire wasn't tired. She was invigorated by her extraordinary experiences – and hungry.

'Mangoes,' said Sapphire. 'I fancy fresh mangoes. It's almost lunchtime but – '

'Lunchtime? Oh, God, maybe I can just make it to the hotel,' said Auralie, anxiously checking her watch. 'A quarter to; I can just make it.'

'Where?' asked Sapphire.

'To the Staples. My meeting with Gerry,' she said, bundling her clothes together.

'Oh God, yes!' exclaimed Sapphire.

'I'll take a quick bath,' said Auralie, running up the glass staircase. 'Ah, *merde*! I've left my make-up in Petrov's room and don't want to go in there.'

'Use some of mine,' said Sapphire, following her up the stairs and handing her her handbag. 'Everything's in the little black wallet.'

'*Merci, chérie*,' said Auralie grabbing it as she ran into the bathroom. 'There are plenty of other bathrooms.' She pointed to an array of doors along the corridor.

Sapphire took less time than Auralie to have her bath. She was sitting quietly in the breakfast room facing on to the peaceful Japanese-style garden, half-way through a mango and telling herself she had no regrets. She had learnt a lot. She was grateful for the experience. She would do it again at the earliest opportunity and she didn't really care a jot about Everett de Bouys. She was thinking all that when she heard Auralie scream.

She jumped up as Auralie tore into the room, fully clothed but her hair awry, and with no make-up.

'Sapphire,' she cried, brandishing her wallet. 'Sapphire, what's this?'

'Jeez, Auralie,' said Sapphire, a little irritated, 'I thought something terrible must have happened – at least the house was on fire! It's only my photographs. I've just had them developed.'

'Where were you?' Auralie demanded. 'Where were you when you took them?'

'Texas,' said Sapphire, put out by the belligerent tone of Auralie's voice. 'That's where I first met Jethro.'

'Texas, Texas – a polo match in Texas?' said Auralie.

'Yes. You're going to be late, Auralie,' said Sapphire, who couldn't quite work out whether Auralie was steamed up with excitement or anger.

'Would you please tell me who this is?' said Auralie, calming down a little as she handed Sapphire the photographs.

'Yes,' said Sapphire, looking at them. 'That's Eduard.'

'Eduard!'

'Yes, Eduard del Sur,' said Sapphire.

'*Non, chérie,*' said Auralie emphatically. '*Non, non, non.*'

'*Non*? Why *non*?' asked Sapphire.

'Because, in my opinion, that is a man called Laurence Vladelsky – Jeanine's supposedly dead husband.'

'No!'

'Exactly,' said Auralie. 'Do you know anything more about him? What was he doing in Texas – apart from playing polo, which he adored?'

'He was coming here to Meriboa.'

'Meriboa? Why?'

'To work on the Exchange as a trader.'

'A trader?'

'Yes, at Minmex.'

'But he's a botanist!'

'A botanist? He's a botanist? Now you've surprised me,' said Sapphire. But then she remembered how Eduard had picked up a little flower and put it in his riding cap. She had thought it an odd thing to do at the time.

For one moment Auralie thought she'd made a mistake. She looked at the picture again. She was quite sure, absolutely sure the man in the photograph was Laurence Vladelsky. He had the same never-to-be-forgotten lopsided smile.

'Ah well,' said Auralie, 'if he can change his identity, he can change his profession! But, *chérie*, do you know what this means?'

'In what way?'

'Laurence was declared dead, but he's alive. Can Jeanine marry again under these circumstances? Sapphy, do you love Everett de Bouys? Answer me truthfully. You've had some fun, *chérie*, but tell the truth. Do you love him?'

'Yes,' said Sapphire.

'Then you've got to fight for him,' said Auralie earnestly. 'And I'll help you. Put some make-up on and come with me. We'll both keep my appointment with Gerry de Bouys and his father Sir Henry.'

'Sir Henry?'

'Yes.'

'Oh,' said Sapphire. 'Sir Henry and my father didn't get on. Well, that's a little understatement, and I don't think I could ask him for help.'

'*Chérie*, your father's enemies are not your enemies. You mustn't make them so. That way lies eternal war. Come, don't be stupid, *chérie*. Don't let Jeanine win.'

Sapphire thought about Auralie's words. 'You're right,' she said.

The two women brushed their hair and put on their make-up. Looking glamorous and elegant, they both headed for the front door.

It opened before them and there stood Jethro Clarke and Everett de Bouys.

'Everett!' exclaimed Sapphire, smiling. He was the last person she expected to see. She wanted to run and kiss him.

'Sapphire Western Untermann,' he said, looking at her coldly. 'I've come across some double-dealing bitches in my time, but I reckon you top the lot in underhandedness and general all-round trickery.'

Chapter Eleven

Zinnia felt as if she were walking on air. To have met Gerry again, albeit in the oddest of circumstances, she found amazing. But then amazing things seemed to be happening in Meriboa.

To have witnessed Eduard del Sur being arrested as Jeanine's thought-to-be-dead husband, Laurence Vladelsky, was odd. For him to have been arrested on the grounds that he had stolen fifty million pounds' sterling worth of bearer bonds from de Bouys bank was bizarre. To discover it was Gerry de Bouys doing the arresting: that was the weirdest thing of all.

Zinnia could hardly believe any of it. Gerry, of all people. Gerry, Jeanine's lapdog and pet wimp, showing strength. Then Zinnia had to remind herself she had sensed something else in him. She had realised there was an intelligence and an integrity in him that she'd suspected he deliberately kept subdued. Of course, it made sense now. He was an undercover agent for de Bouys Bank.

After the initial shock of being surrounded by police, she and Gerry were hurtled into their own private bewilderment. Zinnia had stared at him, quite bemused, watching while he fumbled with the handcuffs he was trying to put on Eduard. In the end one of the policeman had done it and then Eduard had been carted away in a police wagon. And Gerry had told Zinnia she'd better go with him to the police station to verify Eduard as Eduard, so they could prove he was Laurence. Also, she had to state where she was staying.

Zinnia and Gerry had sat side by side in the police car, aware of another's being, body and spirit. She had guessed what he was thinking because of his reaction. He had blushed when she looked at him and she could see goose pimples on his wrist if they touched when the car sped round a corner. She knew then that he fancied her as much as she fancied him.

Having informed the police that she intended to change her hotel, she was told she might be needed again, so she must let the police know where she would be going. Zinnia returned to The Staples, threw her belongings into her suitcase and checked out. Leaving no forwarding address for Caradoc Lewis, she checked into the one next door, The Hotel Lin Chiau. From there, she telephoned the police, giving them the name of her new abode.

The Hotel Lin Chiau provided her with a lovely, expensively-furnished, modern suite with an incredible view of the palm tree edged bay. In the bedroom there was a huge canopied bed, a couple of armchairs and various tables, as well as the ubiquitous television set, telephone and fax machine and personal drinks bar. The walls and soft furnishings were decorated in delicate shades of pink, the chairs and tables were painted in black lacquer.

Zinnia slid open the huge French windows to let the soft sea breeze drift in. Then she settled down on the bed to take a long and much-needed rest. But she was too excited to sleep. Thoughts and ideas were tumbling over themselves. She was thinking about everything. Her life, Jethro; her job; what she would do in future and – most of all – she was thinking about Gerry. Whatever her thoughts, as far as Gerry was concerned, Zinnia's emotions were all over the place. She decided she'd take a long leisurely bath and try and work things out.

Wallowing in the water in the pink marble bath, Zinnia realised there was a deep ache inside her for Gerry. He had a gentle loving sweetness about him that appealed to her maternal instinct. But she knew he needed someone to take control. At least in bed. Since seeing him in London she'd thought about that a lot and had become more and more convinced that the other man screwing her with Kensit earlier in the year had definitely been Gerry.

No-one else had ever given her that extra frisson of excitement, that rush of pure chemistry that had surged through her veins even when she'd been blindfolded. As she lay there, Zinnia's body trembled with erotic thoughts of him. She could feel her wantonness returning as she pictured him kissing her lips and fondling her breasts, his hands strolling over her stomach and down between her thighs. She let her own hands travel where her imagination had been and began to caress and probe her secret flower. Yeah, she thought, the one thing Jeanine always had said was that Gerry was a good fuck; Zinnia knew that to be true.

Her sexual reverie was interrupted when someone started banging on her door. She stepped out of the bath, wrapped herself in an enormous bathrobe and, with a trembling heart, went to see who it was.

There stood Gerry, the handsome object of her day dreams.

'Hi,' he said, giving her a disarming smile.

'How?' she asked. Then they burst out laughing at their ridiculous greetings.

'The police,' he replied.

'Oh, yes; of course, of course,' she said, flustered, blushing and suddenly very shy.

'I came to see if you were okay,' he said.

'Fine, thank you. Would you like a drink?'

'Yes, if you're having one,' he said. 'Vodka, for me, pepper vodka – neat – if you have it.'

241

Zinnia opened the door of the fridge bar and took out a bottle containing liquid the colour of her bright red hair. 'You're in luck,' she said, hunting in the black cabinet under the ice box for the tot glasses.

Their fingers touched when she handed him his glass. The electricity between them was so strong that their skin seemed to fuse. It took a major effort to detach themselves. Shyly they looked away from one another.

'Cheers,' he said.

'Cheers,' she replied, trying to stop the little vibrato in her voice that showed she was excited. 'So where is Laurence now?' she added, sitting opposite Gerry in one of the deep armchairs. She crossed and uncrossed her legs, letting him glimpse her naked flesh; she moved so that her bathrobe gaped and he was able to see the huge swell of her breasts and her dark erect nipples.

Gerry sipped at his vodka while she imagined herself undoing his zip, playing with his dick and sitting astride him, her bare sex poised above his cock then, with tiny pushing movements on its head, pressing down and taking him up to the hilt. Taking him to the top of her womb. Riding him up and down, squirming. And he would hold her big luscious breasts, squeezing her nipples, squeezing them harder and harder. Oh, she would rock and she would roll and the sweat would stream along their bodies, binding them together. He would clutch at her buttocks. She would ride him like a woman possessed.

'What did you say?' he asked.

'Where's Laurence now?' she repeated.

'In Chungee jail,' he replied.

'Oh,' she said; then there was a silence between them. It wasn't awkward, just sexually highly-charged, with neither one wanting to make the first move.

'I must get dressed,' she announced, jumping up.

'Oh yes, of course,' he said, his eyes following her as she walked across the room. 'Do you want me to leave?'

'No.'

Zinnia disappeared into the bathroom and came back

some time later, looking highly desirable in a red and pink zig-zag patterned suit; the jacket was buttoned to the neck and the skirt was short and wrap-over. She was also wearing bright red, extremely high spiky-heeled shoes. She'd guessed he'd find that a turn-on. She was also carrying a large red bag.

'Everybody thought Laurence was dead, so how did you know it was him?' she asked, putting the bag down beside her as she sat in the same armchair again. 'Eduard and Laurence it's not immediately obvious.'

'We had no idea in the beginning. It was when we couldn't find all those bearer bonds. Gradually my uncle and I worked it out that the man responsible for the loss – or, rather, the theft – had to be the one we called Eduard. He was the only one with total access to them, apart from my uncle Cecil. This all started before my cousin Everett joined the company.'

'So you were sent to investigate?'

'Yes,' he said. 'Undercover.'

'Oh, that's for sure,' she laughed. 'Under quite a few covers, at Jeanine's.'

Without warning, Zinnia began unbuttoning her jacket revealing, little by little, her enticing feminine shape. She smiled a smile of come-hither sexuality as his eyes travelled her body, her throat, her sloping shoulders and her huge breasts. She watched him clutch his glass as if his hands were itching to fondle her and to caress her. She saw him swallow hard and his cock move with desire.

Zinnia parted her legs so that he could catch sight of her stocking-tops.

'Why did you leave The Staples?' he asked, gulping at the sight of her thighs.

'Because I went there as an employee of Caradoc Lewis of Hanway's.'

'Him?' exclaimed Gerry. 'He put in a bid for my uncle's company.'

'Did he?'

'Yes; the cheek,' said Gerry. 'But we've seen him off.

243

Unfortunately for us, his bid was topped by somebody else. So you worked for him?'

'Yes. Your use of the past tense is correct; I handed in my notice this morning, early this morning – in fact, just before I saw you standing outside that building with those policemen.'

'What sort of work? What sort of work did you do for Caradoc Lewis?' Gerry asked, with an urgency in his voice – a note that Zinnia thought sounded suspiciously like jealousy.

'Fund manager,' she said, undoing more buttons and letting Gerry catch a hint of her shiny black PVC corset.

'Oh,' he said, slightly hoarse.

'Did you think it was something else? Did you think I was fucking him or whipping him or sucking his cock? Oh, you are a naughty boy if you thought that.'

She saw him put his hands in his lap and adjust his stiff prick.

'You're not replying,' she said. 'In other words, you were thinking that. Oh, you are bad, a real bad boy.'

Gerry took a sip of vodka and tried to clear his throat.

'Do you know what happens to bad boys, Gerry de Bouys?' she asked in a lower, more languid more overtly sexy voice.

'No,' he said, staring at her, completely mesmerised.

'They get punished,' she replied.

Gerry quivered. He held his balls. His cock was straining against the fabric of his trousers, begging for release. And she knew it.

'Come here,' she said, her tone altering. It was more of a command. Gerry stood up. Zinnia pretended not to see his hard-on. 'Come here and stand in front of me,' she ordered.

Staring at her breasts, Gerry obeyed her. Zinnia followed his glance. 'You want to touch my tits, do you?' she asked.

'Yes,' he said hoarsely.

'Touch them and stroke them?'

'Yes.'

'Very well, you may,' she said. 'But you'll have to do it my way. Kneel down and don't move until I give you permission.'

Gerry knelt in front of her. She put her legs close together. 'Put your hands in my lap and close your eyes,' she commanded.

Shaking with delight, Gerry did as he was ordered. Zinnia pulled up her skirt so that when he knelt and touched her legs he was touching her skin through her stockings. He made tiny little circles on her thighs. She smacked his hands hard.

'In my lap, and keep them absolutely still.'

Zinnia could feel the warmth of his fingertips through the silk of her stockings. Very slowly she undid his shirt buttons. Almost as if she had forgotten to take it off completely, she slipped the collar back and the sleeves down to his elbows, severely reducing his freedom of movement. Then she stroked his chest and neck. She knew the touch of her red-nailed fingers was sending shivers of delight down his spine; he broke out in goose-pimples and sighed.

'Keep your eyes closed,' she said.

Zinnia unzipped her handbag and took out a pair of handcuffs. A fraction of a second before she clapped them on his wrists, she let Gerry hear the steel chains jangling, feel that hard cold substance on the fine hairs on his arm. He let out a quick sharp sigh when she locked them shut.

Zinnia delved into her bag once more and drew out a black leather hood. 'Bow your head,' she ordered.

Willingly, submissively, he obeyed her. She pulled it over his head. It had an opening over the nose and mouth but none for his eyes or ears. She wiped her tongue along his mouth as it protruded from the hood. She seemed to have found a special nerve so that, whenever her lips touched his, an instant message was sent to his cock to stand erect. He pushed his tongue out. She nipped it with her teeth. He quickly closed his mouth. Zinnia smiled. He understood. He did what she wanted, not the other way round.

Zinnia leant forward and undid Gerry's zip. She pulled his trousers and his boxer pants down around his knees, immobilising him. His prick was fully erect. She took a pencil from her bag and gave it a sharp tap. It quivered and shrank. She opened her handbag and took out a small, hard rubber ring.

Gerry gave a tremulous shudder as he felt her long cool fingers grasp the tip of his penis and stretch it as far as possible. Then, as she delicately caressed his prick, he felt her roll the ring of rubber along the length of his shaft. Gerry's hands were increasing their pressure on Zinnia's thighs. He tried to let them wander further up her legs but she slapped him hard again for his trouble.

When the ring was firmly in place, she stroked his sac with her soft, gentle and manipulating hands. Gerry gave little moans of pleasure. She brought up one knee and laid it against his chest, slowly pushing him away from her. Then she brought up her other foot, the spikes of the heel digging into his nipple. She gave a sharp thrust with her foot and Gerry fell backwards.

Zinnia left him on the floor. She placed one foot on his stomach, pressing the heel hard down into his skin. She pulled at the waistband of her skirt. The fastening gave way easily. She threw that across the room too. Zinnia stood in front of the hooded Gerry, dressed in a black PVC corset. Her great melon breasts were stuffed into cups ending in harsh, hard points. Her tiny waist was laced firmly, accentuating her large hips and the roundness of her belly. A buckled flap was placed over her sex. The PVC extended down over the tops of her thighs to meet her stocking tops but, at the back, she had left half the studs undone, revealing the dimples at the base of her spine and her enticing full bare bottom.

Zinnia removed her foot from his stomach and pushed the toe of her shoe into his side, indicating to him to turn over, which he did. She then arranged him so that his head was leaning on his handcuffed hands and his bottom was high in the air. She pulled off his trousers and his underpants, his shoes and his socks. She put on a pair of rubber gloves.

She searched again in her bag, brought out a number of instruments and laid them carefully on the floor beside him. Then she took a jar of oil and, standing between his thighs, she slowly massaged his buttocks. Gradually moving her hand down and around, she coated his scrotum and his penis with the oil. His penis grew quickly under her tender ministrations. The ring at the base, as always, gave him an extra sensation but now with Zinnia feeling and touching him it seemed to him that his cock was larger and more sensitive than ever. Her hands knew exactly where to go to heighten every nerve, to have him her complete slave.

She parted his buttocks and, with the same infinite care, she began to rub oil around his small tight hole. Round and around she went, exciting and teasing the sensory muscles surrounding his tight, puckered little place. Taking his prick in one hand and fondling it, she slowly penetrated his anus with a gloved finger.

Gerry licked his lips and held his breath as her rubber-encased hands wandered up and down along his engorged prick and entered his arse. She stopped still. She squeezed his prick but did not push any further upwards nor rub any further downwards. He waited, quivering. She gave the minutest wiggle inside his rectum, enough to entice him, then stayed still again. She knew he was desperate for more. He waited. She did nothing. Then he pressed down, opening himself, allowing her deeper penetration. And he rocked. He rocked hard backwards and forwards as she rubbed on his prick and thrust into his arse.

Gerry's muscles were beginning to contract. She pushed harder. She moved her body, allowing him to feel the sticky coolness of the PVC against his flesh. Through his hard tumescent prick the blood surged. She had his entire body moving snake-like, dancing to the tune of her expert hands.

Zinnia put her mouth beside his covered ears.

'I am allowing you a great privilege,' she said. 'You must thank me.'

She removed her fingers from his prick and put her legs either side of his head. She trailed her rubber-gloved fingers across his mouth. She bent down, stuck out her tongue and licked his mouth, attacking his senses. Zinnia had no intention of stopping.

'You say. "thank you, madam,"' she said.

'Yes, madam, thank you, madam,' he said.

'I told you bad boys are punished,' she said, and raised his flanks higher. 'Stay exactly as you are.'

Zinnia walked away from him and in absolute silence picked up a paddle. The next moment she brought its flatness down hard on his buttocks. 'Naughty boys need spanking,' she said, and brought it down once more with considerable force on his rump.

She told him to remain on all fours. She lifted his head. Then she crawled in front of him, presenting her naked buttocks to his mouth; the sea-smell of her hit his nostrils. She pushed her bottom into his face. He licked her. She pushed harder, spreading her crease so that his tongue was forced to find her small back hole. She knew he wanted his tongue to trail downwards to find her other feminine hole but his way was barred by studs and PVC.

Deciding that for the moment she had been pleasured enough, Zinnia stood up. She picked up the crop and ran it through his crease. Excited, he stiffened, waiting for the blow; but she was teasing him. Instead she stopped, bent down and rubbed his tumescent throbbing cock. Then she fitted a heavily seamed leather sheath over its erect length. The front was attached by a short tie to a belt which she fastened around his waist. She secured it by taking the back tie and drawing it up through the crack in his bottom and fitting it to the belt.

'Naughty boys must receive a very good spanking,' she said. 'What do you say to that?'

'Yes, madam,' he said.

'And you've been a very naughty boy, haven't you?'

'Yes, madam.'

'You will agree to anything I want, won't you Gerry?' Zinnia asked, juggling his balls between her hands.

'Yes, madam.'

'Tell me, then; say "I will agree to anything madam wants", and say it loud,' she said, swishing the crop across his flanks so hard that he screamed and fell flat on the floor. She gave him an extra hard thwack for good measure. He jumped and curled into a ball.

'Tell me,' she demanded.

'I will agree to anything madam wants,' he whimpered.

'Good,' she said. 'Stand up.'

Gerry stood up, his buttocks stinging violently. She covered them with oil then began to rub his cock whilst plying his backside lightly with the crop. Gerry was shaking from top to bottom. The leather covering his prick, her hand rubbing it and the feel of sharp exquisite pain as she wielded the crop on his fleshy expectant bottom, was sending him delirious with pleasure. She was wickedly tormenting him and the ring, tight at the base of his cock, was delaying his climax.

'I'm going to remove your hood.'

For the first time Gerry saw Zinnia in her full dominance. He almost came with surprise. He had smelt her and felt the PVC grazing against his flesh but he had no idea she was totally encased in a corset. He couldn't wait to feel her tits, those huge breasts that were crushed inside and bulging outside the shiny fabric. He didn't know which part of her to grab first. Then he realised without her permission he couldn't touch her at all.

He wanted to pleasure her. He wanted to suck her. He wanted to feel his tongue slobbering at her furls, voyaging inside, finding the spot that would make her squirm. He wanted her squirming. He wanted her crouching over him. His bottom was stinging from the crop and his prick was blood-surging and throbbing.

Sparks flew in Gerry's brain. He had fallen completely

249

and utterly in love. She had skin as soft as down that oozed sex. She had a smell, a sea shell smell that oozed sex. She had a quiet dominance, now activated, that oozed sex. She was sexuality incarnate. She was his goddess. He was her slave. He would be hers forever.

She hit him again. For ever and ever. She hit him again and again. Harder and harder. His tingling buttocks clenching and unclenching were now a delightful bright red. He wanted to kiss her. Kiss her feet, her legs, any part of her that she would allow. Gerry was floating in a mesmeric state of desire. Which part of his body would she touch and stimulate next? Gerry was ecstatic.

'Kneel down, undo my buckles,' she said, pointing at the fastenings over her sex.

Gerry knelt in front of her. With difficulty, as she had not loosened his hands from their manacles, he undid the buckles.

'Suck me,' she said, thrusting her sex at his mouth.

His tongue came out and licked her moist labia, he brought his hands up and parted her sex lips. He lifted the hood to reveal her enlarged clitoris. He flicked it with his tongue. She sighed a long drawn-out sigh. She allowed his hands to wander so that while his tongue was busy, his fingers began their probing search into her inner depths. Her hips began to roll.

Her moisture was easing out over his tongue. Zinnia pushed him away. She lay on the floor. For a moment he looked nonplussed. Had he done something to displease her?

'Fuck me,' she said, opening her legs wide so that he could crawl up between them.

Gerry lay over her body. He put his shackled hands above her head. He trembled as he touched her huge breasts with his chest.

Gerry held his leather-encased prick at the entrance to her sex. She wiggled with desire as she felt the raised seams scraping against her moist walls. She tensed her arse and lifted her hips.

'Now,' she said.

Gerry plunged into her. He took her in one violent thrust, up to the apex of her womb. He ploughed her with every ounce of his pent-up energy and desire. She brought her hands round and slapped his seared and marked bottom as it raged backwards and forwards. The stinging sensation on his buttocks, her hips gyrating, the moistness of her vagina, his leather casing, her PVC, the ring around his cock: everything conspired to make him fuck as he had never fucked before.

She turned her mouth towards his mouth. Their lips met. Bliss. Their tongues entwined. Soldered together wherever they touched, in a dizziness of emotion – almost an annihilation of the senses – they climaxed simultaneously.

Zinnia, too, had found love.

Countess Jacqueline Helitzer checked her watch. It was way past noon. Auralie should have arrived some time ago for her meeting with Gerry and Sir Henry. Jacqueline scanned the dining room of the Staples Hotel. She saw Sir Henry sitting at one table by himself. She looked in the opposite direction and saw Petrov sitting alone. Jacqueline was intrigued and joined him.

'Petrov, darling, hello,' she said, extending her beautifully-manicured hand.

Petrov bowed. 'A drink?' he said.

He was wondering where the hell Jethro was, why he hadn't kept their appointment. He said he was bringing his new partner with him, Eduard del Sur.

'Thank you, no; I've just finished lunch and have another rendezvous,' said the Countess. 'But Petrov, I didn't know you were in Meriboa. Are you staying at the hotel?'

'No,' said Petrov, fumbling in a pocket and bringing out a card. 'I'm at this address. Do come and visit.'

'That would be wonderful, darling,' she said, pocketing the card and feeling extremely pleased with herself. 'Maybe I'll see you later.'

'Yes, and bring Auralie with you,' he said.

Jacqueline looked startled.

'It was obvious that you had helped her escape,' said Petrov. 'I'm glad you did it. She had to get away from Jeanine. Tell her, despite everything, I love her. We love her.'

'You do?'

'Of course,' said Petrov. 'So see you both later.'

'Definitely, darling,' said Jacqueline. 'Until then, *au revoir*.'

Jacqueline decided that, as she was now armed with Petrov's address, there was no further point in staying at the Staples Hotel. She would check to see if Auralie had left a message for her and, if not, would leave one for Auralie and return to the Hotel Lan Chiau. There she would work out her guest list and where she would have her party.

In the vast brown marble foyer of the hotel, she was walking past the ornamental fountain when she saw an elderly man in a wheelchair being pushed along by a handsome young man. She stopped in her tracks. There was something all too familiar about his face. As she racked her brain, she heard his slightly querulous voice saying, 'No, look over there. There. She is over there.'

Caradoc Lewis! The old bastard. What was going on in Meriboa that was attracting the seriously rich men of the world? What was Caradoc Lewis up to?

Jacqueline had no love for him. It was Caradoc Lewis she had fled from many years before when she had asked Rosamund de Bouys for help. He had tried to keep her a prisoner in his castle in Wales. Him and his young flunkeys. Cruel, he was very cruel, thinking that riches bought him the right to do unspeakable things to other people's bodies.

Jacqueline turned to see where the man was pointing. Looking stunningly beautiful, in an azure blue and lime green silk suit and with a spiralling lime green straw confection upon her head, sitting on the far side of the fountain was Jeanine.

How very interesting, thought Jacqueline, watching

the young man wheel Caradoc's chair over to Jeanine. Jacqueline had no idea they knew one another. But with his peccadilloes and his money to indulge them, it wasn't so surprising.

Jacqueline had no desire to meet with Caradoc. She went to the reception desk. There were no messages for her. She left one for Auralie then, as she turned to leave, she noticed Petrov walking out. Caradoc Lewis was nowhere to be seen and Jeanine was sitting by herself, looking remarkably dejected. Jacqueline decided to say a brief hello and then depart quickly.

'Who are you waiting for, darling?' asked the countess, kissing Jeanine on both cheeks.

'Jacqueline, sweetie, darling,' said Jeanine, trying to sound cheerfully normal but Jacqueline caught the hint of relief in her voice. 'My mother. I was waiting for my mother.'

'Your mother?' exclaimed the countess.

'Yes, but I'm very glad to see you, especially as I've just heard she's not coming.'

'Oh?' Obviously, thought the countess, nobody had told Jeanine she was responsible for Auralie's exit from Petrov's establishment.

'My life has fallen apart,' said Jeanine.

'Oh really, darling, don't be so dramatic,' said Jacqueline.

'It's true, it's true,' said Jeanine, almost in tears.

'Have some champagne, darling, and tell me about it,' said Jacqueline.

'No, thank you; I don't want anything,' said Jeanine. 'But I'll tell you what's happened. Remember when you were at the hotel and my mother came in to see me?'

'Yes,' said Jacqueline, throatily, sexily. 'I remember very well I had my best dildo strapped on and was just about to screw you when Jackson announced her arrival.'

'And Auralie said I had gone to France,' said Jeanine butting in, 'and then that bitch disappeared after doing some shopping for you.'

'Yes,' said Jacqueline.

253

'And I told you I'd bought a huge factory in south London and was going to turn it into an hotel.'

'Yes,' said Jacqueline.

'The next day, I went to see my mother,' said Jeanine.

'Yes,' said Jacqueline.

'Well that was the beginning,' said Jeanine.

'Why? What happened?'

'My mother told me that Sir Henry was divorcing her.'

'No!' exclaimed Jacqueline, that was a surprise. She hadn't heard the slightest rumour that anything was wrong with the marriage. 'What for? Why is he divorcing her? I thought he was utterly devoted to her.'

'He was. Unfortunately he came back early from one of his trips and found her in bed with another man.'

'Oh, darling! That is terrible,' said Jacqueline.

'It was, because it wasn't just any man. Maybe any other man he could have coped with but my mother – my mother, who I always thought so clever and so capable – my mother chooses to go to bed with David Lewis.'

'Who?' exclaimed Jacqueline.

'Caradoc Lewis's son.'

'But he's young enough to be her son!'

'Exactly,' said Jeanine, holding back the tears, 'and that didn't go down too well with Sir Henry, who's old enough to be her father! You can't imagine what he's threatening to do and what he's already done.'

'Okay, darling, okay, don't cry,' said Jacqueline, patting her hand. 'Slowly, tell me slowly. What has he done?'

'Sold all his shares in Petolg Holdings. He did that immediately.'

'Is that so bad? I thought you wanted to buy it back?'

'I did. I did,' moaned Jeanine.

'Well so that's okay.'

'No; no, it's not, because he sold such a mass he forced the market down.'

'Darling, then you buy back cheaply.'

'No,' said Jeanine, shaking her head. 'Oh Jacqueline, I

wish it was that simple. But so many other things have happened that I can't do that. I don't want to do that. In fact, I'm now so in debt I most probably wouldn't be allowed to do that. I will be bought out and the company wound up. You see, Auralie has left. She wrote me a letter giving her formal resignation.'

'You have other designers.'

'I had other designers,' said Jeanine wearily. 'They've been poached.'

'Poached?'

'Yes,' said Jeanine. 'A new company's been set up for industrial design and suddenly all my designers have gone.'

'So you find some more.'

'Not so easy,' said Jeanine. 'I thought they were two a penny, but not so. I've even offered them over the top salaries, but no – this new company tops it. And guess who owns this new company?'

'Sir Henry de Bouys?'

'Right in one,' said Jeanine.

'But darling,' said the Countess, trying to be cheerful, 'this is not the end of the world. I mean, you have other things. Your factory, you were going to turn that factory into an hotel, no?

'Don't make me cry,' said Jeanine, dabbing her eyes with a fine lawn handkerchief, 'or my mascara will run.'

'Why should you cry?'

'Because a few days after all this happened my factory fell down.'

'Your factory fell down!' exclaimed Jacqueline. 'But that's absurd.'

Jacqueline thought it was completely absurd. It was so utterly absurd she wanted to laugh but the sight of Jeanine's face, contorted with the effort of not crying, forced Jacqueline to keep even a smile at bay. 'How?' said Jacqueline. 'I mean, darling, how does a whole factory fall down?'

'Well, remember I told you I was so pleased because it was a new building?'

'Yes.'

'What I didn't know was that it was built on the site of a garbage dump and the garbage dump was on the site of an old swampy lake.'

'In London?'

'Yes; in London, south of the river has always been very marshy, and it had never been properly drained. So one day the gases on the dump made the whole thing blow up and then what was left just sank.'

'Oh, *mon Dieu*, darling!' exclaimed the countess.

'And then –'

'There's more?' asked the astonished Countess Helitzer.

'Oh yes,' cried Jeanine. 'Two days later the Ministry of Transport announce their plans for a new road from Dover to the City of London, going right over my land, for people to connect up with the new foot-bridge across the Thames to St Paul's. When the factory was standing there I would have got decent compensation but now, nothing. I've lost millions.'

'But surely you can sue the people who sold it to you?'

'No, I can't,' said Jeanine. 'Because it's a case of purchaser beware. So you understand now when I say my life has fallen apart.'

'Yes, darling, I do.'

'And that bastard Sir Henry sold his shares before any of that happened so he got a good price for them.'

'Oh, that must hurt,' said Jacqueline, secretly pleased that Auralie too had sold her shares in Petolg Holdings and had also got a good price for them. 'But, darling, that doesn't explain why you are here in Meriboa.'

'Because my mother said she was coming here.'

'Why?'

'She wanted to see David Lewis.'

'Why?'

'Because he's been avoiding her. She telephoned me and told me to take the first plane to Meriboa and go to the Staples Hotel; and here I am. And now I've just been told by his father, that his son won't be here and my mother's not coming.'

'Oh!'

'Oh, God! Oh, no! Look, look who's just walking out with Sir Henry!'

'Why, isn't that your Everett, darling?' said Jacqueline.

'What's he doing in Meriboa?' cried Jeanine.

'Let's find out,' said Jacqueline.

'No, please don't,' said Jeanine, earnestly. 'You see, we had a terrible row. Terrible. I got Carola to tell him to come back to England. He did and he told me he'd fallen in love with bloody Sapphire Western.'

'Who's Sapphire Western?' asked the countess.

'A friend of Auralie's. Everett picked her up on a plane or something,' replied Jeanine. 'You see what I mean about my life falling apart? Even my lover's left me. I told him I loved him. And he said tough, he was in love with this – this silly bitch. I told him that wasn't possible, it was only infatuation. He said the infatuation had been with me and he loved her and he believed she loved him. He was going to ask her to marry him when Carola turned up in Geneva. And she fled. She fled and he didn't know where she'd gone. I said I wondered how much she'd love him if she saw the video of him screwing Zinnia last spring.'

'Oh, darling,' said the countess quietly, a sense of despair in her voice, 'blackmail is never wise. You lose friends, customers and lovers when you start blackmailing.'

'I was angry, so angry,' said Jeanine. 'I really loved him. Not as much as I loved Laurence. Laurence will always have a special place in my heart.'

'There always is for one's first love,' said the countess.

'Yes, but Laurence is dead and gone and Everett . . . Anyway, he called me a bitch and said he never, ever wanted to see me again,' she wailed. 'I've tried writing but he doesn't reply. Jacqueline, what shall I do?'

'I've had an idea.' Jacqueline took Petrov's card out of her handbag and waved it in front of Jeanine. 'We'll have a drink and let you calm down, and then we'll go to see Petrov.'

A variety of people were assembled in Petrov's house when Zinnia walked in with Gerry and made her extraordinary announcement. 'Sir Henry de Bouys has taken over Hanway, Rattle and Lewis.'

'What!' they exclaimed in unison.

'It's true,' said Gerry. 'My father was so furious when he found out about David Lewis and Lady Penelope that he started a whispering campaign.'

'Oh, vicious,' observed Ana Tai.

'It happens in business,' said Gerry. 'Anyhow, poor David Lewis couldn't work out why he was getting the cold shoulder. It flustered him and he began making some bad decisions, lost money. And the more he lost, the more he lost. Confidence in Hanway's ebbed away. And on the Exchange, confidence is paramount. Then my father moved in. Old Caradoc, who was here to make a killing – wanted to take over de Bouys, no less – has had to high tail it back to the UK on public airlines.'

'No!' exclaimed Petrov. 'He must have lost a fortune.'

'Or even two or three,' said Gerry, not attempting to hide his glee. 'The jet was the first to go. And he doesn't know whether he's got enough to afford the upkeep of his castle in Wales.'

'Good,' said Zinnia.

'Yes, I agree. But there's always a downside,' added Gerry, smiling fondly at Zinnia and squeezing her hand as they sat down together on the settee.

'What's that?' asked Auralie, who was sitting between Jethro and Ana Tai.

'My father wants to employ Zinnia and put her in charge,' said Gerry.

'*Chérie*, I would have thought that was *une bonne idée*,' said Auralie, gazing at her ex-husband quite fondly.

'It would have been, but I don't want a working wife. Too many distractions for my liking,' Gerry replied, putting an arm around Zinnia.

'Your wife?' said Zinnia, laughing. 'Great, eh? Only he's forgotten something.'

'He sure has,' said Jethro. 'Zinnia's still married to me.'

'But not for much longer,' said Zinnia sweetly. 'We're divorcing remember?'

'Jeez!' cried Jethro, 'Carola Finestein!'

'Ah, Jethro,' said Zinnia, smiling wickedly, 'I didn't tell you? I cited irreconcilable differences.'

'You did?' said Jethro, breathing a sigh of relief. 'In that case, I give Gerry my full permission to ask my wife if he can marry her. But he'd better do it properly. Down on your knees, Gerry.'

Petrov smiled and called for Kim Long. 'Champagne,' he said. And moments later Kim Long returned with a couple of bottles of vintage Krug in ice-buckets.

Gerry slipped off the settee, knelt before Zinnia and, taking one of her hands in his, started to ask Zinnia to be his wife. But he was interrupted.

They had all been so preoccupied they had failed to notice an elegant woman clothed in lime green approaching through the garden until the front door opened.

'Hello, sweeties,' said Jeanine, looking around the room, her eyes falling on the kneeling Gerry. 'Good to see some things don't change! You may get up.'

Zinnia put a hand on Gerry's head.

'Only when you've finished what you've got to say, my darling,' she said.

'Zinnia, will you marry me?'

'I will; yes, I will,' replied Zinnia, bending over and giving Gerry a long kiss on his lips.

Petrov popped the cork and poured out the champagne.

'Oh, how very touching!' spat Jeanine. 'What a lovely little family gathering. Gerry de Bouys, the wimp, Auralie de Bouys, the bitch ... All we need is Everett the rat and Sir Henry the spiteful old cuckold.'

'Everett's here but my father's gone back to the States,' said Gerry. 'By the way, Auralie, he said sorry not to have seen you today but he'll talk to you some other time about various ideas he's got for your new business.'

'What new business?' asked Jeanine.

'Design,' said Auralie curtly.

'Oh, really? And if Everett's here, where is he? Well hidden? Under the table, hm?' Jeanine asked sarcastically.

'Upstairs,' said Auralie.

'Upstairs, eh? Right.' Jeanine rose to go.

'Upstairs with Sapphire Western,' said Auralie.

'Sapphire Western?' exploded Jeanine.

'Sapphire Western Untermann,' said Gerry quietly.

'What did you say?' asked Jeanine, a look of horror crossing her face; she stopped in full flight.

'Sapphire Western Untermann,' Gerry repeated.

'You mean the woman that's just inherited hundreds of millions?' said Jeanine in astonishment.

'The same,' said Auralie. 'But why should you worry where Everett is when your husband, Laurence, is alive?' she said.

'My husband?' exploded Jeanine. 'My husband? My husband is dead.'

'No, he's not. He's alive. Very much alive; and he's in jail,' said Auralie, trying very hard to keep the sound of ultimate triumph out of her voice.

'In jail? Alive and in jail?' exclaimed Jeanine, putting a hand to her forehead as if doing that would stop her fainting.

'Yes, for fraud,' said Gerry.

'Fraud? Fraud? Oh, my poor darling. My poor Laurence. All he must have suffered. How do you know; how do you know this?' asked Jeanine, flinging herself down in the nearest chair.

'Because I helped to catch him,' said Gerry. 'And you're extremely lucky that I spent so much time pandering to you, because I know for certain that you had no idea he didn't die in the Brazilian jungle and were not a party.'

'Party, darlings?' asked Jacqueline, entering the room.

'We'll have one soon in Paris. I want to go home, it's too hot and sticky for me here. And you know? Taxi drivers are the same all over the world — they never have change . . .'

She stopped in mid-sentence, surveying the scene and the champagne glasses. 'What has been happening? darlings, tell me,' said the Countess, scanning the faces of everyone in the room. Every expression was different. 'Is this a celebration? Jeanine? Did somebody buy Petolg Holdings?'

Jethro laughed.

'No,' said Petrov. 'Petolg Holdings has completely crashed.'

'But we wouldn't want you to worry about us,' said Auralie. It was her turn for sarcasm. 'You see, Petrov and I sold our shares before Sir Henry did. We knew about your little scheme to buy back the company and we didn't like it. We got a good price.'

'That's insider dealing,' said Jeanine.

'Is it? No, we just didn't like your attitude. We had no faith in you as Chief Executive. So I'm setting up here with Ana Tai, and Jethro and Petrov are helping with the funding. Oh, and Jethro's staying with us.'

'But I'm going back to England,' said Petrov. 'And the debts are all yours,'

'Oh God! Oh God!' wailed Jeanine. 'What shall I do? What shall I do?'

'Wait for your husband?' said Petrov. 'That should take about twelve years. Well, that is, if he's really lucky.'

With tears streaming down her face, Jeanine stared defiantly at everyone in the room. 'Well, sweeties,' she said. 'I might just do that. Yes, I might.

'Your husband stole bearer bonds worth fifty million pounds sterling from our family, leaving the bank in jeopardy,' said Gerry icily.

'I didn't know. I swear to God I didn't know.'

'Yes I believe you. However, because of his activities, de Bouys bank was unable to meet certain debts —

261

leaving it wide open for a take-over. The bank that has been in my family for generations now belongs to somebody else.'

'One way or another, Jeanine,' said Petrov, putting a hand on her elbow. 'I don't think you're too welcome here.'

Jeanine stared at the faces around her, each regarded her implacably.

'You see, there is such a thing as love,' continued Petrov, guiding her towards the front door. 'Maybe you love Laurence. Maybe with him you can sort things out. But not with us. I think it best if you went now. Perhaps in time you'll learn about love and loyalty and friendship.'

Jeanine swallowed hard, shook off Petrov's hand and threw open the front door. 'Which prison is Laurence in?' she asked.

'Chungee,' said Gerry.

She left the door wide open as she marched through the garden, out of the gate, and out of their lives.

Sapphire and Everett had both calmed down after their row to end all rows.

When he had burst in and proclaimed her news to one and all, Sapphire had been almost as furious with him as he was with her. Accusations had flown backwards and forwards. Words like 'liar' and 'cheat' and 'cheap sexy slut' had been bandied about. She had dived up the glass staircase to get away from him and his remorseless haranguing, and had rushed into the first room she came to, which was Petrov's purple and black bedroom. There she had flung herself down on the bed and sobbed.

Sapphire had cried for all the things she had lost or never known. She had cried for her dead father. She had cried for her mother and then she had cried about her new responsibilities. Slowly, her tears had dried up. She had been in the middle of re-assessing her situation when Everett had stalked into the room.

'I'm sorry,' he said.

'Go away,' she countered.

'No,' he replied, sitting down beside her and attempting to stroke her beautiful red-gold hair. 'We have some things to work out.'

'Talk to my lawyers,' she said, trying to to push him off the bed.

He grabbed hold of her hand and instantly she felt her resistance to him wilting, but she pulled away and walked over to the settee by the window. Sitting straight and upright, she kept her demeanour contained and haughty. She deliberately turned her head away from him and stared out at the garden. She caught sight of Jeanine leaving. Sapphire knew by her walk that she was looking at a woman defiant in defeat.

'Sapphire,' Everett said, annoyed, 'please. I love you. Sapphire, you're not listening to me.'

'Jeanine's been and is now leaving,' said Sapphire, ignoring him.

'Good,' replied Everett. 'Sapphire, did you hear what I said?'

'No; say it again.'

'I was telling you I loved you,' he said.

'Yeah, sure,' she replied, and stared out of the window again, knowing it would anger him.

He tipped her face to his.

'My darling, I'm sorry,' said Everett. 'Listen to me. I fell in love with you on sight. I knew you were the only woman for me.'

'Oh yes?' she said. 'That's why you had that hooker Carola Finestein wrapped around you in your office.'

'Sapphire, believe me, I was waiting for you when she walked in,' Everett said, sitting beside her on the settee. Sapphire got up and went back to the bed.

'Oh, a big surprise, was it?'

'Yes it was. I'd never seen the goddam woman in my life before.'

'Sure, and I believe in men from Mars!'

'Sapphire, will you listen to me for one moment? Let

263

me get a word in edgeways.' He came and sat beside her once more.

'No,' she said.

'Very well, then it's actions that count,' he said. He pushed her back on to the bed, holding her hands above her head, imprisoning her in his grip and kissing her passionately.

The moment he leant over her, Sapphire felt her anger dissipate as his sexuality met hers. But she was determined to resist him. Instead of moulding into him, she lay stiff in his arms.

'Sapphire,' he said, running his hands along her legs and up her thighs, 'Come on, relax; I know you've been screwed by Jethro and Petrov and Auralie and Ana Tai. And I don't mind.'

'You don't mind?' Sapphire exclaimed, endeavouring to wriggle out of his control. 'You don't mind? I don't believe you, you arrogant bastard.'

'Yes, you had some fun because you thought I was a bastard. But I'm not and you're my woman.'

Sapphire carried on struggling but he kept a tight hold of her.

'I know you've been stretched out on the bed with each one of them licking you and enjoying you, sucking your pussy and fucking the life out of you. And I know you enjoyed it, you couldn't have done it so well without enjoying it. But I also know I gave you the best fuck you've ever had in your life. I did, didn't I?' he asked, nibbling at her ear.

Sapphire didn't answer.

'I did, didn't I?' he said, his fingers easing their way under her knicker elastic and gently touching the soft lips of her sex.

'Answer me,' he ordered, one finger sliding inside her moist sex lips and finding her highly sensitive pleasure button.

'Yes,' she sighed.

'So feel my cock,' he said, putting her hand down

between his legs. 'Do as you're told, Sapphire. Undo my flies and take out my cock.'

Sapphire obeyed him.

'Now, suck it,' he commanded, winding his fingers in her beautiful hair and gently pushing her head down so that her mouth was level with his cock-head. She took its rounded smoothness in between her lips.

'Good girl,' he said, opening her suit top so that her beautiful breasts were displayed before him. 'Now open your legs. Lie back and open your legs wide. Because, Sapphire Western Untermann, I want you. You might have spent most of the day screwing but now I'm going to suck you and then I'm going to fuck you.'

Willingly, wantonly, Sapphire lay back on the bed, her skirt rising high; Everett knelt over her, keeping his prick in her mouth while his head went down between her legs. His tongue licked her thighs, then his fingers pushed her knicker-elastic to one side and he ran his lips along her sex-lips, his tongue searching for her pleasure button, and she sighed.

She sucked on his cock, running her fingers along its shaft and cupping his balls in her hand. Sapphire knew she was where she belonged. With Everett. She would do anything for him. She raised her hips so that his tongue could delve deeper into her moist wantoness. Sapphire knew she loved him, wanted him – would always want him. She shuddered and shivered and trembled with delight as the combination of his tongue and fingers opening and playing with her sex sent her emotions and her desires higher and higher.

He withdrew his throbbing and stiff prick from her mouth, swivelled his body and looked at her. Bringing his mouth, which tasted of her own sweet musk, down, he kissed her cheeks, her nose, her eyelids, and then her mouth. He kissed her lips at the same time as the tip of his prick pressed at the opening of her wet sex. Forcing her lips apart, he shot his tongue in between her teeth and echoed the motion with his cock, suddenly thrusting hard into her soft, wet and secret place.

'Me,' he said, thrusting, 'Me. In future you will only have me.'

'Will I?' she asked.

He tweaked her nipples. 'Yes, me and only me.' He flicked her nipples with his tongue, and then with his fingers. He began to thrust harder; she started to squirm and her muscles gripped his cock as it slid back and forth.

'Tell me you love me, Sapphire,' he ordered. 'Tell me you love me as I love you.'

'I love you,' she murmured as he thrust hard; and then neither of them could speak as each gathered momentum. He took his weight on his hands and thrust, pressing his lips to hers as she raised her hips high to take him, every inch of him, so that they were completely one. They screamed and shouted and moaned in ecstasy and came together.

Afterwards they lay quietly resting in each others arms. He gave her butterfly kisses, she nuzzled into his body.

'Darling, darling Sapphire,' he said. 'I love you. I do love you. I was desperate when you left. I telephoned my father, asked him to keep you there when you went back for your clothes. But you never did, did you?'

'No,' she said quietly.

'And then I was angry,' he said. 'Goddam furious, to be exact, knowing you could think so badly of me.'

'Don't talk about it now,' she said, thinking how happy she was to be with him. How well their bodies and their minds fitted together. They enjoyed the same things and had a similar intellectual capacity. They would make a good team.

'But when I heard that news about Untermann's, I went berserk,' said Everett, his words brought her back from her gentle reverie. 'I didn't realise you didn't know – that you had no idea what your father was up to. That it wasn't until this morning that you discovered you were his main beneficiary or that he had made a bid for de Bouys.' He kissed the nape of her neck. 'Marry me, darling,' he said.

'Even though I now own your bank?' she said, laughing.

'I'm sure you'll run it well. You have all the qualifications,' he said. 'Father said if it had to be anybody, he's happy it's you and he's handing you over his art collection.'

'What?' she exclaimed.

'Yes, he told me that earlier. He said you told him you wanted to open it to the public and call it the Olivia de Bouys Collection. He wants you to do it.'

'I can't believe it,' said Sapphire, half-laughing, half-sobbing.

'So will you marry me?' asked Everett.

'Yes,' said Sapphire. 'But you don't have to, just to keep the name in the family, you know.'

'The thought never crossed my mind!' he said, laughing and stroking her face. 'But why not?'

'Because I am a de Bouys.'

'You are what?' he exclaimed.

'That was the other shock I had this morning. I am the illegitimate daughter of Sir Bevis Untermann and Lady Rosamund de Bouys.'

'No! Aunt Rosamund? She's your mother?'

'Yes, and I met her for the first time this morning. And Everett, let me tell you my father wasn't so terrible; because that's the reason why, when he saw what was happening to your bank, he wanted me to own it and nobody else.'

Sapphire was convinced that everything her father had done made perfect sense. He had died leaving all accounts in credit, knowing that she, his clever and capable daughter, would enjoy taking control of his business.

'Oh Sapphire,' said, Everett, holding her tight. 'Oh Sapphire, I can't believe it. This is wonderful, truly wonderful. Come, let's go down and tell the others.'

'Not about my parents, please.'

'No, about our marriage. Come on, my darling: one more kiss and then champagne with friends.'

When Sapphire appeared at the head of the glass staircase it was Jacqueline's first sight of Sir Bevis's daughter. She stared open-mouthed as Sapphire stood in the sunlight, looking glorious in her figure-enhancing, if slightly crumpled, cream chiffon suit.

Jacqueline nudged Auralie. 'Who is she the living image of?' Jacqueline whispered, as the sun picked out the hints of reddish-gold in her thick tumbling blonde hair.

'Oh!' exclaimed Auralie, a hand flying over her mouth in surprise. '*Mon Dieu, chérie*, Lady Rosamund!'

'Exactly, darling, Lady Rosamund Ware de Bouys. And I bet her little family business was to meet her daughter. Look; look at her. The same bone structure, the same mouth and, darling, most of all, the same beautiful hair. I always wanted hair like that,' said Jacqueline wistfully.

'Meet my wife to be,' announced Everett, hugging Sapphire.

Petrov smiled and opened another bottle of Krug. Jethro, Ana Tai, Zinnia and Gerry clapped their hands. Auralie and Jacqueline stayed staring at Sapphire as she, holding Everett's hand and smiling happily, continued on down the stairs.

Sapphire recognised that she had fundamentally changed. A few weeks earlier, her recent sexual escapades would have been unthinkable. Now she was no longer afraid of her most intimate desires. She had let go, lost control and been sexually released. She was a fulfilled woman who had discovered she was capable of loving.

She gazed at the people in the room and realised that most of them had enjoyed her body – but only Everett had enjoyed her mind. She kissed him, at first affectionately and then passionately.

Sapphire knew she could go forward and take charge of her life with knowledge and with her love.

LOOK OUT FOR THE ALL-NEW BLACK LACE BOOKS – AVAILABLE NOW!

All books priced £6.99 in the UK. Please note publication dates apply to the UK only. For other territories, please contact your retailer.

MIXED SIGNALS
Anna Clare
ISBN O 352 33889 X

Adele Western knows what it's like to be an outsider. As a teenager she was teased mercilessly by the sixth-form girls for the size of her lips. Now twenty-six, we follow the ups and downs of her life and loves. There's the cultured restaurateur Paul, whose relationship with his working-class boyfriend raises eyebrows, not least because he is still having sex with his ex-wife. There's former chart-topper Suki, whose career has nosedived and who is venturing on a lesbian affair. Underlying everyone's story is a tale of ambiguous sexuality, and Adele is caught up in some very saucy antics. **The sexy *tour de force* of wild, colourful characters makes this a hugely enjoyable novel of modern sexual dilemmas.**

SWITCHING HANDS
Alaine Hood
ISBN O 352 33896 2

When Melanie Paxton takes over as manager of a vintage clothing shop, she makes the bold decision to add a selection of sex toys and fetish merchandise to her inventory. Sales skyrocket, and so does Mel's popularity, as she teases sexy secrets out of the town's residents. It seems she can do no wrong, until the gossip starts – about her wild past and her experimental sexuality. However, she finds an unlikely – and very hunky – ally called Nathan who works in the history museum next door. **This characterful story about a sassy sexpert and an antiquities scholar is bound to get pulses racing!**

PACKING HEAT
Karina Moore
ISBN O 352 33356 1

When spoilt and pretty Californian Nadine has her allowance stopped by her rich Uncle Willem, she becomes desperate to maintain her expensive lifestyle. She joins forces with her lover, Mark, and together they conspire to steal a vast sum of cash from a flashy businessman and pin the blame on their target's girlfriend. The deed done, the sexual stakes rise as they make their escape. Naturally, their getaway doesn't go entirely to plan, and they are pursued across the desert and into the casinos of Las Vegas, where a showdown is inevitable. The clock is ticking for Nadine, Mark and the guys who are chasing them – but a Ferrari-driving blonde temptress is about to play them all for suckers. **Fast cars and even faster women in this modern pulp fiction classic.**

Published in October 2004

BEDDING THE BURGLAR
Gabrielle Marcola
ISBN 0 352 33911 X

Maggie Quinton is a savvy, sexy architect involved in a building project on a remote island off the Florida panhandle. One day, a gorgeous hunk breaks into the house she's staying in and ties her up. The buff burglar is in search of an item he claims the apartment's owner stole from him. And he keeps coming back. Flustered and aroused, Maggie calls her jet-setting sister in for moral support, but flirty, dark-haired Diane is much more interested in the island's ruggedly handsome police chief, 'Griff' Grifford. And then there's his deputy, Cosgrove, with his bulging biceps and creative uses for handcuffs. There must be something in the water that makes this island's men so good-looking and its women so anxious to get their hooks into them – and Maggie is determined to find out what it is by doing as much research as possible!

MIXED DOUBLES
Zoe le Verdier
ISBN 0 352 33312 X

When Natalie Crawford is offered the job as manager of a tennis club in a wealthy English suburb, she jumps at the chance. There's an extra perk, too: Paul, the club's coach, is handsome and charming, and she wastes no time in making him her lover. Then she hires Chris, a coach from a rival club, whose confidence and sexual prowess swiftly puts Paul in the shade. When Chris embroils Natalie into kinky sex games, will she be able to keep control of her business aims, or will her lust for the arrogant sportsman get out of control?

Also available

THE BLACK LACE SEXY QUIZ BOOK
Maddie Saxon
ISBN 0 352 33884 9
£6.99

- What sexual personality type are you?
- Have you ever faked it because that was easier than explaining what you wanted?
- What kind of fantasy figures turn you on – and does your partner know?
- What sexual signals are you giving out right now?

Today's image-conscious dating scene is a tough call. Our sexual expectations are cranked up to the max, and the sexes seem to have become highly critical of each other in terms of appearance and performance in the bedroom. But even though guys have ditched their nasty Y-fronts and girls are more babe-licious than ever, a huge number of us are still being let down sexually. Sex therapist Maddie Saxon thinks this is because we are finding it harder to relax and let our true sexual selves shine through.

The Black Lace Sexy Quiz Book will help you negotiate the minefield of modern relationships. Through a series of fun, revealing quizzes, you will be able to rate your sexual needs honestly and get what you really want from your partner. The quizzes will get you thinking about and discussing your desires in ways you haven't previously considered. Unlock the mysteries of your sexual psyche in this fun, revealing quiz book designed with today's sex-savvy girl in mind.

Black Lace Booklist

Information is correct at time of printing. To avoid disappointment check availability before ordering. Go to www.blacklace-books.co.uk. All books are priced £6.99 unless another price is given.

BLACK LACE BOOKS WITH A CONTEMPORARY SETTING

To find out the latest information about Black Lace titles, check out the website: www.blacklace-books.co.uk or send for a booklist with complete synopses by writing to:

> Black Lace Booklist, Virgin Books Ltd
> Thames Wharf Studios
> Rainville Road
> London W6 9HA

Please include an SAE of decent size. Please note only British stamps are valid.

Our privacy policy
We will not disclose information you supply us to any other parties. We will not disclose any information which identifies you personally to any person without your express consent.

From time to time we may send out information about Black Lace books and special offers. Please tick here if you do <u>not</u> wish to receive Black Lace information.   ☐

Please send me the books I have ticked above.

Name ....

Address ....

....

....

....

Post Code ....

Send to: Virgin Books Cash Sales, Thames Wharf Studios, Rainville Road, London W6 9HA.

US customers: for prices and details of how to order books for delivery by mail, call 1-800-343-4499.

Please enclose a cheque or postal order, made payable to Virgin Books Ltd, to the value of the books you have ordered plus postage and packing costs as follows:

UK and BFPO – £1.00 for the first book, 50p for each subsequent book.

Overseas (including Republic of Ireland) – £2.00 for the first book, £1.00 for each subsequent book.

If you would prefer to pay by VISA, ACCESS/MASTERCARD, DINERS CLUB, AMEX or SWITCH, please write your card number and expiry date here:

....

Signature ....

Please allow up to 28 days for delivery.